D1590888

And RACHEL *was his wife*

And RACHEL *was his wife*

an anonymous manuscript
revised and edited by

Marsi Tabak

based on the masterwork of Jewish history,
Dorot Harishonim
by Rabbi Yitzchak Eizik Halevy

researched and annotated by
Ben Zion Sobel

FELDHEIM PUBLISHERS Jerusalem / New York

This book was prepared for publication from a manuscript commissioned by the publisher. The author, a talented writer, chose to remain anonymous.

First Published 1990

FELDHEIM PUBLISHERS
200 Airport Executive Park
Nanuet, NY 10954

POB 35002
Jerusalem, Israel

Library of Congress Cataloging-in-Publication Data
Anonymous [Tabak, M., ed.]
And Rachel was his wife.
1. Akiba ben Joseph, ca. 50-ca. 132—Fiction.
2. Palestine—History—70-638—Fiction. I. Title.
PS3563.A784A85 1990 813'.54 88-33598
ISBN 0-87306-488-7

Typeset by Astronel
Printed in Israel

10 9 8

to the Women of Valor everywhere
whose sacrifices for the sake of Torah
have given rise to
generations of Torah scholars

מפרי כפיהן נטעו כרמים

Publisher's Preface

The lessons to be learned from Jewish history are undeniably invaluable, but they have often proved difficult to convey. The primary reason for this is that Jewish history, except in all-too-rare instances, has traditionally been presented in its driest, most unpalatable form. After the first unpleasant taste of it, relatively few willingly consume additional servings. The historical novel, therefore, plays a significant role in Jewish literature: it transforms unpalatable but vital data into a savory, unforgettable dish.

By definition, a historical novel is a work of fiction based on factual events, and preparing such a book for publication requires both a talent for creative writing and a great deal of research. Only after embarking on this project did Feldheim Publishers realize what a challenging undertaking it was. The subject — the life and times of Rabi Akiva — has been dealt with in various forms in the past, and so, it was assumed, there was no dearth of source material. But as the research began, it was soon discovered that earlier authors, some of whom have always been considered reliable, had based their own works on unreliable sources. An examination of the various texts available revealed numerous contradictions and conflicting interpretations of what was presumed to be "historical fact." The challenge, therefore, was to determine which version of history was the accurate one and then to weave the fictional narrative around it.

Rabbi Ben Zion Sobel, a Talmudic scholar of note, was charged with the task of research. A number of years ago, his mentor, Rabbi Yaakov Kamenecki *zt"l*, encouraged him to study the monumental work of Jewish history, *Dorot Harishonim* by Rabbi Yitzchak Eizik Halevy *zt"l*, who was, in the words of Rabbi Kamenecki, "undoubtedly the final authority ('*posek acharon*') on the subject....One should pore over ('*horeveh*') his words as over those of a *rishon*." Further evidence of Halevy's credibility as both a historian and a *talmid chacham* is found in the letters to him from Rabbi Chaim Soloveitchik (the *Brisker Rav*) and Rabbi Chaim Ozer Grodzensky *zt"l*, who held Halevy in the highest esteem. (The same Rabbi Halevy conceived of the idea of Agudas Yisrael, a world organization which would unite religious Jewry everywhere under one banner.) In the light of such outstanding recommendations, and upon consultation with Rabbi Zalman Nechemiah Goldberg, *rosh kollel* of Kollel Shevet U'Mechokek, it was decided that Halevy would be the primary research source for historical accuracy.

The knowledgeable reader will note certain historical novellae, *chiddushim* regarding chronology, personalities, etc. which are at variance with conventional interpretations. These novellae are in accordance with the conclusions of Halevy, who delved deeply into the relevant sources to clarify obscure and contradictory points in the Talmud and the *Midrash*. A thorough study of his work is highly recommended.

In order to reap maximum benefit from *And Rachel Was His Wife*, the reader is advised to examine the extensive references provided. In several instances, however, some of the details in the source cited for a given passage may appear to contradict the rendering of the narrative. This is due to the fact that wherever Halevy's interpretation or understanding of events conflicted with that of the commentaries, Halevy's was the version presented here.

The character "Leah," her family members, servants and close friends, excluding "Rachel," are entirely fictional, as is much of their dialogue, although their intrinsic nature and conduct are typical of the era. Certain other characters were constructed from data compiled from several sources. In some cases, the sequence of events was inferred from various references; however, no fictitious activities were ascribed to genuine personalities mentioned by *Chazal*.

A number of problematic points were resolved with the help of Rabbi Zalman Nechemiah Goldberg, who was the final arbiter of this work. The customs and mores of the period and the geography and topography of the region were verified by Dr. Yehoshua Schwartz, professor of Jewish history at Bar Ilan University. Their assistance contributed significantly to the quality of this book.

It is sincerely hoped that reading this volume will lead to further study of our Holy Torah and the infinite wisdom of the Sages of Israel, and an appreciation of Jewish history as a means for understanding both the past and the present.

CONTENTS

Publisher's Preface

Prologue: *In the morning...*
1

Part One: *...sow your seeds...*
7

Part Two: *...and in the evening...*
129

Part Three: *...do not desist...*
247

Epilogue: *...both shall be good.*
277

Glossary
285

References
295

As you know not the way of the wind,
nor how bones grow in the womb,
you know not the workings of Hashem,
    Who makes all.
In the morning, sow your seeds,
and in the evening do not desist,
for you know not which shall prosper,
    this or that,
or whether they both shall be good.

Ecclesiastes 11:6

PROLOGUE

In the morning...

I AM AN OLD WOMAN NOW, much older than I ever imagined I would become, and I have seen many things in my long life: war, pestilence, the rise and fall of the fortunes of our People — and I have witnessed the most horrendous disaster of all. But I have also seen greatness. Few are so privileged.

I had the tremendous good fortune to have had Rachel as a lifelong friend, Rachel who was so uniquely outstanding that her actions influenced everyone she touched. Like pebbles tossed in a pond, each word she spoke and each deed she performed caused ripples that flowed out in ever-widening circles.

We all admired Rachel, but we envied her too. And I, who admired and loved her more than all the others, was also the most jealous of her.

Beautiful, she always was; she stood out among the young girls of the neighborhood like the radiant full moon among the pale stars of the midnight sky. She looked as we imagined a princess of King David's house must have looked — tall and arrow-straight, with long dark braids that glinted with highlights like the copper-veined rocks at Timna, and clear, bright eyes that seemed to pierce to the center of one's being.

But it was not her beauty that we envied — that was simply a part of her, like the cedar tree's great height, or the way reeds by the water sway gracefully with the breeze.

Was it Rachel's wealth that stirred our envy? Her father was the richest man in the entire district, and she, being his only child, was to inherit everything: the land, the sheep and cattle, the well-stocked barns and houses, even the carved chest of hyssop wood that held the precious scrolls written by the most expert of scribes — and Rachel could read and understand them, and even discuss them with the itinerant scholars who so often were guests at her father's house.

In actual fact, Rachel was the only girl I knew of who could read — until she taught me. And how could she possibly have guessed my secret desire to decipher the little black symbols that danced in neat rows across the parchment? I had never so much as hinted at it; that skill has always been reserved for men, although many of them are even more ignorant than I. And when I had mastered reading, Rachel taught me to write, though I never could equal her beautifully formed letters that looked like embroidery upon the page.

This was to remain our secret for many years. My mother once became quite faint when she came upon me unannounced as I sat scribbling notes in my room. From that time on, I was to be branded "unconventional," a girl noted for her contrariness — which did nothing to discourage me. Of course, the entire matter of reading and writing had nothing whatsoever to do with rebellion, but Imma would never have understood that.

I digress; forgive me. The ability to read and write, which I owe to Rachel, carries me away in so many directions — and not always where I wish to go. I was telling you about Rachel's wealth.

Her father's holdings were vast (people spoke of four *beit kur* — that's some 300,000 square *ammot*!). There is no one today who can compare with him. In addition to a gold-roofed mansion in Jerusalem and storehouses always filled to capacity, he had an estate which extended from our village all the way to the banks of the Yarden, and orchards in the Levonah Valley. His fields and groves yielded more than anyone else's, his ewes regularly bore twins, and his herds gave the richest, creamiest milk. Yes, it seemed there was a special blessing upon everything he owned. But he never hoarded his wealth; he shared it generously, in good times and bad.

No, we were not jealous of her wealth, present or future. She never boasted, never cast it up in our faces; she always behaved like one of us. Her gowns were of the finest linen, spun and woven by her own hand, but they were cut more simply and modestly than all the others. She never wore any jewelry — though her maidservant used to brag about chests full of precious ornaments belonging to her mistress — except for a narrow silver bracelet which was left to her by her mother and which she wore on Shabbat. Rachel never acted the part of a rich girl — she was always just... herself.

And her lineage? Her mother was a descendant of an ancient noble house, and her father was as righteous as he was rich and renowned not only for his philanthropy, but for his integrity and erudition, as well.

Now, don't misunderstand, there's nothing wrong with me. My family background is rather good — I am Leah bat Shaul and my forebears were fine, solid citizens, with quite a few learned men among them, not to mention successful merchants. Unlike Rachel's family, we lived in this area year-'round — for generations, in fact — and our estate, while not nearly as extensive as that of Rachel's family, was far from humble.

I'm not bad-looking either. You should have seen me then — even going around together with Rachel, I must say I made quite an impression on people... but perhaps it was because I was with *her*?

Again I'm wandering. No, we did not envy Rachel her

beauty, or her wealth, or her parentage. What was it, then, that aroused such strong feelings in all her childhood friends, and especially in me? I've thought about it, over and over again, and I believe it was this: We all felt that there was something special about Rachel, some great attribute that no one else possessed — certainly none of the girls and women in our village or in the countryside. Somehow we knew, even then, that she was destined for greatness.

When I was yet a girl, it was suggested to me that I keep a record of my meetings and conversations with Rachel. Well, I did, but I was young and frivolous then and my notes of those encounters surely reflect that immaturity. Still, I maintained my "journal" throughout my lifetime, jotting down an episode here and a thought there, like the weaving I was trained to do but could never quite bring myself to work on with any degree of diligence.

Despite my haphazardness, a pattern of rather touching beauty began to emerge and, as with weaving, the glimpse of wonders at hand gave me the incentive to persevere. This, then, is the story of my friend Rachel, and the story of her husband, whose rise to greatness was Rachel's crowning achievement.

But at the same time, it is the story of our People — of their hopes and dreams, their abandonment of faith and return to it, and of the events that molded their lives. As I reread the earlier pages, I cringe at my silliness, my emptyheadedness, but for the sake of simple honesty, I have not revised my original notes. Undoubtedly, historians will see to that — and there is no question in my mind that Rachel and her Akiva will find their place in history.

But I *knew* Rachel, and you can believe me when I say that Rachel was everything a true daughter of Israel should be, and everything a woman *could* be. Yet she prided herself on only one thing: she was Akiva's wife.

PART ONE

... sow your seeds...

1

THE WEATHER WAS SO PERFECT yesterday that I was determined to get Rachel out of her house. She never went out very much and we were always begging her to go along with us to the marketplace, to see what wares they were showing, but Rachel always had an excuse. She never was interested in going to the fairs either, not the one before Pesach, or the one before Sukkot. But yesterday, the noise, the music, the aromas of the fair were so enticing that I was certain even she could not resist.

"Come on, Rachel," I told her, "there's nothing so bad in those places. Don't you want to see all kinds of different people, people from all over, with red hair and blue eyes, and dressed in animal skins? Or those others, all black from the sun, with heavy copper chains around their necks? And what about the acrobats and the jugglers, and the dwarfs and the giants?" How could she refuse?

"The only place I really enjoy seeing," Rachel replied, "is the *Beit Hamikdash* in Jerusalem, with the *kohanim* bringing the sacrifices, and the *levi'im* singing their holy songs and playing sweet melodies on their harps and psalteries... And how can any marketplace perfume compare to the scent of the *ketoret*?

And the thrill of being part of the hundreds of thousands of Jews from all over *Eretz Yisrael* and abroad, going up to the Holy Temple. And do you know that no matter how many there are, there's room for everyone! To be so close to the *Shechinah*..."

Well! I was flattered that she confided in me, especially since she never spoke about such matters to the other girls, but I told her: "Now listen, Rachel! Of course we all like to see that, but it's not really exciting — it's the same every time. I like to see things that are new, that are different. I heard about a new arcade opening in Shechem — a hundred shops under one roof. You can get anything you want there — if you only have the money. I doubt if Abba would let me go, unless..."

Rachel took my hand. "Leah, do you think that's what life is all about? Running from one shop to another, keeping up with the latest fashions, always looking for excitement? That can't be the purpose of our lives! Yes, we are fortunate to be in our own Land, and to be able to fulfill the will of *Hakadosh Baruch Hu*. But think about how close we came to destruction, when Pompey conquered the Holy City and defiled the Temple, and subjugated our People to Roman rule. And yes, we are lucky to be living as we do — being able to keep all the *mitzvot* of *Eretz Yisrael*; being *oleh regel* three times a year, going up to Jerusalem! Just to see the *Simchat Beit Hashoevah* there — whoever has not seen that has never seen real joy... And what juggler at the fair can match the skill of the torch-juggling Rabbis? But times are hard now, what with the Romans occupying our Land, and the heathens always ready to stir up trouble. Oh, when will we have our own king again, from David's house? Until then, Leah, how can we ever be really happy and carefree, when so many of our People are dispersed among the nations and suffering..."

That was the longest speech I had ever heard her make, and I must say that her words sent a chill up my spine. But still, I felt I had to tell her, for her own good: "Rachel, you're an idealist and I'm a realist. Your fancy ideas won't get you anywhere. Don't you want to get some fun out of life? Always praying, or reading the Psalms, or stuck in the house helping your father! Come to town with us — there's a big sale of second-hand jewelry and clothing, all in the latest style! Helena bat Gurion (you remember — her name used to be Channah) is trying to raise money to redeem her Alexander from the debtors' prison. It's a great chance to buy some really good stuff, and the prices are sure to be low — there are so many others in the same situation!"

"Leah," she said, "I really would go with you, just to make you happy. But I can't. There's a new herdsman coming to ask my father about a job. It'll be around midday, and I should see to it that there's some food and drink waiting. He's coming all the way from Upper Galilee, and that's quite a trip. You know Abba depends on me for all such things. I'm sorry. Maybe next time..."

At first I thought, She can't be serious! Herdsmen come and go all the time, and there are plenty of servants to wait on her father. Then I realized that she was telling me, in her very special way, that even attending the interview of a lowly shepherd was more important to her than my favorite pastime.

Anyone else making such "holy" speeches would sound like a fake, like a goody-goody. But coming from her, every word was just and right and true, and for a moment I felt exactly as she did — but only for a moment. I wanted to be great and noble and idealistic like Rachel, but I knew I never would.

"So have it your way. Stay home and be a good daughter. And good luck with the new herdsman — *if* he gets the job. I'll tell you everything you missed when we get back tonight."

We got back very late last night after the sale — where we only looked, but didn't bid, since there was nothing there that really appealed to us, and there were no bargains, either — and we stopped at a fresh excavation at the edge of town. The foundation of a new building had been started. The stones were smoothly cut, but laid in an unfamiliar pattern. Who could think of putting up a house in these hard times? We asked some elderly men passing by, but they looked at us peculiarly and pretended they didn't know.

Now *there* was a mystery! Finally, we got hold of a young boy, who was dressed in the latest fashion: his sidelocks were trimmed short, and his hair was quite long and curled. He wore a short white *chiton*, but you could still tell he was a nice Jewish child.

"Who is building this house?" I asked. If it were anyone from our circles we would have known about it. But who among the lower classes could afford to even buy a lot, much less put up such a fine, big foundation? The cornerstone alone must have needed four oxen to haul it in place!

The boy just stared at us; he seemed embarrassed. "Well, it's not really a house," he said.

"So what is it, then, if not a house?" Penelope asked. (She's my younger sister, and always puts herself forward.)

"It's going to be a . . . a temple."

"What do you mean, a temple? A synagogue? Here, in the middle of the road? No one would build a *beit knesset* at the edge of town!" I insisted.

"It's not a Jewish temple," the boy continued. "It's a Roman one. Look — you see that big square stone over there? That's going to be an altar to Mercury, the god of travelers. All the Romans passing by here or entering the town will pay tribute or offer a sacrifice. I heard the legionnaires talking about it last night in my father's inn."

"What do you mean?" I was getting very excited. "This isn't one of the garrison cities! It's bad enough that the Romans have the *chutzpah* to build their altars and worship their idols on our holy soil, wherever their soldiers are quartered. But here? There's no garrison anywhere near here!"

It was too dreadful to imagine. We all thought we'd be spared here of having to witness their pagan atrocities. "Well, they'll never catch me passing by here," I said. "Once this abomination is completed, I'll go the other way around." I was indignant.

"Won't help you a bit. They're building another one on the opposite side! So, you'll stay home all day?"

"Enough of your insolence! Too bad you had to pick up such stuff at the inn. If your father had gotten a rabbi to give you lessons, you'd have better manners!" I turned on my heel, dragging along Penelope and Miriam, my friend from the estate next to ours, and strode off so quickly that poor old Bilha (who used to be my nursemaid and now serves as my constant chaperone) and her husband, Shemuel, had to hurry to catch up.

What a horrible boy! I thought. I'll have to speak to Father about providing Aaron, my younger brother, with instruction — I already caught him playing with the assimilated boys, and he had taken off his *tallit kattan*!

We told the whole story when we came home, and my parents were very upset. They wanted to keep me home but I begged them to let me go to Rachel in the morning.

"As long as it's Rachel, I give you permission," my mother said. "You'll only learn good from her." Even *she* seems to realize that Rachel is different.

2

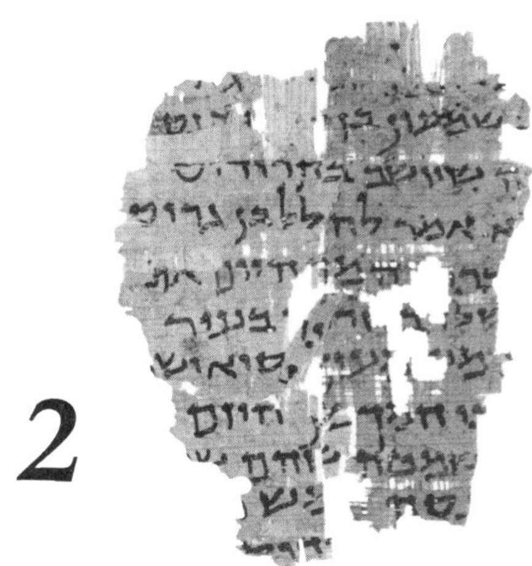

SO I WENT OVER THERE as soon as I'd finished my stint at spinning. I don't know why, with all the poor Jewish women around begging for work, Father insists that I do this menial task — it's so boring.

Rachel was dressed in her gray homespun, made from wool shorn from her father's own sheep. She was happy to see me, and brought out a very good drink, a concoction of date-honey and water flavored with citron. I told her everything that had happened the day before, including the disappointing auction, and the nasty little boy at the excavation.

When I finished, I saw her eyes were full of tears. "Don't be upset, Rachel," I said. "I'm sure that boy was only making up the whole thing to spite me."

"Oh, Leah, how I wish you were right! But that is what is happening all over *Eretz Yisrael*, and it's our own fault!"

"What do you mean? It's the Romans who are to blame, and maybe even that spiteful brat and his like. How can you say it's *our* fault?"

"Because when our People abandon the Torah, and instead devote their time to sports and games with the invaders, *they* gain power over us, and we become their slaves!" She struggled to control her voice, but it trembled and broke.

I tried to remain calm. "We talked about that already, Rachel. For now, we have to accept the Roman occupation. We can still be good Jews. Besides, there's nothing wrong with adapting to modern trends — we're not living in the time of Avraham *Avinu*, after all."

"Leah, let's not talk about this any more — it hurts too much. So are your parents going to hire someone to give Aaron Torah lessons?"

"They're thinking about it. They don't want him to lose out on his secular studies, though — language, mathematics, poetry, philosophy. Perhaps they can find an instructor who is proficient in both religious and secular subjects."

Actually, there'd been quite an argument. The strange thing was that Mother insisted that Aaron study only with the old Hebrew teacher who had taught her brothers, while Father was adamant that he get a good secular education. "After all, he has to make a living!" he had insisted. I wouldn't tell any of that to Rachel, of course.

"What ever happened with your herdsman?" I asked, just to change the subject. "Did he come on time? What did he look like? Did your father give him the job?"

She blushed and nodded, but did not answer.

"Oh, he must be very handsome! How old is he? Is he married? How does he look?" Here was my chance to tease my always-poised, dignified friend.

"First question — first answer: Yes, he came on time, and no, he is not very handsome, or particularly young either. He's tall and burnt by the sun — he's been a shepherd all his life — and he looks tired and worn, and his name is Akiva."

"Well, then, what are you blushing about? There must be something about him, or you'd tell me more." I was very curious; Rachel was acting so agitated, so unlike her usual serene self.

"Well, I'm not sure he's the one, but do you remember there was an Akiva ben Yosef whom everyone was talking about a couple of years ago? His father was descended from Sisera, the heathen general who was killed by Yael, but he became a *ger*, and in those days that was a daring thing to do.

"So, back to Akiva. The story goes that he worked for a man down south for three years, and when the time came for him to collect his wages and go back to his home, he asked his master to pay him what he was owed. But the master told him he had no money. Akiva said, 'Then give me grain.' The master said he had none. 'Then set aside a field as my salary,' Akiva suggested, but the master told him he had no fields. Finally Akiva asked for payment in cattle or even in furniture or bedding. The master said, 'I don't have any such things.'

"Akiva returned to his home emptyhanded; he had served his master for three years without pay!

"After Sukkot, the master took a sack of coins, several donkeys laden with food and drink, sweet fruits and pastries, and went to the home of his former servant. The master gave Akiva his salary, and all the gifts he had brought along. Then he asked: 'What did you think when I refused to give you your salary?'

"Akiva answered, 'I thought that you had no cash; that you hadn't separated the tithe from your grain; that your herds and fields were rented out. But when you wouldn't even give me furniture or bedding, I thought you must have dedicated all your belongings to the Temple.'

"The master said, 'In truth, that is exactly how it was. And how did you guess? My son did not want to study, and I thought I'd force him to do so by pledging all my property to the *Beit Hamikdash*. But the Rabbis agreed to annul my vow. As you have judged me kindly, may the Holy One judge you kindly too!'"

Rachel could see I was impressed. "Leah, I think this must be the same Akiva ben Yosef!" she said. "What a great person, to give his old master the benefit of the doubt like that! Just put yourself in his place — going home with nothing after working faithfully for three whole years! And no complaints! I didn't know that anyone could be so noble and selfless — and he understood and forgave his master's actions without knowing the reason behind them... Doesn't that show something about Akiva?"

"You're right. I don't know anyone like that either. He must be quite educated to know all those *dinim.* Otherwise, he'd never have let the man get away with not paying him."

Rachel's color deepened and she cast down her eyes. "No, he's not educated at all — he doesn't even know an *alef* from a *beit.* All he knows are bits that he picked up here and there in his wanderings. I guess his parents must have been very poor, if they never sent him to a teacher..."

"Oh, Rachel, you always make excuses for everyone." Her way of never criticizing or finding fault could be exasperating. "So he's just a country boor who knows all about sheep and goats and nothing else. So he did a nice thing once — good for him! But I still don't understand why you're so excited about him. And don't try to deny it — I can tell from your face."

"Excited? No, not exactly. But still, it seems to me that he must be someone very special; he's not just a plain shepherd, I'm sure. There must be something more to him."

She still wouldn't look me in the eye, so I said straight out: "Rachel, I think you're really interested in this man! Are you crazy? When every rich young man around is begging your father for your hand, you're even considering this...this *nobody*? What's come over you?" I just couldn't control myself, and the words came tumbling out against my will.

Rachel was quiet. Then she said gently: "I have no intention of marrying anyone right now. I'm definitely *not* interested in any of those young men you mentioned — they only care about sports and games, running off to the Roman gymnasia, dressing up and drinking and gambling. That's not the kind of husband I want. I want a person who has good *middot*, who cares about our People and is devoted to learning and to doing *chessed*. No one around here is like that — they're just silly puppies that want to play all day long."

That hurt, though I'm sure Rachel didn't realize it. For a long time, my parents have been considering Tertius ben Judah for me — Tuvia, he used to be — and they just asked my consent. Now I'll have to think it over, because yes, though he has plenty of money, he is rather silly, always going off to the stadium and the theater with his friends. I'll have to think hard...maybe Rachel is right.

"Rachel, I'm sorry. I was only joking. You deserve the finest and the greatest husband in the world, and I'm sure that you will find him — or rather, that he'll find you. Don't mind my foolish tongue; it often says things I don't really mean. Good-bye — and do try to come and visit me soon."

I hurried down the steps and turned toward the pasture. I must admit I'd become rather curious about this Akiva; if Rachel thought so well of him, he couldn't be just run-of-the-mill.

And then I saw him! I recognized him immediately from her description. He looked old for a shepherd — they're mostly young boys — and he was quite shabby too, and she hadn't bothered to mention that he was nearly *bald*! But despite his appearance, I saw what she meant. He *was* special. The modest way he bore himself, and the gentleness with which he handled the sheep made me think of Moshe *Rabbenu*, how he'd searched for the lost lamb, and carried it back so tenderly in his arms. Of course Rachel would never marry such a poor and ignorant person, but now at least I could understand why he so impressed her.

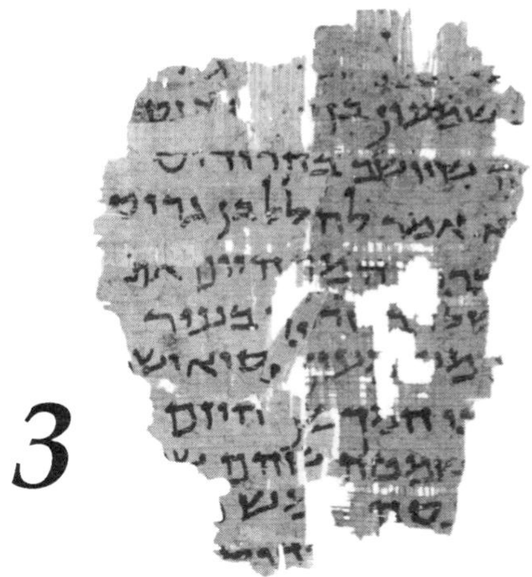

3

HARVEST TIME ARRIVED, and Rachel and I could not meet for quite a while. There were mountains of food to be prepared and taken out to the workers, jugs of drink to be filled and refilled, sacks of fresh straw to be prepared for bedding. Father personally made sure that the men put in a good day's work — if not, we could always find others. He also made sure they abided by the *halachah*: he suspected that one young fellow purposely dropped grain so that his mother could glean it later. Father is a just man, but there's no sense in giving away more than one has to.

So it was busy, busy, busy, with hardly any time to breathe. The last evening of the harvest, who should come over but Devorah, Rachel's servant, with a bowl of fresh white cheese curds. Of course she'd want to chat with our Puah, so I immediately went inside to hear the latest.

"This new shepherd is really the limit!" I heard her tell Puah. "He was arguing with the master and I heard him say, 'Who needs all these scholars and wise men? They only talk all the time, and don't really do anything. And they're so proud of themselves. What's the use of all their learning?' And then he said, 'I'd rather take care of the sheep and earn an honest living. Talk, talk, talk, that's all they do!' "

Puah's eyes were popping out, and frankly, so were mine! How dare Akiva speak that way to the great ben Kalba Savua! (That isn't his real name, of course, but it's been used for so many years that even those who might have heard his real name announced at his *brit* surely have forgotten it by now. It seems an odd name — "the Replete Dog" — but there's a good reason for it: any man who comes to his house, as ravenous as a starving dog, is given nourishment until he's eaten his fill and can eat no more. Ben Kalba Savua is a genuine *tzaddik*!)

"So what did your master say to that?" Puah asked Devorah. "He's got all those Bible scrolls, and they say he knows all of them by heart, almost. He'd know what answer to give to that stupid shepherd!"

"Well, I was surprised," Devorah told us. "He didn't yell or anything — he just said that if Akiva had had more learning, he'd have put him in charge of the slaughterhouse, deciding which animals were fit to be used and so on. As it is, he'll stay out in the fields," she finished.

"Good! That's where he belongs, with his talk against the scholars! Just let him stay out there!" And Puah offered some of that morning's *pittah* to our visitor. It was a bit burnt anyway, so I was sure Father wouldn't mind.

Well! That was interesting: Akiva's only been there a short time, and already he's giving opinions! That'll cure Rachel for sure! I went to bed feeling quite relieved and the next few weeks gave me no cause for worry.

Now all the grain is in the barns, threshed and winnowed. It's time to shear the sheep, but since that's done by the regular farm laborers, we have a few hours each day for visiting. Naturally I wanted to see Rachel — I hadn't met her for two whole months. So I took along Penelope (I didn't want to — she's such a nosy pest — but Imma insisted) and I told her she would have to play outdoors while we talked.

When we arrived, everything seemed to be in the usual perfect order, but I got a funny feeling just the same. I left Penelope outside and asked Devorah if I could see Rachel. She seemed a bit reluctant — said her mistress wasn't feeling so well — but she finally took me to Rachel's room.

Rachel was standing at the window, and when she turned to me, I saw that her eyes were red-rimmed, and her face pale and swollen.

"Rachel! What's the matter? What's happened?" I was thoroughly frightened; my dear Rachel, who usually concealed her emotions so smoothly, looked distraught and miserable.

"Oh, Leah! Haven't you heard? Rabban Gamliel the *Nasi* was *niftar*. A messenger from Hyrcanos brought the news this morning. Oh, oh, oh —" and she burst into tears.

"*Baruch Dayan Ha-emet!*" I gave her the handkerchief I always carry with me (Mother trained us well) and tried to comfort her. "Surely his son, Shimon, will take his place. He's intelligent and creative and capable of leadership."

"Leah, do you think that it is only intelligence and leadership that we have lost? Each Sage is an entire world unto himself! There is no compensation for a scholar's death, certainly not for one of Rabban Gamliel's stature. Listen: You know how it has become customary for families to spend exhorbitant sums for funerals, especially for elaborate burial shrouds woven of gold and silver thread. People have been known to beggar themselves in an effort to demonstrate how devoted they were to their departed relative. Rabban Gamliel decided to put a stop to this and ordered that upon his death he be buried in a simple shroud of linen. Such humility! I'm sure, Leah, that his example will be followed now by everyone. That's the sort of leadership the Nation needs. We must pray that Rabban Shimon will carry on the tradition of the House of David."

Well, of course I couldn't disagree with her about that, but it was getting quite depressing. I fished around for something else to talk about. "How's the harvest this year? And the fleece — did you get the same as last year, or less? Everyone around is complaining."

She lifted her head. "Yes, we all noticed that the grain was poorer, probably due to the drought. But strangely, our sheep gave more wool, and of better quality, than ever before."

"You're lucky. All the others say that the wool this year is so bad it's hardly worth carding and spinning. Could it be that new shepherd of yours, Akiva?" I asked.

That strange look I had noticed weeks ago came back to her face. "Yes, everyone says so," she answered. "Abba never before had a man so devoted to the animals — he cares for them as if they were his children. He carries the newborn lambs in his arms, he brings fodder to the ewes so they'll have plenty of milk, he keeps the rams from fighting, and he stays awake all night to guard the flock from the wolves. Yes, he certainly deserves all the praise he's getting. Hashem seems to bless the work of his hands."

"So this Akiva *is* someone special," I said. "In these bad times, when the workers are lazy and often disregard their masters' commands, that's most unusual. But I heard he argued with your father about learning — didn't that make trouble for him?"

"It did, at first. But Abba realizes that the only reason Akiva is angry at the *talmidei chachamim* is because he has no learning at all, so he cannot understand or appreciate what they do. He only understands action — and all his actions seem to be perfect! Leah, he's so modest, so kind, so good to everyone, even the children of the lowest servants, and especially his own son. Oh, did I tell you he's a widower and he's raised the boy all by himself? Leah, I've never met anyone like him!"

"Rachel, you've said this before — it sounds to me as if you want to marry Akiva. Don't do it! Don't throw your comfortable life away for that...that boor! You'll regret it forever!" I heard my voice growing louder and louder, but I couldn't stop myself.

Rachel went to shut the door, and leaned against it. "Leah, how can you read my mind — or, rather, my heart? My mind tells me he has no education, no property or prospects, and that he's too old for me. But in my heart and soul, I feel that he is destined for me. When we talked about Rabban Gamliel before, I thought: Oh, if only there had been a chance for Akiva to learn when he was young! And then I thought — please don't laugh at me — Akiva will also be great one day. Now isn't that ridiculous? I've always wanted to marry a real *talmid chacham*, and Akiva can't even read! But I can see that he has a wonderful future in store for him. What do you think, Leah?" She looked at me with those big eyes as if she really wanted my advice.

"He'd be a fool not to accept you. You're young, beautiful, intelligent, a prospective heiress — you've got everything anyone could want. Of course he'll want to marry you. He's no fool, that's for sure. But you, Rachel — I don't understand you at all anymore. You're always talking about scholars — and there are plenty of them around who would jump at the chance to make such a good *shidduch*. Why don't you just forget about that Akiva; you can do much better!" It bothered me to have to speak to her like that, but it was for her own good.

"But Leah, I can't forget about him. I've tried and tried, and I just can't," Rachel said. "Leah, I asked him to marry me — and he refused!"

"*You*...asked...*him*...to marry you...and he *refused*?!" I couldn't believe my ears. "I don't know who's crazier, you or Akiva! You both are! Crazy, crazy, crazy!" After that outburst, I fell silent. For once I was speechless.

Rachel, too, was quiet for a long time. Then she took my hand in hers and said, "Leah, it's not the way you think. For a long time I've been observing Akiva from afar, and whenever he comes to the house to speak to my father, I try to hear what they're saying. I feel I really know him well. You remember about his old master, how he didn't pay Akiva for all his hard labor, and Akiva didn't bear him a grudge? That's how he is in everything: absolutely righteous! Oh, if only he'd want to learn Torah — I know he's capable!

"When I spoke to him last week, and said that I'd want to share my life with him if he would agree to study and become a *talmid chacham*, do you know what he answered? He said, 'Thank you for having so much confidence in me, but I never studied, and I'm too old to start now! And besides, I'm just not interested. What have the scholars and wise men ever done for us? They look down on plain, hardworking people. They think they have to purify themselves if we happen to touch their garments. No, I don't want to have anything to do with them. And how would I earn a living? Knowing letters and words doesn't put bread on the table!'

"And when I tried to tell him that the study of Torah is essential for a Jew, that it gives us life in this world and the next, he only answered, 'With all that fancy talk, you still can't put bread on the table'."

"So that's the end of it? Good!" I couldn't conceal the relief in my voice. "Maybe now you'll be interested in my cousin, Elazar — that's what I really wanted to talk to you about. He's coming from Alexandria next month, and I think he's just right for you: he's educated, handsome and quite well-versed in Scripture. Father has written to his family about you, and they've already consented — that is, if you agree, of course." This is the perfect match for Rachel, I thought, and I felt quite smug. It had been my idea all along, but only my parents were aware of that.

So what did Rachel say to that? She released my hand which she had been gripping tightly all this time, and said, "Leah, thank you for thinking of me. It's really very good of you. But your cousin — and I'm sure he's a very fine young man — is not for me. I know that I am destined for Akiva. Perhaps there'll be a miracle and he'll change his mind about learning, and about marrying me. That is what I am praying for." And she actually took out a *Tehillim* and with me still in the room, she started whispering the words!

When I realized there was nothing further to be done there, I took my leave. Foolish, stubborn Rachel. She has a brilliant mind, but no common sense at all!

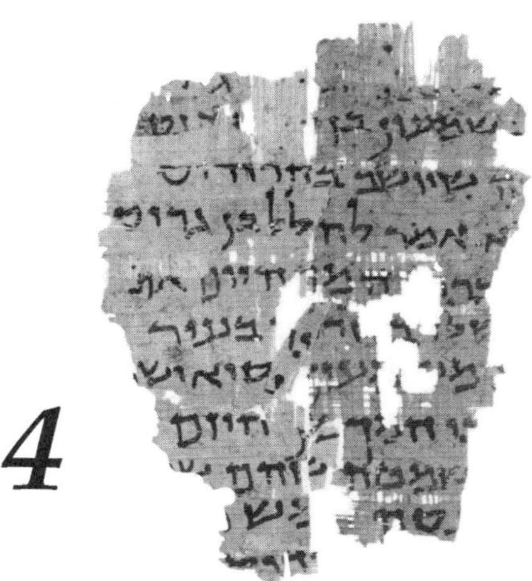

4

THE NEXT THING I HEARD, Rachel and Akiva were married! This was in *Marcheshvan*, just before the beginning of the winter rains. The whole town was talking about it: Rachel, the rich, beautiful, well-bred daughter of Kalba Savua had married a shepherd more than twice her age, descended from heathens, a widower with a young son and without a *prutah* to his name! There must be something wrong with her, people were whispering — how was such a marriage possible? And her father was so opposed to the *shidduch* that he had disinherited her, thrown her out of the house with only the clothes on her back, and sworn that she and that husband of hers would never see even a *zuz* of his money!

All this talk hurt me deeply. Although I had to agree with the general opinion about her marriage, she was still the same great, wonderful, idealistic Rachel whom I admired and loved so much. I quarreled with all my friends who called her insane, even though I'd done the same; and I did not allow anyone in the house to say a word against her. When Penelope repeated a rhyme that all the street urchins were singing at their games, I lost my temper and smacked her. Out of spite, she sang it again:

"Rachel, Rachel, sitting in the straw
Thinks Akiva can learn the Holy Law...
La, la, la, la, la, la..."

and so on. My parents had made me promise never to go to Rachel's house; I guess they were afraid I might do the same thing, marry some poor man without their consent, but they needn't have worried — I'm not Rachel.

I *had* to see her. I heard she was living in Geva, a depressing little hamlet about six *milin* away from our estate, and I decided that I would go there. But what about my promise to my parents? Surely it didn't apply *now*... Still, I was reluctant to reveal my plans and get into a whole discussion with them.

So I waited for the right day, when everyone would be very busy and they wouldn't miss me or ask too many questions. (Bilha, I knew, could be trusted not to let on, although I was less sure of Shemuel, her husband, who was obliged to accompany me for "protection.") I packed up some food: a few flatcakes, dried figs and dates, and a small jug of wine — I find that's always handy, and Rachel surely couldn't afford any, the way things were going now.

Walking along the road, wrapped in my second-best wool shawl, I felt quite light-hearted and adventurous. But as I came nearer to that miserable Geva, I started to worry again.

Would Rachel be glad to see me? Would I be able to control myself, to stop myself from saying, "I told you so!" seeing her in such awful circumstances? I know people exaggerate, but I'd heard the most dreadful things about the way they were living...

Finally, I reached the score or so of dilapidated houses that make up Geva. A shabby old man pointed to the most decrepit one of all — a heap of rough stones plastered with lime — and said with a sneer, "You want to find Rachel, the wife of Akiva? That's where she is!" Oh, my poor Rachel!, I thought. Even this wretched fellow looks down on you!

I knocked on the splintery door and nearly fainted when

that dear, familiar voice called, "Enter!" Somehow, I'd kept believing it was all a dream, and Rachel was still living comfortably in her father's house.

I raised my hand to the *mezuzah* on the doorpost, and immediately saw my friend, busy at her spinning, pulling and twisting the coarse thread with her delicate fingers.

"Oh, Rachel!" I cried. All my good resolves vanished in an instant. I ran to her, threw my arms around her, and started to weep.

"I'm so happy to see you, Leah!" she said. "You're my very first visitor! Here — make a *berachah*," and she offered me water dipped from a clay jug on the floor.

I thanked her, grateful for the distraction. Reciting the *berachah* and drinking gave me a few moments to pull myself together. To think that this girl, who was accustomed to the best, had been reduced to such circumstances — it was unbearable!

"It's so good of you to come all this way to see me. I suppose it's too far for the other girls, and they're probably very busy..."

Same old Rachel, still thinking well of everyone, still finding excuses for them. She knew that the rainy season is slack, with very little to do. She went back to her distaff, and started to twirl the spindle and twist the thread.

"Please forgive my working while you're here," she said. "We can talk just as well, as we always did."

Of course I knew it was because she needed the money so desperately. I had heard that she was supporting her husband while he went off with his son, Yehoshua, to some *alef-beit* teacher for little children. My curiosity got the better of me, and I asked the question that had been bothering me all this time:

"How did you ever get Akiva to change his mind about learning Torah? You wouldn't have married him otherwise, I know. But he was so set against learning, and against the Rabbis..." I felt a little awkward interrogating her so rudely.

After all, we were no longer on our previous more-or-less equal footing. Still, I *had* to find out.

But Rachel was not embarrassed at all. "Do you remember the day you were at my house, and I prayed for a miracle?"

"How could I forget?" I said. "Don't tell me a bolt of lightning struck him and made him change his mind!"

"No, but it was a miracle just the same. That evening, when he took the sheep to drink at the stream, he found himself watching the water splash against the rocks. Then he noticed how the rocks had been polished smooth, and even hollowed out by drops of water — many, many little drops, falling year after year. He picked up a stone, a huge one, and discovered that the water had worn a hole right through it! When he came back to the house, he showed me the stone, and said, 'Rachel, if those gentle droplets of water can pierce a rock, surely the powerful words of Torah can pierce the soft flesh of my heart and mind.'

"That was the miracle I'd been hoping for! I knew that if only he'd *want* to learn, he would succeed. I'd seen how he was with his flock — patient, industrious, devoted. And so we married..."

That was quite a moving story, and I admit I was touched. I looked around at the dingy room. "And is it true, what they're saying about your father? That he forbade you — ?"

"Hush!" Rachel said gently. "He has always been the best, the kindest father in the world. How could he understand that I saw greatness in Akiva? No one else sees it, or understands it."

I had to agree with her there — *I* certainly couldn't. So I decided to talk about cooking and housekeeping. That's always a perfect subject for young brides, though there seemed to be nothing whatsoever to cook in that place, and no furniture or tapestries or dishes or linens to discuss. I saw I'd have to be very tactful.

"You know, Rachel, I just ate a delicious new dish at Shifra's wedding, roast duck stuffed with a quail. I asked the cook for the recipe and it sounds quite easy. Would you like to have it?"

"Thank you, Leah. You're so considerate, but I really don't have the facilities. Besides, Akiva and Yehoshua like simple food, and I really have no time to fuss with fancy dishes. Tell me, how's your family? And all our friends — Miriam, Elisheva, Shifra — oh, she just got married. And what about you, Leah?" She gave me such a loving look, like a kind and true sister. She really cares about me, about my happiness. And so I told her.

"Elazar? Your cousin from Alexandria?" Rachel was surprised. "Isn't he the one you suggested...?"

"Yes. Tertius was out — after hearing you speak about your Akiva, I realized I couldn't possibly marry him. Both sets of parents are in favor of the match, and I'm sure we'll have a pleasant and prosperous life together. Aren't you going to wish me *mazal tov?*"

Rachel embraced me. "*Mazal tov! Mazal tov!* Leah, I'm so delighted for you. I wish you that your life will be as happy and contented as mine and Akiva's!"

Looking at the heaps of straw on which they slept, and the meager pile of kindling that they would use to heat that awful room, I didn't think that was much of a wish. Of course, Rachel could always read my mind.

"Leah, please don't worry about me. You're comparing this room to my father's mansion. You mustn't — everything I've ever wanted is right here. Akiva studies for hours every day, and his progress is just...well, I'm very proud of him. He gathers fallen branches in the woods; half of them he sells and the other half we use ourselves. I'm so happy to be at his side, helping him and encouraging him! Oh, Leah, if only you'll be as fortunate as I am!"

Hearing that speech, I felt the snakebite of envy again, and in a moment the venom had coursed right through me. I burst out: "And do you think I should sleep on bundles of straw, like you? And eat dry bread and vegetables and drink only plain water from the brook? Is that what you want for me? Keep your good wishes — I don't need them!"

Rachel took my hands in that old familiar gesture. "Oh, Leah," she said, "I wish you and Elazar everything good that you wish for yourselves! The straw doesn't matter — I hardly notice it any more. In the beginning, it did disturb me: I couldn't sleep, with the stiff, dry stalks scratching my face and head. I tried to hide my discomfort because I knew how it distressed Akiva — his heart was so filled with pain over the great sacrifices he imagined I'd made by marrying him. And do you know what he said? 'With Hashem's help, I will be able to make it all up to you one day. If He grants me riches, then I'll set a golden crown on your head with an engraving of Jerusalem.' Since then I don't even notice the straw.

"As for the food," she went on, "it's ample for our needs. You know this is not a rich village. Just after we moved in, a stranger named Eliyahu came knocking at our door. His wife had just given birth, he said, and he didn't have even a bit of straw for her and the baby. So Akiva gave him a bundle of straw, and I gave him the bread that I was saving for the next day. He thanked us over and over — and for what? A crust of bread and a handful of hay? Akiva was astonished that there were people who were even poorer than we were. And that's when I knew he was ready to begin learning."

"I'm sorry, Rachel," I said, "but I don't follow you. What does one thing have to do with the other?"

"Don't you see, Leah? Akiva was so overwhelmed by our poverty — all he could see was that everyone else was richer than he was, and this thought would have distracted him from learning. But once he could see himself as a man of means, his mind would open to the words of Torah!

"Oh, Leah," she went on, "I'm certain that stranger was Eliyahu *Hanavi* — in such a subtle way, he showed us the Torah way of life. I feel so rich now, and the bread and water taste like the finest meat and wine."

"Rachel, Rachel! Was there ever a friend, or even a sister,

as good and kind as you? Your wish for me is truly the best one — that I may be as happy and contented as you are!" My words came out in a whisper.

I was afraid she wouldn't accept the package of fruit and wine I'd brought, but she put it on a little stool so it wouldn't spoil from the dampness of the floor. The fruit would go well with the bread, she said, and she'd save the wine for Shabbat.

I tried to persuade her to use a bit of olive oil on her work-worn hands. There's no excuse to let her beauty go to ruin. Rachel's hands were as cracked and rough as a maidservant's. I told her that at this rate, she'd be an old woman in no time.

We parted with smiles and tears and promises to visit one another again soon. I had no idea then that I was going to be so busy!

5

A YEAR AFTER OUR BETROTHAL, we were married in the usual ceremony in the courtyard of my parents' home. (We had had to wait so long because Imma was unwell for quite a while.) Father felt that in these hard times it's not right to be ostentatious, so there were only a hundred and eighty guests invited, including, of course, all Elazar's first and second cousins from our area. I never knew he had so many relatives!

The wedding presents began pouring in as soon as the invitations went out. I received some stunning jewelry from my bridegroom's family, and also a beautifully woven headscarf embroidered with pearls and gold-and-silver leaves from his aunt. I couldn't wait to wear my new gifts! I tried on the scarf, along with the gold hoops for my ears and the gold-and-silver necklace, and when I saw myself in the mirror, I thought I looked like a queen. My wedding day couldn't come soon enough for me — I was so impatient to wear my finery.

There was nothing lacking in my trousseau. I had seven shifts of the best linen, seven gowns, and seven sets of bedding filled with goose feathers. Oh, the countless rainy nights that I'd had to sit with the maidservants, separating the scratchy spines from those feathers! This job is even duller than spinning, but mother kept saying, "Some day you'll be glad I made you do this" — and now I am! Father bought the most modern, up-to-date furniture, without all that tiresome carving that's such a dust-collector, but it has to be transported all the way from the *Galil* and it won't get here for months. I guess I'll just have to be patient!

The wedding feast was simple but delicious: first, broiled fish sprinkled with almonds and raisins, then for the main course, a fat goose stuffed with a small duck (I didn't want it to be too much like Shifra's). The dessert was fresh figs and dates; appropriate wines were served with each course.

As is customary, a number of poor people had been invited. There was not quite enough room, so tables were set up for them near the edge of the road. But they received exactly the same food as the other guests (except for the wines; they were served the new wine, not the stuff that's been aging to perfection for years). My wedding was the talk of the town for weeks afterwards. In fact, when Miriam was finally married, she had almost the exact same menu. I was flattered, but rather annoyed at the same time.

The week after the wedding, when all the *sheva berachot* parties were over, I put on my favorite gift, that exquisite scarf, and went over to my parents' to pick up a few things I had left there: a mirror, an embroidery I had started and never finished, a pair of sandals I had left for Penelope — at the time I had nothing to wear them with, but now I have a new gown edged with silver, and I thought the silver trim on the sandals would match perfectly.

On the way, whom should I meet but Shifra. She complimented me lavishly on my appearance, but kept staring at my scarf.

"What do you think of it?" I asked. "It's a wedding present from Elazar's aunt. She bought it here in town — she said there's nothing like it even in Alexandria or Rome."

"But don't you remember, Leah? This is the kerchief

Rachel's mother left her — the only thing she took out of her father's house. I wonder how your aunt got hold of it?"

"I...I didn't realize...I can't imagine —" I stammered, but I had understood immediately. Rachel, my closest and dearest friend, had not been able to attend my wedding because she had given birth to a son only three days before. The *brit* had been held in their pitiful hovel in Geva and since it had taken place on Shabbat, it was impossible for me to be there.

Rachel must have sold that beautiful scarf, the only thing of her mother's that she had, to support her family, since she'd be unable to work for a while. Akiva still spent practically all of his time learning, so his wood business couldn't even begin to cover their expenses. I did hope that she had gotten a good price for it; she'll need proper nourishment to be able to care for her new baby, and the child will need some swaddling cloths at least, and some kind of cradle, unless he too is sleeping on straw.

Rachel must have bought some cheap rag instead, to cover her head, and here I was, showing off what felt like borrowed feathers! I felt awful. But what could I do? I decided to tell Mother, and ask her advice. Somehow, since I got married, I feel much closer to her, and what she says makes a lot more sense than it used to.

The first thing Mother said when I came to the house was, "Why are you wearing this fancy scarf? You should save it for *Yom Tov*, or at least Shabbat. Elazar's aunt would feel terrible if she knew you were using her expensive present just to walk around in town to do your errands."

"Tell me, Imma, do you know where she bought it? And how much she paid for it? I wonder if I can get another one like this somewhere."

Mother gave me a long, searching look. "Well, I may as well tell you. Elazar's mother mentioned that her sister was planning to buy you some kind of fancy headgear. And I knew Rachel's mother, may she rest in peace, had left her that precious scarf. So I thought I'd combine the two *mitzvot* of trying to get Rachel a good price for it — she surely needs the money, especially now — and saving Elazar's old aunt all the bother of shopping around. She'd never have found anything as exquisite as this."

"And how much did it cost?"

"Rachel asked for two gold *denarii*," Imma said. "That seemed quite fair — a month's wages."

"Then the money must be used up already, what with the *brit* and her not being able to work. I must go to Rachel immediately — I'm ashamed to say that I almost forgot about her, with the wedding and all. Imma, lend me one of your kerchiefs..." I certainly wasn't going to flaunt the pearls and silver in Rachel's face.

I took some bread, hard cheese and honey from the pantry and checked my purse to make sure I had money. Mother didn't say a word; just a couple of weeks ago she would have asked me a million questions, warned me about catching a cold or speaking to strangers, and packed me up with provisions for a week. It's so different now that I'm married!

What a contrast between this visit and the last one I made! Then I was a silly young girl; now I'm a respectable married woman. Rachel then was newly married (respectable, she'd always been) and now she was a mother! I wondered about her husband, and about her son and how she was getting along. I'd soon find out — I was being just as silly as Penelope, who always says, "I wonder who's that knocking at the door," instead of going to answer it.

When I reached Geva, it looked as dejected as ever — maybe even worse. There were trash heaps everywhere; even the weeds looked tired and droopy. The houses appeared to be on the verge of collapse, all except Rachel and Akiva's hut. It was newly limed and the earth around it was swept clean. It was good to see that Rachel still kept up a certain standard.

I hesitated at the door, but at my first knock, a cheerful

voice called, "Come in!" There was Rachel, in the same dress she'd worn the last time, and with a cheap cloth wound around her head, yet she looked more regal than ever. The baby was adorable, with large clear eyes just like Rachel's. (His receding hairline was obviously inherited from his father!)

"Leah, Leah, it's so good to see you! *Mazal tov!* It was *wonderful* hearing about your wedding. I hope you're not angry that I didn't come, but I have the best excuse in the world!" And she hugged the little excuse to her, smiling down at him with such tenderness and love that I had a hard time keeping my tears back.

"Of course I missed you terribly, but you're forgiven. And *mazal tov* to you, too! Maybe when he's a bit older, you'll come to visit me. We're just down the road from my parents — Elazar's family was able to buy the old Simons estate for us. You know that no one's lived there for years? Such a tragedy: their son was killed in a fight in Tiberias, and the son-in-law has his own place on the coast. So it's been neglected terribly, and the price was quite low...

"Oh, there I go, prattling on about myself as usual. You look beautiful, Rachel, but I'm sorry to see you didn't take my advice about your hands — they're so rough and coarse! Are you still working at home, spinning? Or has your father relented, and is he maybe helping you out?"

I don't know why I threw in that last part, since I knew very well that he'd never change his mind once he'd made it up, so I quickly added, "And when will you visit me?"

"Well, right now Shimon keeps me very busy," she answered. "I don't know when I'll be able to come... We planted a little garden in the back —just some leeks and radishes to eat with our bread — and tending that, and washing the baby's clothes and ours, and doing the spinning and a bit of cooking and sweeping somehow seem to take up the whole day. Come look at the cradle Akiva made..." and she showed me a basket woven from twigs and lined with straw. It was suspended by ropes from the beams of the roof, and she set it swinging with just a little push. It looked charming and cozy, and I expressed my admiration.

"If Akiva is so ingenious and capable, why doesn't he become a merchant? I've never seen a cradle as comfortable looking as this, and the idea of hanging it with ropes is excellent. I'm sure if he shows it around to people, everyone will want one."

I was all excited. Already I saw Rachel living in a nice house in town, and the two of us spending hours together, chatting like in the olden days.

"No, Leah. Akiva studies constantly, and that is all I want him to do."

"But with the high prices and all, how do you manage? Flour is much more expensive that last year, and I'm not even talking about poultry and fish." Since I'm supervising my own food shopping now, I'm so much more conscious of prices, and I always count the change the servants bring back — twice.

"Well, I sold one or two things I didn't really need," Rachel said. "When there's nothing left to sell, something else will come along. I'm sure Hashem will provide." This was the opening I'd been waiting for, and I jumped right in.

"Rachel, I know you sold your mother's beautiful head-scarf with the pearls on it. How do I know? Because Elazar's aunt — my aunt now — bought it for me. I forgot all about it until Shifra reminded me. But you only got two gold *denarii* for it — that's ludicrous! It would sell for at least three in Alexandria, and even more in Rome. So let me give you another two *denarii*, or I'll feel too guilty to ever wear it again. Please, Rachel?!" I was surprised to find myself begging her to accept the money, and hoping desperately that she would.

But Rachel said, "No, Leah. I set a fair price, and your aunt paid it without haggling. I wouldn't take another *prutah*. When we'll need money, Hashem will send it to us, I'm certain. We feel so tremendously rich — Akiva is acquiring Torah, the best merchandise in the world. He has already studied half the *Chumash*, and next year, when he finishes, he hopes to begin learning *Mishnah* with Rabi Eliezer and Rabi Yehoshua in Lod."

"In *Lod*!" I exclaimed. "Do you know how far away that is? He'll have to spend half the week traveling just to *get* there, and the other half to get home for Shabbat!"

Rachel smiled serenely. "No, Leah. I wouldn't dream of having him waste all that precious learning time. He'll stay in Lod as others do, for twelve years."

"But — but — but *Rachel*! He has a family now, responsibilities. Hasn't he learned enough already? He didn't even know *alef-beit*, and now he's quite advanced. My Elazar started young, knowing much more and *he'd* be very pleased to have reached this stage. Why must he continue? And how much longer will you struggle like this?" I really felt Akiva was not doing his fair share. Rachel deserved better.

"Akiva is different from most people," Rachel replied. "He doesn't rest and doesn't stop asking questions until he is satisfied with the answer. He's interested in everything that will help him master the sacred Law. When I was spinning once, he asked me to show him exactly how it's done. If he sees a weaver at his loom, or a stonemason, or a potter at his wheel, he'll observe how they do their work, until he knows it perfectly. That way the restrictions concerning the *lamed-tet melachot* forbidden on Shabbat are as clear to him as water from a mountain spring."

"Fine, but what will all his study eventually lead to? What will it accomplish? Doesn't everyone know these laws already? And if they don't, they can ask their rabbi." (That's what Father always says: "Ask the rabbi!" He feels it gives him an opportunity to help out the poor scholars, so he saves up his questions for a while, and when he isn't busy supervising the field hands, or trading at the market, he goes to consult the rabbi. Then he leaves some small gifts and a bit of money with the rabbi's wife.)

"So after your husband studies another twelve years, what will he have achieved? Don't tell me he's planning to be a rabbi!"

"Yes, Leah," came the answer. "That's what I always wished and hoped for; at first for my husband, and now for our sons. How will our Tradition continue, unless there are scholars to pass it on? You know that the only hope for our survival is the knowledge of Torah and the performance of its *mitzvot*. Otherwise, how are we different from the Persians, or the Greeks and the Romans?"

I couldn't answer that, so I said, "But the Romans are so competent and efficient. Of course I can't bear how they are persecuting our People — not only here in Judea but all over the Diaspora — but they do build roads and aqueducts and public baths, and I hear they're planning a postal system that will deliver the mail on time. That's what I call accomplishment — not this endless babbling of the scholars. The Romans stand for improvement and progress."

"Oh, Leah, how can you talk that way? That's what they said about the Egyptians and the Babylonians and the Greeks, too. And where are they now? They've been conquered and subjugated by other nations, and their idols, the ones that they believed would assure them victory and world dominion, crumble in the desert dust."

Rachel was agitated; her eyes flashed and her color was high. "In the name of their gods, they steal and kill and perform the worst abominations. But our Torah teaches only good — what is good for us, and for our fellowmen. You'd trade smooth roads and punctual mail delivery for that?"

"Really, Rachel, you have an odd way of putting things. If we are Hashem's Chosen, why must we suffer so much? Why can't we just have our own country and live peacefully like all the other nations? Every time we're on the verge of independence, along comes a military power superior to ours and conquers us, and then we're enslaved again, just as we were in Egypt." I felt I had scored a point; Rachel surely could not refute my argument...but she did.

"And what makes you think that the gentiles live so peacefully and comfortably in their lands? 'Peace, peace, they cry, but there is no peace,' the prophet Yirmeyahu said, and how right he was! The Persians, Greeks and Romans are all the same: fathers killing sons, and sons murdering fathers, brothers killing one another, friend betraying friend, and kings slaughtering their own people to gain power. Is that what you'd want us to imitate?" She was speaking more softly now, measuring every word. "We are Hashem's Chosen People, and that's why more is expected of us. It is true — we've been conquered again and again, even driven into exile, because of our sins. But *Hakadosh Baruch Hu* will again redeem us 'with a mighty Hand, and with an outstretched Arm' — if we keep His *mitzvot*. And how can we do that, unless we have these 'scholars babbling endlessly' as you say, to preserve and pass on our holy Law?"

As usual, the argument — or shall I call it a discussion? — with Rachel came to no conclusion. Little Shimon very kindly saved me from further debate: he started crying, and his mother was so busy soothing and rocking him that not another word was exchanged on this subject.

6

I RETURNED HOME (it has an altogether different meaning now: my own home, my own husband) and all the way, Rachel's words echoed in my mind. Could she be right? There had been scholars in my family — quite a number of them over the years, as a matter of fact — but these were not the *important* members of the clan. The ones who really counted were the wealthy merchants, the owners of farms and estates, the moneychangers who were knowledgeable about far-away wars, about every mishap — a king murdered, a ship sunk — that could possibly affect the rate of exchange. And yet, what has remained of all their labors? Not even their wealth: some of it was dissipated by prodigal sons, some lost in wartime, and most of it disappeared due to foolish investments and just plain bad luck.

But the rabbis and teachers of generations back — Shemayah and Avtalyon, Hillel and Shammai — their words are remembered and are as true and applicable as they were in centuries past. They are studied by scholars today, and they will be discussed and debated in the next generation, and the next, and the next...

I thought that perhaps I should urge Elazar to stay in the *beit knesset* a while longer after the *maariv* prayers. There's a traveling scholar whose arrival was announced some days ago; surely Elazar would benefit from his discussion of the laws of *shechitah*, and it might help Father too — he wouldn't have to go to the rabbi quite so often.

I prepared an excellent dinner (roast duck with onions and garlic) to put Elazar in a compliant mood. He does love my cooking. When I brought up the idea of his staying later than usual to hear this lecture, he was astonished.

"Leah dear, what's come over you? I never knew you had any interest in these matters. Not that I'd really mind — after all, my tutor in Alexandria taught me all the basics, and some more knowledge surely can't hurt."

I couldn't possibly tell him everything that had happened today — it was too complicated. And besides, I was a bit embarrassed: after all my doubts and criticisms of Akiva, here I was, trying to push my new husband in the same direction...

So I said, "Oh, I just thought it might be interesting for you, and it doesn't cost anything. Anyway, I'd like to spend the evening rearranging all the jars and bowls in my kitchen — that servant girl has no idea how things should look..."

And we left it at that.

I've been kept busy for months and months. Training the maid Rivka has been an endless, thankless job — she was a raw country girl, and I've often thought she must have come from a stable. I wonder how Mother has managed all these years with just Puah to help her. And I guess in the beginning Puah wasn't any better than my Rivka, who still has no idea how to set a table, and once scrubbed my woolen shawl on the rocks until it was full of holes. (I gave it to her as a gift afterwards — maybe it will remind her to be more careful in the future.)

Also, cooking and shopping are not nearly as easy as I

thought they'd be. I burned our dinner several times, and never did get the knack of making those little meal cakes. And spinning — well! It must have been invented especially to torture me. The rough wool chafes my fingers, and just the smell of it makes me itch all over. Being married and running my own house is not exactly the fun I'd imagined.

But one thing I'm almost sure I did right, and that is urging Elazar to learn more. After that first time, he started to go to the study hall regularly every night and, during the rainy season, in the morning as well. Sometimes he comes home all excited — if he understood the teacher's words the very first time, or he asked a good question, or gave a proper answer. Then there are times when he's upset or depressed: if someone challenged him with a difficult *kushiya*, and he couldn't find a solution although he'd racked his brain. But, oh, his happiness when he discovers the *terutz*! His face beams, and I know he'll be in an excellent mood for days afterward.

Yes, I am proud of my husband now. I've often thought of telling Rachel — she'd be so pleased. But then that envious feeling always takes over, and I tell myself: Some other time — what's the rush? And anyway, it's so far to Geva...

She's still living there. Another child was born to her — a daughter, Shulamit. And Akiva has gone to study at the yeshiva in Lod, and learns day and night, and what Rachel and the children live on is a mystery.

All this information was brought to me by Shifra, who lives with her Tertius — I told you that's whom she married, didn't I? — in a big manor house about two *milin* from Rachel. She, too, has a boy and a girl, Julius and Flora.

Julius was named for his grandfather Judah. When the old man died, Tertius went to pieces. He tore out his hair and scratched his face and cried and screamed like those low-class peasants do. But then he had these extravagant golden burial clothes sewn (they cost a fortune, I heard, and were the envy of the town), and that apparently calmed him down. Of course, that was before the white shroud custom became widely accepted. That old grandfather was the backbone of the family; his widow is much younger, and she likes to travel — she's been to Alexandria twice since then. I wonder what's going to happen to them now.

Shifra won't let her children play with Rachel's — she's afraid they might catch some awful disease. (Actually, I'm the only person who still calls her Shifra; she prefers "Silvia." "I don't want to be the only one in the family with a Jewish name," she told me. But since she's my oldest and best friend, next to Rachel of course, she'll always remain Shifra to me.) Her children are very well-dressed, I must say — Florrie had on a charming short pleated dress the other day — and her house is immaculate. I make a special effort to have things clean before Shabbat and *Yom Tov*, but at Shifra's, every corner of every room is absolutely perfect at all times. I'm green with envy.

When I asked Shifra how she does it, she said that she has her girl move all the furniture out of the way before she cleans. That way, no dust and dirt can accumulate under the beds, for example, and then get scattered around the room by the wind.

Some of that furniture looked awfully heavy for one girl to move alone. "Aren't you afraid something might break in the process?" I asked her.

"Oh, I just deduct any breakage from the girl's wages," she said. I thought that was a very good idea, and told Elazar about it, but he said that we mustn't do that. Even though the worker is obligated to pay for her negligence, we must behave *lifnim mishurat hadin* and excuse her.

"Couldn't I at least withhold her wages for a while, so that she'd learn a lesson and be more careful in the future?"

"Absolutely not. The Law is clear: A worker must be paid when the job is done. She depends on those wages for her sustenance, and you mustn't hold them back." He was quite adamant about it.

I said, "What's that old saying — 'In much wisdom there is much vexation'? I never thought you'd take your studying so seriously. I'm a little sorry I encouraged you."

"But *I'm* not!" Elazar retorted, irritated by my remark. "And a person who has Torah knowledge but doesn't keep the *mitzvot* is worse than an ignoramus. Surely you don't want..." He calmed down then, and just in time too. It was the closest we'd ever come to a quarrel, and it frightened me a bit. Deep down, I was glad that Elazar was so careful to observe every commandment properly — I'd hate to have a wishy-washy husband like Shifra's, who went along with all the latest fads, and only made a show of adhering to Torah Law. And to think that I almost...

Time passes slowly. I visit my family often, trying to keep an eye on Penelope and Aaron. His lessons have not taken too well — his tutor, instead of teaching him the *alef-beit*, the prayers and *Chumash*, preferred to talk philosophy and to try out his ridiculous Greek rhymes on my brother. Aaron said he thought Greek was stupid so the tutor made him copy some nonsense a hundred times!

Mother is still pulling for her family's old rabbi, but he's ancient by now, and couldn't possibly make it to our house on his tottering feet; and Father refuses to send Aaron to school with the other boys — private lessons are much classier, he says. And who knows what fanatic ideas he might pick up there? Elazar tried to intercede a few times, but it was no use.

Penelope, in the meanwhile, has improved tremendously. I don't know why — Abba and Imma are much more lenient with her than they ever were with me. She still gets away with everything. She does listen to me occasionally, though; when I said her clothes were too loud, instead of throwing a fit, she asked for my blue shawl, and draped it most becomingly so as to conceal the garish embroidery on her gown. She really has a flair for dressing — now all the girls are wearing shawls draped the same way (but I never did get mine back).

My maid, Rivka, has also settled down, and she's turned out to be quite capable. Mother says that without the training I've given her she wouldn't be anything, but that doesn't stop the neighbors from trying to hire her away from me. I try to keep her happy with all kinds of little presents; I don't know what I'd do if she ever left! I've come to depend on her too much. I really should go back to doing my own *kashering* and cooking, just to keep her in her place.

Elazar's studies are taking up more and more of his time and I really have mixed feelings about it. On the one hand, I *am* proud of him, but he's hardly ever home — out before dawn for study and prayer, at work all day, and back to the *beit knesset* at night. Even at mealtimes, he's often looking at some old scroll, or talking about his latest achievements in learning. Thank goodness he makes a fine living in spite of it, but I'm getting a little tired of being ignored. If only...

7

WITH ELAZAR AWAY so much of the time, I've started to visit my friends more often, mostly Rachel and Shifra, and, since they live near each other, usually on the same day. I really need the distraction; how many hours can a person be expected to devote to supervising the housekeeping? As soon as Elazar leaves, I give Rivka her instructions (I don't dare say orders — servants are so sensitive these days) and set out, with a small basket of food for the way. Sometimes I go to Rachel in the morning and to Shifra in the afternoon, or the other way around.

The contrast between the two is appalling: Rachel in that stone hovel, with the jug of water on the floor and maybe a bit of bread and vegetables on a shelf, and then Shifra's spacious well-ordered house, the wardrobes bursting with clothes and the pantry bulging with food. When she isn't ordering the servants around, she's coloring her nails or trying on some new gown or fussing with a new hairstyle. The children are nowhere to be seen — "My Carmina is excellent with them, and I have no patience. They're *so* demanding," Shifra says. "And besides, they make such a mess, and just when I have things looking exactly the way I want."

At Rachel's, on the other hand, the children are always around. (Where else *could* they be in that tiny hut if not underfoot or right outside in the small yard!) Shimon is getting big — his curly *payot* are adorable, and he is so proud of his *tallit kattan*. Yehoshua — whom Rachel treats as her own flesh and blood — is a serious, studious lad, and Shulie is a little doll, with a sweet, mischievous smile that reminds me of Rachel when she was a child.

I offer Rachel money from time to time (her position is worse than ever) but she always refuses. "*Baruch Hashem*, we're not lacking anything," she says. If it weren't so pathetic, I'd laugh.

Today when I asked Rachel about Akiva, she told me that not only is he progressing well at Rabi Eliezer's academy, but he's also studying with the great Rabi Nachum in Gimzo, not far from Lod. Rachel said it so proudly, and she was right — this was indeed something to be proud of: the great Nachum *Ish Gamzo* is Akiva's teacher! (Elazar said that Rabi Nachum is called *Ish Gamzo* not only after the name of his town, but also because his favorite expression is: *Gam zo l'tovah*, meaning that even an event that seems to be bad is really good, because everything that Hashem does is ultimately for the best.) Akiva would be able to learn quite a lot from such a *tzaddik*, I knew.

Still, I couldn't help feeling that he was ignoring his obligations to his family — and Rachel was encouraging him! "So, is he still in the wood business?" I asked, although the answer was clear.

"Oh, Akiva doesn't have much time for it now," Rachel replied matter-of-factly. (She never reacts to my occasionally biting remarks. I really should make more of an effort to control my tongue!) "He's always in the *beit midrash*, so he can only gather kindling very early in the morning, once in a while."

"So what are you living on, I'd like to know? Surely *you* don't earn enough for what you need..." Why do I *do* this? I knew I was only hurting my dear friend — I can't possibly hope to change her attitude or make her see things as I do.

I had noticed that Rachel looked different somehow when I'd arrived, but I hadn't been able to put my finger on it. Now, when I looked up at her, I realized with a shock what it was.

"Rachel! Your hair! What have you done?!"

She'd always kept her hair tightly gathered under a headscarf, and her thick plaits had formed a high crown across her head, adding to her already regal height. Now her scarf hung limply around her beautiful face.

"You've sold your hair!" I sobbed, and Rachel put her arm around my shoulders to comfort me. Poverty such as hers, need that would compel a woman to sell so precious a possession, was beyond anything I could fathom. How could Akiva subject her to this? How could Kalba Savua?

And on top of this, I had had to say those nasty, hurtful things. Feeling repentant, I pressed her again to accept some money, but as usual she turned me down.

"As long as Akiva keeps learning and growing in knowledge and *yirat Shamayim*," she said, "we'll always have enough."

She did accept some food, though, and some of Aaron's and Penelope's outgrown clothing. Mother had been saving it for me, but there's no need for it...yet.

I walked home, slowly, as I do after each visit, to fill up the day, with Bilha and Shemuel dogging my steps. When I think about my two friends, I realize — oh, this is an awful thing to say — I realize I'm jealous of them both, jealous of Shifra's carefree, uncomplicated existence and of Rachel's total contentment.

But Rachel I love...

8

*M*AZAL *TOV! MAZAL TOV!* A double *mazal tov*!" And again: "*Mazal tov! Mazal tov!*"

I thought if I were to hear that once more, I'd scream. All the neighbors who gave me the double *mazal tov* probably imagined they were being very original and funny. Original, it wasn't, and certainly not funny, but great, beautiful and miraculous it was: the birth of our twins, a son and a daughter. How we had prayed, Elazar and I, for this moment — and to be thus doubly blessed!

"Our cup is overflowing," Elazar said. "May we continue to deserve Hashem's bounty..."

Soon it was time for the *brit*. We had agreed on naming the children Baruch ("blessed") and Batya ("daughter of God") for obvious reasons, and fortunately no one had any complaints about that, although Father felt that we should at least give them additional modern names, or they might be barred from reaching their true potential where it really counted, in Roman society. After a heated discussion, we gave in for the sake of *shalom bayit*.

Then came the busiest, most hectic period of my life. There was no day, there was no night, or rather, day and night seemed to run into each other so rapidly that I couldn't tell the difference. Up early each morning, getting to sleep late or not at all, feeding, changing, putting to bed, picking up, feeding, changing — everything revolved around the needs of my twins. There was seldom a quiet moment, but when there was, I thought of Rachel. How could she possibly cope with *three* children all by herself, with her husband away all the time, and no help from anyone? And with never enough food, and living in that damp, leaky hovel — yet always content, never complaining.

And there I was, with Rivka doing all the housework and cooking, Mother coming in almost daily to check up on the babies and give me a hand, and even Penelope offering to run errands or to hold one twin or the other. She was wonderful with the babies, and had endless patience for them. And yet, I was always exhausted, often cranky, and took for granted everyone's kind offers of assistance — until I thought about Rachel.

Akiva, she had told me during my last visit, was making enormous strides, "although his very first lesson," she added, "was actually a painful one."

I was secretly pleased to hear that Rachel was not the only one to have to suffer, but I said nothing and settled down to hear what I knew would be a good story.

"You see, Akiva was walking along the road when he came upon a corpse." She said this in such a casual way that it took a moment for me to realize she was talking about a dead body! "There was no one else around," she went on, "so he lifted it up in his arms and carried it for four *milin* to the nearest graveyard. It was an innocent mistake, Leah. He only wanted to give the poor man a proper Jewish burial."

I happened to know what the Law was on this matter, because we'd had a similar incident with a worker on our estate a few years back. "The Rabbis must have been furious with him!" I said.

"Worse than that, Leah. When he reported what he'd done to Rabi Eliezer and Rabi Yehoshua, they told him that a *met mitzvah* must be buried on the spot where it's found, and that for every step Akiva had taken, he was considered to have killed the man *himself*! Poor Akiva! How he must have agonized over that. But from this, Leah, he understood how important it is to learn from the Rabbis. And he is now completely immersed in Torah study, sitting in the *beit midrash* day and night and absorbing every word his teachers utter." Her face glowed as she said these words.

"You make it sound quite… well, heavenly!" I said. "But don't the Rabbis argue a lot? And how can they ever decide who is right? We're always hearing about *Beit Hillel* and *Beit Shammai*, and their differences of opinion. What happens when one side decides they're right, and so does the other, and they refuse to compromise?"

For once I wasn't asking just for the sake of argument. I had often heard about their disputes, and wondered how they were ever able to agree on anything, much less to interpret the laws by which we live. How could *Beit Hillel* yield to *Beit Shammai* if they were both absolutely certain of their own position?

"In a way you're right, Leah," Rachel replied and I had to think for a moment what I could possibly have said that she could agree with. "It is quite heavenly, because all their disputes are *l'shem Shamayim*, for the sake of Heaven. However, when things were the way they should be, there were no disputes at all. You see, Leah, when the Sanhedrin was able to function properly, every difference of opinion was brought to a vote by the assembly of the greatest Rabbis of the generation. Since the Torah commands us to accept the rule of the majority, there could not be any ongoing disputes, and *everyone* had to follow the majority's decision.

"But when Herod's father, that *rasha* Antipater, abolished the Sanhedrin, Shammai was appointed head of the *metivta*, the Torah academy, and the B'nei Beteira were appointed the *Nesi'im*. That was almost a hundred years ago, Leah. Later on, during Herod's reign, the great Hillel, who was a descendant of King David, came up from Bavel. The B'nei Beteira immediately transferred their *nesiut* to him, and it has remained with his descendants ever since. I'm sure you know that our *Nasi*, Rabban Shimon ben Gamliel, is Hillel's great-grandson."

Some of this I actually did know, but I had forgotten. "Please go on, Rachel," I said. "This is very interesting. Couldn't Hillel have gotten the *nesiut* and the *metivta* back together, though? That would have made things so much simpler."

"Yes, Leah. His personality and his qualities of leadership would have made that possible, but surely it would have been an affront to the great Shammai. In addition, it was feared that Herod would see this as a new Sanhedrin, which was outlawed. And so, for the first time in the history of our People, we had two independent centers of learning, *Beit Shammai* and *Beit Hillel*."

"Maybe so, but it can't have been the first time in our history that there were ongoing disputes!" Abba always says that arguing is a Jew's favorite pastime.

"That's true, Leah. The differences of opinion between them was nothing new; it's a natural part of learning. What *was* new was that an assembly of all of the great Rabbis could no longer meet to vote and decide between them. Over the last few decades, quite a number of disputes have accumulated. We can only hope that *Mashiach* will come soon, or, at the very least, that some sort of order will preside in the Land, so that the entire Sanhedrin will be able to sit again, as they used to, and settle all of the great Rabbis' disputes — may it be soon, in our days!" Then she got that dreamy look in her eyes. "And may Akiva be among them!"

Same idealistic Rachel, with her head in the clouds. Now that our conversation had finally come full circle, I jumped at the chance to bring her down to earth again. I had been certain that Akiva would not be able to keep up with the scholars and that by this time he would have given up, and come home. Obviously, this was not to be. "Rachel, Rachel," I said, "what will happen to you now that Akiva will be away for years on end? Before, you had a little income from the kindling he gathered. Now you're all alone with nothing at all!"

"No, Leah, we're not alone. Hashem will continue to watch over us. 'Behold! The Guardian of Israel does not sleep nor does He slumber.' Akiva is staying in Lod because I asked him to — I know he's destined for greater things. He's doing this to make me happy; all my happiness is seeing my husband achieving his goal!" Rachel's eyes were shining. I decided to try another tactic.

"I agree that Akiva has made tremendous progress," I said, "but the academy in Lod is a big place. How must he feel, competing with some of the foremost scholars when he's hardly more than a beginner — and an impoverished one, at that?"

Rachel was not at all fazed. "You know that the illustrious Hillel too was a wood-gatherer with no means. Once, when he couldn't even afford the tuition fee at the *beit midrash*, he climbed up to the roof to listen, and stayed there even when it started snowing heavily. They found him the next morning, stiff from the cold..."

"Yes, yes, I know all about it." I'd heard that story a hundred times. "But surely you're not comparing your husband to the great Hillel?!"

"And why not?" I just looked at her. "Leah, you can't imagine how his mind works. He wants to know and understand every part of the Torah as well as I know that one and one is two. Everything he learns, he reviews over and over again, until he's memorized it. He's never satisfied; it's never enough. He's like a fish in the sea that leaps up to gulp a few more drops of the falling rain."

"I wish him luck," I said, "and you too. How long do you think you'll be able to manage without your husband?"

"It doesn't matter to me," Rachel answered. "As long as it takes him to achieve his goal..."

Like most of our conversations, this one had left me puzzled and a bit frustrated.

Baruch was thirty days old and it was time for the *pidyon haben. Everyone* was invited — you must understand, this was the first time in generations that this special occasion had occurred in my family — and of course a lavish feast was arranged. The *kohen* from whom Elazar would redeem our son had real *yichus*: he was none other than Rabi Tzadok, the renowned *tzaddik* and scholar. He happened to be passing through our town and agreed to honor us at our *simchah*. He also brought us news of Akiva, who he said shows real promise.

From near and far people gathered for the feast, and I was thrilled to see Rachel among them. She and the children had been offered a ride in a mule cart for most of the way, and had walked the rest.

"Rachel! How good of you to come!" I said as we embraced. I noticed she looked pale and exhausted. "I hope it wasn't too difficult for you —"

"And when my dearest friend has received such an abundant gift from Hashem, shouldn't I come to share her joy? I'll never forget your visits to me in Geva." And Rachel hugged me again and kissed my cheeks.

I left all the guests to their own devices and sat down in a corner with my Rachel and her children. Rivka brought us refreshments — funny, it was the same date-honey and citron drink that Rachel had served me when she was still a girl in her father's house. It seemed like a hundred years ago...

"So, Leah, you have a son and a daughter now. May they be a source of much *nachat* for you and Elazar, and may you bring them up to Torah, *chuppah* and *ma'asim tovim.* Oh, I'm so happy for you!" Rachel's smile lit up her tired face with the old radiance. Naturally, I conveyed the greetings Rabi Tzadok had brought from her husband, and this pleased her greatly. She told me how happy she is that Akiva's at a yeshiva where some of the greatest men in Israel are teaching. There he would be able to satisfy his tremendous desire for Torah knowledge, she said. There he would become the great scholar that she had envisioned when she asked him to marry her. I still get the chills when I think of that scene...

I didn't dare ask her any questions about how she was able to put food on the table with her husband away, but I decided to put aside part of my housekeeping money and perhaps, in some roundabout way, I'd get Rachel to accept it. Her children looked healthy enough, though somewhat thin, and they were still wearing the same hand-me-downs I had brought a year ago.

Rachel, Rachel, I thought, how can you bear living like this, struggling for every bit of bread? With your husband away, all the responsibility rests on you... and you live for the few scraps of letters that you receive from Lod once in a while. Is that a life? But I said nothing.

Elazar arranged for our wagon driver to take Rachel and the children back to Geva. I didn't want her to leave; strangely, I've come to depend on her, when it seems that it should be the other way around. I pleaded with her to stay with us. But she would not.

9

NOW I HAVE more reason than ever to worry about Rachel. Almost every day brings bad news. In fact, ever since Agrippa II was appointed governor, things have been terrible. It was only natural that he grab the high priesthood for his cohorts, the *Tzadokim*, thereby giving them tremendous power. Because of his policy of permanent tenure, all of his men who ever held the office of *Kohen Hagadol*, even if they served for only a short time, retain the status of High Priest for life. And of course there's nothing we can do about it since he established his own Sanhedrin of *Tzadokim*. With no *beit din* to turn to for justice, there has been a complete breakdown of law and order here in *Eretz Yisrael*; and there's Rachel, alone in Geva with no one to look out for her, or to protect her and the children. Of course I know what she would say to that: "*Hashem Yitbarach* is watching over us," etc., etc.

Maybe the poverty in Geva is a blessing in disguise — what robber would bother with those poor people? And no one would ever kidnap their children for ransom — who has money to redeem them? Still, I'm afraid for Rachel and her family, as much as for my own.

Yes, evil has come upon us in the last years. Because of the high taxes and poor crops, many small farmers here have been driven off their land and into the cities. Some of them were able to learn new trades, but most of them just grew poorer and poorer. These men who had been independent all their lives, tilling the soil with hard labor, have now become beggars. Armed bands of *Tzadokim* roam the streets of our Holy City, looting and thieving and assaulting innocent people, setting themselves above the Law. What is this world coming to?!

But it's an ill wind that blows no man to good. At the same time that the poor are getting poorer, the rich are getting richer. All over the country there are many like Shifra's husband Tertius, opportunists who are buying up the land at ridiculously low prices, and becoming wealthy. Most of them have ties with the Roman district government; they've learned to play the game of politics, and are taking advantage of the terrible situation to enrich themselves.

And the prices are outrageous! Food, drink, clothing, everything is sky-high. Only the very wealthy can still live decently. Even when the price of wheat plummeted recently, there was no money to buy any.

And the cost of pigeons! Today, if you can imagine such a thing, they're considered a luxury, for the really well-to-do or for convalescents. People are complaining bitterly, especially since the birds are needed for the sacrifice after childbirth. Who can afford them now? And just before *Yom Tov*, the dealers especially raised their prices even higher because pigeons were so much in demand — no Jew can partake of the *korbanot* until he's purified from all *tumot* and has brought all the appropriate sacrifices, so many new mothers needed to buy several pairs of birds.

So Rabban Shimon ben Gamliel *Hanasi* did what his ancestor Hillel might have done: he ruled that no woman was required to offer more than one pair of pigeons at the altar, even after more than one birth. Of course, the price dropped immediately, from one gold *denarius* a pair, down to a quarter of a silver *denarius* — about one-fiftieth of that morning's price. Naturally the bird dealers were not particularly pleased; they had some choice words for Rabban Shimon!

In general, people have become, well, discourteous is too mild a description. They're often downright mean to each other. With no recourse to *beit din*, minor disagreements between neighbors and business partners grow into major disputes. In Jerusalem, especially, the populace is split into many factions, and the factions are constantly quarreling. Over what? Nonsense, that's what. It's *sinat chinam*, that's all, baseless hatred and spite, the likes of which I've never seen before.

For once, I'm relieved to be stuck at home with the babies — not that I'm complaining, *chalilah*! I waited so long for this joy that, despite all the endless work, raising children entails, not to mention the endless worries, I don't think there is a happier person in all of *Eretz Yisrael*. Even Abba remarked the other day that motherhood seems to agree with me — imagine Abba noticing a thing like that!

Still, there's no denying that having twin babies tends to cramp one's social life. There are times when I don't even get outdoors for weeks on end, or so it seems.

And Elazar is no help at all. The other night, Baruch, who's teething, began to scream and we both awoke with a start. Of course, Batya immediately joined in, even though there's no evidence that she'll *ever* have a tooth in her mouth. So I ran to comfort Baruch (Imma had suggested giving him a small piece of cloth soaked in sweet wine to suck on. I was appalled at the thought: give a baby wine? I told her I wouldn't dream of it, that if I had to, I'd walk him for hours and rock him in my arms, or fashion a cradle for him like the one Akiva made for Rachel's first child, but I would not give any baby of mine etc., etc. Need I tell you that, once again, Imma was absolutely right?)

Well, by the time I found a clean cloth and dipped it in the wine, Baruch was gasping for breath and Batya was too, only she was turning blue! "Quick, Elazar!" I cried. "Pick her up and pat her or something!"

But Elazar just looked at me helplessly, with perspiration glistening on his brow and no idea whatsoever how to lift her up without breaking her.

I hope Baruch will forgive me for letting him suffer those extra minutes while I tended to his sister. When I saw that she was finally breathing normally again, I gave Baruch his wine-cloth and in moments they were both sleeping soundly. And where was my faithful Rivka throughout all this, you may ask? Sleeping just as soundly as the twins now were, as is her right and privilege, or so she says.

"I'm sorry I wasn't much help, Leah," Elazar said, and he looked so miserable about it that all my annoyance dissolved.

"If you're willing," I told him gently, "I'll show you how to hold the babies. They're not as fragile as you might think."

The next morning, when the twins awoke, Elazar was ready for his lesson. But when I saw him holding his son so tenderly and crooning softly to him a song from the *tefillah*, the tears in my eyes were for Rachel. She had so admired her husband's tenderness with the baby lambs. And what of his own little lambs? Twelve years is such a terribly long time; when he returns, they won't be little lambs at all, but nearly grown. Had Rachel known the heart-swelling joy of seeing Akiva cuddle the babies? She *must* have. But if she's busy all day with her spinning and cooking and everything else, who's cuddling those babies now?

10

THE CHILDREN ARE GROWING OLDER, changing in many ways, and Elazar and I have changed along with them. How often Mother says, when they are being disobedient or playing some little prank: "That's exactly what you used to do, Leah. Why, I remember..."

"Hush, Imma," I tell her (gently, of course) to prevent her from saying more. I'm certain that Mother's memory is failing a bit; I never did those things she mentions. Anyway, even if I did, I surely don't want the children to know about it!

Baruch is full of fun, always teasing his sister, and when he can't find her, he's chasing the chickens and ducks in their pens. Soon he'll be ready for his first haircut. I really would like him to have nice curly *payot* like Rachel's boys, but Father objects. He feels that it is not necessary to make the child look and feel different. (Elazar decided not to make an issue out of it because of respect for Abba.) Most boys now have a neat trim, with the corners of the hair barely grazing their cheekbones. Shifra's son, who is older than Baruch, wears his hair long and curled in the back — he does have beautiful hair. (Baruch's hair is also thick and wavy; only Batya has fine, straight, dull brown hair. Why is it that the boys are always blessed with the pretty hair, while the girls' hair is always impossible and you can't do anything with it? I guess that's another one of those questions for which there is no answer.)

I'm still in contact with Rachel and with Shifra, of course, but my visits are becoming rarer. I'm just so busy at home. I don't understand why — after all, the children have been eating by themselves for a long time now and there are no more sleepless nights, unless they're sick, *chas v'shalom*. Everything is so much easier, yet at the same time, much more difficult.

The last time I went to visit Shifra, I took the twins along, but I don't think I'll do it again. Her son, Julius, was playing what he said was a new game — "Jews and Romans," he called it. He tied a rope around his sister Flora and my twins and chased them, yelling: "Go, go, go!" If they didn't run fast enough, he hit them with a little toy whip. They ran very fast.

"Shifra, do you really think it's a good idea to have them play such games?" I asked their mother. "It makes me feel awfully uncomfortable. It's bad enough that we have Romans ruling over us, but the thought that they might actually enslave us is just too terrible! I would rather the children play games that are more in line with Jewish values, wouldn't you?"

"Please call me Silvia," Shifra said coolly. "I've asked you so often — I do wish you'd remember. It's embarrassing to have such an odd, old-fashioned name. Anyway, I don't see what's wrong. 'Jews and Romans' is no worse than 'Police and Robbers,' and the other children don't seem to mind. Besides, your twins aren't all that perfect, either — I saw your boy break my white vase, and Batya kicked my wine stand and made a dent in it. I really don't mind that much about my furniture, but please take care of your own children before you start criticizing mine." Obviously, she'd been keeping a watchful eye on them, and I was upset.

"I didn't mean to criticize, Shifra — I mean Silvia. It's just that, well, if they get used to such games, chasing and making fun of our own People, I'm afraid..." I didn't know exactly what I was afraid of, and couldn't describe the feeling I had when I saw Julius with his whip, but it lay like a stone on my heart.

"Maybe it's your husband," Shifra remarked. "We all respect Elazar's intelligence and his learning, but you're too much under his influence. Ours is a modern marriage. Tertius has his responsibilities, and I have mine, and together we enjoy a sophisticated lifestyle. We want the children to grow up open-minded and receptive to new ideas. We want them to adjust to the times, and to be able to mingle with whatever society they find themselves in. That's the only way we can assure them of a decent future." Shifra spoke enthusiastically, she who was usually so languid and apparently had little or no enthusiasm for anything. "What do I want for my children? Success, happiness, a prosperous and easy life. Is that too much to ask? And we both feel that this — our way of life and the atmosphere of tolerance in which we raise our children — is the only way to achieve our goal."

I didn't know what to say. I felt she was wrong, but at the same time her words seemed to make so much sense. Isn't she much better off than Rachel who is carrying such a heavy burden, while her husband is away studying the Holy Scripture? Shifra lives in comfort, and plans comfortably for the future. And Rachel?

Shifra had mentioned Elazar, so I thought I'd ask her about Tertius. "And how is your husband's business going? I hear he just bought another abandoned estate — they say he got it for a very good price. He must be doing well." I thought that would pacify her.

"Oh, yes, he's doing quite well. We now own all the land on either side of our estate. And believe me, we need it — the riffraff are moving closer and closer all the time. Did you notice how that sordid Geva is spreading? More and more Jews are moving to that slum; they can't afford to keep up their villas and ornamental gardens, you know." She might have been speaking about some inferior race instead of her own People! "And real estate prices are dropping in the Galilee, too," she went on. "It's a buyers' market, and Tertius is working day and night to take full advantage of it." Her voice was inflated with pride; I couldn't resist puncturing it.

"Is that why he doesn't come to prayers any more? He used to attend at least on Rosh Hashanah and Yom Kippur, but this year I hear he didn't come at all. I wonder how his father would feel, if he could see what's happening to his son?" I thought perhaps I shouldn't have said quite so much, and I was sure of it when I saw how red-in-the-face Shifra became.

"Tertius' father was old-fashioned. He retained all his outdated ideas from his yeshiva days. Perhaps it's better that he's... gone. I'm sure he'd only be unhappy and disappointed in his son and in his grandchildren. It's a pity — Tertius *did* love his father — but we must move with the times."

It was getting late, and the children were tired and cranky. I made them thank Shifra politely for the good time they had, and we left for home. All the way, I chastised myself: Why hadn't I answered Shifra? I knew she was wrong, but I couldn't find the words to tell her. Maybe I should ask Rachel; she always seems to have the right answers.

A long time passed before I saw Rachel again. After my unpleasant experience with Shifra, I was eager to speak to Rachel, and to get her opinion. I didn't want to take the children along though; this talk was not for their ears. What with one thing and another, I couldn't get away on my own for days and days.

When at last I had a free morning, I prepared the usual basket of food and used clothing, and added to it a small sum from the cash box, hoping that Rachel would accept it. How little it meant to me, and how much it would mean to her!

Walking to Geva is so much easier now since the roads have been vastly improved in the last few years. When I got there, I went directly to Rachel's hut. The village had spread just as Shifra said, and I saw the son of a former neighbor playing in a dusty yard. He hid when he saw me; maybe he was ashamed of living in such a poor section.

There was no one home at Rachel's. I knocked and knocked but there was no answer, so I went to the little garden in the back, hoping to find her working there. Then I remembered that it's harvest time — could she be gleaning the fields, picking up the grain dropped during the harvest? Miserable thought! But I had to find out.

That old man I had met on my first visit to Geva saw me searching for her — he must spend all his time snooping on the neighbors. "If you're looking for Rachel," he cackled, "she's out in the fields with her children picking grain off the ground along with the rest of the poor trash!" He seemed to get satisfaction out of telling me that. I wonder why? Perhaps he, too, has glimpsed Rachel's greatness — and can't bear it.

I couldn't decide what to do. Should I go to the fields in the hope of coming upon Rachel? Maybe she'd be embarrassed at being found like that, though I thought not — gleaning the fallen or forgotten wheat and stalks and the corners of the field is her right; it wouldn't disturb her. But maybe someone would mistake me, with my basket, for one of those poor gleaners? I'd die of shame!

Anyway, I didn't know in which direction to go, and I'd never ask that nasty fellow — he'd probably send me to the wrong place, out of pure spite. I left the food and clothing in back of the hut, and started walking home slowly, hoping that I'd meet Rachel on the way. But I didn't. The main reason for my visit had been to discuss Shifra with her and now I have to work this out for myself.

Should I make up with Shifra? Not that I ever really quarreled with her, but there has been a coldness between us since that day. Maybe I'll be able to influence her for the good, I thought. But what about my children? Seeing how Shifra's offspring behave might be harmful to them; yet there are those like my father, who say: "Let your children be exposed to the rest of the world. You can't shelter them forever. If you don't give them the opportunity to observe all kinds of people, how can they ever make their own judgments or draw their own conclusions?"

But I *want* to shelter them; I want to keep them safe and secure in my arms for as long as I am able. I decided to go alone, without the twins — not today, but soon. In a strange sort of way, Shifra is now my only link with Rachel.

"Man proposes, God disposes." Months passed. The rainy season set in, with colds and fevers, and it's been ages since I've gone anywhere, much less had time to visit. As soon as the children recovered from one thing, there was another emergency. Also, they were never both sick at the same time. If Batya was well, she wanted me to take her out to play, while Baruch whined for me to sit at his bedside and hold his hand; when he felt better, he wanted me to do a puzzle with him or pull him in his wooden cart, while Batya pleaded from her bed for a drink or some sweets. I thought the rains would never end — I don't remember ever being housebound for such a long time.

But now, finally, spring has come and what a perfect spring it is, straight out of *Shir Hashirim*:

> "For lo, the winter is past, the rain is over and gone. The flowers appear on the earth; the time of singing is come and the voice of the turtledove is heard in our land. The fig tree puts forth its green figs, and the vines in blossom give off their fragrance..."

Yes, now there are no more excuses. The children are well again and the weather is fine. I'll make it my business to visit my friends at the first opportunity.

11

I HAD PROMISED MYSELF that as soon as Baruch was back in school, I'd take Batya and visit either Rachel or Shifra or both of them; I couldn't decide. I *had* to know how Rachel had fared through this bitter winter, and I also wanted to hear how Akiva was doing in his present surroundings. At the same time, I still needed to clear the air with Shifra. So when the opportunity finally arose, I packed the usual basket, fixed Batya's hair — it's still hopelessly thin and straight — and set out early, more eager than ever.

The decision as to which of my friends to visit was made for me by Batya, who became quite tired and irritable before we had gone even halfway, so we stopped in at Shifra's first. Actually, Batya preferred Shifra's house to Rachel's since there were always plenty of toys there, and she *did* like Flora, who she said was more fun than Shulamit. But we ended up staying there too long, and the sun was low when we started back. Still, it was worth it — I returned with interesting news about Rachel's husband.

At Lod, Shifra told me, Akiva was continuing his unusual manner of learning which had brought him so far in such a short time. Other students concentrate on only one facet of

Torah at a time, but Akiva is different. He sits at the feet of his teachers, listening to every word, regardless of the topic, and storing it all in his phenomenal memory. They say he resembles a poor man who goes out to the field with his basket, picking up everything that he finds — wheat, barley, beans and lentils. When the poor man returns home, he sorts the items, wheat in one pile, barley in another, and so on. Akiva does the same: he'll absorb everything he has the opportunity to learn, regardless of the topic, and then he'll divide his accumulated knowledge into the appropriate categories.

They also say that Akiva's behavior sometimes seems odd and overly bold. One day, when the aged Rabi Nechuniah the Great visited the yeshiva, Akiva stepped up to him and asked: "Rabi, Rabi, what did you do to merit the blessing of long life?"

The Rav's servants wanted to grab Akiva and beat him for his *chutzpah*, but he escaped by climbing up a tree! From the top he called down, "Rabi, Rabi, since the word *keves* means 'one lamb,' why is it followed by the word *echad*, 'one'?"

"Let him be," Rabi Nechuniah told his servants. "He asked me, not out of idle curiosity, but in order to learn."

So Akiva came down from the tree, and Rabi Nechuniah said, "I will answer both your questions. The word 'one' indicates that the best lamb of the flock must be set aside to be used as a *korban*. And how did I reach such an old age? I never accepted gifts, as it is written in the Scriptures: 'He who despises gifts will live.' I have never repaid evil for evil and I have not been miserly."

"Thank you for your instruction," Akiva said. "I will try to do as you have done." Akiva always tries to learn from any person or incident, and he adds the results to his storehouse of Torah.

Shifra related all this to me, word for word, and much more that she had heard, which is why we were so late leaving her estate. Strange, how curious she is about Rachel and Akiva and everything that's happening to them, even though their paths diverged years ago and have continued in opposite directions. Shifra seems to care only for wealth and her position in Roman society, while Rachel's life is dedicated to her husband's learning and to her children — in what order, I couldn't say.

It seems that whenever a traveler comes to our village, Shifra will try to find out if he's been to Lod. Then she'll pump him for information, and always questions him about Akiva. Why should she care about him? And why should she be so interested in Rachel's doings, and in her children's? She still doesn't permit her own children to associate with Rachel's, but she questioned me about them at great length. Come to think of it, she always does, whenever we see each other. It seems like an obsession, her constant interest in every aspect of Rachel's life.

But if Shifra's obsessed, so am I. I also interrogate anyone who comes from Lod for news about Akiva. Whenever I visit Rachel, bringing her some wine, or honey, or flour, or some outgrown clothing, and she tells me about her husband's progress, I always feel I've gotten the better bargain. I only bring her food for the body, but I carry back with me food for the spirit.

Rachel never accepts any money; she always says she has enough. How could she have enough, with the little that she and her daughter earn, and the oh-so-rare letters from her husband with a few *prutot* enclosed?

I made it my business to visit her the next day. As always, my offer of money was refused. "Rachel," I suggested, "why don't you send the boys to work? It's time they started learning a trade. And I know that you can't afford the *sechar limud* you pay their private tutor."

"I want the Torah to be their trade," Rachel answered. "It's the best trade in the world! And with the coins I pay their *melamed*, I get the greatest *metziah* of all, one that assures a good life in this world *and* in the next."

That annoyed me. "You call this a good life? You and Shulamit working your fingers to the bone digging the earth in the spring, pulling weeds all summer, just for a few vegetables to eat with your bread? And at harvest time, both of you stooping to find some leftover wheat kernels — don't deny it, I've seen you do it! Rachel, you'll be old before your time —" but when I looked at her, *really* looked at her, I saw that she is not old at all. Her face is thinner, but her eyes are still the same — clear, undaunted, and her expression is as serene as ever.

I'm only a year older than Rachel and my life has been easy; first my parents always protected me, even spoiled me, and then my husband took over. And what are my worries? That a child has a sniffle? That my maid will leave me? That Elazar spends too much time in the house of study, and not enough at home or in the business? Nobody should have it worse, *beli ayin hara*! And yet, I feel that, compared to Rachel, I look old. Of course, I'm a bit overweight — I've learned to be a very good cook now, and I really enjoy it. And what with our frequent visitors — traveling scholars, business guests and so on — I'm preparing more elaborate meals. How would I know if a recipe is good unless I taste it? Sometimes it takes a lot of tasting to get the seasoning just right.

Anyway, I'd rather be a bit heavy than gaunt like Shifra. She's absolutely determined to stay young-looking forever. There was a time when I suspected that she used the vomitorium regularly — all the Roman matrons were doing it. They'd eat and eat until they were stuffed and then disgorge everything. That way, they were able to try all the new dishes, indulge themselves day and night, yet never gain a *sela*. But no Jewish woman — no matter how assimilated — would do such a disgusting thing. She's as thin as ever though, and she eats twice as much as I do. Maybe she's had a tapeworm inserted — that's the latest.

So I got nowhere with Rachel, as usual. She said that the important expenses were all taken care of: she had money put away for the boys' tuition; the harvest had been good, so she had enough flour to last a while; and the honey I'd brought her would make their bread taste "better than the finest cake." She asked about my children and was happy to hear about Baruch's progress in learning. I told her about Penelope — my parents are beginning to look for a *shidduch* for her. She's young, but, as Father says: "It's never too soon to start looking."

Two more pieces of good news I was able to tell her: Aaron's tutor has left — he said he could never make a Roman aristocrat out of this uncouth Jewish boy. So now he goes to school with the other boys, and at last is beginning to learn something. And my little Batya who was always so disobedient and wild, chasing chickens in the yard, running over the fields, climbing trees like a boy, is finally beginning to act like a girl. Imagine: last week, she combed her hair without being told! And when she misplaced her thimble, she looked and looked until she found it.

All this I told Rachel, and she congratulated me. Then we said goodbye — a bit sadly, because we knew we wouldn't be seeing each other again for a long time. Pesach is almost upon us!

So I had to leave sooner than I would have liked, but I came home with rather a good feeling. Elazar says he can always tell by my face if it was a successful visit. I guess he's right.

12

WE'VE BEEN BLESSED with a few days of sunshine, so I grabbed the chance to see Rachel again, but this time I came home extremely depressed. That in itself is nothing new, but usually I'm able to console myself: she seems happy, the children are thriving, Akiva is making good progress in the yeshiva, and so on. I can always find good reasons for her way of life, or at least good excuses. But this latest incident was just too much! Listen to what she told me:

You remember that fellow, ben Buri, who's always hanging around in Geva, keeping tabs on everyone's comings and goings? Whenever he sees Rachel passing by, he asks her a hundred snide questions:

"Did you pick up a lot of grain today? Your sack looks half empty!"

"Is that a new dress you're wearing? I saw your friend wearing the exact same one, the last time she was here."

"What do you live on, anyway?"

"When is Akiva coming back? It must be twelve years already!"

Rachel is too polite to ignore the old man, or to insult him, so she'll always tell him a bit of news. She says she does that out of respect for his gray hair, and for fear of hurting the feelings of a poor man. I've told her, time and time again, not to bother with him. Lots of people are gray (I noticed a few gray hairs in Elazar's beard just yesterday, and even more in his *payot*) but they still work and try to support themselves. If that old good-for-nothing is capable of being on his feet all day, asking everyone their business and running to tell it to the next one, then he's surely able to do some work and make an honest living. It's his own fault he's poor.

But you know Rachel by now — always making excuses for everyone.

Well, one day she gets a message from Lod. Right away this ben Buri wants to know what's in it. (He always stops the *shaliach* and asks him whom it's for, where it's from, and anything else he can find out.) So Rachel tells him that Akiva might be coming home one of these days soon — she doesn't know exactly when.

That's all this troublemaker needs. Every day he's watching the roads in all directions, waiting for Akiva to come. Why? What concern is it of his? He loves to make mischief, that's why!

One morning, he sees a tall stranger with a bald head approaching the village from a distance. Of course, he recognized Akiva immediately. So what does this nuisance do? Just picture this:

He runs to Rachel's house and starts yelling, "You've been miserable ever since you married that man! You're a living widow! He doesn't care about you at all — goes away for twelve years to learn, and lets you starve! You could have been living like a queen all these years, and instead you're a beggar!

"Get rid of him! Go to your father and ask him to forgive you. Maybe he'll be kind enough to take you and the children back into the house. That so-called husband of yours has ruined your life..." and he keeps screaming on and on, and doesn't let her say a word.

Finally he's so hoarse he has to stop, and Rachel, not knowing Akiva's right outside, answers him: "I am happy that Akiva has already spent twelve years studying. Look what he's accomplished! I wouldn't mind at all if he were to stay away another twelve years!"

That's all that *rasha* needs to hear. He starts braying like a mule. "Ha, ha, ha! You want him to stay away another twelve years! You don't care if you and your brats die of hunger — you want him to stay away another twelve years! Ha, ha, ha!" He's laughing so hard he almost chokes.

Apparently, Akiva overheard every word of that conversation. Without even stepping foot in his house or greeting his family, he turned right around and went back to Lod — that's what his Rachel wanted, wasn't it?

And when that *tzorer* discovered what had happened, he ran back and told Rachel: "Your husband was here. He came, just like he said he would, and you sent him away! Fool that you are — the daughter of the richest man around, and living worse than the beggars in Jerusalem! Another twelve years like this, ha! You'll never make it!" And he's laughing to split his sides: his scheme had worked out even better than he'd hoped!

Rachel told me all this — of course, she tried to cover up for that old man, and to be perfectly honest, she never did say it was ben Buri, but I guessed right away. (She would not confirm my suspicions, but really, who else *could* it have been?) She was utterly calm about the whole thing, even tried to find excuses for that awful person.

"It's actually fortunate it turned out this way," she said. "Akiva has been learning at Lod, studying day and night, and in this short time —" (twelve years is a short time to her!) "he's accumulated so much Torah! Now he'll be able to pass it on to others. This neighbor was sent to test me, and *baruch Hashem*, I withstood the *nisayon*. So you see, I'm grateful to him — now Akiva will grow and grow in learning, and he knows that really is what I want. Oh, Leah, I'm so happy!" And she threw her arms around me, her eyes full of tears.

Happy, happy, happy! Her husband is going away for another twelve years, and she's happy! *Can* you believe it?

13

ANOTHER YEAR HAS PASSED since then. How endless each day, each week, each month must have seemed to my dear Rachel! But when I asked her about it yesterday, she smiled and answered: "On the contrary! Each day that Akiva is away learning Torah is precious to me. Imagine your Elazar leaving you, going to a faraway country where precious stones were almost as common as pebbles are here. If you knew that every day that he was gone, he was finding treasures there — one day a diamond, one day a ruby, one day a sapphire — would you object to his going? And would you complain about his absence?"

Well, I do like jewelry, especially diamonds, so Rachel's question wasn't hard to answer.

"Of course I wouldn't mind, but I'd be satisfied with a handful or two. So let him pick them up and return a few months later with some nice jewels. But I certainly wouldn't let him go for so many years!"

"I guess I didn't describe it the right way," Rachel said. "Learning Torah is not like finding pebbles on the ground. It's more like mining — digging deep into the earth with great effort, splitting rocks, and then sifting through tons of ore, discarding the shiny quartz in order to discover just a few precious stones. Would you let your husband do that, in the hope that he'd bring back a fortune of diamonds in the end?"

That was different. I had to think a while before answering. "If I were sure, absolutely sure," I said, "that he'd return laden with jewels, I might possibly let him go for such a long time, although... But you said, 'In the *hope* that he'd return with a treasure.' That wouldn't be enough for me. No, I'd never let my husband do what yours is doing. *Hoping* is not the same as being *certain*." Now I was positive that I was right. Rachel could not dispute me.

But — "Leah, I *am* certain. I was certain almost from the first moment I saw him." She said it with such conviction and with such a glow of happiness on her face that I saw the young, beautiful Rachel before me again saying:

I know that I am destined for Akiva. Perhaps there'll be a miracle...

I'm tired of fighting the whole world. Who would ever have thought that my friendship with Rachel would lead to this?! Elazar has got this idea in his head that he wants to go to Lod to learn!

Can you imagine? Here he is, with a flourishing business, a wife and two children, a respectable position and a good reputation, and he wants to give it all up — and for what?

"You're an important person here," I told him, "with a family depending on you. Everyone in town respects you. Who'll even look at you over there, with thousands of *talmidim* all over the place? You'll be just another face in the crowd."

"So?"

"So why would you want to do such a ridiculous thing? Do you think you're still eighteen? Just because you know more than our local *melamed* does, do you really think you can compete with all those youngsters? I don't know what's come over you!"

I was indignant, and didn't mind showing it. I *wanted* him to realize the seriousness of what he was considering.

"Are you sure it's not your father's influence that makes you so angry at me?" Elazar asked in that calm, reasonable manner that he knows infuriates me. "After all, we've talked about this before, and you never seemed upset about it the way you are now."

Well, I can be reasonable too. I sat up straight on the couch, composed myself and said in a voice as sweet as date-honey:

"Elazar dear, Father is a man who has the wisdom that comes with age and experience. He says that this would be a foolish step at the present. You have responsibilities here at home; this is no time to be running off to Lod. There are many business opportunities opening up now, especially in real estate, but you have to be here if you want to take advantage of them."

I didn't tell Elazar that Father almost had a fit when I brought up the subject. He was furious! He said that ever since Elazar started going to the *beit midrash* at night to learn, he was a changed person: always reading something, always scribbling notes, not tending to his business.

"But Abba," I'd protested, "I was the one who sent him there in the first place, and you seemed so happy about it. You said it's such a good idea to have a *talmid chacham* around the place, that you never know when some question of *halachah* will come up. And just the other day, when you met that tax collector, Tadai ben Yerucham, you were bragging about your son-in-law, how he spends all his spare time learning, instead of frittering away hours on small talk like all those good-for-nothings around town do."

Why didn't I want to admit to my husband that I had defended him, that in a way I agreed with his ideas? Was it that streak of contrariness that I thought I'd suppressed long ago?

Elazar didn't say a word; he just stared at me with that measuring look that made me feel like two *prutot*. Finally he asked: "Leah, have you ever wanted for anything?"

"No, I can't say I have."

"Did it ever occur to you that maybe it's *because* I spend so much time in the *beit midrash* that Hashem has blessed us with everything we need? Look around you, Leah. These are not easy times. We've had to work so hard to keep our land, but the harvest is still not as good as it was before the drought, and the taxes are rising. Between the low market price we get for our produce and the Roman tax collectors, we're in a tight squeeze.

"As far as real estate goes, people are losing their robes! How many of them bought houses, and then had to sell out at depressed prices because they couldn't afford the upkeep? Yes, if I were to try to get in with the procurator's clique, I'd probably make a bundle, like Tertius and all the others. But I don't want that! That's not what my life is all about!"

"And what about *my* life? And the children's? "

"Aren't our lives about the same thing? To serve *Hakadosh Baruch Hu*, to be good Jews and decent people? It's all one and the same, isn't it? What more is there?"

I couldn't answer that. Elazar was right. But still I wouldn't give up.

"It's true we're quite comfortable, compared to the people in Geva, let's say. But what about the others? Everyone I know seems to be getting ahead, making money and spending it, traveling. And we're still stuck here. I've only been to Alexandria twice, and never to Rome."

Elazar was being patient again. "So what's in Alexandria?"

"But Elazar —" He wouldn't let me get a word in edgewise. My usually quiet husband was about to deliver a lecture, and there was no stopping him.

"Let me finish, please," he said. "I grew up there, you know. Politics, crime, people literally stabbing each other in the back

— *that's* what's in Alexandria! Remember what my father wrote us about the Sicarii, how they go around Alexandria with their daggers, murdering their own Jewish brothers? And Rome is even worse. What's wrong with living here? The valley is beautiful all year 'round. There's plenty to eat, *baruch Hashem*: the grapevines and fig trees bear fruit almost without anyone tending them. Our children are safer here than in the big cities, where, as we've heard, crime is rampant and there's been a breakdown of law and order." He ended with one of those pathetic sighs — you know what I mean. "I just don't know what's come over you, Leah."

I knew what had come over me. The day before yesterday, I had met Shifra and Miriam in town. They were both dressed in the latest fashions from Rome, and they looked gorgeous! I felt like a housemaid next to them. And all they talked about was the Roman architecture, and the theaters they'd been to, and the fancy vases and things they'd brought back with them. No wonder I felt jealous!

But I couldn't tell Elazar *that*. I was determined to show him how reasonable I was and how well thought-out my position. "It's not only Abba who feels that way," I said gently. "All my friends agree that it would be utterly ridiculous for you to give up everything you have here and go off to learn. I discussed it with them, and they said it's simply out of the question."

"So who are these friends?"

I was afraid he'd ask me that. "Shifra and Miriam. Their husbands are doing so well —"

"Ha!" Now Elazar was being scornful. "That's who you ask for advice? Your father is your father, and you have to respect him. But to ask *them*, to tell *them* about our private affairs... I'm surprised at you."

"Well," I stalled, feeling a bit ashamed, "we've been friends for so many years, and I know they have my welfare at heart."

But Elazar wasn't impressed. "Do you want our children to grow up like theirs? Running around with the gentiles, imitating their way of dress and their lifestyle? Julius is only fifteen, but I heard he's never home at night. They say he's always getting into trouble."

"Shifra says it's not his fault. It's the low-class element in town that's influencing him. If they hadn't opened that new tavern, this never would have happened." I was repeating Shifra's words, but I knew Elazar was right. I also knew exactly what he would say next, and he did.

"And what about Rachel? What does she say about all this?"

That husband of mine can see right through me. He knew very well that I hadn't asked Rachel, and he knew why. So did I. I also knew I had lost this particular argument.

"All right, Elazar," I sighed, "if it means so much to you, I'll let you go. But remember, only for two months, and only in the rainy season. I'll have to manage with the children somehow..."

The next day Elazar set off for Lod.

14

IT'S BORING AND LONELY with Elazar away. Baruch is in school full time now, and needs little of my attention. Batya has no interest at all in studying; she spends her time trailing after me in the house, running outdoors with her friends, playing with the new lambs and ducklings. The rest of the time she hangs around the kitchen with the servants. Am I glad I have my faithful Rivka!

We hired another maid, Dina. I had argued with Elazar about that: I said that the peasant girls from the back country are stronger than our local girls, and willing to work for less. Also, you have to be so careful with the local servants, not to hurt their feelings. But Elazar insisted; he didn't want the children picking up that vulgar peasant speech and manner. I said he was prejudiced, but in the end I have to admit that he was right.

It's true that Rivka, and now Dina, took a long time to train: Rivka was oversensitive and sometimes cranky, and Dina was young and silly. But at least I don't have to worry about Batya spending time in their company: they're decent and reliable, and I know she's safe with them.

I decided to visit Penelope. I hadn't seen her since her *sheva berachot* — I forgot to tell you she married Chanania ben Rav Avraham, from Yaffo. You must want to know how that *shidduch* came about.

Well, Father had been in Yaffo on business; he'd made a number of lucrative cash purchases, and had given his small change to the beggars who hung around the market. In the evening, when he went to the *beit knesset*, he was approached by yet another poor man, but he discovered that he hadn't a single *prutah* in his purse. He was appalled: not only couldn't he give the beggar anything, but he couldn't buy himself a meal or pay for lodging! (You know that Abba always stays in the best inns when he travels.)

I suppose his distress must have shown on his face. A young fellow in the *beit knesset* came over to him and said, "You must be a stranger here. Do you need a place to stay? Come to our house. My parents are always happy to have guests."

Naturally, Father hesitated. Maybe these people were really out to rob him? But by this time he was starving and exhausted. He figured he had nothing to lose, since he had no money on him, and besides, where could he go so late at night? Also, he told us, the young man had an honest face. So he went along with him.

The house was quite plain compared to ours: no grounds to speak of, a tiny reception room, and only one maid. But Abba was impressed by the library, where there were rows and rows of Bible scrolls, all well used. (No one we know has a "library," certainly not as extensive as this! Apparently, Rav Avraham had a complete set of *Tanach* for every one of his sons — all *eight* of them!)

So after supper, Abba started talking to his host, and it turned out that the man's uncle (Chanania's great uncle) had done business with Abba's father years and years ago. Also, Rav Avraham had been in our town several times to lecture in the synagogue, and he knew of our family. He had met Elazar on one of his visits, and had been impressed with his knowledge. So one thing led to another, and Abba came home all excited about Chanania. He told us that the young man had studied in Lod for several years, and was planning to become a scribe, and also to continue learning.

Actually, Abba wasn't too thrilled about that. He thought it wouldn't be much of a *parnassah*, but he liked the young man and his family, and so did Imma, and of course Penelope. So they were married in *Elul*.

The wedding was not quite as elaborate as mine; even my parents are feeling the pinch, and also, Chanania doesn't have nearly as many relatives as Elazar. Still, it was a lovely *chatunnah*, and my parents were proud and pleased to have such esteemed *mechutanim*.

So I went over to Penelope's. Chanania wants her to be called by her real name, Penina, but I haven't gotten accustomed to it yet. Mother did right away and I guess eventually I will, too.

Their new furniture still hadn't come so I had lent them an old table of mine, and Imma had given them the extra cushions and linens from her house. I told Penelope not to think about it; my furniture had taken months to arrive but I was so pleasantly surprised with Abba's selections when it finally did come, that I forgot all about the waiting. (Now, it's starting to look altogether old-fashioned; the styles have changed in the intervening years and I really would prefer a more modern look.) But on the whole, it's only a minor matter, I told her.

"You can make the house look quite decent," I said, "even without the new furniture. Just cover that scratched table with the embroidered cloth you were working on, the one I gave you that I had started. (I never finish all those projects I begin; I blame it on the twins.) And put up some small rugs or tapestries, and it'll look fine."

Then Penelope showed me her trousseau. She had gotten

twelve gowns to my seven, but I think the quality and workmanship are not nearly as good. But what is, nowadays? The clothing I got when I was married still looks almost new; they knew how to weave and sew in those days. Of course, my gowns are rather outmoded, and don't fit quite right (they must have shrunk in the closet somehow, but I'll hold on to them for a while yet; I'm planning to lose weight soon).

So we talked about this and that, and she said she's very happy with her Chanania, and doesn't mind that he goes off to the *beit knesset* at night. She asked me how Rachel is doing, and I started to tell her, but just then Aaron dropped by.

"Hello, big sister!" It was nice to get such a warm greeting from him. "This is a surprise! I haven't seen you in ages! How's Elazar, and how're the twins?"

This brother of mine has improved enormously, I must say. He's let his *payot* grow out, and he's just beginning to sprout a beard. Also, his manner is much more courteous than it used to be. Before, the first thing with him was always, "What's there to eat?" and he'd gobble down whatever it was without a *berachah* or anything. Now, he shows me the proper respect due an older sister and he treats our parents respectfully too. Most significant is the fact that he has stopped hanging around with Julius. Despite their age difference, or maybe because of it, Julius was a very bad influence. Mother had been very upset about that friendship, and had begged Aaron not to associate with that type of boy, but he would just laugh. But when his *teacher* told him, it was a different story altogether. So there's been a big change in Aaron, and all for the better.

"You're still talking about your friend Rachel, and about Akiva? Seems to me that's all I hear whenever I see you. Why don't you write it down — keep a diary or something? Maybe you'll leave it to your children, so they'll know what it was like when you were young."

"Maybe I will, at that." (I wasn't about to tell him I've been writing for years.) "You know I've saved every note I ever got from Rachel. And now that Elazar is in Lod, I guess I'll be saving his letters also. But Aaron, I have a good idea: why don't *you* start writing things down? Your handwriting could stand improvement, and that'll give you some practice."

"Elazar is still in Lod? How could I have forgotten! Good! And maybe I *will* start writing stuff down — there's a lot happening now, and it's good to remember. When I think of what a brat I used to be..."

This opened a new subject, and we spent the rest of the afternoon talking about it; it was almost dark when I came home, and I had to rush around preparing supper. It was really so annoying: couldn't I spend an afternoon with my family without having to pay for it? I wouldn't dream of letting the servants handle meal preparation any more, now that I've learned to cook so well myself, but they *could* have heated up the oven. And Batya really should start to help a little in the house; she's certainly old enough. But how will she ever learn if I don't teach her?

A messenger had brought a letter from Elazar while I was out and I didn't have a chance to look at it until supper was cleared away. First the usual things: How are you, and the children, and your parents, and the weather. I'm fine *baruch Hashem*, very busy. Sorry I didn't write before, etc., etc.

But then came the thunderbolt: Elazar wants to stay in Lod another month!

It's so amazing, the letter said, he never knew how wonderful it could be to learn in a real yeshiva, where every single student knows more than all the local *melamedim* put together, and to be surrounded by such tremendous *talmidei chachamim*...but most of all: Akiva!

That's whom the letter was all about — Akiva! How could it be that he never realized what a great man this Akiva was, Elazar wrote. And the rest of the letter was a series of raptures on the same subject, pages and pages of it. I'll give you the gist of it; it would take too long to put in every "great," "wonderful," "supreme," "overpowering," and all those other adjectives Elazar used. So here it is, approximately.

A miracle has come to pass. In his twelve years of study at Lod, Akiva has accumulated a treasure trove filled with Torah. Until now, his intellect was hidden; he seldom spoke, except to ask questions of his teachers, to make sure that he understood perfectly each word of the *halachah* and of the Tradition.

Rabi Eliezer had not recognized Akiva's potential, but Rabi Yehoshua ben Chanania saw his tremendous will and desire for learning, and took Akiva under his wing. Akiva followed him everywhere in order to learn from his conduct, as well as from his vast Torah knowledge.

Akiva had been splitting rocks and sifting through the rubble from his very first days of studying *alef-beit*; now he has begun to take out his gems, to polish them to perfection, and to exhibit them to the astonished eyes of his teachers and fellow students.

In his thirteenth year at Lod, Akiva gave an opinion of his own, in opposition to his teacher, Rabi Eliezer. All the Sages had agreed that the *korban Pesach* should be offered even on Shabbat; Rabi Eliezer argued, however, that even the preparations for the *korban* which could have been done before Shabbat, may be performed on Shabbat, if their observance constitutes only a *shevut*, a Rabbinical transgression of the Shabbat. Akiva attempted to prove to Rabi Eliezer, however, from something Rabi Eliezer himself had once taught them, that only the actual offering of the sacrifice was permissible on Shabbat.

From then on, he has been looked upon by both teachers and pupils with entirely different eyes. Rabi Yehoshua said to Rabi Eliezer, in the words of the Scripture:"This is the People which you have disdained; now go forth and do battle with it!"

The student who was so persistent in is learning has now become a teacher, but he is still the same simple, modest Akiva who walked behind the plow, who guarded the flocks, who sold bundles of fallen twigs and branches for a livelihood.

Yes, the yeshiva at Lod has a new star rising. Akiva is not young: his back is bent from years of hard physical labor, and from the additional years of poring over the parchment scrolls, studying and analyzing every word for its exact translation and its hidden meanings. But there is a youthful strength and vigor in his teaching and in his learning. With quick long strides he walks around the huge rotunda of the *beit midrash*, explaining each word to the pupils so that even the least of them can understand and repeat his interpretation.

Akiva labors from dawn to darkness, just as he labored in the fields of his masters. He pursues knowledge, just as he used to run after the sheep to gather in a stray lamb. He guards his pupils, and guides them to the wellsprings of Torah just as he led his thirsty flock to streams of water. So now the former *am ha'aretz* has been promoted to the rank of master, and many young men, eager to learn, are gathering around him.

Once Akiva came late to the *beit midrash* and, not wanting to disturb the others, he sat himself down outside, instead of at his usual place in the front rows. When a question of *halachah* was asked, everyone said, "*Halachah* is outside." When a second question was asked, they said, "Torah is outside." And when a third question was asked, they said, "Akiva is outside — make way for him." The students moved aside and allowed Akiva to pass and he sat down at the feet of Rabi Eliezer.

Yes, it was indeed a miracle — but it seems that only Elazar and I were aware of the extent of it:

By now, everyone in the Land knows about this Akiva who came, a middle-aged beginner, to study at Lod. He has never spoken about his past, though; in the first twelve years here, all his time was devoted to listening and learning. And now he is constantly surrounded by students eager to acquire the gems of knowledge from his treasury.

That's what Elazar wrote, and that's why he wants to stay

longer: he has attached himself to Akiva — now *Rabi* Akiva — and is memorizing every word he says, and trying to emulate his conduct. How could he return in less than two months, Elazar asked, when he's just beginning to get a taste of what learning is all about?

Reading his letter, I got the feeling that he wasn't asking me; he was telling me.

Since the rain looks as if it will never let up, and there isn't too much work on the estate, and since I have no choice anyway, I agreed that he stay.

15

AFTER THREE MONTHS, Elazar returned from Lod. He's thinner now and he speaks more rapidly than he used to, and he goes to the *beit knesset* earlier and stays later. Also he now studies with Chanania, his new brother-in-law, in the middle of the day, before dinner. Otherwise, everything is the same.

But I keep hearing about Akiva, or rather Rabi Akiva ben Yosef, as he is called now, not only from Elazar but from others as well. Every traveler from Lod brings reports of this brilliant middle-aged student-turned-teacher, and his name is now mentioned along with Rabban Shimon ben Gamliel, and Rabi Eliezer and Rabi Yehoshua. Yet no one seems to be aware that this giant of Torah was once an ignorant shepherd whom Rachel had married.

It's so unfair! Shouldn't Rachel reap some of the benefits? Akiva is becoming famous, and she's still struggling along, raising her family on the little she earns, and the pittance that Akiva — *Rabi* Akiva — sends her. I'll have to talk to her about that; surely she deserves some share in his fame.

I've tried to picture myself in her place. Of course, I never would have been able to make the sacrifices that Rachel has made, but if my Elazar were ever to become an eminent scholar, I'd want the whole world to know that I was married to him. Not that I'm looking for glory, you understand; I'm not that type. But still, it would make my parents so happy, and Elazar's family too. And when the time for weddings would roll around, as it is beginning to for Rachel's children, it would make a tremendous difference in the type of *shidduchim* we could expect.

Yes, I decided, I'll have to do something about this. But what? And when? Now, with Pesach practically upon us, Rivka has decided to get engaged. Imagine, after all these years! And to Reuven, our herdsman, no less. And the wedding is set for three weeks before Pesach! Couldn't she have picked a better time? Of course, as far as she's concerned, the timing is perfect. All the Pesach preparations are now in my lap.

But besides having to remove all the *chametz* myself, bake the *matzot*, cook the other special foods, see to it that the seamstress has the children's new spring clothes ready on time, and do some decorating in the dining room, I have another project: to find a wife for Aaron.

Now don't laugh; believe it or not he's almost twenty, and Father says it's high time we started looking. Since he's far too busy on his estate and was never one for socializing, he asked me to lend a hand. It makes good sense anyway: who is better suited to pick out a good woman than another woman? I suppose Abba has finally come to recognize some of my talents. But you can't imagine how much work this matchmaking takes: I have to go to all the weddings and look for eligible girls. Now that Aaron has turned into such a fine young man, we have to make sure he gets the right kind of wife. It'll make all the difference to his future.

Shifra has mentioned her Flora a few times, but I'm less than enthusiastic. She seems a sweet girl, although a bit too flighty for my taste. And her brother's reputation isn't much help. Still, Abba says we shouldn't be too hasty in rejecting the offer. Tertius is now one of the richest men in the area, and if

Aaron wants to continue learning, as he says he does, a wealthy father-in-law is essential. Abba can't support another couple when he's still helping Penina and Chanania, and their family is growing, *beli ayin hara*.

All this is just too much for me. I can't appear in the same gown at every wedding, so I'm always busy with shopping for fabrics and with fittings. I can't neglect the house either; Elazar has absolutely no interest and leaves it all in my hands. He has no idea what finding a new maid, and training her, entails. Dina has never worked out as well as Rivka did, somehow. She's still the same silly, giggly girl she's always been. In a way, though, I'm relieved that Rivka is getting married: she's often cranky, and though she does a good job of running the house, she acts as if it belongs to her. Yes, it's really the best thing, and I wish her all the luck in the world. Still, she could have waited until after Pesach.

Also, we'll need a new herdsman soon. Reuven says now that he's getting married, he wants to be working for himself, and wants to rent part of our land, and raise wheat and barley. He doesn't seem to realize that it's much harder to be a boss than a worker: there are so many more responsibilities. Reuven also used to fix a lot of things around the house, and it won't be easy to find someone as skillful, who can take care of the sheep and cattle too. When I speak to Elazar about these things, he just shrugs and says, "Hashem will provide!"

Still, if I didn't worry about all these things, the estate would probably collapse. So I really don't know when I'll have a chance to visit Rachel. It'll have to be after Shavuot, for sure, when we return from the pilgrimage to Yerushalayim.

And when I see her, what will I tell her? I'm so confused, and it's all Elazar's fault. I wish he hadn't told me about Akiva.

16

FIRST IT WAS PESACH, and then it was Shavuot, and before we knew it, the High Holy Days rolled around. If I wasn't busy preparing for holiday guests, then I was packing or unpacking from the Sukkot pilgrimage. And then Elazar announced his plans to return to Lod.

"But Elazar," I argued, "how can you leave the estate when things are so bad?"

"What's 'so bad,' Leah?" he asked in that innocent tone that always makes me say things I regret later.

"Oh, Elazar, you know they're all saying there won't be any rain this year, that we'll have to cart in water from somewhere and maybe dig new wells to irrigate the fields. How am I to cope with all that if you're to be away? What if..."

"Calm yourself, Leah," Elazar said soothingly. "I've already made all the arrangements necessary for the estate. And I know you'll handle everything in my absence as well as you did last year."

Well, I certainly couldn't argue with that.

Amazingly, the time flew by, and I still had not gone to see Rachel. There were many good reasons, the primary one being that we had not yet found a *shidduch* for Aaron, and so in addition to dealing with estate affairs, I was going to many out-of-town weddings. I had seen the local girls, and there was no one that really appealed to me. We all felt that Aaron deserved somebody very special and I was determined to find the right one, no matter how far I'd have to look.

I was also very busy training Hadassah, the new girl, and trying to pacify Dina, who was being very bossy and critical.

"Hadassah has no polish," Dina said to me when we were alone in the kitchen one day. How quickly she's forgotten her own rough manners when she first came! And she hasn't improved that much since then, either.

"Polish? Better no polish and a good Jewish heart, than those heathens from back in the hills," I told Dina. "They can't be trusted with the children, or anything else, for that matter."

Eventually, Hadassah became quite skillful, but it's taken a lot out of me. I'm grateful, though, that Batya likes her; my once sweet-tempered daughter is becoming picky and irritable, not to mention irritating! There are daily arguments about nothing at all; not serious fights, but they're annoying and upsetting just the same.

"I have nothing to wear!" Every single morning I hear the same song, and the girl has a closetful of clothes!

"Imma, tell Baruch to stop breathing so loud. He's bothering me!" Baruch is hardly ever home, yet his presence seems to make her even more petulant than usual.

My friends tell me their daughters are the same. I can't remember ever acting that way myself. I was always respectful to my parents. I don't recall ever quarreling with Penina; we are very close and the best of friends. And I don't have to tell you what high regard I have for Aaron — he's certainly the best boy in his yeshiva. So having my own child fighting with her only brother — and her twin, yet — hurts me and worries me terribly. And that's another reason I must visit Rachel: I want to get her advice.

When I realized that almost a year had passed since I

resolved to visit Geva, I told myself: No more excuses — just go! I still hadn't decided what I would tell Rachel, so on the long walk there, I tried to plan my words. I'd have to be very subtle.

I never have the wagon driver take me to Rachel's, partly because all the wagons are needed for estate business most of the time, and partly because it's embarrassing to let the workers see me go to that deplorable slum. (I can trust my chaperones, but who can trust a wagon driver not to gossip?) But now I was particularly glad I had gone on foot. The road which had been improved but never maintained properly was virtually crumbling to pieces, there was no doubt about that, and I'm certain we would have lost a wheel or lamed the mule.

As I walked, I noticed that the fields on either side looked gray and dried-out. Even the new leaves of the fig trees hung down, dull and dusty, and there were barely any blossoms on the fruit trees, which by now should have been in full bloom. What's happening to the land? There used to be grapes, and figs, and almonds just growing wild. The drought this year has made everything look barren and empty.

I didn't pay that much attention, though, because I was worried about Rachel, and what effect my words would have on her. I was absolutely certain that even after all this time, Akiva had never told her about his success — he was far too modest — nor would any traveler from Lod bother stopping in Geva to spread the news. There was nothing of interest to a traveler in that dreadful little hamlet, not even an inn.

When I arrived in Geva, I was almost hoping to meet that awful ben Buri. I wanted to give him a piece of my mind for making so much trouble for my dear Rachel! If he hadn't gone to the house and screamed at her, she wouldn't have given the answer that Akiva overheard, and Akiva would be safely home with his family now. Maybe. But I couldn't find the old trouble-maker. Typical — always around at the wrong time, but never there when you want him!

Rachel was at home. Strange, how she never seems to

change! The only indication of time passing was in the condition of the house: everything looked smaller and shabbier than I remembered it from last time. She greeted me with the same fond attention as ever; it seemed as if we were still two girls together, instead of a matron with grown children, in her case, and one with troublesome youngsters, in mine.

Rachel quickly offered me a cool drink, and she seemed as anxious as I was to catch up on everything that had happened since the last time we met.

"So, Rachel, how are things with you?" I wanted to get a clue about Akiva before I said anything, and find out if she was aware of his fame.

"*Baruch Hashem*, everything is just fine. The boys are in yeshiva, learning well, and Shulamit is down the street, helping a neighbor." Rachel was busy, as usual; she was sorting dried peas on the table and I could see there were many wormy ones. She must have sold all the good ones that grew in her little garden.

The very thought of it upset me so that I burst out: "And what about Akiva? About him you say nothing? Don't tell me you haven't heard from him!"

But Rachel answered calmly: "Of course I heard from him. I got a note with some money just a couple of weeks ago."

"And what did he write?" I couldn't contain my curiosity. Was she or was she not aware of her husband's greatness? Had he told her that he had hundreds, maybe even thousands, of *talmidim*? That his words were being repeated and memorized as if they were *Torat Moshe*?

"Akiva writes that he is learning well. He found an answer to something that was bothering him for a long time, and his teachers agreed with him, so he's very happy. And he sends fond regards to me and the children." That's what she answered. But had I really expected anything different?

"Rachel," I said, choosing my words carefully, "are you aware of the fact that your husband is not a student any longer, but a teacher? Not only that, but he's in the top rank, together with Rabban Shimon ben Gamliel and Rabi Eliezer and Rabi Yehoshua. All *Eretz Yisrael* is talking about him. Every sentence he utters is repeated and discussed by the whole yeshiva. And he hasn't written a word to you about all this?"

Rachel's eyes flooded with tears. She threw her arms around me, and kissed me again and again.

"Leah, Leah, you've always been my dearest, most loyal friend!" she cried. "It's only right that you should bring me this wonderful *besorah*. I always knew that this would happen one day, but that you should be the one to tell me?! It makes my happiness even greater. Why am I *zochah*, what did I do to deserve all this?" And Rachel was smiling — no, laughing! — even as she wiped the tears from her face.

I must admit that I was crying too. If ever a person deserved complete happiness, it was my precious Rachel. Her husband had been away now, let's see, it must be fourteen years or more. All this time she's had to carry the burden of *parnassah* and the responsibility of the children. She had never asked for anything or complained about her circumstances. I was completely delighted for her and with her. And for once, there was no trace of my old envy; I rejoiced in her joy.

"*Baruch Hashem*, dear, dear Rachel, that you have seen this day! And lucky me, that I was the *shaliach* to bring you the good news! But now you must be practical: you should get rid of this place, and move to Lod immediately. There, you'll —"

I was rushing along with my plans for Rachel, when I realized that she wasn't even listening. She had taken out her little *Tehillim* scroll, and was quietly reciting a psalm of thanksgiving:

> "I thank You because You have answered me
> And have been my salvation;
> The stone which the builders rejected
> Has become the chief cornerstone.

This is Hashem's doing; it is wondrous in our eyes,
This is the day Hashem made;
Let us be glad and rejoice in Him..."

While Rachel was murmuring the words with a look of absolute bliss on her face, I took a quick inventory of the room. There was no point in her taking along anything but a few pots and bowls, and possibly the table. It was a bit unsteady, but it could be fixed. The rest she should give away. To whom?

Why, to ben Buri, of course!

Why did I pick him? Because suddenly I understood. I had been blind, but Rachel had always seen clearly. If that terrible man hadn't purposely made a fuss just when he knew Akiva would be coming home, would she ever have said that her husband should stay away for another twelve years? And if Akiva hadn't overheard her, he *would* have stayed home and probably settled down nicely with his family. He would not have returned to Lod. And he would have missed his chance at greatness!

Strange are the ways of Hashem, and even stranger are the people He uses to fulfill His plan!

I couldn't wait for Rachel to finish her prayers so I could explain my new insight to her; I thought she'd be overwhelmed by my brilliant deduction.

But — "Leah," she said, "I never doubted that there was a reason for that scene. I tried to explain that at the time, but you were so upset and depressed then that I was sorry I had told you about it. I was sure there was a purpose, that whatever Hashem does is ultimately for the good!"

So what it took me years to discover, Rachel had known all along. Good! Now I'd help her to plan the next step: the move to Lod.

"Rachel, I think you shouldn't bother packing these things. It really doesn't pay. Hiring a carter is a big expense, and there are plenty of good shops in Lod. You should buy the best —

they say those Tabor iron pots are good — because it always pays in the end. You'll need some new clothes..." and I started to make a list.

Rachel gently stopped me. "Leah dear, I'm not planning to move. Why should I? I'm very comfortable here, and I have everything I need — including you!" And she gave me that sweet smile.

That was too much for me. Just when I thought I was beginning to understand, I realized that I knew nothing at all. "You're not planning to join your husband in Lod? Now that he's finally reached the heights that you've always hoped he would, you're going to stay here — alone?" It was beyond human comprehension.

"And why not? Here our needs are very small. This little cottage costs practically nothing, and a lot of our food is free. And my good, generous Leah always has us in mind." Again the sweet smile, but I was almost in tears, tears of utter frustration!

"Rachel, you can't mean that. You *must* go to Lod. You waited so long for this, and you deserve it — you deserve the best of everything! Now is your chance!" I put all my heart, all my conviction into those words, but to no avail.

"We'll stay here. Don't you see? If you hadn't told me, that's what we would have done anyway. Just because Lod is becoming aware of Akiva's greatness doesn't mean we have to run there. Having the family with him would only distract him from his learning, and prevent him from reaching his true potential. I said another twelve years, and I meant it."

I saw there was no reasoning with Rachel. And...perhaps...she was right...

17

AT HOME, EVERYTHING was as usual. Elazar was preparing for his yearly trip to Lod, his fifth one now. He had been staying for three months each time, but now he asked for four.

"It seems that just as I'm about to get my teeth into something, it's time to turn around and go home again. I'll make arrangements with Reuven, so that he can take care of any emergencies." (As a wedding gift, we had given Reuven and Rivka a small parcel of land on our estate, instead of leasing it to them, so they've remained close by.) "And if you're lonely, you can visit your parents, or Penina or Rachel."

"What about Shifra? And Miriam?" I asked.

"You know exactly how I feel about that," Elazar said. "But I won't tell you what to do; you'll suit yourself anyway."

He can't possibly know how much this conversation annoyed me. Other women are always saying: "My husband doesn't let me do this, my husband doesn't let me do that," when they're really talking about things *they* don't want to do. Elazar lets me do everything, so I have to make my own decisions; it's so much more difficult, and when something turns out badly, there's no one to blame!

After he left, I gave the house a thorough cleaning, with Dina and Hadassah helping, of course. Batya also gave me a hand; I hope she's coming out of that moody stage now. It's gone on for far too long. The other day she even laughed at one of Baruch's jokes, which I think is a good sign.

I decided it was high time I taught her to spin. After all, I learned how to do it when I was much younger than she is. It's the kind of skill every girl should have; you never know when it'll come in handy. But after all these years, I was rather rusty and I wasn't at all sure that I had demonstrated it well enough for her to grasp. But to my surprise, she got the hang of it immediately, and became an expert almost overnight! Not only that, she *liked* it!

"Batya, I'm proud of you," I said. "I never expected you to catch on so quickly."

"Imma, remember when we used to go together to Rachel's? I always watched her doing it, and wished that you'd let me. When Shulamit got to be old enough to learn spinning, I thought she was the luckiest girl in the world because it looked like so much fun." Batya said this in a normal, cheerful voice, without a trace of the sarcasm that had become so habitual that I hardly noticed it any more.

Will wonders never cease? My little girl wants to spin! Maybe she has other interests or talents I've never been aware of; I'll have to find out. Perhaps I could get someone to teach her weaving. I never learned to do it well enough, to Mother's eternal frustration. Who would have thought I'd need to teach it to my own daughter?

I'm starting to realize something: I'm not Batya, and Batya is not me. Why do I always try to impose my feelings and opinions on her? I'll have to remember that the fact that she's my child does not mean she has to be the same as me in everything. Yes, I'll definitely begin asking around tomorrow for a weaving expert, and start lessons right away.

Only if Batya wants to, that is.

In the meantime, I'm enjoying the new peace that has come to the household, and I've postponed my visiting for another time.

Of course I miss Elazar, and the children long for their father, but by now we've become so accustomed to his absences that it makes little difference. Baruch goes to the *beit midrash* very day, comes home, eats his dinner, goes to prayers and some more study, and then to sleep. When Elazar is home, he wakes Baruch early, at dawn, and they do a bit of learning together. I felt the poor child could use some extra sleep since he's up so late every night, so I told Reuven not to wake him until it's time for the minyan. So what happens? Baruch wakes up even earlier!

At the rooster's first crow, he's out of bed; when it's time to go to prayers, he has already spent a good hour bent over his *sefarim*. I worry about his posture; his back is already quite rounded and I'm afraid he'll look like an old man before his time. But since he started attending this *beit midrash*, he behaves much better at home, and is also getting along well with Batya. Maybe it's because he's away all day. Since he's been *bar mitzvah*, he's been talking about switching to an out-of-town yeshiva, but I feel he's much too young.

The matter of finding a *shidduch* for Aaron has become more pressing. Should we think seriously about Flora for him?

I went to my parents' last night (Penina and Chanania were there too) and the subject took up the entire evening. Father thinks it might be a very good match. He says Flora's grandfather, Judah, was a well-known and highly respected businessman, and Tertius takes after him in his ability to make money. "But unfortunately not in any other way," I muttered to myself.

Still, I don't think that this is really the right girl for my brother; I begged Father to wait until Elazar's return before making such an important decision. "He should be back by now, shouldn't he?" Abba asked. "Isn't it three months already?"

"Well, Elazar asked for another month, and I agreed." I was a bit reluctant to tell Abba since I knew he wouldn't be too happy about my answer.

"I don't know what the world is coming to. Where I come from, a boy studied until he was old enough to work and make some money, and that was that. As soon as I was able, I started to learn a trade; I knew that I'd have to support a family eventually, and I wanted to be ready. Believe me, I'm worried about Aaron: he only wants to sit and learn, and has no interest in business. And is Chanania any different? 'Don't worry, Abba,' Penina tells me. 'Even though my husband only works part-time, we manage.'

"Manage, ha! Crowded into that little house, with babies all over the place and not a *prutah* of savings!" This is actually Abba's pet peeve. Once he gets started on the subject, there's no stopping him. "And even your Elazar! When I took him for a son-in-law, I expected him to make a good living for his family, not to keep running off to Lod to learn! What's come over everybody?"

Imma, I saw, was a bit embarrassed at this outburst and tried to interrupt Abba, but he was totally carried away. I decided it was my duty as the eldest and the one who's always been closest to him, to speak for the others.

"Abba dear," I began, "Penina is telling the truth when she says she manages, and quite well, as a matter of fact. The house is so orderly and looks so pretty, and the children are polite and always neatly dressed. But most of all, they're happy! They're a happy family, and they're not lacking for anything. Penina knows that her husband is *learning* when he's away at night, not gambling and carousing or running to the theater, and the children are not spoiled and bratty, like so many of her rich friends' children are. From the time they can talk, they learn to make a *berachah*; they know to be grateful for everything they get. Isn't that worth more than a bigger house, or gold buried in a clay jar?"

Father was surprised. Hardly anyone ever contradicts him.

"But what about the future?" he asked. "And about you and Elazar — don't tell me you're happy to have him away for such a long time!"

"True, Abba, I must admit that it was very difficult at first. I was so accustomed to running to him with every little problem — the children, the house, the servants, even the weather, as if he could do anything about that! But now I've learned to cope and to make decisions myself, and it's working out quite well." I was a bit astonished at my own words; I never realized how much I had changed in the last few years, and everything I'd said to Abba was true.

"And what about the children? You used to complain about them constantly. I even remember your saying, the first time he went to Lod, that all their problems stemmed from Elazar's being away; you said you never were able to control them, and only threats of 'Wait till your father gets back' would keep them in line." Abba looked triumphant. He felt he had scored a significant point.

Well, just a few months ago he would have been right. But now the situation at home is so much better: Batya is busy with her spinning and weaving, and she even designed a new pattern that made a big hit with all her friends. Baruch is really progressing in his studies. The two of them have stopped quarreling, and are respectful to their elders. All this I told Father.

"You know something, Abba? I think it's Elazar's going to Lod that has made them change for the better. What went on before was just the typical pre-teenage trouble. My friends' children are worse than the twins ever were. Baruch and Batya are very proud of their father, proud that he's becoming a genuine *talmid chacham*, and this gives them a certain standard to look up to. Now they wait for his return eagerly, not to get showered with his attention but to show him what they've accomplished and hear what *he's* accomplished. When he *is* home, he spends a lot of time with them; you know he learns with Baruch every morning, and he takes a big interest in Batya's doings. When she wants to talk to him, he always has the time, not like most fathers who say, 'Don't bother me, I'm busy.' *Baruch Hashem*, I have no complaints."

I guess this is the longest speech I've ever made to Abba; he's usually the one who makes speeches. I thought he'd answer with a flood of criticisms and objections, but all he said was: "I don't know, you all live from day to day, from hand to mouth. Aren't you concerned with the future? Who do you think will take care of you?"

And now Rachel's words came back to me:

The same One Who's been taking care of us all this time — the Ribbono shel Olam!

On this note we parted. Penina, Chanania and I walked home together and Chanania said, "I never knew you were such an orator. You expressed our feelings so perfectly, much better than I could have."

"I hate to disillusion you," I told him, "but there was nothing original about my speech. I've heard those words from Rachel so many times. Do you think Abba was convinced?" I personally doubted it.

But Chanania said, "Well, it's the first time I know of that he didn't insist on having the last word."

That's progress, I suppose.

18

WE COULDN'T WAIT for Elazar to return. Baruch wanted to exhibit his learning ability, Batya was weaving a *tallit* bag for her father, with his initials on it (slightly lopsided, but still quite an accomplishment) and I had to speak to him very seriously about Flora, for my brother Aaron. Father had been asking me about this almost every day.

So when Elazar finally walked in the door, one bright day in *Adar*, we all jumped on him at once.

"Look, Abba, look! It's not finished yet, but can you see...?" That was Batya, dragging Elazar to the workroom, where the half-finished strip of weaving was stretched on the loom.

"Abba, you must come with me to my yeshiva. I think I found the answer, with proofs, to the *kushiya* we talked about just before you left." Baruch had grabbed Elazar's elbow, and was pulling him in the opposite direction, so I thought I'd better take over.

"Children, let Abba sit down and catch his breath. He's just come from Lod — your things will have to wait." And I immediately started bombarding him with my news.

"Very interesting," Elazar said. "But we'll have to talk about all this later. Let me tell you what happened at Lod..."

And he told me...and he told me...and he told me...

He said "Rabi Akiva" was rising like the sun in the morning. He said that the most illustrious Rabbis consulted with him on every question. He told us that Rabi Akiva was systematizing the Midrash *halachot* and *aggadot* and the principles on which they were built. His students are the greatest in the yeshiva. They call him "one of the fathers of the world" and he is known as a "sealed treasury" with separate compartments for each treasure stored within. "You see, Leah, he teaches his students every topic separately: *mikra, halachah, aggadah,* and so forth. That way, they can attend all of his *shiurim* without being confused by different topics and can learn the subject matter thoroughly."

All this, and much more Elazar reported. He was aflame with enthusiasm and excitement, and none of us could get a word in edgewise, so we didn't even try. It occurred to me that perhaps Elazar was thinking of following Akiva's example... He's younger than Akiva was when he'd begun learning, and even before Elazar began to study in Lod he already knew the basics that Akiva took years to acquire...

But I am not Rachel!

The next day, after the children had shown their achievements to their father, and he had expressed proper admiration and appreciation, I tackled him on the subject of Aaron and Flora. (Father had already stopped by to remind me on the way to morning prayers. I guess he's really getting anxious.)

"You know Aaron is almost *twenty-five*," I began. "Most of the boys in his class are married, and some of them are already fathers. Not that Aaron ever complains — he's much too refined, but it must be worrying him..."

"So?" Elazar asked with a dismissive shrug. Husbands can be so exasperating!

"So, I've been looking at all the girls in the neighborhood, and I've been going to weddings all over. In fact, I especially went to Emmaus because there are so many fine Jewish families there, and I inquired of all the *shadchanim*, and I checked out quite a few girls. Abba is too busy, and Imma simply isn't up to it, you know, so the burden is all on me. But there was no one that I thought suitable for Aaron."

"And so?"

"And so Abba keeps bringing up the name of Shifra's daughter, Flora. In fact he's been waiting for you to come home, to get your opinion."

"So..."

"Well, somehow I'm not too happy about that choice. You know Tertius — no use discussing him. And Shifra is in with that clique from the west side of town. All they do is shop, shop, shop and visit each other to admire one another's new clothes and jewelry."

I like pretty things too, and I've been talking for ages about buying some new furnishings for the parlor, but Elazar is so stubborn! He says the tables and chairs we got when we were married are just fine, and I tell him that I'm embarrassed for people to come to the house. We've reached an impasse but I haven't given up...

"Leah, we're not talking about furniture, we're talking about Flora for Aaron."

How that man can read my mind! Are my thoughts written on my face? It seems that way when I'm talking to Elazar; Rachel too, for that matter. I had no intention of dragging the new furniture into this discussion, though, lest Elazar think me to be as frivolous and emptyheaded as some of my friends are.

"Elazar, this is serious. I just don't know about Flora. She seems a sweet girl, always friendly and pleasant, with a nice smile. But I think she's flighty, always going off to shop and fussing with her hair and clothes all the time..."

"I know other people who like to go to shopping, and there's nothing wrong with *them*." Whom could he have meant? "That's not enough reason to reject a *shidduch*. Why don't you go over to Shifra's one of these days soon, and take a good look at Flora, and try to have a talk with her. You can take Batya along so it'll seem more natural."

"Excellent idea!" I said. I wonder why I hadn't thought of that, instead of all this speculating and worrying. "I'll go tomorrow morning." How pleasant it was to be doing my husband's bidding, while at the same time obeying my father and also getting out of the house and visiting an old friend. Perfect!

Batya wasn't at all eager to go with me. She said she was nearly finished with the *tallit* bag and didn't want to waste the whole morning, when the light is good. "Besides," she added, "I don't really like Flora so much any more. I haven't seen her for more than a year, and all she talks about is clothes."

What a short memory teenagers have, I thought. Who was it that was making a scene every morning about not having a thing to wear just a few months ago? But I didn't say a word.

"Imma, if you really want me to go, though, I'll do it gladly. I can work on the weaving when we get back."

Goodness gracious! Will wonders never cease?

So we put on our second-best gowns (visiting clothes, as Mother calls them) and were on our way. The walk was delightful. It was such a good feeling, talking to Batya comfortably, without the tension that was ever-present last year. Why, she spoke so sensibly, almost like an adult! In fact, more sensibly than many adults I know.

When we arrived at Shifra's, I sensed a change in the atmosphere of her house. Everything looked the same: furniture and silver polished to perfection, a lavishly laden table that appeared within minutes of our entering, the set smile on Shifra's face; and yet there was a difference.

What was it? While talking to Shifra about the usual subjects (the weather, the crops, the new fashions) I tried to analyze my strange feeling. There were a few lines on Shifra's face that hadn't been there before, and her gown was not new. In fact, I've seen her in it twice before. Maybe Tertius was having financial troubles? No, that couldn't be it. Father had mentioned that Shifra's husband had just bought another big piece of land in the most expensive part of town.

It was something else. There was an uncomfortable aura, almost a sadness in the air; the feeling was so strong that I was certain Batya, too, must be aware of it.

"Where is Flora?" she asked in a subdued voice. "I haven't seen her in ages! She hasn't been to any affairs lately, has she?"

"I think she's in her room," Shifra said moodily. "That's where she usually is. She's become so serious and withdrawn. I don't know what to do with her."

I was astonished. Was this the same Flora who wasn't happy unless she could do something different or exciting every day?

"But Batya came especially to see her," I said. A little white lie, but for a good purpose.

"Well, in that case I'll send the maid to tell her." She turned to Batya. "Maybe she'll be willing to come out for you. She used to like it when you visited her years ago, when you were both little girls." Shifra rang for the maid, and gave her instructions that Flora was to come out to greet the visitors.

Quite a while passed before Flora put in an appearance. In the interim, a strained conversation was going on between Shifra and me. When I asked her about Rachel, her face became blank, and she quickly changed the subject. The tension was almost tangible.

What a relief it was when Flora finally entered the room! But I was stunned by her appearance — I almost didn't recognize her. Her hair, which she always wore elaborately puffed and curled, was drawn back and tied with a cord. In place of her usual silk gowns in the latest Roman fashion, adorned with elaborate gold and silver embroidery, she now wore a plain linen dress, simpler than any my Batya owned. But the most shocking change was in her face: her cheeks were hollow, her lips were pale, and her eyes had lost their sparkle.

"It's so good of you to come," she murmured. Then there was an awkward silence; no one seemed to know what to say.

"Flora, why don't you go outside with Batya?" Shifra suggested. "You can show her the new herb garden."

The two girls left, and Shifra launched into a detailed description of the garden. It was laid out in the shape of a knot, she said, with graveled paths between. In it grew thyme, sage, rosemary, cardamom and who knows what else, all maintained by a gardener hired especially for this purpose.

"The expense is inordinate, but it's worth it. No one else here in town has anything like it, and we have fresh herbs at every meal." There was a note of pride in her voice, but also a sense of urgency, as if she were trying to distract my attention to trivial things.

"And how is Julius?" I asked pointedly. "He used to like working outside, or at least instructing the estate men. Does he take an interest in the garden?"

"Oh, Julius doesn't live at home any more." She said it lightly, but her expression revealed that I had inadvertently struck a nerve.

We went on chattering about this and that, and I found myself getting more and more tense. Shifra must have felt the same; when the girls finally returned, we both nearly jumped from our chairs.

Flora's face was even paler, and Batya's was red. They both looked as if they'd been crying.

We said polite and hurried goodbyes, and made a swift departure. It was a great relief to be outdoors, and the two of us just walked on, breathing in the fresh spring breeze without saying anything. Then Batya took my hand. "Imma," she said desperately, "I don't know if I should tell you, but Flora is so unhappy!"

"That was obvious. I felt something was wrong as soon as we came into the house. But what is it? Flora looks like a different person. What's happened to her?" I really was worried; deep down I still considered Shifra the carefree girl with whom I'd run around through all our childhood years. I'd known Flora since she was a newborn, and I'd always been fond of her.

"Well, Julius doesn't live at home any more."

"Yes, Shifra told me that already, and if you ask me, good riddance! He's been in and out of trouble for years. It must be a relief not to have him in the house." Everyone knows about his delinquency, so I didn't consider it *lashon hara,* but I'm sure Elazar would have disagreed.

"But, Imma! It's much worse than that! He ran off to join the local militia attached to the Tenth Legion! Those murderers and oppressors — how can a Jewish boy want to be a part of that? And Flora says they're afraid he might even marry a gentile girl..." Now Batya started to cry, really cry, the way she did when she was a baby, so I did what I had done then: I took her in my arms, cradled her and soothed her. "There, there, Batti," I crooned, "don't cry. Shh, shh, there, there..."

After a long while, she stopped. Then she told me the rest of what Flora had told her.

"You know that his parents always encouraged him to play with the gentile boys. They sent him off to the Greek school before he'd even learned *alef-beit.* They felt that way he'd get ahead in life, and be a success. 'Those *Perushim*' (meaning us) 'are being persecuted,' they said, 'and they deserve it. They don't seem to realize that these are modern times, that you have to fit in,' and so on. So of course Julius hardly even knew that he was a Jew. Then he started to get into trouble, staying out late at night, drinking, gambling. His father was always able to get him off with bribes to the police and to the praetor.

"He didn't obey his parents at all, and why should he? He never had any real Jewish education. So one day there was a big argument. Tertius tried to lay down the law and get him to go straight. When he grabbed his arm, Julius shoved his father and knocked him to the floor. Then he ran out of the house.

The next day they got word that he'd joined the Tenth Legion's local militia and..."

"Poor, poor Shifra!" I also started to cry — I couldn't help myself. True, she'd always been vain and ambitious (I couldn't help blaming it on Tertius) but she didn't deserve this! No Jewish mother, no matter how un-Jewish her conduct, should ever have to go through what my friend was going through. Now I understood the strain in the house.

"But what about Flora? She seems to be taking it much worse than her mother. Isn't that odd?"

"Well," Batya said, "she and Julius were very close. He used to tell her things her parents never knew about. She feels guilty, as if it's her fault, somehow. She just cried and cried the first few weeks after it happened, and she hardly goes out of the house. In fact, we're the first visitors she's seen in months."

"And she told you all this?" It seemed so strange: with all her fancy friends, Flora picks my little Batti to confide in. "Wasn't she embarrassed?"

"She said she just *had* to tell me, that she still feels close to me from when we were little. All their former friends are shunning them because they're afraid their sons might do the same as Julius. No one wants that to happen..."

Yes, I understood, all too well. No matter how friendly some of our People are with the Romans, no matter how big the profits of doing business with them, or how enticing their culture, or how pleasant their social life, no Jewish parent wants *that* to happen...

But Batya wasn't finished with her revelations and the next was almost more shocking than the first.

"Imma," she said, "they do have one friend, though. You know how Shifra was always asking about Rachel, and that she even went to Geva once in a while, although she wouldn't let their children play together? Well, she took Flora along to see Rachel. She told her everything."

"And what did Rachel say?" I really wanted to know. For

once I was at a complete loss. In *my* life, *baruch Hashem,* nothing had prepared me to be able to give advice in such a situation.

"Rachel just listened. She didn't say a word until she had heard the whole story. Then she took Shifra's hand in hers — you know how she does — and said: 'Shifra, don't give up. Hashem's help can come in the blink of an eye. Call on Him, and He will answer.' Flora asked what that meant, and Rachel said, 'It means that you must call on Him, with a pure heart, and ask for help. Hashem is a loving Father to His children. And even one who has been led astray by false gods can return...'

"Shifra asked her, 'Do you really think there's any hope?' And Rachel told her, 'Certainly! You've always kept Shabbat and observed the *kashrut* laws. And Tertius has never drunk wine with the Romans, although that must be a great temptation for him. But he has withstood it. All these *zechuyot* will now stand by you, and help you. We cannot always understand Hashem's ways, but have trust, and pray to Him, and you'll see...'

"Then Rachel asked Shifra: 'Your son's name is really Yehudah, isn't it? And Flora's is Shoshanah?' (How did she know that? We'd completely forgotten. But of course: Rachel is a local girl. She'd remember Yehudah, the grandfather, and Shoshanah, Shifra's mother.) And she took her *Tehillim* scroll, and told them to say the words along with her, since they could read only Greek: '*Ya'ancha Hashem b'yom tzarah.* Hashem will answer you in the day of trouble; the name of the God of Jacob will raise you on high...May Hashem grant salvation; as the King will He answer us on the day on which we call upon Him.'

"Since then, Flora-Shoshanah has gone to Geva many times. She's become friendly with Shulamit, and wants to be just like her. That's why the change in dress, and so on..." She really looks much better this way, to tell the truth, if not for her pallor and that air of sadness. She was always pretty, but with all that fussy hair and fancy clothing, she looked overdone.

With a jolt, I realized that I had completely forgotten the reason we'd gone to see Shifra, but now it came back to me with a vengeance. Oh, my! What will I tell Elazar? It's very complicated, much more complicated than before!

19

ALTHOUGH I HAD DECIDED to think about the business of Aaron and Flora-Shoshanah for a while, I told Elazar the whole story that very night. Why? One, because it had distressed me so much that I couldn't stop thinking about it for a moment. Two, because Father sent Mother over to remind me about Flora, as if I needed a reminder! Three, because after hearing about Julius, I thought the match had no chance at all. (Really, why should Aaron get involved in this sticky situation?) We'd have to find someone else, and soon. I had been against the *shidduch* from the start; it was only my father's and Elazar's urging that made me pursue the matter.

So I told Elazar everything. And do you know what he said? "Great! I think they should meet and if they like each other, they should get married immediately!"

"Elazar, I'll never understand you! Great? What's great about it? And you're all set for them to get married. How do you think Aaron will feel, having such a brother-in-law? And what about Flora herself? You know how she was brought up. I'm surprised at you!" I made no attempt to hide my outrage, but Elazar just smiled.

"Well, Leah, I'm glad I can still surprise you. Please don't misunderstand me: what *happened* here is not great; it's terrible and tragic. But because of it, Flora, or rather Shoshanah, is a different person. She understands what this kind of upbringing can lead to. She'll be the best, the most careful Jewish wife. She'll bring up the children to keep all the *mitzvot* perfectly. She'll guard against any outside influences. Don't you see?"

"Elazar, you're right." Once he'd said it, there was no doubt about it. He *was* right and I didn't mind telling him so. I must say, I'm not a sore loser.

I was beginning to feel very happy about this *shidduch*, and hoping that both sides would be agreeable. But nothing goes that easily. Father, in the meanwhile, had heard about Julius, and refused to have his son marry into such a family. There were some pretty heated discussions; Abba had switched sides: as much as he had wanted this match before, he was now against it. It took all of Elazar's powers of persuasion to convince him, and after a full week of arguing about it, my father finally gave in.

He went to Zevulun ben Perachia, our local *shadchan*, to tell him to speak to Tertius. This ben Perachia is a peculiar creature, eccentric, some might say. He speaks with a lisp (I'm sure it's an affectation, not a genuine speech defect) and he carries a carved walking stick all the time, looped over his arm, although he never seems to use it to walk with. All the best people patronize him, though, so Abba asked him to see Tertius on Aaron's behalf.

Ben Perachia was surprised. "Haven't you heard about...?"

"Never mind that," Abba told him. "Just speak to him about his daughter."

"Well, if you thay tho. Do you know what my fee ith?"

"I was told five gold *denarii* — if you're successful, that is." Abba, of course, had investigated in advance. He thought it was too much money, just for carrying messages back and forth between the two interested parties, and had grumbled about it quite a bit.

But Imma said, "Well, you didn't have to pay any *shadchan* fees for our girls. Elazar is our nephew, so it's all in the family, and Chanania you picked out yourself. So, you'll pay for Aaron. It's worth it."

Father had to agree. Still, he was annoyed when ben Perachia said, "And if I fail? If Tertiuth ith not interethted, or the two young people don't like each other?"

"What do you mean? Of course he'll be interested! Aaron is the best boy in his yeshiva, he's tall and handsome, and he comes from an excellent family. Why, his grandfather was..."

Ben Perachia interrupted him. "Yeth, yeth, I know all about it. I have both families on file for five generations back. But just in case it doethn't work, my fee ith twenty thilver *denarii*."

Abba didn't like that at all, but since he was convinced that Tertius would jump at the chance, he didn't argue. Also, he had to admit that a man should get paid for the hours he spent; after all, he could have been earning some money in that time.

So it was agreed that ben Perachia would go the next morning and would report back to Abba in the afternoon. We were all waiting expectantly at the house when he came.

The *shadchan* looked very hot and red. He wiped his brow a few times and asked for a drink. Then he said: "They're not interethted."

"What? It can't be!" That was Father.

"Maybe you're making a mistake, or you misunderstood?" Mother.

"Are you sure you presented it the right way?" Elazar.

"I knew all along she's not right for Aaron!" Me.

When the hubbub died down, ben Perachia said, "Well, maybe I didn't put it right. What I *should* have said is, 'Tertiuth ith interethted, but Flora ithn't.'"

"What?!" Father was turning purple. "Who asked her anyway? I never heard of such a thing — a snip of a girl refusing my Aaron!"

Elazar said, "Let's hear exactly what happened."

So ben Perachia told us: They received him very nicely and right away he saw they were pleased with the idea. (Tertius knows everyone's business affairs, and he knows Abba's well-fixed.) Then Shifra said she has to ask her daughter. A minute later she came out, all white, and said, "Flora doesn't agree!"

We all looked at each other. "Did she say why?" Elazar asked.

But ben Perachia had no answer. As soon as he'd seen how upset the parents were, he'd picked up his walking stick and gone.

"I think you should go back and ask why," Elazar said. "Maybe there's a good reason. Maybe it's something that can be changed or corrected."

Father was furious. He said he wouldn't go begging to anyone; with a son like Aaron he didn't have to. But Mother kept pleading with him, in that gentle way she has, and finally he yielded.

"It'll cotht you another twenty *denarii*," says ben Perachia, "and cheap at twithe the prithe. I don't appreciate little girlth like that taking matterth into their own handth."

That almost started a new argument, but Elazar gently pushed the *shadchan* out the door.

We sat down to wait. I almost started to bite my nails but remembered just in time that I had a fresh manicure. An hour and a half later ben Perachia reappeared.

"I rented an ox-cart. You'll reimburse me, of course." He was so nervous that he completely forgot to lisp.

"Yes, yes. So what did she say?" For someone who wouldn't go begging, Abba seemed very anxious.

"She says she only wants to marry someone who'll sit and learn, who wants to be a great scholar some day. Now I know you're fine, educated people, but you've built up a good business, and you'll surely want your only son to inherit it. And how will he be able to run it, if he sits in the yeshiva? And that's what I told them. So it's no." He was huffing and puffing as if he'd run the three miles, instead of riding comfortably in a cart.

Abba was beside himself. I was afraid he was going to have a stroke. Elazar quickly offered him some water. "Here, Abba, drink this. It'll make you feel better." Then he suggested that he go along with ben Perachia this time. "We'll take the horses — we'll be back soon."

Imma brought an armload of pillows, and Father reclined on the couch. I fanned him slowly, and gradually he began to look better. Then he started getting excited all over again: "That ben Perachia — I never should have let him..." But Imma gently placed her finger on his lips and Father stopped talking. In a few minutes he was snoring softly. I guess all the storm of emotions was just too much for him.

Pretty soon Elazar returned, without the *shadchan*. As usual, he didn't mince words. "*Mazal tov! Mazal tov!* He agreed, I mean, *she* agreed, that is, *they* agreed! *Mazal tov!*"

Father popped up from the couch.

"*Mazal tov!*" Elazar said again.

Tertius, of course, had been in favor right along, and so had Shifra (she'd certainly hinted often enough). But when Elazar told Flora-Shoshanah that Aaron has been learning day and night since he became *bar mitzvah*, and that he's the best boy in his yeshiva, and that he's planning to continue his studies until he becomes a great scholar, she said, "Yes! Yes! Yes!"

Ben Perachia was stunned, Elazar told us.

"Don't you want to meet him, have thome converthation with him, thee if you have any common interetht?" he'd asked.

But Shoshanah had said, "I remember Aaron well, from when we were children. I always liked him then. And I want a husband who's a real *talmid chacham*."

Ben Perachia had stayed there, talking to Tertius about

some business or other, but my good Elazar had come back immediately to bring us the good *besorah*. I'm so proud of him.

Four weeks after the *tena'im* were signed, Aaron and Shoshanah were married. It was a beautiful wedding; everyone came, many even traveling great distances to attend. But the most important person, the one who was responsible for the change in my new sister-in-law, wasn't there. I mean Rachel, of course. She sent me a lovely letter of congratulations, but said she couldn't attend, giving no reason. I resolved to visit her right after the festivities were over.

But like many of my resolutions, this did not turn out the way I planned it. Mother's having some back trouble, so I'm over there every day to help out, and Penina is expecting (twins, from the look of things) and I offered to take the older children occasionally. She accepted gladly, of course, so I just don't have the time now.

20

THE MARRIAGE OF Aaron and Shoshanah has turned out exceptionally well. It seems they were made for each other: he's completely devoted to her, and she to him. Every time he finishes a portion of his learning, she makes a little party, a *seudat siyyum*, she calls it. Only the family and a few friends are invited, but she's made many of these parties over the years.

Elazar was able to attend the most recent one, when he returned from Lod before Pesach. (He spends four or five months there every year, and by now I have not only come to terms with his long absences but am actually enormously proud of his accomplishments.) At the party I told him that Aaron was planning to go to Lod to see this famous "Rabi Akiva" that we're always talking about. I still haven't gotten used to his title, although I do have tremendous respect for him.

Elazar said, "Aaron won't have to go. I heard in Lod that Ṛabi Akiva is coming home, together with all his *talmidim*."

I couldn't believe it! Had so many years passed already? "Oh, Elazar!" I cried. "I must go to Rachel immediately! I must tell her!"

I was so excited, I thought I'd faint. I ran to get my shawl. If

Reuven could spare the ox-cart, I'd take it and get there faster. I told Dina and Hadassah to clean the house from top to bottom and to cook all the meat we had planned to use for Pesach — there was plenty of time to prepare more later. I told Batti to put flowers in all the rooms, and to change the bedding, and to put out the best silver.

I was still giving instructions when Elazar said, "Never mind."

"What do you mean, 'never mind'? Akiva is returning after all these years, and I shouldn't tell Rachel, and I shouldn't..."

"Never mind, because he's almost here right now." Elazar was standing by the window. "I can see some of his pupils, hundreds and hundreds of them. I recognize some of them from Lod."

Not even taking my shawl, I ran out the door. As far as the eye could see there were yeshiva students, young and old, tall and short, dark and fair. They filled the wide road completely, ranks and ranks, marching like an army with banners.

And there, at their head, was Rabi Akiva!

He towered over them like an oak tree above the seedlings on the forest floor. His beard was almost white, but otherwise he looked the same, with that gentle, loving glow to his face, the serious intelligence in his eyes.

Everyone had rushed out for a better view: Elazar, Baruch and Batti, Dina and Hadassah. We all joined the crowd, following along the road to Geva. We didn't even bother bolting the door.

I wish I could make you see that scene. It was overwhelming! Thousands upon thousands of men, with their *tzitziyot* dancing in the breeze. They rolled along and surged like the waves of the sea. Yes, it was like gazing at *Yam Hagadol* for the first time, and I felt that a special *berachah* should be recited. More and more people from the town and the countryside joined them, overflowing the highway and spilling out onto the adjoining fields.

Then the students started singing: "*Amar Rabi Akiva! Amar Rabi Akiva! V'ahavta l're'acha kamocha-a-a, zeh klal gadol baTorah! Amar Rabi Akiva!*"

Their voices rose like foaming breakers crashing on the shore. There were children, boys and girls, running alongside, like schools of tiny fish swimming with the tide. Men and women poured out of their houses, out of their shops and fields. The procession grew ever wider, longer, louder, stronger, and my heart pounded to the rhythm of the marching feet until I thought it would burst.

"*Amar Rabi Akiva! Amar Rabi Akiva!*" I thought the sound must surely reach to Heaven; surely *Rachel* must hear it — we were very close to Geva now. I noticed that even Tertius and Shifra and all their servants had joined the procession.

"*Amar Rabi Akiva! Amar Rabi Akiva!*" Countless voices, countless feet marching closer and closer. How could she not hear?

She heard. I saw a lone white figure coming out of the house, running down the road, coming closer and closer. Then the *talmidim* blocked her way. They tried to hold her back, but they could not.

What superhuman strength did this Rachel possess? The same strength that had driven Akiva to learn, that had kept her going through all the lonely years, now came to her aid. She was unstoppable. She hurled herself to the ground before her husband to kiss the hem of his cloak.

The students were furious! They shouted at this madwoman and tried to drag her away from their beloved teacher.

But Rabi Akiva said, in his deep voice that carried all the way to where we were standing:

"Leave her be! If not for her, I'd still be an ignorant shepherd. All the Torah I have learned, and all that *you* have learned, belongs to Rachel, my wife!"

Kalba Savua, too, had heard the commotion, although his mansion, at the far end of town, is more isolated and set further back from the road than other less stately houses. He came out to meet and greet this new and obviously famous Rabbi and, as he is the *gvir* of the city, everyone made way for him. Rabi Akiva turned to him respectfully and a hush fell over the crowd.

"Honored teacher of thousands," Kalba Savua began (he always did have a flair for fancy language), "I must ask your advice. Many years ago, I made a vow concerning the allocation of my estate, after a hundred and twenty, and now I wish to annul it."

"And what was that vow, sir?"

"I had a daughter," Kalba Savua replied, "but I disinherited her. Against my will she married a poor, ignorant shepherd, completely unsuitable for an educated, well-to-do girl, and I vowed then that she'd never have any benefit from my wealth. It wasn't so much his poverty. I knew that could change in an instant. Hashem gives and Hashem takes away. But his ignorance — he didn't even know the *alef-beit*! That's what made me disinherit my daughter." Clearly he had no idea that this great Rabbi was his own son-in-law!

"And if that poor shepherd had tried to learn a bit, and had perhaps even become a scholar, and you had known then that he would succeed, would you have made such a vow?" Rabi Akiva asked.

"Oh, if I had thought that one day he might know even one chapter of the *mishnayot*, or even one *halachah*, I'd have been satisfied!"

"I am he, Akiva ben Yosef, your former shepherd, the man your daughter married. Will you forgive her?"

Kalba Savua's face paled, and then he started to cry like a baby. "Akiva, Akiva, can you ever forgive *me*?" he said. "Oh, if I had only known —" and he started crying again, and couldn't stop.

"There is nothing to forgive. You had a right to do this. But now I hope you will welcome us back into your home and your heart."

"May *Hakadosh Baruch Hu* bless you, Akiva! He has already blessed you with the best wife in the world..." Kalba Savua paused. He shook his head from side to side in dismay. "How could I have let her live in such misery all these years? I always hoped she'd give up her foolish dream, and come back to me. And she had to suffer hunger, and cold, and humiliation... Half my wealth I give to you and your wife, Akiva; my Rachel will never be in need again.

"But where *is* my beloved child, and my grandchildren? Oh, how I regret all those empty, wasted years." And again he wept.

"Father, comfort yourself. Your daughter is here, and the children too." And Rachel approached the man who had shunned her for so many years, and the children followed her.

What happened next she would not tell me — she said that every time she thinks of it she starts crying. And with all the jostling going on, I had lost my vantage point, so the rest is what I heard from others and what I myself could surmise.

Rachel's father recognized her instantly — she hasn't changed much over the years. He reached out to embrace her and his eyes shone with tears of joy mingled with sorrow. And then he saw his beautiful grandchildren. "They are like olive shoots around the table!" he exclaimed. They look so much like him, that it must have been like seeing his own reflection in a series of mirrors. Then he placed his hands on Rachel's head, and on theirs, and blessed them.

You can't imagine the happiness I felt at this reunion. It was as if a stone had been lifted from my heart, knowing that my dear, dear Rachel's suffering was over at last. But all she said was: "I never suffered. *Kol d'avid Rachamana l'tav avid* — Everything the Merciful One does is good."

PART TWO

... and in the evening...

21

FOR MONTHS AFTER, Rabi Akiva's triumphant return was all everyone could talk about. It was the high point in our lives. His students were spread out from here to Antipatras and he would travel from town to town, teaching them and learning with them, disseminating Torah the length and breadth of the Land. It was glorious! And then, a terrible thing happened.

It was not long after Nechama was born — oh, did I tell you Rachel had another girl? This one is truly a beauty, with dark, dark eyes and a very serious disposition. Perhaps this child somehow knew what the future held. What a pity to have one's earliest memories be marred by death, and so much death at that!

Right after Pesach, the plague came. People were terrified — they kept the boys home from school, the women hardly went outdoors except to buy food, and then they'd hurry back without exchanging even a few pleasantries with their neighbors. After all, what was there to be pleasant about? Week after week, the death toll rose.

Oh, the anguish! For thirty-three days during the Counting of the Omer, we awoke to wails of sorrow. At night we buried the dead, the mourners' cries piercing the air and rending our hearts. No one knew where the plague might strike next, who would be next to succumb. Almost until Shavuot the whole Nation was mourning, and then, as mysteriously as it had begun, the dying ceased.

Elazar brought me the shocking news: the death toll was *24,000*! And all of them — *all of them* — Rabi Akiva's *talmidim*!

I *had* to see Rachel. But how could I now? I was so distressed that I could hardly get our things together for the pilgrimage to Yerushalayim. The *Beit Hamikdash* will no doubt be as mobbed as ever, so I know it will be impossible to find her in the crowds. As soon as we get back, I'll go to her.

22

OH, WHAT DISASTER has befallen us! The worst, the absolute worst tragedy of all time! How can I find words to describe it? But I must. And I must try to tell it in sequence so you'll know just what happened.

Remember what I said a while back about *sinat chinam*? Well, there's no doubt in my mind that that's what brought about the terrible war; still, there are many who say that Rabi Zechariah's forbearance was the cause. You can decide for yourself:

Not long ago, when people were still in the habit of throwing lavish banquets and inviting all their friends (it's hard to imagine that happening *now*), this rich fellow sent an invitation to his friend, Kamtza, to come to a party. By mistake, the servant delivered the invitation to *bar* Kamtza, who was certainly no friend and in fact was one of Agrippa's men.

Anyway, bar Kamtza dressed up in his best and came to the feast, all excited — he had never expected to be invited by his enemy. All the great and would-be-great of Jerusalem were present, and he was thrilled to be in their company.

But when the host spotted him he shouted at his servants: "I never invited that man! Throw him out!"

Bar Kamtza realized he had been invited by mistake, so he offered to pay for his own food and drink, if only they'd let him stay, but the host refused. He offered to cover half the cost of the banquet itself, even the *entire* cost! But it did no good. While everyone watched, the host personally removed the uninvited guest.

It's not surprising that bar Kamtza went home with bitter thoughts of revenge. "All the great people of the city were there," he must have told himself, "rabbis, judges, noblemen, and they all saw my shame. Yet no one stood up for me. I'll show them!" And did he ever!

He went to the Emperor and told him the Jews were planning to rebel against Rome. And what proof did he offer? "See for yourself how they disdain the Emperor," he said. "They will not accept your sacrifice in the Temple!"

The Emperor couldn't take any chances, so he sent an unblemished yearling to the Temple with bar Kamtza. On the way, we later learned, bar Kamtza wounded the animal slightly — it was all right for a non-Jew to sacrifice such an animal on his own altar, but forbidden for a Jew to bring to the *mizbe'ach* in the *Beit Hamikdash*. (The Emperor could not have known about this distinction, but bar Kamtza surely did.) Naturally, the *kohanim* spotted the damage during their routine examination, and consulted the Sages about bringing the yearling as a *korban*. This of course started off a whole debate.

Some said, "It is better to sacrifice it for the sake of peace. Who knows what they might do to us if we refuse?"

But Rabi Zechariah ben Avkulos said, "What?! Are we now to bring animals with a blemish as sacrifices? Others who see this will be misled and believe that it is permissible to do so under *any* circumstances. No, we must not!"

Some Rabbis suggested that they *kill* bar Kamtza to prevent him from distorting the truth in his report to Emperor Nero! As drastic as that idea seemed, the danger of the situation was truly great. But Rabi Zechariah again protested. "We must not kill him. People will think that the penalty for blemishing a sacrifice is death," he said.

The majority agreed with Rabi Zechariah, and bar Kamtza wasted no time in taking his "proof" to Nero that the Jews were indeed preparing to revolt against the Roman Empire. "It is as I predicted," he told the Emperor. "They rejected your sacrifice!"

This, of course, was precisely what Agrippa had been hoping for. You see, just before the bar Kamtza affair, we had succeeded in expelling Agrippa from Yerushalayim, and he was looking for an opportunity to regain his position of power. He also wanted to punish us for the insult to his honor, although he'd brought it on himself. The crimes that evil governor knew he had committed against our People had made him more and more fearful that we would rebel against him, but all his requests to Rome to send him reinforcements had been denied.

Agrippa's fear had been so great that he had even built a huge tower over his palace so that he could see over the wall around *Har Habayit* and observe whether the Rabbis were meeting to plot against him. (This had really angered the Rabbis and they had built a wall in the courtyard of the *Beit Hamikdash* to obstruct his view!) Then he had gotten Florus Gessius, the procurator of Jerusalem, into the act:

Agrippa appealed to Florus, with whom he was on very good terms, for help in suppressing us. The two of them conspired to break our spirit, and without any provocation, Florus raided Jerusalem and massacred thousands of helpless men, women and children. Naturally, in his report to his superior, the legate Cestius Gallus, that massacre became the quelling of a Jewish "revolt" against the Empire. Gallus, who was stationed in Syria, must have had his doubts; he sent his personal emissary to verify Florus's report, but the emissary discovered that we were as loyal to Rome as ever.

The Rabbis then requested permission from Agrippa to

travel to Rome; they wanted to lodge an official complaint with Emperor Nero about Florus's unprovoked massacre, lest Nero believe that we had been at fault. Not surprisingly, Agrippa refused to grant them permission to go; it would mean risking the loss of Florus as an ally, at the very least. He told the Rabbis that we should simply continue to quietly submit to Florus's tyranny and wait patiently until Rome chose to replace him.

Clearly, if we could not have the opportunity to explain to Rome what Florus had done, Nero would have no reason to replace him. The situation called for action: Agrippa had to be removed! The people demanded that Agrippa leave Yerushalayim immediately, and some even threw stones at him!

At last Agrippa realized that he had pushed us too far and that the uprising he had feared was now a reality. But since our loyalty to Rome had been confirmed by the Syrian legate's emissary, Agrippa could no longer claim that "the Jews are revolting against Rome" in order to gain Nero's support. He had no choice but to leave Yerushalayim and return to his homeland, incensed over the insult to his honor.

After his departure, Agrippa's strongmen and his *Kohanim Gedolim* sent two delegations, one to Agrippa and one to Florus, asking them to quell the uprising and restore the *Tzadokim* to power. Florus wisely did not intervene; obviously he couldn't pretend that this was a revolution against *Rome*. But Agrippa sent an army of three thousand to Yerushalayim and they recaptured the upper city; the lower city, though, and the *Beit Hamikdash* and its surrounding area, remained in our hands. There was tremendous bloodshed on both sides.

As soon as the fighting broke out, our Greek neighbors, always happy and ready to massacre Jews, joined Agrippa's men in the slaughter of innocent civilians. Only the Roman legions stood aside and did not join in the battles, since they knew that the Jews were only fighting Agrippa, not challenging Rome's authority.

And that's when the bar Kamtza affair occurred (oh, if only

the Rabbis *had* killed him!), and the situation played right into Agrippa's hands. It was just the thing that would enable him to convince Cestius Gallus to bring the Twelfth Legion to his aid. At the same time, Nero dispatched one of his most experienced generals, Vespasian, and the general's son, Titus, to Caesarea to assess the situation.

Although we were now forced to fight against the Romans, while defending ourselves from Agrippa and his band, we were confident that if our forces could only rout the *Tzadokim* from their positions of authority in *Eretz Yisrael*, we could then convince Rome of the truth: that it was *not* against the Empire that we had revolted, and that we wanted only peace with the Romans and would accept their rule, as long as our internal affairs would be governed by fair, reputable men.

And we almost succeeded. Yochanan ben Levi from Gush Chalav — a brilliant warrior who was loyal to the Rabbis and especially to the *Nasi*, Rabban Shimon ben Gamliel — was totally committed to the salvation of our People from oppression. Encouraged by the great Rabbis and all of the *Perushim*, he and his men fought against the *Tzadokim* and their many allies, and won victory after victory until they succeeded in consolidating the rule of Yerushalayim under Yochanan's able hands.

Word was sent to General Vespasian, pleading with him to give us a free hand to rout the oppressors from the Holy Land, bring order among the populace, and show our loyalty to the Emperor. He heard our messengers out, but he could not take action without direct orders from Rome.

Then, to add to the confusion, Nero died suddenly and a new Emperor was appointed, so Vespasian sent his son Titus to Rome to greet the new Caesar and receive new orders concerning Jerusalem. But on the way Titus learned that the new Emperor had been assassinated and someone else was on the throne in Rome. He went back to Caesarea to confer with his father.

With the *Tzadokim* almost totally defeated, and Vespasian leaning sympathetically towards our cause, there really was some hope that peace and tranquillity were on the horizon.

And then, suddenly, that hope was dashed. The *Tzadokim*, in desperation, sent for Shimon ben Giora to come and save the day for them. It was a move that was to prove not only *our* undoing, but their own as well.

Ben Giora believed that he and his zealots, the *biryonim*, had the manpower, the weapons and the skills not only to unseat Yochanan ben Levi, but to drive the entire Roman Legion from *Eretz Yisrael*, and then ben Giora would become the sole ruler of the Holy Land. Knowing that even the *Tzadokim* did not want that, he considered them his enemies too, and he turned against the very people who had brought him to Yerushalayim. Drunk with power, he declared a full-scale war on Rome.

Now, the Jewish revolt against the Romans was no longer a fiction, but a very sad reality. Vespasian and Titus pleaded for reason. "Fools!" they said. "Why do you want to destroy this city and the Holy Temple? What do we ask of you — only that each of you send a sign of submission to Roman rule, and we will leave you in peace."

But the *biryonim* were not about to do this, for they really had this mad fantasy of evicting the Romans from our Land. They surrounded the walls of Yerushalayim from within, to prevent anyone from accepting the Roman offer of peace. Then they burnt down the storehouses of the richest men of Yerushalayim, Nakdimon ben Guriyon, ben Tzitzit Hakesset, and Rachel's father. Those storehouses had held enough supplies to sustain the residents of Yerushalayim for *years*! Can you imagine such craziness?

When the aged Rabban Yochanan ben Zakkai saw how the situation had deteriorated, he too appealed to the senses of the zealots, but they turned a deaf ear. War with Rome, he knew, would be disastrous, so he began to plan for the preservation of the remnants who would somehow survive the coming conflagration and help rebuild the Nation. The only possibility was to negotiate with Vespasian, before he laid siege to the city.

The problem was, how to get out of Yerushalayim with the *biryonim* blocking the gates from within?

Rabban Yochanan turned to his nephew, Abba Sikra, for help. Now, Abba Sikra was the leader of a local band of *biryonim*, but out of respect for his uncle, he agreed to meet with him secretly. Although Abba Sikra would not dare confront his own *biryonim* and order them to cease their activities as Rabban Yochanan urged, he provided his uncle with the means to escape. At his suggestion, Rabban Yochanan pretended to be ill (he was a very old man, you see, over a hundred years old, and surely did not have long to live) and then a rumor was spread that he had died. It sped through the city like wildfire. His two *talmidim*, Rabi Eliezer ben Hurkanos and Rabi Yehoshua ben Chanania, wrapped him in a burial shroud and placed him on a bier. Alongside him, under the shroud, they placed a piece of rotting meat, to simulate the odor of a decaying corpse, and took him to the city gates, pretending that they were going outside to bury him.

A *biryon* guard challenged them. "I'll stab him and make sure he's really dead!" the guard said to Abba Sikra.

"No, no!" Abba Sikra commanded. "The Romans will say the rebels have desecrated the body of their own master!"

"Well, then," the guard suggested, "at least let me push him a bit. Maybe he's still alive and this is just a trick to get him out of the city."

"No, no," Abba Sikra insisted. "They will still say that the rebels have disgraced the body of their master." The guard relented and the "funeral cortege" was permitted to leave through the city gate. Soon Rabban Yochanan was on his way to Caesarea to see Vespasian.

The Roman soldiers brought the elderly Sage before the

general. "Hail, Emperor!" Rabban Yochanan greeted Vespasian.

The general responded angrily: "I should condemn you to death on two counts," he said. "First of all, I am not the Emperor. And second of all, if you thought I was, why did you not come to me sooner to declare your allegiance?"

"But you must be the Emperor. It is written: 'The Lebanon,' our Holy Temple, 'will fall only to a great one,' meaning an emperor. And I could not come sooner as the zealots would not permit it."

While Vespasian pondered this, messengers arrived from Rome to report that the Emperor had died, and that the Senate had elected him the new ruler.

Vespasian, as you might imagine, was very pleased. He turned to Rabban Yochanan and said: "I wish to reward you for bringing me the good news. What is your desire?"

Without a moment's hesitation, Rabban Yochanan replied, "Give me Yavneh and its Sages, spare the progeny of Rabban Gamliel, and send doctors to heal Rabi Tzadok!"

And so it was. In spite of the terror which hung over our Land like black smoke, the *metivta* at Yavneh was established and many students came to join the great teachers there. This was the only bright spot; years of sorrow were yet in store for us. Perhaps we will never stop mourning...

Vespasian had no choice but to put down the rebellion — Rome could not risk allowing the tiniest of its many provinces to revolt; it would be a sign of weakness that would encourage all the others to do the same and in no time the mighty empire would topple.

Vespasian's armies swept through most of *Eretz Yisrael* like a stiff broom on a packed-earth floor. Even up north, where the farmers fought back like the best trained warriors, the sheer numbers of the Roman soldiers gave them the advantage. They decimated the population of the Galilee, burning, plundering and slaughtering everything in their path. Then

Titus laid siege to Jerusalem. A huge army surrounded the city so that no one could enter or leave. Knowing that the zealots would never surrender, he tried to starve them out, and with the storehouses gone, this proved a most successful strategy.

On the ninth day of *Av*, that *rasha*, Titus, broke into the *Beit Hamikdash*, ransacked it, and burned it to the ground. Our sacred gold and silver vessels were taken along to Rome by the soldiers, to be used for who knows what unholy purpose. The *kohanim* and *levi'im* fought desperately to defend the Temple. Many were tortured and killed; some were sold as slaves. Men, women and even little children were slaughtered in the streets of the city! Hashem's glory was in the dust, and the blood of His People ran in rivers.

There's so much more, but I can't bring myself to tell it. I tried again and again to write it all down, but each time I was so overcome with grief that I couldn't bear it. Even now, so long after the events, my hand trembles uncontrollably as I record them.

While all of this was going on, my family and I remained blessedly ignorant; throughout the war we were in hiding. My wise husband had seen the disaster that was coming and had taken every precaution to protect his loved ones. He had evacuated our entire household to the safety of a secret cave some distance from town. Others had done the same, but oh, too, too few.

When Elazar had revealed this plan to me, for once I kept my mouth closed. Instead of arguing, I began organizing, and soon great quantities of food, water, clothing, utensils, and just about every precious thing we possessed were packed and loaded onto the ox-cart. No one spoke the whole way there; I held the children close to me, my heart pounding wildly.

Imma and Abba and their household were already settled in when we arrived, Abba reclining on a pile of blankets and cushions and Imma stacking crockery on the rock ledges. The cave was much larger than I had imagined — actually, I hadn't thought about it at all since all thought had been blocked out by fear. It was really a series of caves, one chamber leading to the next. The largest chamber of all became a sort of family room, where we cooked and ate and prayed and talked, and the smaller chambers served as sleeping quarters. In the smallest cave, deep into the mountain, we buried the jewelry and jars of gold and silver coins.

Too soon, Elazar left us to join the battle. Reuven, our herdsman, remained behind to defend us if necessary, armed with an axe and a club. He was strong, I knew, and fierce as most of the local men, but it was clear that even he would be powerless against the mighty legionnaires. Our salvation would come only from *Hakadosh Baruch Hu*, that was certain, so we passed the time fervently praying for His help, while the war raged around us.

23

HERE IN THE COUNTRYSIDE, it was a long time before we realized the full extent of what had happened in Jerusalem. The survivors had scattered, and those who reached us told tales that were beyond belief. It was only when we pieced together their reports that we began to grasp the magnitude of the disaster. Earlier on, Elazar had been sent home, wounded in battle, so until the handful of survivors came, we had no real news of the war.

When we emerged from the caves, we looked around the valley below us in stunned silence. The rolling green pastures and fields were now a smoldering grey carpet of ash. A dark cloud of smoke hung over the hills and the terrible stench of death was everywhere. A lump lodged in my throat, but my eyes were dry. This was no time for tears; it was time to rebuild.

As soon as the cart was unloaded and I'd set the girls to cleaning out the house, I hurried off with Elazar to see how our friends and neighbors had fared. The general mood was like our own — to put the past behind us and start anew — and everywhere the sad story was the same: almost every family had lost a father, a son, a brother. *Baruch Hashem*, Elazar's wounds were minor and healing quickly, but we learned that Shalom ben Reuven had been killed with all four of his sons, trying to bring water into the besieged capital before it fell.

"Jerusalem? Captured?" I said. The news of the *Churban* struck us like lightning. I just stared at Miriam when she told us about it. Elazar tore his garments.

"And the Sages?" he asked urgently. "Are they safe?" When he found out about Rabban Yochanan's rescue of the *metivta* in Yavneh, Elazar did something I'd never seen him do before: he buried his face in his hands and wept.

Miriam's brother Netanel, that young *levi* with the beautiful voice, had been "lucky" — he had survived the massacre after the destruction of the *Beit Hamikdash* and was taken to Rome in chains.

Other friends and neighbors added details to the little we already knew of the events preceding the *Churban*, until the complete picture emerged. The power struggle of Jew against Jew, *Tzadokim* against *Perushim*, had sparked a conflagration, and now all that was left for us to do was to sift through the dying embers.

In the months that followed, there were reports of Netanel's being sold from one Roman aristocrat to another; apparently everyone wanted this Jewish slave who was known to have the most melodious voice. But he stubbornly refused to sing, saying his voice was dedicated only to *Hashem*'s service. Each master tried to persuade him — some with bribery, some with force — but he remained defiant.

Finally, the last owner gave Netanel an ultimatum: to sing before the pagan idols, or to take his chances in the arena. For over a year he was brought to the arena daily to witness the slaughter, in the hope that the horrible sight of unarmed men being ravaged by wild beasts would make him change his mind, but no, Netanel did not yield. His young life ended there, in the arena.

Netanel's story was one of so many that had tragic conclusions, but his touched me deeply. I've known Miriam and her family all my life.

I was desperate to see Rachel but for a long, long time it was unsafe to leave one's house: one might never return. Bands of marauding soldiers still roamed our country, sacking farms and plundering villages; many local farmers resisted the occupation and chose to fight to the death. It seemed like forever until some semblance of law and order emerged, but there is constant fear in our hearts now. We know that our lives can never be the same.

When I finally knocked on Rachel's door and she opened it, I was so relieved to see her that I collapsed in her arms and wept.

"Leah, Leah! How good it is to see you again!" She held me close until I was able to regain my composure, and then she said: "*Baruch Hashem*, that we have lived to see this day!" Her eyes were dry and there was a gentle smile on her lips.

"How can you smile, Rachel?" I asked her, astonished. "With everything that's happened in the last few years, how can anyone ever smile again? The countless lives that were lost, our Holy Temple burned down to the ground, the Roman *resha'im* ruling over us — and you're smiling?" I never would figure her out.

"Listen, Leah," she said calmly. "We have shed our tears, but tears will not resurrect the dead. Only after the *Mashiach* comes will Hashem bring the martyrs back to life. Surely their souls dwell peacefully in *Gan Eden*. And the Holy Temple? The *Beit Hamikdash* was built of wood and stone. Hashem in his compassion chose to allow its destruction as punishment for our sins. If we are deserving, He will rebuild it! And the stolen vessels? They were only metal, mined from the earth, and they can be replaced. The Romans may have robbed us of everything else, but they did not rob us of our holy Torah.

"Look what's happening in Yavneh, Leah. Just look! Rabban Yochanan's *metivta* is growing steadily, and soon there will be new generations of great men who will arise and defend the Torah and uphold its laws! So why should we be downcast?"

"But, Rachel," I said, "Elazar told me that only if we mourn for the Holy City that is covered with ashes will we merit to see it rebuilt!"

"Yes, Leah, Elazar is right, but mourning can take many forms. There were those who decided to mourn by refraining from eating any meat or drinking wine because these were used for offerings on the *mizbe'ach*. But Rabi Yehoshua taught that the proper way to mourn is by leaving a bare, unpainted patch on a wall of our homes" — she pointed to a rough square near the door — "and by omitting part of our normal meals and by wearing less jewelry." (My hand flew self-consciously to my ornate necklace. With things the way they were, I couldn't very well have left it at home, to be stolen, could I? True, it might have tempted a thief on the road...)

"Yes, my dear, dear friend, we must never forget the lessons of the *Churban* and we must mourn our loss," Rachel added with a gentle sigh, "but life must go on, and we must look to the future!"

Her words moved me deeply. She was right; somehow we had to get on with our lives. I wiped my tears and pulled myself together.

"Tell me, Rachel, how is your husband? How is Rabi Akiva?" I had seen the children when I arrived. They were really quite grown-up already and I almost didn't recognize them when I came upon them digging up the bit of earth in the back. Rachel told me that the vegetables they grew there had helped to keep them alive during the troubles.

"Akiva? *Baruch Hashem!*" The glow of happiness was there, stronger than ever.

"Rachel, I will never, never understand you! All of his students died in that terrible plague, brilliant *talmidim*, young men with their whole lives ahead of them..."

"Leah, they were not only brilliant students," Rachel said softly, "they were *talmidei chachamim* of the highest order. From men such as they, Hashem demands more than from us simple folk, and apparently He was displeased with their lack of respect for one another. Akiva was inconsolable. Imagine, 24,000 students, and all of them gone in the space of seven weeks...

"Akiva felt responsible, somehow. He reproached himself for failing to impart the importance of the *mitzvot* between man and his fellowman. And then, suddenly, it was as if the clouds had parted and a ray of sunshine broke through. 'In the morning plant your seeds,' Akiva said in the words of *Kohelet*, 'and in the evening do not desist!' Those words were his comfort. He understood them to mean that if in his earlier years he could produce students, then he must continue to do so even in his later years. And that is precisely what he is determined to do."

"Will he be joining the Rabbis in Yavneh, then?" I asked.

"Soon, Leah," she replied. "But now he has embarked on a fund-raising mission — there are so many homeless because of the war, there are families to be reunited, slaves to be redeemed — you've heard about Yishmael ben Elisha, haven't you?"

The name was not familiar to me. It was getting late and I had to get back home, but surely I could spare a few moments. I just knew she was going to tell me a story about this *talmid*, and I was not disappointed.

"Yishmael ben Elisha is a descendant of a noble family of *kohanim*. During the war, he was carried off by Roman soldiers and imprisoned. Possibly, he was an orphan, or perhaps his family believed him dead, as he languished in prison for some time before Rabi Yehoshua ben Chanania came to Rome to redeem Jewish prisoners. He heard about a good-looking boy who'd been captured and so he hurried to the jailhouse. There he saw a handsome lad staring out through the prison bars.

"Rabi Yehoshua called out in Hebrew: '*Who has given Jacob for plundering and Israel as a prey for robbers?*' And immediately the boy answered: '*Is it not God, against whom we have sinned? For they did not wish to walk in His ways, or obey His teachings.*'

"Of course, the Romans were reluctant to give up such a clever, fine-looking Jewish boy and they demanded an enormous ransom for him. But Rabi Yehoshua realized immediately that Yishmael had great potential, so he collected money from everyone he could until he had enough for the ransom. He brought the boy back to *Eretz Yisrael* and enrolled him in the *metivta* in Yavneh. In no time at all, Yishmael has become an outstanding student, and everyone vies to be his study partner."

"Thank God he was rescued!" I exclaimed. "Who knows what terrible things they might have done to him in jail!" The image of my Baruch in such a place came to mind unbidden and I shuddered at the thought.

I was eager to know more, but Rachel had nothing to add. Instead, she asked about my parents, about Penina and Aaron, about Elazar and the children.

Yes, there had been some very hard times, I told her, but *baruch Hashem*, we had pulled through. We were alive, and we were together. That was the main thing...

We agreed that we would say the complete *Tehillim* each day, in thanksgiving and in hope...

24

ELAZAR, DID YOU KNOW that Rabi Akiva is now traveling all over, raising funds for the needy?" I had hoped to impress my husband with this bit of news, but one look at his face told me that the information had come as no surprise.

"Of course, Leah. And I was among the first to make a contribution to the cause. *Baruch Hashem*, we're in a position to help our less fortunate brethren and even participate in the *mitzvah rabbah* of *pidyon shevuyim*." I felt wonderful about that. I knew without asking that Elazar's donation had been a generous one.

Still, I thought the whole thing was a bit odd. After investing all those years in Torah study, and proving himself to be such an unbelievably great teacher, Rabi Akiva has now abandoned that vital task for a job that others might do just as well. I had pondered this the entire way home from Rachel's; we hadn't had time to discuss it during my visit.

Before I had a chance to ask Elazar what he thought about it, he looked up from his dinner and said, "With Hashem's help, the necessary funds will be raised quickly. Everyone is hoping that Rabi Akiva will be able to return to *chinnuch* soon — he's a masterful teacher and his lessons are sorely missed."

"Oh, yes," I said, remembering the other bit of news I'd saved. "Rachel said he's planning to join the others in Yavneh when his mission is done."

Elazar's face lit up. "Are you sure, Leah?"

I didn't understand my husband's reaction to this, and frankly I was a little hesitant to question him — I can't say why. But he pushed aside his plate and his expression became thoughtful and he began to pace the room, gesturing with his hand from time to time as though he were carrying on a debate with himself. I decided to wait until he was done and then change the subject. Why had I brought this up in the first place? I chastised myself. If I wanted more details about how and when and why Rabi Akiva was doing what he was doing, Rachel would surely provide them, and I could go and ask her next week. But this quiet midday meal with Elazar had somehow become tension-laden.

As usual, my scheduled visit to Rachel was delayed somewhat and it was almost two months before I saw her again, but I hadn't forgotten about wanting to ask her how Rabi Akiva came to be a fund-raiser. I was just working up to the question when a messenger arrived with word that Rabi Yehoshua ben Alam was *niftar.* It was obvious from Rachel's reaction that he had been an important person, but I had never heard his name before.

"Who was this Rabi Yehoshua?" I asked her and she got that look in her eye I so loved to see, the one that meant I was in for a good story. Once again, she did not fail me and I was glad I'd left the stew on a low fire.

"He was a very special man, Leah," she began. "From his earliest youth, Rabi Yehoshua ben Alam spent all his time learning Torah. He had eighty devoted students who called him their *Rav*, and all his life he did not move *dalet ammot* without *tzitzit* and *tefillin.*

"One night, they say, he had a strange dream. A Heavenly Voice announced: 'Rejoice, Yehoshua! Your companion in *Gan Eden* will be the butcher, Nannes.'

"Rabi Yehoshua was puzzled. 'After all these years of studying and learning, will I be the neighbor of a common butcher?' he asked himself. 'I must see this man, and find out why he was chosen to be my neighbor in Paradise.'

"So he went from town to town with his students, searching for the butcher Nannes. Finally he came to a village where there was a butcher by that name. Rabi Yehoshua said: 'I want to speak to him.'

"The villagers were astonished. 'Why should the honored Rabi Yehoshua want to see this ordinary butcher?' they asked.

"Rabi Yehoshua inquired of them: 'What does he do?' And they replied: 'Our master, do not ask anything about him until you see him.'

"So Rabi Yehoshua sent the villagers to get Nannes. 'What would the great Rabbi want with a plain man like me?' the butcher asked them. 'Who am I and who are my ancestors in Israel that Rabi Yehoshua should ask for me?' And he refused to come. I'm sure he didn't mean to show disrespect, Leah; he thought the villagers were making sport of him."

Rachel paused then — for dramatic effect, I think. I was on the edge of my seat by this time but I didn't say a word; I might break the spell and never hear the end of the story. At last, she went on.

"So Rabi Yehoshua ben Alam decided to go himself. He found the butcher, a humble man, who threw himself to the ground in awe when he saw the great scholar.

"'What is the reason for your coming, honored Rabbi?' he asked. 'I'm but a simple tradesman. Why should you want to speak to me?'

"Rabi Yehoshua was even more puzzled than before — this was a very plain man indeed, surely not a fit companion for a scholar like himself. 'Tell me, my friend, what are your deeds and what is your work? I had a dream about you, and I want to know its meaning.'

"'Well,' said Nannes, thinking for a moment, 'there's nothing *extraordinary* that I do. I am a butcher by trade. I have parents who are old and weak and I dress them and feed them and take care of all their needs — I, and not a servant. It's been many years now, and I hope to have the *zechut* to do it for many, many more.'

"Rabi Yehoshua embraced the man and kissed him on his head. 'My son, lucky are you and fortunate is your lot, how good and sweet indeed, and how fortunate indeed am I to have been chosen to be your neighbor in *Gan Eden*! May there be many more like you among our People!'" Rachel's face was glowing and her eyes shone. "Ah, Leah," she sighed, "our treasury of Torah scholars has suffered a terrible loss with Rabi Yehoshua's passing."

"That was a great story, Rachel," I said. "And speaking of treasuries, you reminded me of something I've been meaning to ask. You told me that your husband is now the new treasurer of the *tzedakah* fund for all *Eretz Yisrael*. I know that charity is one of the cornerstones of his teachings, but isn't his place in the yeshiva?"

"Leah, you know how vital this undertaking is. I'm sure Akiva will carry out his trust as *gabbai tzedakah* with the greatest care. Can you imagine being responsible for the distribution of all that money? Not merely raising it — that would be difficult enough — but making sure it's allocated properly and fairly."

It was ironic. Kalba Savua's former penniless shepherd now controlled and disbursed the vast sums in the charity coffers. I wondered if he was qualified for the position, having had so little experience with money.

"But Rachel," I said, "how can Rabi Akiva abandon his teaching and his learning to take over this job?"

Rachel laughed, a soft burbling sound like a clear brook in

a green meadow, and her bright eyes twinkled. "He's certainly not doing if for the *kavod*, Leah!" And I joined her laughter. We both knew what an arduous, thankless job this was.

We became serious again. After all, it was a serious matter. "When they asked Akiva to be the new *gabbai tzedakah*," Rachel said, "he told them he would first ask my consent. I believe he felt he needed my permission because he had promised me he would devote his whole life to Torah. In these difficult times of low income and high taxes, fund raising, he knew, would be particularly hard. Since he would have to give up time from his studies to fulfill his duties properly, he may have thought the decision should be mine.

"I was surprised to see him home in the middle of the day, but even more surprised when he told me why he'd come. 'I'll have to spend much time collecting and distributing the money,' he said, 'And I'll probably have to travel — maybe even out of the country. Would you agree to that?'"

"Don't leave me hanging, Rachel. What did you say?"

"Leah, the purpose of learning Torah is the practice of the *mitzvot* we learn. When an opportunity to perform a *mitzvah* arises, and no one else is as capable or competent to perform it, one is obligated to seize the opportunity — even if he must temporarily disrupt his learning to do so. The Sages assured Akiva that *he* was the most capable and I believe they were right. And if he would have to be away again, so be it! I warned him, though, that he would have to be prepared to accept people's curses and insults; that, unfortunately, is the way of the world."

"Then what happened, Rachel?" I urged.

She looked at me for a moment and said, "Why, Leah, we bade one another farewell, and Akiva left on his mission. May *Hakadosh Baruch Hu* help him to succeed!"

I couldn't believe it! For Rachel, of course, it was perfectly consistent with everything she'd done before and everything she held dear. But here I was, so happy to be together with my husband, and there she was letting hers go again. Oh, sure, I understood that it was for a very good cause. But I know I could never be that altruistic. Who could?

Rachel.

And so began another long interval of separations for Rachel and her husband. Rabi Akiva traveled wherever there were Jewish communities, to collect money for the poverty-stricken of Judea. The Romans never for a moment ease up on the financial pressure they apply, always finding some new tax they can levy. Oh, there are plenty of people who are well-off, and *baruch Hashem*, we still have our gold and jewels, but there are lots of needy people too. If not for Kalba Savua's timely advice before the war and Abba's good business sense, we'd be no better off than many of our Jewish brethren. It doesn't matter that it would be unseemly to spend our money ostentatiously; the important thing is that it's *there*. And from the look of things, we're going to need it: the harvests have been less abundant since the *Churban* — and farming is still our major source of income.

Rabi Akiva really has his work cut out for him. Abba too has contributed generously to the *tzedakah* fund, but our family can't be expected to support the whole country! Contributions must come from the wealthy Jewish communities outside the land too. Rabi Akiva does not spare himself; he travels by caravan, by ship, and even on foot to raise the necessary funds.

He went to Arabia, to Gaul, to Africa, to Tyre and Cyprus and returned with vast sums of money, but it's all been spent; more, much more is needed. Rachel told me that Rabi Akiva approached Rabi Tarfon, his former teacher and now his friend, for a donation. I thought the way he asked for it shows that Rabi Akiva really has style. Listen:

"My esteemed colleague," Rabi Akiva said, "you have been blessed with great wealth..." (Everyone knows Rabi Tarfon is well-off, but only someone as close to him as Rabi Akiva could talk about it so openly.) "...I have an excellent investment opportunity for you, but it requires a substantial sum of money."

"Here are four thousand gold pieces," said Rabi Tarfon. "Go and invest them as you see fit." Such blind trust! Well, it wasn't misplaced.

Some days later, Rabi Tarfon asked, "So, Akiva, where is my investment?" and Rabi Akiva took him to the *beit midrash*, called over a child who was holding a *Tehillim* scroll in his hand, and had the boy read aloud the ninth verse of Psalm 112: "He scatters around and gives to the needy. His righteousness endures forever."

I imagine Rabi Tarfon was well-pleased with these dividends!

Rachel and I savored this little story over a warm herbal brew. "Tell me more, Rachel," I pleaded. "I'm sure your husband has had many fascinating experiences in his travels."

Rachel smiled. "I didn't want to bore you, Leah," she teased, "but if you insist." And she related a wonderful episode about a *gvir* named Barboohin.

Rabi Akiva and his companion had heard that Barboohin was very rich, so they decided to approach him for a sizeable contribution. When they arrived at his house, they overheard a servant ask him, "What shall I buy for your supper?"

"Some vegetables," the master said, "but make sure to buy the wilted ones — they're cheaper."

"How can we expect to get any money from this man?" Rabi Akiva asked.

"Well, let's see how we make out here in town," his companion replied. "If we're still short of funds, we'll try Barboohin."

So at the end of their rounds, they went to his house. He sent them to his wife, with a message that she was to give them a measure of *denarii*.

"Did he say a level measure, or a heaped one?" she asked.

"He did not specify," they answered.

"In that case, I'll give you a heaped measure. If my husband complains, I'll tell him to deduct it from my *ketubbah*." And she filled a purse to overflowing with gold coins.

When they went to Barboohin to thank him for his generous gift, he asked them why they hadn't come to him first. Rabi Akiva replied that they had indeed come to his house before anyone else's, but that they had inadvertently overheard his instructions to his servant. "We felt that if you found it necessary to be so frugal with your food, then surely a request for a donation would be an imposition upon you."

Barboohin laughed. "I can deny myself anything that's not really necessary, but how can I refuse to fulfill the commands of my Creator?" Then the *gvir* leaned over and whispered conspiratorially, "By the way, how much did my wife give you?"

"A heaped measure," they replied, and Barboohin laughed even more heartily than before. "A true Woman of Valor! For that, I'm going to double her *ketubbah*!"

In Antioch, the *tzedakah* committee always went to Abba Yudan, a constant and generous donor. When they called on him recently, though, they learned that he had lost all his wealth and was embarrassed that he could not contribute. But his wife said to him, "Look, we still have one field left. Let's sell half of it, and give the money for charity."

And so they did. The Rabbis blessed him, saying: "May Hashem restore to you your losses."

When Abba Yudan went to plow the half of the field left him, the ground suddenly opened up beneath him and his cow fell into the crevice and broke her leg. Abba Yudan leaped into the breach to pull her out, and there, before his very eyes, lay a treasure. Abba Yudan understood that this was a reward from Hashem.

On a subsequent visit, the Rabbis discovered that Abba Yudan had become tremendously wealthy again. When they asked about him in town, the local people said, "Abba Yudan? He's the owner of cattle, camels, donkeys, land, houses. Who can compare to him?" And Abba Yudan came before the Rabbis and said, "Your prayers for me yielded multiple fruits."

The Rabbis accorded Abba Yudan a place of honor at their table, for it is said: "A man's gifts make room for him."

"Oh, Rachel," I sighed, "I could listen to you all day, but I must be going. May I share these episodes with my family?"

"Of course, Leah," she said. "There are such important lessons to be learned from the righteous ones who give so unstintingly to those less fortunate than they, that Akiva relates these stories himself at every opportunity. The Sages say even a poor person is obliged to give *tzedakah*, you know. No matter how little one has, there's always someone with less."

I couldn't help but remember my dear Rachel's situation of not so long ago. Her words had a familiar ring.

"I know what you're thinking, Leah. About when Akiva and I were first married, and that stranger came to visit us. I, too, recall that moment vividly, and Akiva will never forget it either. It was certainly a turning point in our life."

In mine as well, I wanted to add, but the words wouldn't come.

"Yes, Leah, by all means tell your family these stories," Rachel said. "And please mention this too: Akiva says that no one should ever accept charity needlessly. Better a Shabbat without celebration, than one celebrated with alms."

May we all be spared ever having to make that choice!

25

I'M GOING TO YAVNEH to be with Rabi Akiva," Elazar announced, and for once I agreed wholeheartedly. But this time I decided to go along with him — not because I was forced to, but because I wanted to.

So much has happened in the last five years, so many changes in our lives. The *Beit Hamikdash* is gone, and for a time many people even believed that this would be the end of our existence in *Eretz Yisrael.* Truth to tell, if not for the great wisdom of Rabban Yochanan, this might have been the case.

Remember when he greeted Vespasian as Emperor, and the Roman was so pleased that he agreed to grant the Sage's wishes as a reward? Oh, the cleverness and foresight that went into Rabban Yochanan's reply! One cannot but be amazed. "I only ask of you Yavneh," he said, "that I may go there and teach my students, institute prayer, and practice all of the *mitzvot* of the Torah." Such a simple request; how could the Emperor refuse? The Sage hadn't asked for gold, or precious jewels, or even power.

Vespasian must have thought: It's no big thing. The Rabbi is old and feeble, not to mention peace-loving. After all, Rabban Yochanan was the one who had wanted to avert war with

Rome at all cost. So he'll pray and learn with his handful of students for the few months, at most, that he has yet to live. No threat to the great Roman Empire in that. But little did he know that *because* of Rabban Yochanan's advanced years, the term "my students" applied to virtually every Torah scholar in the entire generation, in the entire Land of Israel!

The choice of Yavneh as the site for his yeshiva was another means of allaying the Roman's suspicions. Yavneh even then was a well-populated city, with many large synagogues, and the Sanhedrin had met there on occasion. So, to Vespasian's mind, setting up a small yeshiva in that town did not constitute "new construction" or the establishment of a new religious entity where none had existed before.

The result was that Rabban Yochanan now had official sanction for his project, and what a farsighted, blessed project it was! He invited all of the greatest Torah scholars to join him in Yavneh, and help him create a new Torah center, to serve as the "heart of the People" when Jerusalem would be no more, and it was clear to him even then that the Holy City was doomed.

When he spoke of "instituting prayer," he envisioned a place where Jews from all over *Eretz Yisrael* would eventually come on every *Yom Tov*, just as they had come to Yerushalayim. When he spoke of "practicing all of the *mitzvot* of the Torah," his intention was to reinstate the Sanhedrin, which would enforce the observance of the Torah commandments among all of *Klal Yisrael.* He planned to make Yavneh a place where the *shofar* could be blown even when Rosh Hashanah fell on Shabbat, something that had only been done in the Sanhedrin's halls of the *Beit Hamikdash* complex. But that's not all.

When Rabban Yochanan asked Vespasian for the "progeny of Rabban Gamliel," he was preparing Yavneh to be the place where the *Nasi*, descended from the family of King David, would sit and rule, just as the kings had always done in

Jerusalem. Since Rabban Shimon ben Gamliel Hazaken was no longer alive, his son Rabban Gamliel was the newly crowned Prince. Once duly enthroned in Yavneh, he would appoint the mayors of all of the towns, and all of the communal leaders, and they would all be answerable to him. In this way, the unity of the People, under one able ruler, would be assured. By asking for the "progeny of Rabban Gamliel," Rabban Yochanan made it sound merely like a request to spare a family of Torah scholars, and Vespasian had no inkling that this meant a royal dynasty.

In the same breath, Rabban Yochanan had asked for doctors to heal Rabi Tzadok; Elazar told me that in military terms, this was called a "diversionary tactic." Vespasian probably equated the progeny of Rabban Gamliel with Rabi Tzadok, never realizing the true importance and future significance of the House of the *Nasi.*

That was the plan: Yavneh was to replace Jerusalem, in every way possible.

And now Rabban Yochanan is gone, may his memory be a blessing. Before he died, his own *talmid*, Rabban Gamliel, indeed became Prince and Rabban Yochanan accepted for himself the lesser role of *Av Beit Din.* And to ensure the growth of and respect for the new *Nasi*, he humbly withdrew to Bror Chayil with his five great students: Rabi Eliezer, Rabi Yehoshua, Rabi Yosei Hakohen, Rabi Shimon ben Netanel and Rabi Elazar ben Arach. With their teacher's passing, these scholars have now returned to the *metivta* in Yavneh. (All except Rabi Elazar, that is. Rabban Yochanan's demise must have hit him very hard — they say he went to some far-off place and forgot all his Torah!)

Yes, the great Sage is gone, but what a legacy he has left his People! Because of his foresight, the Torah lives on.

I wouldn't want you to think I figured this all out myself; I haven't turned overnight into a brilliant strategist. It was my beloved Rachel who told it all to us when she came by with little Nechama (still a serious but beautiful child) to say goodbye. "We're moving to Yavneh," she said, her face aglow.

"Can you tell us about the yeshiva, Rachel?" I asked. "Have you seen it yet?"

"Oh, yes, my dear friends, I have seen it, and it is unbelievably beautiful." Rachel's eyes shone as she described "*Kerem B'Yavneh*," a house of study as tranquil and exquisite as a vineyard before the harvest. Students sit before their teachers in neat rows like grapevines planted in a *kerem*, the high dome of the huge edifice protecting the tender fruits from the elements. All the students' needs are seen to, so that nothing might distract them from their vital work. The building is airy and flooded with sunlight during the day, and a thousand oil lamps burn in wall niches all night long.

"And Rabban Gamliel's house," she went on, "is a palace, as befits the Prince of the Jews. I have never seen such a place before. Akiva told me that a thousand members of the royal family live there, and many of them know several languages so that they may mingle with foreign aristocrats. Of course, the *Nasi* didn't start with a house full of his family and servants, for fear of the Romans, but when it was deemed safe enough, the palace was erected. Oh, Leah, you must come and see. This is only the beginning, I'm sure. We will yet have our king and our sovereignty, as Hashem intended for us."

"May it be soon, in our days," Elazar and I responded together. But I couldn't help feeling slightly uneasy about the whole thing. What if Rome...

I thrust aside my fears and kissed my Rachel goodbye.

Now, when Elazar made his announcement about joining Rabi Akiva, I was not at all surprised. I think I knew this was coming all along, at least since that day when I told him about Rabi Akiva's plans to go to Yavneh. When Elazar had become so distant, I must have sensed that he was thinking that his place was at the feet of his *Rav*, but I was afraid then, afraid to say a word about it.

You see, it was so soon after the war. I couldn't bear to be separated from Elazar again.

But now, the situation is different — *I'm* different. And now I have good reason to go together with my husband to the "new Jerusalem." Besides, I want to see with my own eyes Rachel's new life, I want to share her happiness, and most of all I want to repay the debt I owe her. All these years, I imagined that I was helping *her*, bringing her bits of food and clothing, giving her advice. How wrong I've been!

Rachel, *Rachel* was the one who had helped *me*. Rachel had pulled me out of my shallow, self-centered routine, and taught me to yearn for higher things. From her little hut in Geva, she changed my entire existence. How different my children would have turned out, if not for Rachel! Why, even Elazar, as studious and capable as he is, was first urged in that direction — when? When I returned from Geva, full of Rachel's words about her wish for Akiva to become a *talmid chacham*.

And my father, and Penina and Chanania, and Aaron with his precious Shoshanah — aren't all the changes in them due to Rachel? Even Shifra and Tertius: she has stopped going to the theater, and is learning to read Hebrew, and he has started to come to the *minyan* almost every day. Rachel is like a candle, I thought, that with its flame ignites new fires all around it, but its own glow is not diminished.

So we have come to Yavneh (but only for a short time, I'm sure). Elazar has put Reuven in charge of the estate, and Rivka will supervise the running of the house. (I still haven't found any household help that can compare to her. I'm glad she's willing to give me some of her time — she is very much in demand, and Reuven acts as if he's doing us the biggest favor, letting her come to the house a few hours a day. He seems to have forgotten that everything she knows, I taught her.) Batya is staying with my parents.

We packed up only the bare minimum: six gowns with matching shawls for me, and Elazar's weekday and Shabbat garments, my set of Tabor pots, a number of clay jars and bowls, the small mortar and pestle, and several sets of linen. I *do* like to have my own things around me; for instance, I could never manage without my little vegetable knife that I got from Mother, that fits my hand so exactly. Elazar feels the same way about his *kiddush* cup: it's scratched and dented, but he received it from his grandfather when he became *bar mitzvah*, so it's very precious to him...

Why do I always go off on a tangent? Well, never mind.

When we arrived in Yavneh, the whole town was talking about the beautiful gold ornament that Rabi Akiva had given his wife. Do you remember his pledge when they were first married, and they slept on straw? Well, he kept that promise. It's exquisite — the greatest artisan in the district was hired to engrave the Holy City on it. Rachel wears it on Shabbat and *Yom Tov*, not to show off, you realize, but to remind our Jewish girls that the sacrifices made for Torah are ultimately rewarded.

There's a story going around Yavneh. It seems that the wife of Rabban Gamliel the *Nasi* saw Rachel wearing her gold ornament one Shabbat, and asked her husband, "Why did you never give me anything like that? It's the most beautiful thing I've ever seen!"

And Rabban Gamliel answered: "Ah, but neither have you sold your hair that I might learn, as Rachel did for Akiva..."

He was right, of course. No one could do all the things that Rachel has done; but her example has begun to inspire others. Girls now are less quick to reject a *shidduch* with someone unlearned, and after their marriage they encourage their husbands to study more and more, just as I did. Those who could not endure the separation have moved here to Yavneh too.

Every day new students arrive, and many of them come just so that they might learn from Rabi Akiva. The halls of learning are filled to overflowing.

The seeds that Rabi Akiva planted "in the evening" have already begun to blossom.

26

NEEDLESS TO SAY, the best part of being in Yavneh is being close to Rachel, and we see each other almost every day. The very brief *Yom Tov* encounters we've had over the intervening years, when Elazar and I made the triannual pilgrimage to Yavneh, were never very satisfying. With people coming from all over to the "new Jerusalem," her house was always filled with guests and we couldn't really talk.

Rachel is content now, of course (but, then, when was she not?) although her life here in Yavneh has been far from uneventful. When we first came to Yavneh, she told me that Rabi Akiva had started looking among the best boys in the yeshiva for a suitable husband for Shulamit. Let me tell you, she is another jewel in her mother's crown. When I saw her all grown up, it was like seeing the young Rachel all over again. The hard years in Geva had only refined and strengthened her, and one could glimpse the future Woman of Valor in her clear, steady gaze. Many had asked for Shulamit's hand in marriage, Rachel told me, but she appeared indifferent to all of them.

One day, shortly after our arrival, Rabi Akiva said to her: "How much longer will you reject every *shidduch*? Each one about whom we have spoken is a *talmid chacham*; each one has good character; any one of them would make a fine husband of whom you could be proud."

But Shulamit answered: "Father, my choice was made long ago. He is great in learning — he cannot rest, day or night, until he understands each word perfectly. His whole life is Torah, and I want to join my life to his."

Her father smiled. "*Rachila batar rachila azla.* The lamb follows the ewe," he said. "And who is the fortunate man whom you have chosen?"

"His name is Shimon, the son of Azzai."

"A fine choice, daughter. They call him 'the uprooter of mountains.' His grasp of learning is immediate and brilliant; it is surpassed only by the depth and thoroughness of his research. We will send a messenger to tell him the good news."

But when ben Azzai received the offer of marriage from Rabi Akiva, he was upset. He didn't know how to respond, because even greater than his knowledge was his love for Torah.

Rachel said: "I know he was afraid of the responsibility of marriage and of raising a family only because he felt it might hamper his studies. He teaches too, you know, and once, when he was impressing upon his students the first *mitzvah* in the Torah, to marry and be fruitful, his students asked him: 'Honored *Rav*, why don't you practice what you preach? Why are you telling *us*, when you yourself are not married?'

"And do you know what ben Azzai said, Leah? 'My soul yearns for Torah. Let others continue the human race!' Possibly, if we had listened more carefully to those words, we would all have been spared some pain." Rachel sighed gently and continued her story.

After several days of soul-searching, Shimon ben Azzai decided, reluctantly, to accept Rabi Akiva's proposal that he marry Shulamit, and the wedding was celebrated in great happiness and splendor. (Abba and Imma were both unwell at the time, so we hadn't attended, although we did send a nice gift from the whole family.) The Sages of Israel came from near and far to see ben Azzai married to the daughter of Rabi Akiva.

When the week of *sheva berachot* drew to a close, the guests returned to their homes. Shulamit and her husband began to settle down, and she cheerfully started arranging, improving and beautifying their new home. But Shimon, her husband, did not appear happy. In fact, Rachel said, he seemed gloomy and despondent.

"What is the matter?" Shulamit asked him. "You seem so sad. Is it anything I have done? Please tell me!"

"No, no. You are goodness and kindness itself," said Shimon. "I don't really know..." And she did not question him further.

But day by day, he seemed to sink deeper and deeper into a mood of melancholy, and others, too, began to notice the change in him. "Even Akiva saw that something was amiss. So I urged Shulamit to speak to Shimon again."

And Shulamit asked once more: "Please tell me what's troubling you."

"I'm afraid to say it — it would make you unhappy," Shimon answered.

"It is *not* knowing that's making me worry so much. Even my parents have said that you're not the same. What is it?"

"Do you remember that I had promised you I would devote my life to Torah? My love for learning is so great that there is no room in my heart for anything else. I begrudge every moment that I'm not at my studies. And yet, I want to be a good husband to you. It's the conflict that's tearing me apart."

Tears rose in her eyes. "You know that all I want is for you to study," Shulamit said, "to learn Torah day and night so that you can reach your true potential. The more you study, the happier I will be."

"Any other man in the world would count himself blessed

to have a wife like you," Shimon said. "But I cannot bear being encumbered with responsibilites, being away from my studies, and that is what marriage entails. I can't give you what you need. All my being is dedicated to the holy Torah."

Shulamit was quiet for a long time. Then she said, "Your spirit is bound up with the Torah, and cannot be separated from it. I would never want to feel that I prevented you from reaching the heights which you are capable of attaining. I cannot hold you back..." and she asked him to give her a letter of divorce, so that he would be completely free to pursue his studies.

When Rachel told me this, I tried to restrain myself from crying but in the end, I succumbed. The tears poured down my cheeks. "Oh, Rachel! Your poor Shulamit! And ben Azzai, too! How could she bear it? And did he...?" I couldn't continue.

But Rachel remained calm and dry-eyed. She told it as if it had happened to someone else, not to her own child. "Yes, he gave her the *get*. And she accepted it."

"But how did you console her? What could you say to her?" I was completely bewildered. How could a mother bear her daughter's unhappiness so...so serenely?

"I told her: 'Your sacrifice is a thousand times greater than mine,'" Rachel said. "'I gave up only wealth and comfort to win my husband for Torah, while you gave up your life with your husband so as not to hold him back. May *Hakadosh Baruch Hu* bless you for it!'"

I couldn't speak. I know Rachel so well — the pain for her daughter must have been unbearable, and yet she seemed to be bearing it quite well. Her faith in the Almighty's kindness is so steadfast that nothing, apparently, can shake it.

"But Rachel," I cried, "what if other men will decide to do the same thing, for the same pure motive? What if our greatest *talmidei chachamim* will remain unmarried, in their pursuit of learning? The world — *our* world — would come to an end!" Already I pictured in my mind thousands of our finest girls, alone and unwed. The whole matter was distressing — and it wasn't just theoretical. After all, my Batya is of marriageable age, and she, too, wants to marry a *talmid chacham.*

"Please don't worry, Leah. There is only one ben Azzai, whose love for Torah is so great that it excludes all else. You're probably imagining that there'll be countless old maids because of this, and you must be thinking about your Batya —"

"Rachel, can you see what I'm thinking?" No, Rachel does not have magical powers. She only knows me through and through, better than anyone else. "Yes, I *am* concerned, and not only about Batya but other good Jewish girls like her. What if every young scholar decides to do the same? If the great Shimon ben Azzai, Rabi Akiva's son-in-law, could do it, why shouldn't others follow in his footsteps?"

A little smile crossed Rachel's lips. "There's nothing to be concerned about," she said tenderly. "The first *mitzvah* we were given is to be fruitful and multiply. No one else will do as ben Azzai did — there is no one else in the whole world with his all-consuming yearning for Torah. A *talmid chacham*'s obligation is to observe *every* commandment. So don't worry about Batya, or about Baruch either."

So instead of me comforting *her*, Rachel had comforted me...as usual.

27

I AM REALLY SURPRISED at myself: I love being here in Yavneh! We're living very simply, of course, more or less as we did when we were first married, but I don't mind it at all. In a way, it makes me feel young again. The most beautiful thing is that the entire city seems immersed in learning. Our Shabbat guests are *talmidim* from the yeshiva and all through the meals the house resounds with the music of Torah study. Even the women I meet in the marketplace "talk Torah," repeating their husbands' clever *derashot* and tales of the great scholars.

We've rented a small cottage, very modestly furnished. (It was a bargain, although we had to give the owner a sizeable deposit.) Of course, I have no household help, but our day begins quite early and the housework is usually done by noon. I asked Elazar if he'd let me have Dina, at least, but he just gave me that *look* and I realized I was being silly. Where would I *put* her? She'd just be underfoot.

Naturally, having Elazar close by is wonderful: I don't feel so left out of his life any more. I try to take a rest during the heat of the day so that I can be awake when he comes home late from the yeshiva; that's when he regales me with the latest from Rabi Akiva. I never tire of hearing his *chiddushim*.

Rabi Akiva has continued his studies and his teaching with unflagging diligence, Elazar says. Since every syllable of every word is important, and each letter is analyzed, Rabi Akiva declared that "the *Masorah,* which provides the accurate rendering of Scripture, is a fence to the Torah. Only in accordance with the correct text can we interpret the laws stemming from it."

I didn't quite understand that, so Elazar gave me this example: "In the commandment '*Kabed et avicha v'et imecha* — Honor your father and your mother,' the *et,* which might be considered superfluous, implies that a step-parent must also be honored, and the additional *vav* in *v'et* teaches us that so must an older brother." (I'm sure he meant "older sister" too. I'll remember to tell that to Penina the next time I give her some unsolicited advice!) "Also, in the verse '*et Hashem Elokecha tira* — you shall fear the Lord, your God,' the *et* before *Hashem* indicates that one must respect and obey the Sages, who are His representatives here on earth."

It's so flattering when my husband shows some respect for my intelligence and takes the time to explain these things to me, that I pay extra close attention. "Rabi Akiva says that even the *tagim* — the crowns of the letters — hold secret meanings. And *Shir Hashirim* is for him the 'holy of holies' because it describes the eternal bond between Hashem and Yisrael." When Elazar told me that, I smiled and nodded, but truthfully I didn't know what he was talking about. So the next day I borrowed the scroll from Rachel and studied it from start to finish. How could I have missed the true meaning of those precious words? But I suppose others do, too.

There are thousands of young scholars in Yavneh, you know, and so many of them gather around Rabi Akiva to drink from his well of Torah, but he is the same modest, quiet person he's always been. "A fence for wisdom is silence," he says, and he lives by his own words. If every syllable in the Torah has a special meaning, should not a person's words also be counted?

If there is not one superfluous word in the Torah, should we not also take care to utter no superfluous words? I wondered if Elazar was trying to tell me something when he quoted that to me. But no, he hadn't placed any special emphasis on it. He's always repeating quotes from the great master. My favorite one, however, is still: "*V'ahavta l're'acha kamocha* — Love your fellowman as yourself; this is a great principle of the Torah." That's something I'll have no trouble with here in Yavneh. The people are as nice as can be.

Maybe this is the one good thing that has come out of the war. Remember how awful it was before the *Churban*, when everyone was spiteful and mean to everyone else? Perhaps we've all learned a lesson. Let's hope!

Rabi Akiva urges his students to be close to one another, to care for each other, to exert themselves for each other, as much as each would for himself. One of our guests said that Rabi Akiva's many years of hardship had taught him that this was the basis of every *mitzvah*. This is what Hillel had meant, he said, when a heathen demanded that he be taught the whole Torah while standing on one foot. Hillel had replied, "Don't do to others what is hateful to you. All the rest is commentary. Now go and learn!"

I'm sure a lot of husbands and sons repeat Rabi Akiva's words to their families, because everyone in town goes out of their way to be kind and helpful. Well, almost everyone. Some old-timers do seem to resent having all these students crowding their town, arguing and gesticulating as they walk down the streets together. When I overheard a woman in the market saying, "Why don't they go to work and make something of themselves?" — and several others agreed with her — I felt terrible. Of course, I went to consult with Rachel.

"Perhaps she thinks the *talmidim* are just wasting time, when they're actually discussing Torah," Rachel said. "I'll ask Akiva about this. I'm sure he'll know what to do."

That evening, Elazar came home very agitated. "Leah,

listen to what happened today," he said. "After *minchah*, Rabi Akiva called together all the older *talmidim*, the ones who are closest to him. We all wondered: What could be the meaning of this? What new insight would our Rav reveal to us? You can imagine the excitement. Well, as soon as Rabi Akiva entered, he began lecturing us. 'My students!' he said. 'I hear that there are people in town who are upset about the yeshiva. Now, that's not surprising — they are hard-working farmers and merchants, good, observant Jews, but ignorant of learning. They are unaccustomed to seeing young men walking around in the middle of the day, doing nothing — or so they think. Why, I remember, before I began to learn Torah, when I was still an ignorant shepherd, I actually wanted to *bite* the scholars like a wild donkey!'

"The students were astonished," Elazar continued. "Elchanan, who's always been outspoken, ventured to ask: 'But my teacher, why *like a wild donkey*? Why not *like a dog*?'

"Everyone looked at him. But Rabi Akiva just smiled and said, 'Because a dog only nips the skin, or at worst, penetrates the flesh. But a wild donkey's bite cracks the very bones of its prey!'"

"Elazar!" I gasped. "Can it be that an *am ha'aretz* feels that way about people who learn?" I recall having had a few doubts myself about the value of learning, but I *never* felt *that* hateful.

"So it seems, Leah, although we students couldn't believe it of our esteemed *Rav*. We just stared at one another, stunned. Then Rabi Akiva went on: 'My friends,' he said, 'you must realize that it is difficult for people to understand or accept a way of life that is different from their own. As representatives of the Torah way of life, we bear a very important responsibilty: to apply our learning to every aspect of our life. Therefore, a student must take care to always be dressed in spotless garments, to always speak in a pleasant manner, and most of all, to always be decent and honest in his dealings. There is no reason for anyone here to be proud of his scholarship or his *yichus*; there have been great people before you, and there will be great ones after you.'"

"So what happened?" I asked anxiously. "How did the students react?"

Elazar thought for a moment. "Well," he said, "some of them hung their heads in shame, and the odd thing was that these were the modest ones who never offend anyone. But I saw others looking down their noses haughtily. They seemed to be saying, 'Surely our *Rav* doesn't mean me!' But he did; he meant everyone, including himself!"

Well, I told myself, if Rabi Akiva meant *everyone*, then what he said applied to women, too. So I made a resolution: from now on, I will be extra careful in my speech, in my dress, in my manners. I will try to live up to the standard that Rabi Akiva has set for his students, and perhaps, eventually, *all* the people here will accept us and recognize the value of Torah learning. I don't expect it to happen overnight; how long has it taken me?

The very next day, you could see the effect of Rabi Akiva's words. The boys milling around during their break spoke in softer tones than usual; their robes looked neater and free of stains; I even saw two *talmidim* who had been engaged in a serious discussion stop to help an elderly woman carry her heavy shopping baskets.

All this is evidence of Rabi Akiva's influence. He demands from his pupils that the laws concerning the dealings between man and his fellowman be as strictly observed as the laws between man and Hashem. Kindness and charity, he says, are essential *mitzvot*.

I remembered what Rachel had said about the plague that had claimed the lives of Rabi Akiva's 24,000 students, that it was their punishment for the lack of respect they had shown one another. No doubt Rabi Akiva would see to it that such behavior would never again be tolerated.

When I walked past the *beit midrash* yesterday, I was surprised to find it so quiet. Normally the yeshiva study hall is so noisy that I often wondered how the students could hear themselves think, what with all the arguing going on.

"Why *is* it so tranquil, Rachel?" I asked when I stopped in this morning. "Have they run out of things to argue about?"

Rachel smiled warmly. "I'm sure it does seem comparatively quiet now," she said. "Yes, you might say they've temporarily run out of things to argue about. Until now, the yeshiva had been dealing with all those long-standing disagreements between *Beit Hillel* and *Beit Shammai* — this was impossible before Yavneh was established, because the Sanhedrin couldn't meet to decide them. For the past three years or so, while these deliberations were taking place, the arguments were quite heated, but now, *baruch Hashem*, almost everything has been settled. Now the Sages all know exactly what the *halachah* is, and the students are learning the laws by heart. And do you know *how* the debating was resolved? A Heavenly Voice came down and announced that they were to rule according to *Beit Hillel*! What more could we ask as a sign of Hashem's favor?"

I thought this was really wonderful. It was one more positive step toward unifying the Nation. You can't have half the people observing the *halachah* one way, and the other half observing it another way. Elazar had been so pleased when he'd heard that Rabi Shimon Hapekuli had standardized the *Shemoneh Esreh* prayer; because people may make up their own additions and private supplications, the precise wording of the *Shemoneh Esreh* had nearly been forgotten. Now, thanks to Rabi Shimon and his committee, everyone may still add their personal prayers but they know and recite exactly the same eighteen original *berachot* handed down from the time of Ezra.

I said as much to Rachel, and she remarked, "And the *nineteenth* one as well. You do know about the additional *berachah* concerning the 'informers,' don't you? The one Shemuel Hakatan composed?"

"Oh, yes," I remembered. "*V'lamalshinim* — yes, of course. But why was that added?"

"It was because of an incident that occurred shortly before your arrival," she said. "I was sure you must have heard about it — it was almost the end for Yavneh! You see, people from all over the country pass through the city, including many apostates. They used to be our own Jewish brothers and sisters, but now they have renounced our Faith and taken on strange customs. May Hashem one day return them to the fold."

"But straying from the path doesn't make them *informers*, does it?" That was a pretty harsh term, even for heretics. Are we supposed to suspect every non-Jew of plotting against us?

"In this case, Leah, they *did* plot against us." As always, Rachel was reading my mind. "These former Jewish brothers, people who know and understand our ways, took one look at the yeshiva and the *Nasi*'s palace and went straight to Rome to inform the authorities that a revitalized Nation of Israel was emerging. That's why the Romans immediately ordered the commander of the legionnaires, Turnus Rufus, to plow the Temple Mount and obliterate the site where our Holy Temple had stood. Then they sought to arrest Rabban Gamliel and have him killed, along with his entire family, the descendants of King David."

Everyone knew about the plowing of Jerusalem and *Har Habayit* on Tisha b'Av, but how could I have missed this part about Rabban Gamliel? "What happened, Rachel? You must tell me!"

"At the last moment, a Roman senator repented and warned the *Nasi* of the danger, so Rabban Gamliel was able to escape just in time. The soldiers would have continued searching for him until they'd carried out their orders, so the senator suggested a means by which Rabban Gamliel's life could be spared. In exchange, he begged the *Nasi* to guarantee him a share in the World to Come, and Rabban Gamliel agreed. Then the senator committed suicide, thereby rendering the edict against the *Nasi* null and void, according to Roman law. Since then, *baruch Hashem*, we've been allowed to continue here unmolested."

It was time for me to go, but Rachel had certainly given me a lot to think about. That's one thing about Rachel that's always been true: she's never allowed me to be ordinary or complacent. It would have been so simple for me to think only about what shawl I would wear with which gown, or whether to buy a new toy for the twins when they were small, or what new recipe I should try for dinner, instead of the lofty matters that occupied the men.

But Rachel always was special, and when I was with her, I felt special too.

28

MORE THAN A YEAR has passed since we first came to Yavneh, and what a glorious time it has been! We have to be getting back to the estate soon, so I'm making the most of my last few weeks by spending as much time as I can with Rachel. I don't have to tell you how much I enjoy her company, but to be perfectly honest, this morning I had an ulterior motive: a *shidduch* for Batya.

Yes, Batya. As much as I hate to admit it to myself, she's unquestionably of marriageable age. A number of her friends are already married — some even have children! I could go on and on about why the vital matter of my only daughter's *shidduch* has been neglected: so many fine prospects for her had lost their lives, *Rachamana litzlan*, during the plague, or the war, or in the aftermath, and every time I would bring up the subject with Elazar, he would say, "Our Batti? But she's just a child!" or "It's too soon, Leah. Things are still so unsettled..."

Now, you know Batya has always been outstanding and none of her friends can compare with her in talent and intelligence and charm. About her lovely appearance, I'm not even talking, *beli ayin hara*. And you can't imagine how beautifully she weaves. Each of the girls who got married received a gorgeous tablecloth from her, and she has never repeated a design. She's so mature and understanding; I can talk to her like a friend. I've come to depend on her more and more in the last few years — could I possibly have left my parents alone and come here to Yavneh if not for Batti staying with them? She's so responsible that I knew she would make sure they dress warmly when they go out, and don't overexert themselves, and so on.

But why am I prattling about her talents and her qualities? The real reason why we haven't married her off until now is that Batya keeps insisting that she isn't ready yet.

Just before we left home, I decided it was time I had a serious talk with her, but I knew I'd have to go the long way around. "Did you hear about Chaya?" I asked her, trying to sound casual. "She just had her second boy."

"*Mazal tov!* That's wonderful!" Batya exclaimed. "I'll visit her and take her some of the quince-and-citron jelly. Didn't you tell me it's good for new mothers?"

"Yes, that's what they say. Her older one is so cute — he's exactly like his grandmother. I wonder what the second one looks like? I hope he doesn't have his father's nose. It would be way too big for such a small face. And what if he gets his mother's red hair? And all her freckles? And..."

"Imma, I'm sure he's adorable," Batya interrupted, stemming the flow of my babbling. "And why should you worry, anyway?"

"That's not really what I'm worried about," I told her truthfully.

"So then what *are* you really worried about?"

And before I realized what I was saying, it all burst out. "It's *you* I'm worried about, Batya darling. Here Chaya has her second child already, and you're not even engaged. And everyone knows that you're smarter and better than all of them... I'd love to have a grandchild already; when will you let us start looking for a *shidduch*? I can almost *feel* your baby in my arms!"

I was practically in tears, but Batya smiled. "Even if he — or she — has a big nose, red hair and freckles?" she asked mischievously.

"Well, we don't have those things in our family, *baruch Hashem*," I said. "Even the straight, fine hair that you had when you were small is beautiful and thick now. But since you asked, yes! Isn't it time for you to get married and give us some *nachat*? What are you waiting for, anyway?"

Now I was really sniffling, and Batya gave me her handkerchief. It had a very pretty blue embroidered border. She must have finished it quite recently; I had never seen it before.

"I'm waiting for someone like Abba," she said. "Maybe I'm being unrealistic — how can a young *bachur yeshiva* measure up to someone like Abba? But that's what I want. And I hope, *b'ezrat Hashem*, to give you loads of *nachat* one day..."

"Oh, Batya! You *do* already, all the time! You're the best daughter in the whole world!" And I hugged her and smiled; but inside I felt like crying. She was right. She needs a very special sort of husband, and there's no one like that back home.

So, ever since our arrival in Yavneh, I've kept an eye out for a potential *chatan* — can you think of a more likely place to find one? Of course Batti still believes she's "not ready," but between you and me, if the right young man were to come along, she'd be ready. And even though I have always allowed her to be independent and never tried to make her over in my own image (not like some pushy mothers I know), there comes a time in a parent's life when one simply must help things along.

Still, none of the many *bachurim* I've met has seemed to be *the one*. And now that we were about to leave, I felt as though the opportunity was slipping through my fingers. I had decided that I would simply come right out and ask Rachel if she could recommend someone, but when I arrived at her house, I noticed that there were several young men milling about. A few were engaged in a discussion in the front courtyard, and some were seated at the long table in the main room, getting what appeared to be private instruction from Rabi Akiva. The house was often full of *talmidim* when I visited, but this seemed to be a new batch.

"Who are those boys, Rachel?" I asked.

She knew right away whom I meant. Without even looking up from her embroidery, she answered, "They're recent arrivals from Rome and the provinces. When Akiva returned from his recent fund-raising trip, they came along to further their studies, and they're staying with us until they get accustomed to their new surroundings. Many of them have weak backgrounds in learning. You know, Leah, the boys from Rome don't have the educational advantages our own boys have and there's a lot they must learn before they can start attending regular classes."

One of the newcomers especially caught my eye. He was older, taller and broader than most of the others and his beard and *payot* were short, but that did not surprise me. Most out-of-town boys are clean-shaven, like the Romans, when they arrive in Yavneh. Usually, in a few months' time, they look like everyone else. I decided to watch this one.

And I made sure I had plenty of opportunity to do so. I'm practically a member of Rachel's household anyway, and throughout our stay in Yavneh I suppose I've spent more time at her place than in my own cottage. Now, I practically moved in! After all, time was running out.

On several occasions I noticed how diligent this tall young man was; he seemed to study continuously, getting up in the morning before anyone else, and going to sleep last. I couldn't control my curiosity. "Who is this boy?" I asked Rachel. "He looks different from the others, yet he has such a familiar face. Where have I seen him before?"

"Oh, maybe on one of your trips?" Rachel was vague, and went on to speak of something else. That was not like her, keeping secrets. I was determined to find out everything I could about this boy, but before my investigations had gotten anywhere, it was time to pack up for home.

Our farewell this time was not a tearful one, for a change. We knew we would stay in touch no matter what, and I felt certain that Rachel had grasped my unvoiced concerns. Surely she would...

29

SO WE WERE BACK HOME and life was quite humdrum and boring: taking care of the house, giving the servants their instructions for the day, putting away the summer clothing and taking out the winter things, drying dates and figs and putting up jars of vegetables to pickle. It seemed as if I'd been doing the same things forever and ever. Nothing had changed.

And there was no word from Rachel about that boy in Yavneh.

There's one thing I didn't tell you about Yavneh: Baruch is learning there. He actually started learning in the *metivta* a few months before we left, but Elazar and I had very little contact with him except to exchange a few words in passing from time to time. Now, I know this sounds a bit odd, and I wouldn't want you to think there's anything wrong with our relationship, *chalilah*, but this was what we had agreed.

When Baruch wrote to us in Yavneh saying that he was very anxious to attend yeshiva there but that he had "certain reservations," we understood immediately. Elazar and I had a long discussion about it.

"If he's here, and we're here," Elazar said, "he's going to feel obligated to spend time with us on Shabbat and so on. We will be a constant distraction from his studies. That's why he's hesitating."

I knew just what my husband meant by "we." He was being diplomatic. "Elazar, don't you think I'm aware of that?" I said. "The last thing I would want is to take him away from his learning. Do you imagine I would insist on his staying with us, or demand his attention? He's no longer a baby, you know, or even a child — he's an adult."

"That's just the point, Leah. All these other boys have left home to be at the greatest Torah academy in the Land, and Baruch would have his Imma close by, packing up food for him, and doing his wash, and cooking lavish meals. And he's such a respectful boy, he would of course want to please you."

Packing up food? Well, maybe a nice fruit, I had thought. But obviously this was out of the question. "You're absolutely right, Elazar. It would not only distract him; it would embarrass him terribly." I wrote back to Baruch the very next day and told him that we understood his "reservations." I assured him we would be there for him if he needed us, but would otherwise keep our distance.

It wasn't easy maintaining our part of the bargain, believe me.

But last week's mail brought wonderful news: Baruch is coming home for Chanukah! It's only been a few months since I saw him, if you can call barely making out his face in a crowd of *talmidim* and a hasty farewell "seeing" him, and now I won't have to pretend we're strangers. I can be his Imma again!

Suddenly, there was so much supervising to do: preparing the *chanukiyot* (we like to use the best oil from our own olive groves), getting everyone's winter clothing ready (I didn't even have time to have anything new made up for the season), readying Baruch's room, and all the food and linens for our other guests. I thought I'd never be finished in time.

When Baruch arrived on *erev* Chanukah, I couldn't believe

my eyes. He's changed so much and seems so mature and adult — somehow I've retained the image of a much more youthful Baruch in my mind. He's quiet and more serious now; only with Batya does he still joke as in the old days. And of course, just like his father, all he can talk about is Rabi Akiva, and that was all we heard throughout the festival.

"Do you know what Rabi Dosa ben Harkinas said to him when Rabi Yehoshua introduced them? He said, 'Are you the Akiva ben Yosef whose name is known from one end of the world to the other?' It's such an honor to have a *Rav* who is so famous!

"You were so right about Yavneh, Abba," Baruch went on. "The yeshiva is tremendous! Almost every day new boys and men come from all over the country, and from many places in the *galut* also. It must be all because of Rabi Akiva. He's so kind to everybody. He never loses patience, even when they ask the silliest questions...

"And his humility! I told you what Rabi Dosa said about him. Well, I heard that when Rabi Akiva and Rabi Yehoshua and Rabi Elazar ben Azariah went to see him, they started discussing the *inyan* of *tzarat habat*. So they asked Rabi Dosa, 'How do you rule?' And he answered, 'Like the school of Hillel.'

"The Sages were surprised. 'But we heard that you ruled according to the school of Shammai,' they said.

"And Rabi Dosa asked, 'Who says so? They must have said *ben Harkinas*, meaning my brother Yonatan. *He* says to follow *Beit Shammai*. But I say: The *navi* Chaggai dwelt on this problem and taught that the marriage of a brother-in-law with the co-wife of his own daughter is forbidden. Now establish the law accordingly! But watch out — if you should meet my brother, he may best you in the debate, as he has three hundred proofs to support his opinion!'"

I was having trouble following all this but I knew Baruch would get to the point about Akiva's humility soon. And he did.

"So Rabi Akiva left the house," Baruch continued, "and whom should he meet but this Rabi Yonatan. Right away, they started discussing the matter, and Rabi Akiva was not able to get the better of him. Then Rabi Yonatan asked him, 'Are you the famous Rabi Akiva that everyone's talking about? Well, you are lucky to have gotten a good name for yourself, although you have not yet reached the level even of a cattleherder.'

"And Rabi Akiva replied: 'Not even of a shepherd.' I wish I'd been there — I would have told that Rabi Yonatan..."

"Well, I'm glad you weren't," Elazar said. "Rabi Akiva doesn't need anyone to defend him. As for his humility, remember that he sat at his *Rav*'s feet for twelve years in Lod and Rabi Eliezer had no idea how brilliant he was." Elazar smiled and placed his arm on Baruch's shoulder. "I'm pleased, though, that you admire him so much, son. As it is said, 'Make for yourself a *Rav*'..."

Well, I found all this very interesting, but in the back of my mind was the constant worry about Batya, so as soon as the maids had cleared the table, I told Elazar that I had to speak to him — urgently! I had hoped Baruch would bring some word from Yavneh, but obviously his mind was on other things.

"If this is about buying something, or fixing something in the house, Leah," Elazar said, "it'll have to wait till after Chanukah."

"No. It's much more important than that. And I have to speak to you in private." That was a bit difficult, because there were guests all over the house. "Let's go for a walk," I suggested, "like we used to when we were first married."

"Fine. Do you know where my winter headscarf is? It's windy out." Elazar never used to care about the weather. I guess we're both getting older.

So I gave Elazar his headscarf and wrapped myself in my good woolen shawl, and we left the house and started to walk towards the road. "Every time I go outside," I said, "I notice how things are falling apart. The old trees seem to be dying, and no new ones are growing. And the stone paving is crumbling in front of our house. I just feel like closing my eyes..."

"Did you want to discuss the outdoors?" Elazar asked impatiently. "For this you needed privacy?"

"No, Elazar, it's about Batya. We really have to think about a *shidduch* for her, even though she claims she's not ready. It's time. Most of the women my age are grandmothers already, and plenty who are even younger than I. Of course, everyone tells me I don't look my age..."

"You're right. About Batya, I mean. She still seems to me to be the little girl who used to climb trees and chase the ducks. I guess I just didn't realize she's old enough to get married. It's high time we did something about it. But there's no one for her around here, you can be sure of that." My husband, who is usually calm, seemed tense and worried.

"Well, you can't expect me to take care of that too," I complained. "It's the father's job. Don't I have enough to do with the house, and the servants and all? Why don't you speak to Abba? He might have some good ideas. You remember when he went specially to Yaffo and picked out Chanania for Penina? Look how well *that* turned out!"

"Oh, is that what he did? You have such a selective memory, Leah. Well, I'll think about it." Elazar was very quiet for the rest of our walk, and when it started to rain, we hurried back to the house.

Baruch was still up. "Why aren't you in bed yet?" I asked him. "You hardly sleep a wink in yeshiva, I know. At least try to catch up while you're home."

"I've been waiting up for you," he said, meaning both of us. "I didn't finish telling you about the yeshiva. For instance —"

"I'm sure it's very interesting," I said, "but I'm awfully tired. Maybe you'll tell me some other day?"

"But, Imma, this is important!"

I was too exhausted to stay up another minute. Elazar, though, said he wanted to hear everything that Baruch had to say, even if it meant staying up all night. So I went to bed, and left them talking.

In the morning, I heard Elazar pacing back and forth in the bedroom, the way he does when he has something on his mind.

"Are you awake?" he asked. How could I *not* be awake. "I have to talk to you."

"This early? The sun is barely up. Can't it wait until you're back from *shacharit*?" I couldn't get my eyes open.

"I *am* back, Leah. Now listen: It's about a *shidduch* for Batya."

The magic word! "In that case, I'm all ears." And I was. That's all I'd been thinking about since before we left Yavneh; I even dreamed about it. "So let's hear."

"What Baruch wanted to tell us last night was about a friend of his. He hasn't been in the yeshiva long; he only came from Rome several months ago. Baruch says he's great: takes his learning very seriously, prays with tremendous *kavanah*, never says a word that's unnecessary or unpleasant. Well, you can imagine what I was thinking..."

"That maybe it's something for our Batya?" I ventured.

"Exactly. So I asked him more questions: how does the boy get along with the *rabbanim* and the other *talmidim*, what about his appearance, his manners, his background..."

"And?" Oh, I was wide awake now!

"Baruch said that everyone likes him. He noticed that Rabi Akiva gives him special attention — that's surely a good sign. His appearance is good: tall, pleasant face, very neat and clean, fine manners. Baruch doesn't know much about his background, only that he comes from Rome, and started learning late. But he's more than made up for it."

"Did you ask Baruch his name? And what about his age? Does he know how old he is? I'm glad he's tall — not that Batya would mind if he were a bit shorter..." Already I saw her standing under the *chuppah*, and I was planning what to wear to the wedding.

"His name is Yehudah. Baruch doesn't know his age exactly; he says he's surely older than most of the others who started together with him; and several years ahead of Baruch."

I was very excited; this must be the boy I had my eye on! "So, he's older than Batya too, of course. That's good, because she's very mature. He learns well, he's serious, he's well liked — it sounds interesting. So what's the next step?"

"Well, we really don't know anything about this boy's background. He's quiet, Baruch says, doesn't talk about himself. Let's see what we can find out before we go any further." Elazar was analyzing the situation in his usual organized manner. "When Baruch goes back to the yeshiva, he'll talk to the boy and get more information about him. Maybe he can even ask Rabi Akiva... No, that would be presumptuous. We'll just have to wait until we hear from Baruch."

"Isn't there anything we can do *now*?" I was too impatient to wait. "First *Shabbat Chanukah*, and then the long trip back to Yavneh, and then waiting for Baruch to find out — he won't realize how important this is to me! Baruch is shy — he might not even ask right away. And what if he writes back and the letter gets lost in the mail? The postal service is getting worse and worse. And what if the answer he gets is not what we want to hear? What if the boy's parents are not our type?" I was getting very agitated.

"Elazar, what if...?"

"Please go back to bed, Leah," Elazar urged. "You can't arrange things like this in ten minutes, so don't even try."

I went back to bed, but you can be sure I didn't sleep.

30

SHABBAT CHANUKAH was soon behind us but the days until Baruch's departure could not pass quickly enough for me. I usually love the festival: the joyful spirit, the family all together, and especially having my son home. But this time it was different. I was counting the days until Baruch would return to Yavneh; I couldn't wait to hear more about this Yehudah. At the same time, I continued to look around in our own neighborhood for someone suitable, although I knew that Elazar and Batya had been right: there was no one.

Well, since there was no way to hurry the days, I tried to relax and enjoy them. Abba and Imma came over several times for meals. Father is not nearly as opinionated as he was years ago. He now listens to Elazar, and even respects him. Mother seems tired. She's still working hard, with only Puah to help her. And the maid isn't so young any more, either. Once Abba and Imma showed up while Chanania and Penina and their brood were visiting. The noise was deafening, and my parents left earlier than usual. We sent the children outside and settled down for a nice chat.

I told my sister about everything that was going on. She said Yehudah sounded all right, but she had some doubts. "Is it enough that Baruch thinks highly of him, and that the teachers and students like him? What do you know about his background? How do you know he'll make a good husband?" She kept hurling questions at me until I became quite upset and asked her to stop.

"We'll try to find out about his family and everything," I said. "But as far as what kind of husband he'll be, how can anyone tell in advance? Did you know that Chanania would turn out to be so good? And what did I know about Elazar? True, he's our cousin, and his parents are nice people, of course, but that's about it. How can we guarantee our children's happiness?" I was thinking about ben Azzai. "Do we ever know what fate has in store for them?"

"No, of course not, Leah. But we can try to help them by investigating their potential partner's background very thoroughly, and making sure it's right. And even then..." her voice trailed off.

"Listen, Penina, this conversation is making me very nervous. If Elazar's parents had known what a silly girl I was then, they never would have let him marry me. Everyone says that making a *shidduch* is as difficult as *kriat Yam Suf*, splitting the Red Sea. I think it's as difficult as *crossing* the Red Sea, because you have to jump right in, without worrying too much. If everyone thought the way you do, no one would ever let their children get married. We just have to have *bitachon*!"

Even though I tried to sound very firm and big-sisterly, I didn't really feel sure of myself, so I tried to change the subject. Selecting a new topic was no problem.

"My, the children are getting big," I said. "How old is Yehudit now? Fourteen?"

"No, she's fifteen, almost sixteen."

How could I have forgotten? But I hadn't noticed my own children growing up either. Lately, time seems to be running faster and faster.

"And how old is the baby? Two already? It seems to me we just went to his *brit*. Unbelievable!"

Then Penina told me all about her children, from the oldest to the youngest. She said her Yehudit had just started to learn how to weave — she was trying to copy my Batya. As if she could! She's also very good at embroidery, Penina said, and she often helps out with the younger children. The only problem is that she prays a lot — so much that she hardly has time for her friends.

"So what's bad about that?" I asked. "My Batya does the same. Girls are growing up differently now than when we were young. Who even knew how to read? The only ones who did were a few daughters of rich Roman families, and they only read Greek, not Hebrew. If not for Rachel, what would I know today? She taught me everything, right from the beginning. Anyway, isn't it better that Yehudit spend her time talking to the *Ribbono shel Olam*, instead of engaging in silly gossiping like we did when we were girls?"

"Speak for yourself, Leah," said Penina in her old snippy way. "But I guess you're right — our girls are better than we were."

The little ones came in, clamoring for cake and drinks. I served poppyseed half-moons, made by Batya, and that good old date-honey and citron drink. Then Aaron and Shoshanah arrived. It was really a pleasure to see them, with their young family, but the noise! So Penina rounded up her gang, and they left. I rehashed the whole business of the *shidduch* with Shoshanah, and came to the same conclusion. We'd have to trust in *Hakadosh Baruch Hu*.

So finally Baruch went back to the yeshiva. Yavneh is quite a distance away, but I packed three times as much food as he needed for the trip. After he left with all his bundles, I had to smile: I remembered how Imma would make me take a day's supply of food for a two-hour walk, just in case...

From the moment Baruch left, I was impatient for the messenger to arrive. Each day that passed without a letter seemed like a century. Finally, weeks later, it came, and I tore it open frantically, but the little news it contained was disappointing. All he'd been able to find out was that Yehudah had come from Rome and that his father's name was Tovia. Baruch had questioned the other students, but no one knew anything. Yehudah was friendly, but never spoke about himself. Being a good son and brother, Baruch had even tried to ask Rabi Akiva, but no luck. Yehudah's appearance, however, he described in great detail. I had thought it might be the young man I'd noticed at Rachel's house in Yavneh, the one who learned so diligently; now I was certain of it. Perhaps it was a sign? Anyway, I showed the letter to Elazar. As he read it, his brow furrowed in consternation.

"Well, it seems that I have to speak to Rabi Akiva myself," he said. "I'd better go to Yavneh now, while we have a break in the rains. And what if someone else has an eye on this Yehudah? After all, Baruch writes that he has become one of the best in the yeshiva."

There was nothing for me to say. Foolishly, I'd gotten my heart set on this boy, a total stranger who might turn out to be unsuitable, and I didn't want to think about "what if"s. So I packed for a trip for several days, and sent along some honey cakes for Baruch, and also some more warm winter clothing. Baruch catches cold so easily...

Then I settled down to being *really* nervous. I marked off the date early each morning, as if somehow that would make time move faster. Batya did not know the reason for her father's trip (I was afraid of a disappointment, so I purposely did not tell her) and she thought it was just the usual visit to Rabi Akiva, but she noticed something was amiss.

"What's the matter, Imma?" she asked. "You're so jumpy these days. Is it because Abba is away? You could have gone along again, you know — I'm a big girl now."

I forced a smile. "I guess I am nervous without Abba this time," I said, trying to sound casual, "but anyway, he'll be back soon." I realized that I still wasn't very good at hiding my emotions. I'd have to try harder.

31

WHEN ELAZAR RETURNED AT LAST, I was shocked at his appearance. He looked exhausted, completely drained. Ordinarily, I would have put a hot meal in front of him, and saved the questions for later. But now I couldn't wait.

"What did you find out from Rabi Akiva? Who are the boy's parents? And does he want to continue learning? And what about —?"

Elazar put up his hand to stave off the barrage of questions. "Wait a minute, Leah. I can't talk now. It's very complicated, and I don't know what to do. I have to think; we'll talk later. Anyway, it's time for *minchah*." And without even taking a drink or a bite of food, he left for the synagogue.

I was in agony. What could have happened? What had Rabi Akiva said to him to make him so upset? I decided I'd make him tell me everything the minute he came home. That took a long time, though; and it was already dark when I saw him coming up the walk. I threw open the door.

"What took you so long?" I cried, slightly hysterical. "Here I've been waiting on pins and needles and you don't even say a word! *Baruch Hashem*, you look much better than when you first came in. Did you have anything to eat? Here! All day I'm slaving over a hot stove, and you just peck at the food — you don't even appreciate how hard I work. So let's hear already what happened in Yavneh!" Even though I was upset, I thought I controlled my emotions very well.

"Well, Leah, which do you want me to do? Talk or eat? I can't do both." And he gave me that *look* — you know!

"Oh, talk, of course! But you must be starved! Better eat first. But I just can't wait to find out —" Then I saw Elazar smiling down at his plate. I smiled too, and waited until he'd taken a few bites.

"As I told you," Elazar began, "it's very complicated. When I spoke to Rabi Akiva, and he made me aware of the *bachur*'s background, I didn't know what to do. All the way home, different thoughts kept running through my mind: yes, no, maybe — I was completely confused, and I felt terrible. But then I went to *minchah*, and after the service I heard an excellent *shiur* from an itinerant *maggid*, and then I went to *maariv*. Now I can see more clearly, and I feel much better."

"You still haven't said anything!" I tried to lower my voice. "What—happened—in Yavneh?!"

Finally he told me. Rabi Akiva had received him in a very friendly manner, as always. They talked about Baruch (he's doing well, Rabi Akiva said), about the situation with the Romans, about a *chiddush* that Rabi Tarfon had discussed. Then Rabi Akiva asked why Elazar was honoring him with this visit, and Elazar brought up the subject of Yehudah.

"Excellent! Excellent!" Rabi Akiva said. "Excellent in Torah, in character, in *yirat Shamayim*! He's one of the best here — and he accomplished it in almost no time." And then, "Excellent!" again.

But when Elazar asked about his background, Rabi Akiva was silent for a long time. "It's about a *shidduch*, I suppose?" he asked quietly. "Then I'll have to tell you; otherwise I would not be permitted."

He said that Yehudah came from good Jewish stock — in

fact, his grandfather had been a *tzaddik*. His parents were more modern; at one time, they'd actually been quite friendly with the Romans, but with conditions as they are today, they've discontinued their business and social relations with them, at a significant loss of income.

"Well, that doesn't sound too bad," I said, though I'd always hoped my children would marry into one of our good local families. I still think that's the best. "So what's the problem?"

"Before he came to the yeshiva" — Elazar paused and watched carefully for my reaction — "Yehudah was a Roman soldier. He was attached to the Tenth Legion here, and because he was such an outstanding soldier, he was later transferred to Rome. He signed up for seven years, and he served his full term."

"What?!" I was speechless. "A Jewish boy — a *bachur yeshiva*, and you say he was once a...once a...one of them?" It was impossible! That fine-looking student of Rabi Akiva's had been in the army of our enemies, had maybe even — no! I refused to believe it!

"Yes. You'd best believe it." Again Elazar was reading my thoughts! He said the boy had always been difficult and rebellious, and had run away from home in his teens to join the Roman forces. But once he reached the pagan capital, he realized that he'd made a terrible mistake. Those soldiers whom he'd often admired from afar, were nothing but depraved drunkards and murderers. Their language was appalling, and their actions were worse. The discipline was merciless: a soldier would be whipped, or even killed, for the slightest infraction of the rules. In turn, the legionnaires behaved cruelly towards the lower ranks, and even more so to the natives of the lands they occupied.

But worst of all, they had no God. They worshiped a pantheon of beings who were jealous, lustful, capricious and bloodthirsty. And every legionnaire had to profess devotion to these idols, or face death!

So the teachings of Yehudah's early youth came back to him. He remembered: "You shall have no other gods before Me."

"You shall not kill."

"You shall not steal."

"You shall not covet."

"Honor your father and your mother."

"Love your fellowman as yourself."

And all around him, his comrades were doing just the opposite. Suddenly, he regretted his wasted youth, and his hasty decision to join the Legion. But he could not turn back — to desert meant certain death.

He started to look for places where Jews assembled — synagogues, houses of learning, even the marketplace — to hear his own language again, to absorb some words of Torah. He tried to keep the *mitzvot*, and never ate meat or fowl, though his fellow soldiers thought it strange, and he often went hungry. He rose in rank to a position where he was sometimes able to choose his assignments. Then he would go to the prisons where Jews were incarcerated, smuggling in kosher food so they wouldn't starve, dressing their wounds, and even burying the dead.

And so the years passed. When Yishmael ben Elisha was arrested, Yehudah was part of the detail guarding the jail and he supplied the boy with food and drink. But out of fear for both Yishmael's life and his own, he did not reveal himself as a Jew.

When Rabi Yehoshua ransomed Yishmael, Yehudah learned that the boy was going to study in Yavneh. Even he knew of the academy there, and he started thinking about what it would be like to learn Torah, to return to the faith of his fathers.

Finally, his tour of duty ended and he was honorably discharged. He sought out Rabi Akiva, who was fund raising in Rome at the time, and told him everything.

"You must go to a yeshiva and learn Torah," Rabi Akiva said. "Come with me."

"But it's too late!" Yehudah protested. "I'm too old for that. And I've led a sinful life..."

"It's never too late, even at the last moment. '*Ein kol davar omed bifnei ba'alei teshuvah* — There isn't a thing that can stand in the way of the penitent.' And," Rabi Akiva added with a smile, "I was much older than you, and knew far less, when *I* began. Come!"

And so Yehudah arrived in Yavneh.

There, Rabi Akiva said, he applied himself with such tremendous *hatmadah* that he soon was first among the students who had arrived with him. But most outstanding of all was his *tefillah*!

"To see him saying the *Shemoneh Esreh*," Elazar said, "was like watching an angel. No; it was even more than that. *Malachim* have no temptations, so they need not do *teshuvah*. When I stood near Yehudah, I felt as if I were standing next to the *Kohen Hagadol* on Yom Kippur..."

I had heard my husband out without saying a word. But now it was my turn. "Listen, Elazar. I see you're quite taken with this young man. I appreciate that he has become a great *talmid chacham* in a short time. And I'm sure his prayers are all you say they are. But a Roman soldier! How do we know he didn't...you know. And we still don't know who his parents are. I doubt that we'll see eye to eye with them. They live in Rome, so how can we find out? And what about Batya? How will she feel about it? And what did Rabi Akiva say about the *shidduch*?"

"Believe me, Leah, I had all the same doubts and fears. I was completely confused, just like you. And when I asked Rabi Akiva, he only said: 'I know what I would do. But the decision has to be yours — and your daughter's!' The whole way home I was eaten up by indecision. How could I take this responsibility upon myself? Especially since Batya is such a good child, and would probably agree to whatever I told her. Yes, no. Yes, no! The problem of his past went around and around in my head, until I thought I would burst.

"So when I came home, it was no wonder you thought I looked awful. But luckily it was time for *minchah.* I spoke to the *Ribbono shel Olam* and I placed my burden on His shoulders. I prayed for a solution, and it came — immediately! After *minchah,* I told you, a new *maggid* gave this really wonderful *shiur* about *teshuvah,* and he said: '*Makom sheba'alei teshuvah omdin, tzaddikim gemurim einam omdin* — In the place where the penitent stand, the perfectly righteous cannot stand.'

"There was my answer! I had no more doubts. *Hakadosh Baruch Hu* Himself had decided. I hope that Batya will agree — and you too, of course..."

Did I have a choice? The story had moved me to tears. But I still wasn't satisfied. "I always hoped to have *mechutanim* living nearby," I said. "It's so good to have someone of your own type, someone you can communicate with. And what if he wants to live in Rome, near his parents? We'll never get a chance to be together. Anyway, I still don't know about his family," I finished and waited for Elazar's answer.

"Oh, didn't I mention it? He is Yehudah ben Tovia — you know, Tertius. His mother is your friend, Shifra."

32

NOW I HAVE TWO — no, three — children in Yavneh. Baruch had been doing very well and now, inspired by dear Yehudah, he is doing even better. Batya is happy, and very proud of her husband. Her home is a pretty little nest, and all the walls are hung with beautiful tapestries that she wove with her own hands. She has such an excellent sense of color, and she uses the best materials, so her work is becoming very popular, and people come from all over to buy it. Maybe, some day, she'll earn enough to support Yehudah while he learns...

And this, too, I owe to Rachel. To tell the truth, I never liked having to spin; as for weaving, although I'd done a few simple designs as a girl, it was always the farthest thing from my mind. But Batti remembered seeing Rachel and her daughter do it, and she thought it looked like fun! Now, perhaps she'll have a decent *parnassah* from it. That would be good, because our income is dwindling. The crops are poor, and the people can't afford to buy; many go hungry. And Elazar isn't getting any younger. He finds it difficult to deal with the government, the tax collector, the new Roman laws. Still, we have it better than most.

Rachel wrote me a very long letter that went on and on

about the Sages' delegation to Rome but on the same day, I received a letter from Batti as well, and Batti's had such great significance for me personally, that I put Rachel's aside and promptly mislaid it.

And what earthshaking news did my daughter have? Well, she didn't quite come out and say as much, but I'm certain that I'm about to become a grandmother at last. So you can understand why the Roman machinations failed to capture my interest. Still, since all I've got to do now is WAIT (and Elazar has forbidden me to utter a word to anyone about the impending "event," especially since we're not even *sure*), I spent the whole morning searching for Rachel's letter. It was right where I'd put it, of course, in the chest where I keep my journal. Here's what she wrote:

When the Rabbis of Yavneh finished all the deliberations and clarifications of the disputed *halachot*, Vespasian died and his son Titus became Emperor. Somehow, his ascent to power transformed him from a bloodthirsty *rasha* into a kind and benevolent ruler. (I think only someone as pure and lacking in cynicism as Rachel could write those words and mean them. "Can the Ethiopian change the color of his skin?") Yes, the sadistic mass-murderer who had slaughtered hundreds of thousands of innocent people and had reveled at the sight of his captives' flesh being torn from their bones by raging animals in the arena, turned overnight into a peace-loving caesar, concerned for the welfare of all his subjects.

The leaders of the generation wasted no time; they organized a delegation to Rome, comprised of Rabban Gamliel, Rabi Eliezer and Rabi Yehoshua, whose mission it was to bring the greetings of *Klal Yisrael* to Titus and entreat him to deal kindly with our People as well. (I think they also wanted to see with their own eyes this leopard who'd changed his spots.)

Upon their arrival in Rome, the Sages sought out friends and supporters among the senators and other government officials, people of influence who could speak in our favor to the Emperor. These efforts were successful; there were a number of Roman statesmen who were favorably disposed to our cause.

However, before the Rabbis' scheduled audience with Titus, his vicious brother Domitian had him assassinated, and he became Emperor in Titus's stead. Then, the Rabbis later learned, he called a clandestine session of the Senate and passed into law a decree for the annihilation of every Jew in the Empire, to be carried out within thirty days! It was *min Hashamayim* that one of the Romans whom the Rabbis had befriended was the Emperor's trusted advisor, a man who was secretly God-fearing, and he revealed this dastardly plan to them.

The Rabbis sank into despair when they heard Domitian's evil scheme, but the God-fearing senator comforted them. "Do not be distressed," he said. "The God of the Jews will not abandon His People."

"Who is this Domitian?" the Rabbis asked. "What do you know of him? Is there any way that we could influence him to change his mind?"

The senator gave them a pitiful look. "Influence a madman?" he scoffed. "Since the days of Haman there has never been such peril for the Jews. Domitian is slavishly devoted to the Roman gods and demands the same devotion from his subjects, on penalty of death. He is taking special vengeance on the great philosophers because they are outspoken and oppose him publicly. The noblest Romans are trembling for their lives. He's so insane that he has even killed many of his own relatives! His anger is directed most particularly towards those of us who convert or abandon idol-worship. The Jews pose a threat to him because many Romans have lately become God-fearing. My life is as much in jeopardy, my friends, as yours."

Day by day, Domitian became more and more tyrannical, persecuting the senators and noblemen of Rome. Many were assassinated on the slightest pretext, or on no pretext at all. They trembled before him, fearing his volatile temper; a look or a word could arouse his anger, often with fatal consequences.

At the same time, Domitian tried to win the favor of the lower classes. He doubled the pay of the soldiers. He gave the population of Rome all kinds of athletic displays, sports and circuses, and paid for the entertainment with the money he appropriated from the slain senators. He had himself proclaimed a god, and he filled the city with statues in his image. An enormous one was erected in the Forum, before the temple of his family, the Flavii. The head of this statue reached to the heavens, and could be seen from every part of the capital.

Upon the completion of the new statue of the Emperor, a poetry contest honoring the Roman gods was announced. But Domitian demanded that he, being one of the gods, should be the main subject of the verses. He sat on a golden throne and awarded crowns of golden oak leaves to the winners; these, of course were the poets who had praised and glorified him the most. He seemed happy, smiling at the throngs who had assembled to pay him homage, but then he condemned two poets to death because they had praised a man he disliked, and a third because he had written a satire that made a few sly references to Domitian's wife. The three men were executed before the entire Senate.

If the Emperor exhibited friendship toward anyone, that person became terrified, for he knew that the friendship would soon turn to hatred, and the object of the Emperor's hatred would not have long to live. So the senators and patricians obeyed his every whim and avoided antagonizing the madman. No one knew how this reign of terror would end, but they felt that it would have to end soon, or there would be none left alive of the upper class, including even Domitian's own relatives.

(*Ribbono shel Olam*, I thought, to this Amalek-incarnate our delegates would present their plea for mercy!)

It was clear that the Emperor couldn't be approached directly. The Sages knew that if they were able to reach him at all, it would be only through one of the courtiers or the philosophers — the former, because they had easy access to Domitian; the latter because their class was persecuted by the ruler, so they might make common cause with the Jews.

They first sought the advice of Artemidorus, a famous geographer and philosopher who had been banished from Rome, suspected of harboring traitorous thoughts against Domitian. He greeted them graciously.

"Welcome to you, wise men of Israel, with Rabbi Gamliel at your head," he said. "To what do I owe this honor?"

The Rabbis quickly told him about Domitian's edict against the Jews.

"Rome is as full of gossips and spies as a pomegranate is full of seeds," Artemidorus said, "and yet I knew nothing of this. Ah, Roman intrigue — is there no end to it? The senators, the noblemen, the military, the governors of the provinces — all of them are buzzing like flies around the capital, trying to gain money and power. No one seems to care about what is good for the country. Only we philosophers try to remain aloof from politics, yet we are drawn in, even against our will.

"Allow me to explain to you what kind of person Domitian is. We were not unhappy when Titus died, you know. He had become quite mad. They said there was a gnat eating away at his brain. His father, Vespasian, wasn't much better: an absolute tyrant. But Domitian, unfortunately, has the worst traits of both his father and his brother, and some terrible ones all his own. Vespasian was of humble origin; he was born in Reate, in the Sabine province. His son's ambition is to restore the religious and moral conditions of the old Republic, as in his father's day, although he himself violates them constantly. He has declared himself a god, and punishes with death anyone who criticizes him.

"Domitian has also proclaimed himself the guardian of the people's behavior," Artemidorus continued, "though his own is cruel and corrupt. No one is safe from him, and he especially hates the Jews. Why? Many Romans ridicule the gods which he pretends to revere. They are turning to other religions, including Judaism, and the Emperor is furious.

"Those suspected of wanting to become Jews, he orders executed or exiled. But he has not succeeded in preventing Roman nobles from converting. I suppose he is now seeking other means..."

"It is as you say," Rabban Gamliel said. "We need your advice. What can be done to prevent him from carrying out his vile plan?"

For a long time Artemidorus was silent. Then he said, "How can I advise you? This man is without pity. He may act very kindly towards you, and promise you everything, and in the next moment, have you arrested and tortured. There is only one hope: the senators! Many of their class have been executed. They are at the end of their patience. I believe they're planning to get rid of Domitian before he gets rid of them. It's only a matter of time now..."

"But what if, God forbid, he acts upon the decree against our People before he is killed?"

Artemidorus had no answer for them.

The philosopher had confirmed all that the God-fearing senator had told them about Domitian, and the Sages were again plunged into a state of despair. They returned to their lodgings to fast and pray for Divine intervention.

And their prayers were soon answered, but not in any way they had imagined.

The God-fearing senator had spoken to no one else of the plot, not even to his wife, until the time period had almost elapsed and still no solution was in sight. When he broke the terrible news to her, his wife cried in dismay, "But twenty-five days have already passed!" And the senator replied, "Yes, my dear, but there are yet five more days. The salvation can come in the blink of an eye."

The senator's wife, who was even more righteous than her husband, realized that action was called for. "Do you not possess a poison ring?" And the senator understood immediately. The edict would not be rescinded; however, according to the law, if any senator were to die before the edict was carried out, it would instantly be annulled.

The couple bade one another farewell, and the senator drank the droplets of poison from the hollow of his ring and died, thereby bringing about our salvation.

Rachel's letter went on:

When the Rabbis heard what he had done, they went to visit the senator's wife to console her. Knowing that there were spies everywhere, they chose their words cautiously. "What a shame that the ship has set sail without paying her duty!" they said, meaning that this righteous man had given up his life for Judaism, but had not been circumcised. And the senator's wife replied, "I assure you that the ship did indeed pay her duty," and she provided evidence confirming her statement.

The Sages gave her their blessings and said, "Your husband was greater even than Avraham our Father. May his memory be your consolation."

The Rabbis returned to Yavneh, Rachel concluded, with heavy hearts. Although the edict was annulled, Domitian was still Emperor and the danger was only temporarily averted. The madman could strike again at any time, especially now that Rome was looking differently upon the yeshiva. It was no secret that the concept of Yavneh was succeeding, just as Rabban Yochanan ben Zakkai had intended, and now its continued existence was threatened.

And so it was decided that the full assembly of seventy-two Sages from all the neighboring cities would not meet again in Yavneh, at least until the prevailing conditions allowed them to convene in safety. Only those members who reside in Yavneh would gather to discuss Torah issues and national policy.

I thrust Rachel's letter into the wooden chest, tears stinging my eyes. I was suddenly very tired. Is this what the future holds for us, that every moment of joy must be mingled with sorrow and fear? Only this morning, my heart was bursting with happiness at the prospect of holding Batya's baby in my arms, and now I'm trembling with terror.

Ribbono shel Olam, please watch over my children!

33

THINGS ARE SO MUCH EASIER now that Elazar is learning in a yeshiva close to home. He would have continued spending part of every year in Yavneh — not only because of the high level of the *shiurim* there but because it gave him an opportunity to look in on the children — but Rabi Elazar ben Matya asked him especially to join his local *beit midrash*. (Do you know, Rabi Elazar speaks *seventy* languages? I thing there are only three or four people in the whole world like that!) He told Elazar that with the situation in Rome as it is, he himself would be spending less time in Yavneh and more time organizing his study group here. He would need *talmidei chachamim* like Elazar to help him.

I'm so proud of my husband! Oh, I know he's no Rabi Akiva, but he's become a respected scholar, one whose presence will add prestige to a Torah institute. Imagine where he'd be today if I hadn't encouraged him! Well, that's not entirely true; it did take me a long time to come around. But didn't I defend him to Abba, rest his soul, even though I myself had no idea then where all his learning would lead?

Still, there was one serious matter that required Elazar's attention before he got involved in all his new responsibilities, and I told him so.

"And what is that, Leah?" he asked.

"Baruch," I said emphatically, expecting an argument.

"You are absolutely right. We've put this off for far too long already. Now, whom do you have in mind?"

"Whom do *I* have...!?" I exclaimed. "Elazar, if I had someone, don't you think... Oh, what's the use. Don't you see, this is the whole point. There *is* no one."

"Don't be ridiculous, Leah," Elazar said dismissively. "The Sages teach that forty days before a male child is created, the identity of his future wife is Divinely decreed. That doesn't mean we don't have to make an effort on Baruch's behalf, of course. Now, you're his mother; what kind of girl is he looking for?"

Did I ever mention how exasperating my husband can be when he sets his mind to it? How was I supposed to know what Baruch wanted — remember, we had to play at being strangers back in Yavneh, and how much time did we have to talk when he was home? First, it was about Batya's *shidduch*, and since then, his learning, and the situation in Rome, and so forth. *Elazar* should know his son's preferences far better than *I* could.

Rather than continuing this pointless "discussion," however, I simply said, "I'll ask him." And when he finally came home, I did.

Now, you know Baruch. He's very refined; he has never hinted or said anything about a *shidduch*, but I know he's ready. Most of his friends are married and have children.

The next time he came home, I brought up the subject and Baruch blushed a bit and said, "Yes, Imma. You're right. It's time already. But it's not easy to find the right kind of girl..." There he stopped.

"What kind of girl would you like?"

"Well, she should be a girl who sincerely wants me to learn, who values Torah, who is willing to live modestly... I guess someone like Batti or Aunt Penina or Aunt Shoshanah." I was a little disappointed — I'd hoped he'd say someone like me — but I managed to hide my feelings.

"Excellent!" I said. On second thought, I felt quite flattered. Batti and Penina take after me, of course, and Shoshanah was hand-picked by me for my brother. No wonder Baruch holds them in such high esteem.

But knowing the *kind* of girl he was looking for didn't bring us any closer to knowing her identity.

I went over to my sister's house. We talked about this and that and she showed me the latest thing Yehudit had made: a white woolen shawl, with a border of green and gold. Ravishing! I admired it so much that Penina gave it to me as a gift, though I really didn't have that in mind at the time.

Then Penina told me she was worried about her Yehudit. All her friends are getting engaged, and Chanania has been looking for a suitable young man for ages! "But he says he can't find anyone good enough for his daughter. So I tell him that anyone married to Yehudit would *have* to become good, but that's not enough for Chanania. I wish there were someone like your Baruch around here..."

I tried to console Penina. I told her that it often takes longer for some of the best girls — look at my Batya! And surely the right one would come along very soon. Yehudit has plenty of time; she's hardly more than a child! Still, I decided to speak to Elazar about it; after all, my sister's problem is mine too, isn't it?

After supper that night, Elazar turned to me and asked, "So what's on your mind? What do you want to talk to me about?"

"What makes you think I want to talk to you about anything special?" I said, trying to sound my most casual.

"Oh, something told me." Husbands! "Well, so let's have it."

"All right, Elazar. It's about Penina. She's so worried about her Yehudit because there just don't seem to be any good boys around for her. At least that's what Chanania says, but he's so critical and picky. Penina feels Yehudit can turn any young man into a decent husband. That's her side of the argument. I don't even know what they're arguing about — you'd think their daughter was an old maid!"

Elazar looked at me queerly, then shrugged. "Anything else bothering you?" he asked (at last!).

"I asked Baruch what kind of wife he'd like, and what he wants simply doesn't exist," I said. "Do you realize that our son is the only one in his group who's not married yet? He's not even engaged. And unlike his cousin, Baruch is no longer a child — far from it!

"*You're* going to have to deal with this, Elazar, because I don't know where to *begin* to look. For my brother Aaron, I went to all the weddings and celebrations, looking over all the girls. But I can't do that any more; people are limiting themselves and only inviting the immediate family to their *semachot*. So how will we ever find anyone for him?" The more I talked about it, the more worried I became.

"Hmm, now that you mention it," Elazar said, "I do have someone in mind...perhaps it will work. I'll speak to ben Perachia tomorrow." Yes, that old *shadchan* was still around, walking stick, lisp and all.

"Well, who is it?! Don't you think you should tell *me* first? After all, he's my son too. I should have some say in the matter." I was growing quite indignant.

"Don't worry, Leah. If it works out, you'll know soon enough." With that, my husband left the house and headed for the *beit knesset*. Lucky men — they always have an excuse to end a conversation.

Bright and early the next morning, ben Perachia appeared. "They agree," he declared, "and they're willing to thare all the expentheth."

"Fine," Elazar said, smiling broadly and clapping the *shadchan* on the back. "So let's all meet, and make it official."

"Would — you — kindly — tell — me — who it is?!" Does he

do these things on purpose, or does it just seem that way?

"Oh, I thought you knew," Elazar said in his most exasperating tone. "Yehudit, of course. If the young people like each other, that's it! Something tells me they will, though."

"Yehudit!" I screamed excitedly. "Who would ever have thought of her? Of course, she's our own niece, and she's lovely, and skillful too, like Batya. It's funny — I didn't used to like the name Yehudit — it's so old-fashioned. But now I love it, and it goes so well with Baruch. And she's very religious: she prays often, not just on *Yamim Tovim*..." I do tend to babble when I'm excited.

All in all, it was an excellent idea. When they became engaged, the whole town came to congratulate us. I graciously accepted their good wishes and their praise. I now had a fourth *shidduch* to my credit, and I was very happy.

34

ELAZAR SAYS HE'S GETTING too old for all this traveling back and forth. I, on the other hand, thrive on it. From the first moment after we return from visiting the grandchildren in Yavneh, I am busy shopping for toys and other surprises in preparation for our next trip. And almost any excuse will do. Whether it is for an upcoming *Yom Tov*, or a *brit*, or simply a spate of spring-like weather in the midst of the rainy season, I will drop everything and gladly endure the long journey for the pleasure of holding the babies. With three little ones, *beli ayin hara*, it's impossible for Batya to come to us, of course, so we are constantly on the move.

And despite all his grumbling, it's obvious that Elazar enjoys being a grandparent just as much as I do. You should see him with his Binyamin! Can you imagine my dignified, scholarly, even-tempered husband giving that child "donkey rides" on his back? Oh, the laughter, the sheer glee that bubbles out of that darling boy — what can I say? That's *nachat*.

On our most recent visit to Yavneh, we had an extra bit of pleasure that I'm sure you'll want to hear about: the wedding of Rachel's daughter, Nechama. Well, I don't have to tell you that I love Rachel's children like my own, and this raven-haired beauty, Nechama, perhaps most of all. So when we heard of the planned *simchah*, we scheduled a longer visit than usual so that we would be able to spend time with Batya and Yehuda and the babies, and also attend the wedding.

And what a wedding it was!

Batya said that Nechama had been engaged to Yehoshua ben Kefusai for a relatively long time. They were only awaiting her father's return from a trip to Rome to schedule the wedding. Then, it seemed, Rabi Akiva had been reluctant to agree to a date. (I could understand his reluctance after Shulamit's unpleasant experience, but I wasn't sure that had anything to do with it.) Finally the day was set for the end of the *z'man* at the yeshiva.

The preparations began. Old Kalba Savua insisted on financing the whole affair; he wanted his granddaughter's wedding to be truly splendid. The greatest men in Israel were invited, and rooms were prepared for them all over town. Cattle and sheep, lambs and kids were slaughtered for the feast. Fish — the largest I've ever seen — were brought by the local fisherman and steamed over huge kettles outdoors. Cooks and bakers were hired, and Rachel's house was filled with the smells of breads, pastries, and every kind of rare delicacy.

There was no space inside the house, large though it is, to accommodate the expected crowd, so tables were set up on the grounds. Colorful awnings, supported by poles wreathed in flowers, provided shade for the guests.

Ah, my dear, we don't have weddings like that any more! Kalba Savua spent lavishly for this occasion, and nothing was lacking from the feast.

While the reception was going on, and the waiters were rushing about, carrying platters of food and baskets of bread, a poor man came to the gate. No one heard him ask to be admitted or paid him any attention at all. Everyone was too busy to notice.

The bride, however, saw him and invited him in. With her own hands, she brought him her own portion of food, and served it to him with a smile. When he had eaten his fill, she said, "Come! We'll be honored to have you at the wedding ceremony." A true granddaughter of Kalba Savua!

In the hubbub of the preparations, no one else was aware of this incident. At last, all was ready and the marriage ceremony could begin.

The *chatan* and *kallah* stood under the *chuppah*, surrounded by a huge crowd of the noblest people in the land. A choir of children's voices, accompanied by harps and lutes, sang a sweet melody honoring the bride and groom. It was like a day in *Gan Eden*, full of beauty and happiness.

Suddenly the *kallah* felt something pricking her. It was a jeweled pin fastening her headdress. She drew it out and, without looking, stabbed it into the wall behind her, thinking to retrieve it later.

After the ceremony, a magnificent celebration took place. Rachel noticed that one of the pair of jeweled pins which her daughter had received as a wedding gift was missing from her headdress. "My dear, there's only one pin holding your veil," she said. "I wonder what could have happened to the other one?"

"Oh, I remember. I stuck it in the wall in back of the *chuppah*," Nechama answered. "I'll get it tomorrow."

The following morning Nechama went to retrieve the ornament. She appeared at her parents' house moments later, ashen-faced, with the jeweled pin in her hand. Impaled on the point of the pin was a poisonous snake — quite dead, thank God. The pin had pierced it through.

"*Baruch Hashem*," Rabi Akiva exclaimed. "You have been saved from certain death. Blessed be Hashem's holy Name! When you were born, a stargazer predicted that your wedding day would be your last." (When I heard this, I thought: So *that* was why he'd hesitated over setting the date!) "What special act of yours brought about this miraculous rescue?" he asked.

"I don't remember doing anything unusual," his daughter replied. "Oh, there was a poor fellow here yesterday evening, during the reception. No one had time to serve him, so I did. But that's nothing..."

"It's everything!" Rabi Akiva said. "I had always believed that the adage 'Charity delivers from death' refers only to a *mitah meshunah*, an unnatural death. And indeed your act of charity delivered you from such a death — death by snakebite. But your wedding day has passed and, despite the stargazer's dire prediction, you are alive and well, *baruch Hashem*. This means that *tzedakah* delivered you as well from any natural death that might have occurred during the night."

That day, you can be sure, I had Elazar donate a sizeable contribution to the *tzedakah* fund in the names of each of our children and grandchildren.

There's no point in taking chances.

35

YOU'LL NEVER GUESS what we've done: our entire family has moved to Usha! Yes, Baruch and Yehudit, Batya and Yehuda, the grandchildren, Elazar and I, and even the servants and Reuven and Rivka. Penina and Aaron and their families will be joining us soon too, *b'ezrat Hashem.* We sold everything — the estate, the herds, and many household goods that were too cumbersome to transport to the *Galil.* It was a difficult decision to make, believe me, and even more difficult to carry out, but now that all the hard work is behind me, I can truthfully say that I'm delighted we did it.

You see, Artemidorus's prediction that Domitian would not rule very long was not entirely accurate. That despicable *rasha* is still Emperor and more powerful than ever, especially since he's gotten rid of just about everyone who opposed him. The Rabbis decided it was far too dangerous for the yeshiva to continue functioning as it had in Yavneh, and so they organized its relocation to a part of the country remote from the capital.

Well, what can I say? Once it was determined that the yeshiva was moving, we really had no choice but to do the same. Traveling back and forth to Yavneh was one thing, but a journey to the *Galil* every *Yom Tov* was more than we grandparents could handle. Fortunately, we got a good price for our property, and with land values up north so much lower than in the center of the country, we were able to purchase a huge estate with plenty of space for the children and grandchildren to live with us.

Reuven knew some very clever stonemasons in the area. They renovated this old structure to suit our needs and now there's a completely separate set of rooms for each family and one very spacious room where we can all be together for *Shabbatot* and *chagim*. Perfect!

Getting here was a story in inself, but suffice it to say that I will *never* get on a camel again as long as I live! However, once we arrived, I knew it had all been worthwhile. I'd never been to this part of the country before, although I'd always heard it was beautiful. Well, "beautiful" is inadequate by far to describe the lush greenery, the sweet clear waters of the Kinneret, the fragrant valleys and forested hills, the graceful deer, and flocks of birds soaring overhead.

Elazar and the boys learn in the yeshiva, of course, but it is vastly different now from what it was back in Yavneh, and for good reason. The *metivta* and the *Nasi*'s palace were extraordinarily impressive edifices there; in fact when I first saw them I felt a bit uneasy, thinking that they might attract just the sort of attention from Rome that we did not want. But in the end, I was only partially right.

What *did* attract Rome's attention was the tumult over the *nesiut*. Rachel (who is once again my next-door neighbor, to my unending joy) told me that the trouble began not long after it was decided that the full assembly of seventy-two should not meet routinely. Once again, with no legal body to adjudicate halachic disputes, serious conflicts arose, this time between Rabi Eliezer (who was the *Chacham Hava'ad*, in charge of the enactment of *halachah l'ma'aseh*) and Rabban Gamliel the *Nasi* and Rabi Yehoshua the *Av Beit Din*. The Rabbis separated themselves from Rabi Eliezer, and he returned to his home and yeshiva in Lod with a number of his *talmidim*.

"How could they do that to such a scholar and Sage as Rabi Eliezer?" I asked, taken aback at such a drastic move.

"It all comes down to a matter of authority, Leah," Rachel replied. "Halachic decisions have always been made according to the rule of the majority of the entire Sanhedrin. Now, since the ruling body has been reduced to a fraction of its former size, Rabi Eliezer, as *Chacham Hava'ad*, did not feel compelled to abide by its decisions."

I could see her point. Rabi Eliezer's actions would seriously undermine the authority of the Sages of Yavneh. "But why should Rome care one way or the other about Rabi Eliezer being sent away?"

"That was only the beginning, Leah," she said. "After Rabi Eliezer left, the situation deteriorated further. Conflicts arose between the *Nasi* and Rabi Yehoshua — in public, no less — and the people began to demand Rabban Gamliel's removal. Without the Nation's support, the *nesiut* could not function, so obviously Rabban Gamliel had to be replaced by someone who could command everyone's respect." Rachel was quiet for a moment, her thoughts far away.

"For once, I think I can read *your* mind, Rachel," I said gently. "You felt your husband was the ideal candidate, right?"

"Oh, but he couldn't be, Leah," she said quickly. "You know his father was a *ger*, and that means he is lacking in *zechut avot*." She concealed her disappointment well, but I know Rachel better than anyone and you can be sure the denial of Rabi Akiva's candidacy had hurt her deeply. "Finally, Rabi Elazar ben Azariah was chosen."

"Rabi Elazar?!" I exclaimed. "But he's only a boy of eighteen!"

"Eighteen in years, perhaps," she said, "but like seventy in wisdom, and he has excellent *yichus*. And furthermore, he's very well-to-do."

"What does *that* have to do with anything?" I was getting quite indignant.

"Calm yourself, Leah, please. Money means influence, and we need a leader who can influence Rome on behalf of our People."

"You're right, as usual," I said, regaining my composure. "But how was it decided that Rabi Elazar would be the one?"

"The Sages felt that although it was dangerous for them all to meet publicly, the issue was too pressing to delay. So the full assembly gathered and elected the new *Nasi*, and while they were together, they settled a number of outstanding halachic disputes that had accumulated. At the same time, Rabban Gamliel and Rabi Yehoshua resolved their differences, *baruch Hashem*, and the Rabbis invited Rabban Gamliel to serve alongside Rabi Elazar as co-*Nasi*."

"I can imagine how all this to-do might have attracted Rome's attention," I said. "They must have understood that such a tremendous fuss would not be made simply to select the head of an insignificant Torah school. And once they'd taken a good look at the *Nasi*'s palace, the Romans would have known it was the Royal Residence — built right under their noses!"

"Precisely. They even began to suspect Yavneh of being our headquarters for planning a revolution. In fact, on Rosh Hashanah, when the *shofar* was blown, the Roman soldiers, who had become our ever-present watchdogs, believed we were sounding the trumpet to call the People to war!"

"*Ribbono shel Olam*! What happened then?" I immediately regretted having asked.

"It was a massacre, Leah! There was blood everywhere. Our beautiful yeshiva was defiled and countless students were the *korbanot*."

I began to tremble uncontrollably. *My children had been there!* And I'd been kept in the dark all this time. They must have agreed among themselves not to tell me about it, knowing how it would affect me. Penina and Aaron and I used to protect Imma, rest her soul, from terrible news for the same reason. Now I understood why the yeshiva here in Usha consists of only a fraction of the students and teachers that had populated *Kerem B'Yavneh*; why it is housed in an aging, crumbling structure; why *shiurim* are occasionally held in cramped attics and cellars, and sometimes even in nearby towns. Fear. Again.

Rachel took my hands in hers. "It's all right, Leah," she soothed. "We're safe here, *baruch Hashem*."

But all I could think was, Safe, yes...for the time being.

36

WHEN I HEARD THAT Rabi Akiva had left for Rome, I flew to Rachel's house. Surely she realized how dangerous conditions are today. How could she have allowed her husband to walk into the lion's den! And he'd gone *alone*! What can he hope to accomplish by himself?

"Leah, Leah," she said calmly, "it's not good for you to get so excited." And she handed me a cool drink to refresh myself.

When I had settled down a bit, Rachel said, "Although we're relatively safe here in Usha, we cannot allow ourselves to become complacent. Every effort must be made to prevent disaster, regardless of the perils. And you must have misunderstood — Akiva did not go; he could not possibly leave the yeshiva at this time. He sent a *shaliach*."

"A *shaliach*? One man, alone?! But —"

"Leah, he is a *shaliach mitzvah*; Hashem will protect him from harm. It was vital for him to go now, and far better that he not travel with a large retinue. That would only call attention to him. Things are heating up in Rome and someone reliable must be there to keep an eye on the situation and maintain contact with our Roman friends."

Rachel said that when her husband had come home to tell

her that the Sages wanted to send someone to Rome on a special mission, she knew immediately who the right man for the job was.

Her husband recognized the look on her face. "You probably have someone in mind," he had said, "and you probably have a good reason for choosing him. Who is it?"

That was just what I wanted to know. "Well, Rachel, whom *did* you have in mind?" I asked, running through a whole list of "possibles" in my head. But I was in for a shock. When she announced the nominee, I nearly fell off my seat!

Anyway, Rabi Akiva agreed to send ben Buri to Rome, and Rachel had said to him, "Now you have lifted up one of the fallen of our People. In that *zechut, Hakadosh Baruch Hu* will surely uplift you and help you to succeed in all your endeavors."

"But Rachel," I exclaimed, "ben Buri, of all people! That old meddler, that gossip peddler! Why him? Can you please explain that to me?" What reason could she possibly have had for choosing that troublemaker to represent our People? I'll never understand her, never!

"If you knew his whole story," Rachel said quietly, "you would understand. He's had a very hard life..."

"What! Standing around in the street, minding everyone's business? You call that a hard life!?" But I couldn't help smiling at Rachel. After all these years she was still finding excuses for everyone.

"Please promise me to keep this a secret — at least until he returns." I nodded at once. I knew Rachel wasn't going to speak *lashon hara*, but at the same time I knew that what she was about to reveal would be special — she had never sworn me to secrecy before! Had I remembered to tell the servants to hang up the linens to dry before I left home, I wondered, or were they lying in the basket getting wrinkled? Oh, who cares! "I'm only telling you this to correct your bad impression of that man," Rachel said. "There was a reason ben Buri was always asking so many questions. Back in those days, he was a spy for the Romans —"

"What!" You could have knocked me over with a feather. "Him — a spy!? And you've sent him on this mission —" I was aghast.

"Leah, listen. He was all alone, no wife, no children. And no one would give him work because he wasn't strong, and he looked much older than he actually was. So when one of *them* approached him, and offered to pay him well just for watching the crossroads and stopping wayfarers to find out what was going on, he agreed..."

Well! That explained a lot of things. Still... "But how is it that he's here with you? I never noticed him. And I always thought he hated you! So now you pick *him* to go to Rome? What can you be thinking of, Rachel?"

Rachel gave me that sweet smile. "He told me that he *did* hate us, at first," she said. "He'd always felt sorry for himself — no money, no education, no family — and he blamed that for all his troubles in life. And then along comes a poor shepherd, a man no better than he, who has the temerity to go off and learn! *And* he has a wife, and then children, too! Ben Buri just couldn't bear it. Yes, he felt bitter towards us for a long time. But then, he told me, because I was the only one who ever treated him decently, he started to change. When Akiva came back after twelve years, and I never reproached ben Buri for what he did then, he began to feel remorseful."

"All right, Rachel, so he started doing *teshuvah.* But what about —"

"Wait until I tell you the rest. Remember when Akiva came back to Geva with all the *talmidim*?" (How could I forget?) "Well, ben Buri came to me, with tears in his eyes, and begged to be my husband's servant — 'his devoted slave,' he said. And ever since then he's been with us, helping out with small things like mending the fence before we've even noticed that it was broken. And he has always been careful to stay out of the way. We almost never saw him working — we would just wake up in the morning to find some annoying little chore already done.

"Later on, during the war," she continued, "he helped our side by carrying messages, risking his life again and again. But the Romans never suspected him; they believed he was still part of their spy network because he carried the documents to prove it.

"So when I heard about this mission to Rome, I immediately thought of ben Buri. He knows their language and the lay of the land, and he has many contacts there. Besides, I knew it would make him so happy..."

"Rachel," I said, "what ever made me think you're impractical and unworldly? Why, you're just the opposite. You're like our ancestress Rivkah — you have the eyes that see clearly what others cannot see at all..."

So ben Buri went to Rome and, as it turned out, it was the best thing that could have happened. No one ever suspected that he had any connection with our People. He did have contacts everywhere, and through some of them we were kept informed about events almost as soon as they occurred. Messages were carried back and forth by the most unlikely *shelichim* and we were spared much anxiety. But we didn't realize until much later what a good plan it was — and all her idea!

The Ben Buri Express Mail Service was amazingly efficient and Rachel received regular reports. He wrote in a peculiar kind of code, addressing each installment "To my dear Auntie" and referring to his master as "the shepherd," to the *Nesi'im* as "the brothers," and so forth. The code was simple enough for us to decipher, and this way Rabi Akiva and the Sages were protected in case the mail was intercepted. Rachel and I managed to piece together the following from those reports:

The journey to Rome had been blessedly uneventful, but upon his arrival ben Buri learned that Domitian had become even more insane and wicked, if such were possible. No one was safe. The executions had continued without letup, and tension was high throughout the city. Several former friends of the Jews had been killed; others had gone into hiding. At great risk to himself, the philosopher Artemidorus agreed to see our *shaliach*, but ben Buri had had to reveal his true identity to Artemidorus, thereby placing himself at risk as well.

"There is virtually nothing I can do to help you," Artemidorus said regretfully. "I surely have no sway with that madman and it is only a matter of time before he sets in motion his evil plan to annihilate your People. Until now he has been preoccupied with eliminating his local adversaries and has satisfied himself with exacting intolerable taxes from Judea and the other provinces. But he is bound to run out of Roman victims soon. I am not one to advocate violence; however, Domitian needs to be assassinated, and the sooner the better."

"Are any of our allies still alive?" ben Buri asked. "Or do you know of anyone who might be encouraged to support our cause?"

Artemidorus thought for a moment. "I have been told that the next on the executioner's list is Marcus Cocceius Nerva," he said. "He is old, well-liked among the members of the Senate, and respected by all. If he is killed, then no one is safe. If you can get the message to Nerva, I'm certain that the senators will rally behind him and find a way to get rid of Domitian. And there is another one who might help..."

"Who is that? I must try all possible channels!"

"The Emperor's kinsman, Flavius Clemens. He and his wife, Domitilla, have long been suspected of wanting to convert. Perhaps they have done so already. I've heard that whenever your Rabbi Akiva visits Rome, Clemens makes a point of seeing him. Since Flavius Clemens is the Consul, second only to the Emperor, he may be able to sway the Senate in your favor. It's worth trying."

Ben Buri went first to the house of the great senator Marcus Cocceius Nerva, where he was reluctantly admitted by a surly manservant. In the antechamber, waiting for the senator, ben Buri silently prayed for guidance.

The senator entered. He had recognized ben Buri's name from his spying days and had therefore agreed to see him, but ben Buri hardly recognized *him*. Nerva had aged considerably. His face was deeply marked with many fine lines, and his thin gray hair was combed forward in the Roman fashion. "I can only give you a few minutes," he said importantly. "You must realize I'm a very busy man. All the cares of government..."

"I won't take much of your time," ben Buri said. "I've come to warn you: your name is next on the Emperor's list."

The senator's face turned white, and he grasped the arm of a chair to steady himself. "How did you find this out?" His voice, which had been so full of self-assurance, was suddenly weak and tremulous.

"It's my business to find things out," ben Buri said, "and this I heard from someone who is completely reliable. I came here immediately so that you could take steps to save yourself."

"But what ever made you come?" Nerva asked. "Why should you endanger yourself to help me?"

"Because I am a Jew. Of our People the Almighty has said: 'And all the nations of the earth shall bless themselves in you.' We are obliged to care for the well-being of our fellowmen. But there is another reason for my coming here: I was sent by the Sages of Israel to enlist your aid. Domitian despises my People; he has threatened to annihilate all the Jews in the Empire. He is our common enemy — perhaps together we can find a way to defeat him." Ben Buri stood silent, awaiting Nerva's reply.

But the senator, too, was silent. He nervously pulled at the loop of his toga, looking around the room as if help were to be found in the rich furnishings or the heavy tapestries.

"And what do you advise me to do to save my life?" he finally asked.

"That I cannot tell you. I hear you're popular among the senators — surely they'll realize that if it can happen to you, a man who is so well-liked, it can happen to them as well. Speak to your friends. Perhaps they can think of a plan."

"You are right. I will consult with my fellow senators. Too many have been executed by the Emperor in the past year. I thought I'd be able to pass my old age peacefully; instead, I'm being hunted like an aging stag in the forest. Still, the astrologers have told me that I'll die quietly in my own bed." Nerva was now much calmer.

"If that's what the stargazers said," ben Buri exclaimed, "then you must tell it to the Emperor! He's very superstitious, I'm told, so he'll be afraid to tamper with your fate."

"Blessings upon you, Jew," said Nerva. "You will be well rewarded if your advice proves to be good."

'It's not reward I seek," ben Buri replied. "But if you should ever reach a position of power, my masters beg that you be gracious to our People. They bade me to say: the Almighty will be gracious to you if you will protect the Jews of the Empire."

There was no faulting ben Buri's reporting, even if he did exaggerate a bit, which I suspected he did. His selection as Rabi Akiva's *shaliach* had been absolutely inspired, and I congratulated Rachel on her foresight. Who else could have gained access to the Roman upper classes? And who could have been so clever about getting word to us?

I didn't know that we were in for a long delay before we'd hear from Rome again.

37

DAYS PASSED, THEN WEEKS, and we still hadn't gotten any new reports. I was tearing my hair out and biting my nails to the quick, but Rachel was impassive. "Ben Buri is in Hashem's service, Leah," she said, "and He will watch over him." At last, three letters came together, one with a peddler, one with a troupe of traveling jugglers, and one with a camel driver in a caravan of Arabs. This batch of correspondence made us all painfully aware of how truly dangerous the situation was in Rome.

On the day Nerva received ben Buri's warning, the members of the Senate Secret Council were summoned to the Emperor's palace. His custom was to treat prospective victims in an especially charming and friendly manner, so when Marcus Cocceius Nerva entered the room, the evil Domitian embraced him and kissed him, and held his hand longer than usual.

"Nerva, my dear friend! You look so sad and depressed. Is it possible that there is something troubling you?"

"Yes, gracious Emperor. I am indeed sad. The stargazers have forecast that my life will soon be over."

The Emperor tried unsuccessfully to hide a smile. "Your words cause me great sorrow, dearest friend," he said facetiously. "Let us hope that, although the stars are never in error regarding human fate, the stargazers' reading of them will prove wrong in your case. Have they also predicted the manner of your death?"

"Here," said Nerva, exhibiting an elaborately drawn chart which he extracted from the folds of his toga. "This is the forecast which was made by the Chaldean stargazers at the time of my birth."

Domitian looked at the horoscope, paying special attention to the final part. "It is true," he said. "It seems that the stars predict your death within a short time. But your star seems to descend while still shining brightly. That means you will die peacefully in your bed, with no disturbance or misfortune to spoil your few remaining days. May you enjoy the time allotted to you, dear friend!"

Nerva drew a breath of profound relief. He knew the Emperor through and through, and was convinced he would not do anything that might challenge the forecast of the astrologers. Ben Buri's advice had proved correct: Nerva had gotten his reprieve.

Now Domitian mounted his throne. Reclining on lounges as was their custom, the senators were assembled before him, awaiting their Emperor's commands.

"My friends," he began, "what shall a man do when he suffers a painful sore on his foot? Should he leave the infection alone until it has spread through his entire body and brought him to his death, or should he take a sharp knife and cut it out, thereby saving his life?"

The senators sat in silence. No one wished to be the first to answer. They knew well their ruler's terrible and capricious temper; one wrong word, one wrong gesture, might mean death.

Finally, Mauricius, one of the younger men whom the

Emperor had once favored, but not too much, plucked up his courage. "Surely Your Imperial Majesty alludes to some other matter. Naturally, everyone understands that the boil must be lanced and excised completely. That way the whole body will be saved."

"You have grasped my meaning precisely, Mauricius. Now, you all know that the religion of our ancestors is in great jeopardy. In Rome, many are beginning to doubt the power of Jupiter, and my gracious patroness Minerva is not getting the homage which is her due. I have driven the philosophers from the city, for they have been misleading our youth, poisoning their minds with their false teachings. But there are far more dangerous enemies in our midst, and we benignly tolerate them!

"Who are these enemies? The Jews!

"Unlike all other nations, the Jews do not worship the gods. The gods of the Chaldeans, the Greeks, the Gauls, the Germans are like our own; only their names differ. But those Jews have no gods before whom they bow down. They worship instead some invisible thing, a being with neither body nor form. And they have always been the enemies of the Roman Empire. My father conquered their land and Titus, my brother, burned their Temple to the ground. Still, they persist in worshiping their invisible being, and even worse, some of our own people are embracing that accursed religion, in defiance of my edicts. The Jews are a festering sore on the foot of our holy Empire, and we must excise them before the infection spreads and destroys our entire domain."

The senators nodded in agreement. "Kill the Jews!" they declared in unison.

"Yes, my colleagues, this cancer must be removed completely; not the tiniest trace of it shall remain to further poison our citizens! Every Jew in the Empire, whether in Rome itself, or in Judea, Egypt, Syria, Greece or Spain, every man, woman and child shall be exterminated, like the vermin they are.

"Since we are all agreed, we may begin to carry out the plan that will restore the Empire to good health. The Jews will be annihilated. All property belonging to Jews will be confiscated by the State. Their dwelling places will be plowed into the earth, so that there will remain no remembrance of them forever after."

Again the senators cheered. Then Flavius Clemens, the Emperor's Consul, rose to speak. "Permit me, great and glorious Caesar..."

"I warn you, Clemens," the Emperor said in the slow and pleasant voice that signaled his most dangerous moods, "don't try my patience! I have received reports about you: You have been secretly associating with their clerics; you have been studying their heretical writings. If your wife were not my kin, if I had not once considered your sons my worthy successors, you would not be here today."

Despite Domitian's warning, Clemens dared to speak. "Great and gracious Caesar!" he began again. "You are my kinsman; my wife Domitilla is your niece. We ask you, for the sake of your father, to whom you were so devoted, do not do this terrible deed! You will never be able to destroy them all, in any case; they are everywhere. In their Scripture it is written: 'For like the four winds I have scattered you.'"

"You speak in riddles, Clemens," Domitian scoffed. "This only proves that their God cares as little for them as I do; that's why he scattered these wretches throughout my Empire."

"No, Caesar, not only throughout the Empire, but throughout the entire world. And there is additional meaning to that verse. If it only meant that the Jews were scattered, the verse would read: '*to* the four winds.' But it says '*like* the four winds,' meaning that just as the world cannot exist without the four winds, the world cannot exist without the Jews. It was not because their God cares little for them that he scattered them; it was because he regards them so highly."

"Well then," Domitian countered, "I shall have to be content with their eradication from my domain, and as the Empire expands, I will see to it that their numbers decrease."

"If you attempt to destroy the Jews," Clemens replied, "the God of Israel will take vengeance upon you and your Empire will be destroyed. It will become known throughout the world as the 'truncated nation,' the nation from which the Jews were cut off. There is still time! I beg you to reconsider!"

A murmur of dissent rose in the senate chamber. No one wanted the Empire to go down in history with its honor so badly tarnished.

Domitian silenced the assemblage and nonchalantly popped a grape into his mouth. "You may be right, Clemens, but you seem quite agitated. Why should the fate of these wretched people concern you at all? Unless you're one of them! Don't bother denying it. Now I advise you to withdraw your argument, for you know the penalty for besting your Emperor in a debate. It is a crime punishable by death in a house filled with sand.

"Think carefully, my dear Consul," Domitian threatened. "You have one last chance to recant. If not, you will be arrested and dragged to prison like a common criminal. You will be sentenced — by your own fellow senators! — and you will serve as an example to any others who might foolishly consider abandoning our ancient gods and challenging Caesar's authority. You will be as dust under the chariot wheels of history!"

Flavius stood erect, his head held high, and drew a deep breath. "My argument is irrefutable, as even you, mighty Emperor, have attested. I shall not withdraw it."

"Seize him!" Domitian roared, and his guards quickly surrounded Flavius and marched him out of the palace.

While all this was going on, ben Buri had gone to the Consul's home to enlist his aid, as Artemidorus had suggested. There he was told that Clemens was attending a special session of the Senate and so he quickly made his way to the Forum.

As he approached, he saw that a great crowd had gathered. He slipped in among the people. All were talking excitedly about the Emperor's Consul being sentenced to death. "Their eyes glittered," ben Buri wrote, "in anticipation of witnessing the execution."

Edging toward the front rows of the throng, ben Buri was soon in position, and when the phalanx of guards came close, he thrust a hastily scrawled note into Flavius's hand. The note read: "Rabbi Akiva and the Sages of Israel bless the one who has brought salvation to our People."

Flavius gripped the note tightly and then, before the astonished eyes of the Roman masses, he circumcised himself! He searched the crowd for ben Buri and when his gaze fell upon our *shaliach* he declared: "All my possessions I bequeath to your master, the great Rabbi Akiva, and his colleagues, the illustrious Sages of Israel. Tell them that I, Flavius Clemens, gave my life so that Israel may live." The guards brutally shoved him into the house of sand where he died a horrible death. Not once did he cry out.

"When the soul of Flavius Clemens ascended," ben Buri's report concluded, "a Heavenly Voice was heard. 'Ketiah bar Shalom,' it said, 'has earned a place in the World to Come.'"

Rachel explained that this new name was Divinely ordained for Flavius, a name which glorified his courageous act and his just reward.

38

THE NEWS OF Flavius Clemens's execution spread like wildfire, ben Buri wrote, and all of Rome was seized with terror and wonder. The Emperor's kinsman, the Consul, husband of the Emperor's niece — had died a Jew, giving up his life for his ideals. The city was in turmoil. And now they were preparing for elections for a new Consul to take Clemens's place. Many wanted the honor, it seemed, although they knew it might cost them dearly, perhaps even cost them their lives.

So now the political campaign was in full swing. It was to be a general election, with every Roman citizen entitled to vote, and in the streets and marketplaces all conversation centered on the candidates. But the Jews of Rome sat trembling in their houses. Domitian's evil design was now public knowledge and although he had been prevented from carrying it out, the delay was only temporary.

Through his contacts, ben Buri learned that a secret meeting of some of the key senators was called at the home of Marcus Cocceius Nerva, with only one item on the agenda: to find some way of getting rid of Domitian. The senators were terrified; if word of their plot leaked out, the Emperor would have them put to death, but not before subjecting them to horrible tortures. There was no doubt that he had to be assassinated, but they could not risk an unsuccessful attempt. Even if they succeeded, they'd have to face the vengeance of the legionnaires; the Emperor had always treated his soldiers generously, both in the matter of salaries and of dividing the spoils of war, and they were completely loyal to him.

And if, against all odds, the senators' plot should succeed, who would be the new Emperor? There were no heirs, no relatives left. In the vacuum left by his demise, another power-mad tyrant might seize the throne. No, they would first have to choose Domitian's successor.

They talked and discussed and argued, back and forth, back and forth, but could come to no conclusion. No one wanted the honor of taking Domitian's place.

Then the aged Cocceius Nerva arose, and spoke in a trembling voice: "I am old and had hoped to pass the time remaining to me in peace and quiet. I wish that one of you would assume the burden of state. However, since I surely do not have long to live, I am willing to take the risks. If your choice falls upon me, I will accept and devote the remainder of my life to the good of the Empire."

The Senators congratulated Nerva, without a trace of envy. They were relieved, though still fearful. They still had no concrete plan for eliminating Domitian, but there was satisfaction in knowing that their murdered colleagues would soon be avenged and that the Empire would be ruled by someone worthy of their respect.

Domitian, as if aware that his days were numbered, became like a raging beast. He had the head of the palace guard arrested and killed, together with some of his own spies; the Emperor had become suspicious of them too, and had set others to spy on them. Even the lowest servant in the palace now trembled in fear.

Then one young palace employee found a scrap of parchment hidden behind a tapestry in the Emperor's antechamber.

It was a list of new victims, and the first name on it was Domitia, the Emperor's own wife. Next was Parthenius, his most trusted servant.

"I never dreamed it would come to this," the Empress said when she was shown the list. "It was always someone else. I was happy when he got rid of Clemens — he might have stood in my way later, with his stupid Jewish morals. But that Domitian should have the audacity to do *this*! We must find someone to kill him, and quickly!"

"You have spoken truly!" Parthenius agreed. And together they plotted the Emperor's assassination.

The election day for the new Consul had been set for the eighteenth day of the Roman month September, which coincided with our *Tishrei*. Throughout the days of *Elul*, the prayer houses were full to capacity, and on Rosh Hashanah, the wail of the *shofar* was a cry from the heart of every Jew, pleading for Hashem's mercy. The Emperor had announced that immediately after the selection of the new Consul, a vote on the fate of the Jews would be taken. It was no surprise that the eighteenth of September — the day the verdict would be sealed — was Yom Kippur. Domitian was not only mad, we told ourselves, but he was also a fool; he believed we'd be most vulnerable on that day, when in fact, the opposite was true.

The Yom Kippur prayers took on an extra special meaning for all of us and I can't remember ever reciting them with such fervor. The Rabbis composed special supplications for the occasion, just as Rabi Akiva had once done to end a terrible drought. His prayers had caused the floodgates of Heaven to open; perhaps ours too would be answered.

"*Avinu Malkenu* — our Father, our King! Nullify all evil decrees against us;

"Our Father, our King! Nullify the plans of those who despise us;

"Our Father, our King! Make the counsel of our enemies of no effect;

"Our Father, our King! Rid us of every oppressor and adversary...

"*Avinu Malkenu!....*"

In Cologne, a stargazer named Mardonius predicted that the Emperor would be assassinated in the fifth hour of the eighteenth day of September. When Domitian heard this, he consulted his own astrologists and they disputed Mardonius. So Domitian ordered that Mardonius be arrested and brought in chains to Rome, where he was sentenced to death by hanging.

Mardonius only laughed. "I will not die by the hangman's rope," he declared. "The stars have foretold that I will be torn to pieces by dogs." So the Emperor ordered that he be burned at the stake.

Mardonius was bound to a stake in the marketplace and a great pile of wood was heaped up around him. When many spectators had assembled, the pile was set alight. Flames flared up all around Mardonius, and the smell of burning flesh rose in the air. At almost the same moment, there was a tremendous cloudburst. Rains poured down from the heavens in rivers, and swiftly extinguished the fire. Seizing the opportunity, the soothsayer freed himself from the scorched ropes, and threw himself at the Emperor's feet, but just then a pack of wild dogs appeared and tore his body to pieces.

The color drained from Domitian's face (ben Buri's report said), but not from weakness at the sight of blood. If Mardonius had accurately prophesied his own fate, would not his prediction about the Emperor also come true?

Domitian spent the following days and nights in terror. He permitted no one near him. All his food was first given to servants to taste, and only then, when he saw that it was safe, would he nibble a morsel. The rest he sent back, untouched.

On the eighteenth of September, the Jews all over the Empire were in their synagogues, fasting and praying, imploring Hashem for mercy and for a good verdict, while Domitian paced anxiously in his room. When the fifth hour passed and he found himself still very much alive, he was seized by a mood of crazed elation. He clapped his hands and danced for joy: he had triumphed over fate itself!

The Emperor ordered that a bath be drawn for him, and that fresh clothing be laid out. He called for a meal to be prepared and brought to him at once.

It was the last order he was to issue. At Domitia's command, the Emperor's own bodyguards stabbed him to death.

With lightning speed, the word spread through Rome. The senators, who had assembled for the election, greeted the death of the tyrant with shouts of joy. They cursed and vilified him and smashed the statue of Domitian which stood in the Senate chamber.

All over the city the Emperor's portraits were pulled down, and his standards broken and trampled in the dust. The populace that had cheered him and honored him as a god only the day before, now sought to erase every trace of his memory.

And when the excitement had died down, the senators hastened to bestow the highest honor in the land upon Marcus Cocceius Nerva. He was proclaimed Caesar, Emperor of Rome and all her possessions.

The Jews of Rome were still in the synagogue and the Day of Atonement was drawing to an end, when the din of rejoicing over Domitian's death was heard in the streets. "He is dead!" the people were screaming. "Domitian is dead! The Emperor is dead! Long live the new Emperor!"

The Jews prostrated themselves on the ground and cried out seven times: "*Hashem, Hu HaElokim!* — Hashem is the Almighty!"

The reign of Emperor Nerva did not begin tranquilly. Domitian's loyal legionnaires avenged their ruler's death by killing Parthenius and Maximus, who were the primary perpetrators of the assassination. (Those Romans can take a life like you or I can take a headache potion, with no more thought or hesitation or concern about the consequences. I started to count up all the Romans who had been put to death during the period of ben Buri's mission alone, but I had to stop. It's much too awful to think about. Even if they *were* Romans, they were still human beings created in Hashem's image!) There was an attempt by Calpurnius Crassus to overthrow Nerva and seize the throne, but order was soon restored.

Finally, it appeared that peace had come to the land. Nerva was indeed a benevolent ruler and he did fulfill his pledge. He rescinded the unjust laws and recalled to Rome those whom Domitian had banished. But for Domitilla, it was too late; the wife of Flavius Clemens had died of grief in exile on the isle of Pandateria.

The new Emperor called for ben Buri and received him in the palace with great honor. "Now I can repay the good that you have done for me," Nerva said. "Your warning saved my life — I will never forget!"

I breathed a sigh of relief as Rachel read the last of ben Buri's reports. That fellow had certainly acquitted himself well, and I congratulated my friend once again on her foresight. "Do you think we'll really see peace now, Rachel?" It was hard to imagine, after living in terror for what seemed an eternity.

Rachel gave me one of her enigmatic smiles. "Leah, we are like clay in the potter's hands. He shapes our destiny according to His will. For now, let us rejoice that our heartfelt prayers have been answered, but we must never, ever forget how close we came to tragedy."

39

UPON RECEIVING WORD that Nerva had been crowned Emperor, the Sages immediately organized a delegation to Rome, to plead our cause. For once, there was hope that we would have a receptive audience.

With Emperor Nerva as old and, apparently, as sick as he is, there was reason to hasten. Who knows how long his reign might last? So, although it was almost Sukkot, Rabban Gamliel, Rabi Elazar ben Azariah, Rabi Yehoshua and, of course, Rabi Akiva rushed off to greet the new Caesar.

"How will we know what's happening?" I asked Rachel anxiously. "Ben Buri has spoiled us with his terrific reports."

"Akiva promised he would write as often as possible," she said, "and the delegates will meet ben Buri in Rome. I'm sure he won't let us down."

Frankly, I was less confident, so when Rachel appeared at my doorstep with a long letter in her hand and a smile on her face, I was taken by surprise. We sat down to read it together.

After leaving Usha, the Sages' first stop was Jerusalem, where they visited the site of the ruined Temple. Even though it was very much out of their way, they couldn't leave *Eretz*

Yisrael before seeing the Holy City one more time and praying for the success of their mission.

When they climbed the hill, and the dreadful scene of destruction unfolded before them, their eyes overflowed with tears. The massive stone walls had been torn down, and the area was strewn with rubble. The Romans had used some of the blocks as paving stones, for people and animals to step on. Such a desecration!

From the cracks between the stones, thorn bushes had sprouted, forming a tangle of brambles. Only a portion of the western wall that surrounded the Temple Mount remained intact, but all of that glorious edifice was gone, shattered and defiled by the invaders. Thistles now grew in the place where the *kohanim* had brought the sacrifices. The vessels of the Temple, of course, were gone; they had long since been carried off to Rome, to be used for their idolatrous ceremonies. Nothing was left of the former splendor; all around them the earth was covered with a deep layer of ash.

(Rachel started to cry when she read this, and so did I. Oh, the awful desolation!) The Sages rent their garments in mourning. Suddenly, a fox scampered out of the innermost part of the ruins, the place where the *Kodesh Hakodashim* had been. Rabban Gamliel, Rabi Yehoshua, and Rabi Elazar ben Azariah wailed in anguish at the sight of this wild beast in what had been the Holy of Holies. But Rabi Akiva *laughed.*

They turned to him, aghast. "How can you laugh, Akiva, here in this place of death and destruction?"

Rabi Akiva replied with a question: "And you, my masters, why do you cry?"

"The *Kodesh Hakodashim,*" they answered, "which was entered only by the *Kohen Hagadol,* in purity and holiness, only one day each year, has become a lair of foxes; the place about which it is written: 'The stranger who comes near shall be put to death,' and now wild animals roam freely over it. Should not our eyes overflow with tears?"

"My teachers," Rabi Akiva said, "that is the very reason why I am laughing. It is written in Scripture: 'And I will take true witnesses, Uriah the Priest and Zechariah, the son of Berechiah.' What is the connection between these two? Was not Uriah at the time of the First Temple, and Zechariah at the time of the Second Temple?

"Concerning Uriah, it is written: 'In truth, because of you, Zion will be plowed like a field, Jerusalem will be a desert, and the Temple Mount like the forested heights.' But in *Zechariah* it is written: 'Thus spoke the Eternal One: I will return to Zion, and dwell in the center of Jerusalem; then Jerusalem will be called the city of truth, and the mountain of the Lord of Hosts the holy mountain. There shall yet sit old men and women in the open places of Jerusalem, leaning on their staffs because of their great age; and the streets of Jerusalem will be full of boys and girls playing in the open places.'

"Do you see, my teachers? As long as Uriah's prophecy was not fulfilled, I was afraid that Zechariah's, too, would not be. But now that we see that the Temple Mount has indeed become a forest, a lair of foxes, as Hashem declared through Uriah, we know that He will rebuild His Holy Temple and His Holy City, as He promised through His prophet Zechariah."

The Sages agreed. "You have comforted us, Akiva," they said, "you have comforted us."

Full of hope and confidence, they continued their journey. They boarded ship in Yaffo and Rabi Akiva immediately began to build a *sukkah*. Rabban Gamliel argued that a *sukkah* on a boat is unacceptable, but Rabi Akiva built one all the same. The following day, it was toppled by a strong wind.

I wanted to ask Rachel if this meant that Rabban Gamliel was correct, but decided it would not be tactful. We read on.

With or without a *sukkah*, the Sages were determined to observe the *chag* as best they could. Although they had spared no time for elaborate preparations before their departure, they apparently had managed to acquire a *lulav* along the way.

Rabi Akiva wrote that Rabban Gamliel had paid *a thousand zuz* for it, and each of the Sages used it in turn to fulfill the *mitzvah.*

When the Rabbis arrived in Rome, a great feast was being held to celebrate Nerva's victory. The din was overwhelming: screaming, singing, trumpets blaring, cymbals clanging, the tramp of countless marching feet. Three of the Sages stopped, and again tears came to their eyes. But again Rabi Akiva did not weep. Instead, there was a smile on his face.

"Why do you smile?" they asked him.

And Rabi Akiva said: "Why do you weep?"

"These heathens," the Rabbis answered, "who bow to abominations and sacrifice to idols, are living safely and soundly, while we witness the House which was the Footstool of Hashem, burnt by fire. How can we not cry?"

"That is the very reason I am smiling," Rabi Akiva said. "If Hashem shows kindness to those who daily transgress His laws, how much more goodness must there be in store for His servants who live according to His will!"

Again the Sages agreed. "You have comforted us, Akiva," they said, "you have comforted us!"

Among Nerva's first decrees as Emperor was a new law concerning slander: slanderous or libelous accusations would not be accepted at face value; they would have to be proven by positive evidence and investigated thoroughly before any action would be taken. The best-known slander of the day, of course, was directed at our religion, and the Sages were instantly deluged by Romans with questions about our faith in Hashem. They took this as a positive sign and they were more convinced than ever that they would be welcomed warmly by the new Caesar.

And they were right. They were hailed into the palace as visiting dignitaries should be, and brought before the Emperor. Nerva greeted them graciously and declared that the

Jews would have increased rights. He promised to see to our welfare, and not to hinder our religious observance. He showed the delegation a new coin which was soon to be minted, proclaiming his new policy. It was inscribed: "*Fisci Judaica calumnia sublata* — The injustice of the Jewish tax is withdrawn."

The Sages thanked the Emperor, and gave him their blessing. Then, at last, they set out on the long journey home.

You can imagine the jubilation in Judea when the delegation returned from Rome. But no, unless you had been there to see it, you cannot possibly. The Sages' report of all that had happened was greeted with unrestrained excitement and a tremendous surge of hope for the future. Word spread to every corner of the land within a few days. In the marketplace, the shopkeepers had no time to attend to their customers, and the customers had no time to shop. They were all busy talking about Rabi Akiva and Rabban Gamliel, and Rabi Yehoshua and Rabi Elazar. Everyone wanted to hear about the debates with the Romans on Judaism.

Ben Buri, needless to say, enjoyed his role as "man of the hour," reporting everything in great detail to anyone who would listen.

Of course, I was in a special position to know more of the events in Rome than almost anyone else, but even I took pleasure in hearing about them from those who had witnessed it all in person. It made everything seem more real.

And now, for the first time in years, there is talk of reestablishing the *metivta* in Yavneh.

I suppose everyone senses, as I do, that we've come to the end of an era. The frightful and exciting things that have taken place in the last few months have really fired up the people: all the news coming from Rome; the conspiracies, the intrigue, the threat of annihilation, and finally the death of the tyrant, Domitian, *yimmach shemo*. Imagine, the ruler of almost the entire world, and he was a madman! It's a terrifying thought, that a brute like that could attain such tremendous power.

And what about Flavius Clemens? You know, I cry every time I think of him. Would we — I mean Elazar and myself — be capable of such sacrifice? Elazar, maybe: being with Rabi Akiva so much and modeling himself after him, Elazar has elevated himself; he is becoming quite famous in his own right for his Torah knowledge, and his character has always been impeccable. Yes, he is capable of great things.

And I? Well, I've improved a lot over the years, I know that. But compared to Rachel, I'm like a faint reflection in a hand mirror on the far side of a tremendous hall. I pray to the Almighty that we will never be tested. I'm afraid that I might fail.

As for the *metivta* moving back to Yavneh, I don't have to tell you that I have mixed feelings. Here in Usha, the yeshiva is, well, modest (to put it kindly), so of course I understand the yearning to return it to its former glory. But even if we now have a ruler who is truly benevolent, everyone knows he's ancient and unwell. What if, *chas v'shalom*, his successor is not... Oh, it's too horrible to contemplate.

If the yeshiva does return to Yavneh, I'm sure my children will, too. Elazar and I, however, will remain where we are. We're too old for all this upheaval — packing and unpacking and getting settled all over again — and we're very comfortable and content here in the *Galil*.

I can't imagine what our life will be like without the children and grandchildren close by, or what it will mean to me to be separated from Rachel again — for she would certainly want to be wherever her husband is — but I guess we'll just have to manage somehow.

PART THREE

... do not desist...

40

ONE OF THE PROBLEMS with keeping a journal is that you have got to *keep* it — that is, write everything down as it happens. Otherwise, you end up as I do, having to rack your memory to try and reconstruct all the events you forgot to record which led up to the one you want to write about. Now, I don't know about you, but my memory is not what it once was, so you'll have to bear with me.

What prompted me to pick up my journal again after all these years was — as it has often been — my recent visit to Rachel, this time in Bnei Brak, where her husband has established his own yeshiva. Of course, I must tell you how that came about.

Things had been looking up for a while when Nerva became Emperor, and the *metivta* did move back to Yavneh, but the return to glory was short-lived. Today the future is as uncertain for us Jews as it ever was. Oh, to have our own rulers once more! Why must we forever be at the mercy of one foreign sovereign or another? Judea is like some bauble, to be played with or cast aside at the whim of a power-mad Caesar. No one is ever neutral on the subject of the Jews.

The benevolent rule of Emperor Nerva unfortunately

lasted only sixteen months. Since he had no children, he adopted Marcus Ulpius Trajan as his successor, and while Nerva had been kind and tolerant, the new Emperor was not well-disposed towards us at all. The brief respite was over.

Trajan loved war and glory. He conquered many provinces, built harbors, bridges and highways, so that merchandise could be transported from one part of the Empire to another. Before he could embark on a campaign of foreign conquest, however, he had to be certain of the loyalty of his subjects. And when he examined the various provinces in the Empire, he found that formerly submissive Judea was undergoing a revitalization.

It was obvious to Trajan that the yeshiva in Yavneh, and the *nesiut* of Rabban Gamliel in particular, were at the core of our renaissance, so he passed a law abolishing the *metivta*. I had hoped this would mean a return to Usha (I get to see the children so rarely now), but the Rabbis decided it was best to disperse. Many of them, including Rabban Gamliel and Rabi Akiva, relocated to Lod, where Rabi Tarfon already had a *beit midrash*. There, they hoped, they could live as private citizens and still be a part of an existing yeshiva without attracting any attention.

From time to time, when there was a need to resolve halachic issues, the five elders — Rabban Gamliel and Rabi Elazar ben Azariah, the co-*Nesi'im*, Rabi Yehoshua, the *Av Beit Din*, Rabi Akiva and Rabi Tarfon — would meet. The situation was far from ideal, but at least, until Rabban Gamliel's passing, we didn't find ourselves with an accumulation of unresolved disputes.

I must digress to tell you a story Elazar brought back after visiting Rabban Gamliel's family during the *shivah*. You know how people always bring up remembered incidents about the *niftar* at the house of mourning? Well, this one happened back in Yavneh, not very long after the *Churban*, at the wedding of Rabban Gamliel's son.

All the great men of Israel had come to the wedding feast, and Rabban Gamliel stood to pour wine for Rabi Eliezer, Rabi Yehoshua and Rabi Tzadok. When Rabi Eliezer saw this, he became indignant. "How can we sit and allow the Prince to stand and serve us?" he demanded.

Rabi Yehoshua said, "About Avraham *Avinu*, it is written: 'He set it before them, and he stood next to them.' And all the time, Avraham thought his three guests were only passing Arabs, idol-worshipers. Therefore, why should not the great Rabban Gamliel serve us?"

Then Rabi Tzadok spoke to them angrily. "How long will you neglect the honor of the *Ribbono shel Olam*, and regard only the honor of men?!" he exclaimed. "The Almighty causes the wind to blow, the clouds to ascend, the rain to fall, and the wheat to grow; He sets a table before *everyone*. Why, then, should Rabban Gamliel not stand and serve us?"

I was very impressed with this story. It showed that despite the great honors bestowed upon Rabban Gamliel, as is the *Nasi*'s due, despite the opulent palace, the clothes, the servants, he retained his humility, just as his grandfather Rabban Gamliel Hazaken had.

It wasn't long after Rabban Gamliel's *petirah* that Rabi Eliezer became ill. His colleagues hurried to his bedside in Caesarea, where he had gone in the hope that the sea air would improve his condition, to offer their prayers and good wishes.

But even the Sages' blessings didn't help. Rabi Eliezer died in Caesarea, on Shabbat. After the Sabbath, his body was carried to Lod to be eulogized at his own yeshiva. His former student, Rabi Akiva, followed the coffin, crying as Elisha had done when Eliyahu *Hanavi* was taken from this earth:

"My father, my father... you strove and fought for us. Your prayers gave us more protection than mighty armies! I have so much to ask still, but the one who could answer is no longer here!"

After Rabban Gamliel's passing, Rabi Elazar ben Azariah

thought it was safe to begin to expand the yeshiva in Lod. When I heard this, shivers went up and down my spine; the same sense of foreboding filled me as when I had first seen the glorious yeshiva in Yavneh.

None of my husband's reassurances could allay my fears. "Rabi Elazar is sure the Romans won't object," he said. "It was the *nesiut* from the House of King David that made them suspicious, and since Rabi Elazar is not a descendant of David and has no royal blood, they won't view him as a threat. It will be all right, Leah, you'll see."

For once, Elazar was wrong, and so was Rabi Elazar. Rome was quick to react to the reports of their Christian spies (the Rabbis had been under constant surveillance), and most of the thirty-two Sages who had assembled in Lod had to flee for their lives. A few chose to remain because it was their hometown, and they would meet secretly on the upper floor of someone's house, away from watchful Roman eyes. Rabi Akiva resettled his family in nearby Bnei Brak, where he established his own yeshiva.

Our suffering during Trajan's reign did not end with the dispersion of the Sages. The persecutions continued until his dying day, persecutions not just of the Jews of *Eretz Yisrael*, but of our brethren throughout the Empire. Trajan needed more money to finance his wars and to pay his soldiers, so taxes were raised again, and the people grew poorer and poorer. His military victories went to his head and he decided to conquer Babylonia, something no Emperor before him had dared to attempt. Along with their fellow Babylonians, the Jews of Babylonia fought back against the Roman invaders, providing an excuse — if one were needed — for attacks on Jews throughout the Empire.

The Greeks were particularly enthusiastic about killing Jews; they slaughtered hundreds of thousands. In Alexandria, where Elazar still had relatives, they destroyed the exquisite *beit knesset* and massacred the entire community. But when they attacked Cyrene and Cyprus, the Jews there were ready for them and drove the invaders back. The Greeks called for reinforcements from Rome, claiming the Jews were revolting. Trajan, however, had his hands full in Babylonia, so he denied their request. Besides, he didn't lend much credence to the Greeks' report.

Desperate for Trajan's support, the Greeks turned to Plotina, the Empress, with a message that was sure to kindle her fury. (Rachel told me about it. You see, Trajan had a son and a daughter. When the son was born, it was Tisha b'Av, and while the whole Empire was celebrating, the Jews were fasting and lamenting the destruction of the Holy Temples. When the daughter died, it was Chanukah and the Jewish homes were filled with light.)

Plotina read the message from the Greeks and immediately sent word to her husband in Babylonia. "Look at these Jews!" she wrote. "When our son was born, they fasted and lamented, and now when our daughter is dead, they light up their dwelling places to celebrate!"

That was all Trajan needed to hear. He dispatched Lucius Quietus to help the Greeks quash the "rebellion." The Jewish communities of Cyrene and Cyprus suffered a fate similar to Alexandria's.

Word of Trajan's demise did not bring us relief because we were sure that Lucius Quietus, the evil oppressor, would take his place, but instead the nobleman, Publius Aelius Hadrianus was named Emperor, through some typical Roman intrigue. Hadrian's first act as Caesar was to have Lucius Quietus executed, before Quietus could carry out his diabolical plans for us, *baruch Hashem*.

Now Hadrian, unlike his predecessor, appears to be favorably disposed towards us. When he was a commander of the Roman troops in Syria, he met Rabi Yehoshua and the two engaged in several theological debates. Naturally, Rabi Yehoshua impressed him, and Hadrian was big enough to admit it.

There has been plenty of evidence that the new Emperor is sympathetic to our cause. For example, when the survivors of the Alexandria massacre reported to him on what had transpired there, he had the perpetrators of the massacre executed and ordered the reconstruction of the beautiful buildings and homes in the community.

Feeling secure about traveling for the first time in years, I convinced Elazar that we should visit the children in Bnei Brak. Yehudah and Baruch are learning in Rabi Akiva's yeshiva, so everyone I care about most is living there now, including Rachel.

The trip was harder than I thought it would be, but blessedly uneventful. I won't say one word about the grandchildren, *beli ayin hara*, except that *Hakadosh Baruch Hu* has granted me tremendous *nachat*. I could hardly tear myself away from them.

As ever, the boys regaled us with "Rabi Akiva stories," one of which I found particularly meaningful. It was about two of Rabi Akiva's *talmidim*, Chanania ben Chachinai and Shimon bar Yochai. They had come to the yeshiva to learn for thirteen years, both of them leaving families behind in their hometowns. During their stay, Yehudah told us, Shimon sent letters home regularly, but Chanania did not.

"I don't think students really understand how much those letters mean to us back home," I commented. "They must become so engrossed in their studies that no other thoughts can penetrate. They can't possibly realize how we are affected by the separation."

"But, Imma," Baruch replied a bit defensively, "there's so much to learn! We can't afford the luxury of taking time out for trivial things like letter-writing. It's *bittul Torah*!

"Stop right there, son," Elazar interjected. "There is nothing trivial about *derech eretz*. In fact, the Sages teach that courteous behavior precedes Torah. And furthermore, there is nothing to say that your letters can't *contain* Torah. I am a strong advocate of sharing one's Torah thoughts and yeshiva experiences with one's family. I have always done it, and believe me, the benefits are immeasurable."

Elazar and I exchanged a knowing smile. "Please continue your story, Yehudah," Elazar said (courteously).

"Right. So Rabi Chanania got this letter from his wife, begging him to come home because their daughter had come of age and it was time to find her a *shidduch*, but he just ignored it. I wonder if he even *read* the letter — he's such a serious student, I doubt if he took the time." Seeing the look on Elazar's face, Yehudah immediately corrected himself. "What I mean is, he's simply so involved that it's possible... Well, no matter what I say in his defense, I can't really justify his actions. But that's the whole point."

"Exactly," Baruch agreed, picking up the threads of the story. "Rabi Akiva came into the *beit midrash* and announced that anyone who had a daughter of marriageable age was to go home to attend to the matter of finding her a *shidduch*. He must have had *Ruach Hakodesh*! How else could he have known about the letter? Needless to say, Chanania complied, and quite a few others seemed to be reconsidering their own circumstances."

"Does this mean we'll be hearing from you more often now?" I asked pointedly.

The boys looked sheepish. "We'll try," they replied in unison.

Gazing around at my family, I allowed myself a sigh of pleasure and, I have to admit, a small measure of pride. I haven't done too badly, have I? *Baruch Hashem*.

When I finally got around to visiting Rachel, I was surprised to find that she was not her usual self. She seemed tired, and her smile didn't come as quickly as it used to. Only her eyes were as bright and untroubled as always. Those eyes, that had seen so much sorrow, poverty and pain, were clear and happy like a young girl's. I thought of Sarah *Immenu*: at a hundred she was as twenty in beauty; and at twenty she was pure and innocent as a seven-year-old girl. But neither Rachel nor I would see twenty again.

We had much to talk about. Rachel told me of her husband's yeshiva, we discussed our children and grandchildren, and then, inevitably, the conversation turned to the political situation. I could not believe my ears when Rachel told me the news: It seems that Hadrian is going to grant us permission to rebuild the Holy Temple! May we see it soon, in our days!

When it was time for me to go, Rachel took my hand in hers, in that dear familiar way, and held it for a long, long while.

It was only on the way home that I realized that Rachel hadn't said a word about herself. I started to think about that. Had she ever? No. It was only when I was telling her what to do — don't marry this ignorant shepherd, don't give up your inheritance, tell your husband to stop learning, move to Yavneh — that she ever spoke about her own affairs. Even that time, after the painful experience with her daughter and ben Azzai, she had comforted me, rather than the other way around. And she never once complained...

41

ELAZAR RESPONDED with his usual equanimity, and I with my usual outrage, when we heard that Hadrian had changed his mind about rebuilding the *Beit Hamikdash.* "If we've learned anything in our old age, Leah," my husband said, "it is that one should never take a Roman at his word."

It wasn't entirely Hadrian's fault, though. Our "great friends," the *malshinim*, offered all sorts of dire warnings about what would happen to the Empire if we were allowed to rebuild our Holy Temple, and Hadrian, for whatever reason, agreed with them even though it meant antagonizing us. He amended his decree so that we could only build the structure on a site other than *Har Habayit*, and the dimensions he specified were contrary to those ordained by the Torah. Of course, this was tantamount to rescinding the decree.

And I wasn't the only one to be outraged by the new orders. The People almost rose up in rebellion! Only when Rabi Yehoshua spoke to them placatingly did they calm down. This was his parable:

"The lion, king of beasts, swallowed a bone which stuck in his throat. A crane came along, placed his head in the lion's mouth and, with his long bill, removed the obstruction. When the crane asked for his reward for saving the lion's life, the beast roared: 'Go and boast that you placed your head in the lion's mouth and escaped unharmed. Is it not enough for you that you were not torn to pieces by my sharp teeth?'

"We, too, have escaped from the lion's mouth," Rabi Yehoshua explained.

His point was clear: even though the Emperor had failed to grant us our heart's desire, we should be content that he was doing us no harm.

All this came to me in a long-awaited letter from Rachel, in which she also wrote with great joy about her husband's burgeoning yeshiva: students were coming to Bnei Brak from every part of the country and even from the Diaspora!

But on the same day that that letter arrived, we received the terrible *besorah*: Rachel had died in her sleep. Her husband, her children and grandchildren had all been close at hand. They said there was a smile on her lips.

I cried and cried and cried. Why did Rachel have to die now? She was so good! It was too soon! It wasn't fair! Then I thought about the way she had lived all her life, without resentment or complaint, with kind, loving words for everyone, and the pain in my heart began to ease. Her letter had spoken of her pride in her husband's achievements: this was all she had longed for in life, and she had lived to see it. Even now, she was still comforting me.

"*Deracheha darchei noam* — all her ways are pleasant, and all her paths are peace." Those words are said about our holy Torah, but they clearly applied to Rachel as well. She was like a living *sefer Torah*, an embodiment of all its goodness. And in that peaceful, pleasant way of hers, she had always encouraged her husband to strive to reach his true potential.

All of us — Elazar and the children and grandchildren, too — mourned for her. She was my dearest friend, my sister — no, my mother! My whole life I owe to her, and now she is gone. No one will ever be able to take her place. I feel as if a part of me had died with her.

Rachel's passing seemed to be a harbinger of other sad news. Not long after, Rabi Elazar ben Azariah left us, and then Rabi Yehoshua. The Sages decided that the political atmosphere was right for reestablishing the *metivta*, but not in Lod; nor could they chance Yavneh again. This time it would be back in Usha, with Rabi Akiva, who is now the undisputed leader of the Nation, at its head.

This was the true fulfillment of Rachel's lifelong dream and for a while the depressing thought that she had missed this moment occupied my mind so, that I found I could barely function. At a time when I should have been so happy and busy with my children and grandchildren moving back into our big house (everything was just as they had left it), I spent my days walking absentmindedly in the garden and orchards with a stone on my heart and tears in my eyes.

Then Rabi Akiva suffered another mighty blow, and all at once I was grateful that Rachel had died when she did: at least she was spared this agony. Their son Shimon, who had grown to be a great teacher in Israel, was *niftar*. He had always been frail as a child, I recalled. Elazar, of course, stayed at Rabi Akiva's side the entire time.

At the funeral it seemed that all of Israel had come to comfort Rabi Shimon's father, and Rabi Akiva was astonished at the large turn-out. "My friends," he said, "you have come from great distances to share my sorrow. Who am I to deserve this honor? There are many others like me. No; you are not honoring me, but Hashem's Law, which it has been my privilege to teach. Therefore, I am consoled. Return now in peace to your homes!"

"In peace..." Rabi Akiva had said. Is it peace that *Hakadosh Baruch Hu* has in store for us? Somehow, I have my doubts.

42

By RIGHTS, MY STORY should end here, since I'd intended from the start only to tell you about Rachel. But, as I've always said, Rachel was so wise and so special that she was able to influence everyone who came in contact with her. Rabi Akiva, of course, is the prime example of this; about me, you already know; then there's ben Buri, Shifra — oh, the list goes on and on.

The fact is that each of us, in turn — especially Rabi Akiva — influenced others, so that events which occurred even long after Rachel's death could be traced back to her. You might not agree, but, well, that's the way I see it.

After the *Churban*, Rachel had comforted me by saying that the *Beit Hamikdash* was only a building of wood and stone that could one day be rebuilt, if Hashem wills it. "The entire universe and beyond is His dwelling place," she said. "Although the *Beit Hamikdash* symbolized Hashem's connection to His People on earth, as long as His holy Torah remains intact and there are scholars and Sages alive to learn it and teach it and pass it on to future generations, that vital connection is assured."

Rachel was right, of course, but for the Nation, the *Beit Hamikdash* had been the focus of our faith and our prayers. The sacrifices, bringing the first fruits, the Yom Kippur services — they were all so much a part of Judaism that their absence left a void. The People never stopped yearning for their reinstitution in a new Holy Temple; "May it be rebuilt swiftly in our days" was a phrase that was always on our lips. Even Hadrian's revocation of permission to rebuild failed to destroy our dream. In fact, with the reestablishment of the *metivta*, under the superb leadership of Rabi Akiva, the Nation felt stronger, unified, and more confident than ever that fulfillment of the dream was not far off.

The fact that we had come so close to reestablishing Jewish sovereignty — and with official Roman sanction, no less! — was observed with growing fear and fury by our enemies. They were quick to advise the Emperor to take the necessary steps to prevent "disaster." The time had come, they told him, to put us down once and for all and thereby eliminate the threat to the Empire.

When Baruch brought us the news, Elazar was napping peacefully in a chair with the newest addition to our family — our first great-granddaughter, Rachel — sleeping softly in his arms. She looks nothing like her namesake, but she is the rapture of our existence and I pray that she will grow to be like Rachel in *middot.* I gazed at her with tears in my eyes, fearing for her future.

Elazar stirred, and so did tiny Rachel, and Baruch took her in his arms as he repeated the latest report to his father. Hadrian had announced that he would rebuild Jerusalem himself and call it Aelia Capitolina, and erect on the Temple Mount an altar to the Roman god Jupiter! And all this on top of new edicts banning the performance of the *mitzvot* most essential to our existence. Oh, Hadrian had been well-advised, yes, by those apostates who knew precisely how to strike at our heart.

We cried together in that room, with tiny Rachel turning her head from one to the other, not knowing what was happening but sensing our pain and fear. She too began to cry and I took her to her mother while Baruch returned to the *metivta.*

Overnight our peaceful, idyllic *Galil* has turned into a *Gei Hinnom.* Few people considered for a moment actually obeying Hadrian's vicious laws; the question was not "How can we stop observing Shabbat?" but "How can we continue to observe Shabbat without the Romans finding out?" And the answer was: secretly, in underground tunnels, cellars and caves. To this end, an intricate network of tunnels was dug beneath the town and its outskirts, with every able-bodied male lending a hand.

But despite our cunning, many were followed and their hiding places discovered. The legionnaires are particularly dedicated to serving their Caesar and tracking down lawbreakers. Soldiers are everywhere, and again and again people have been caught in the act of performing a *brit milah* or reciting *Kiddush* on Shabbat. They were viciously punished, and some even summarily executed for their "crimes," and the cave or cellar in which they were found was sealed.

Each day brought more bad news — another friend or neighbor killed for daring to defy the Emperor — until I could stand no more. "Elazar!" I whispered urgently. (We've all taken to speaking only in hushed voices, if at all, for fear our words will be overheard.) "We can't go on like this! And it's not only here in the *Galil* — all over the country this slaughter is going on. Why don't the people fight back? There are more of us here than there are Romans!" I felt my voice rising in spite of my efforts. "Isn't the Torah worth *fighting* for, not just *dying* for?"

"Leah!" Elazar exclaimed, fear written all over his face. "You must speak softly! Yes, of course it's worth fighting for. And that's just what's beginning to happen now — our People are fighting back. They're also getting more organized, posting guards at the tunnel entrances, armed and ready to defend themselves if necessary. Now, if you promise not to shout, I'll tell you who was the first to rise up to defend the honor of our Torah."

I nodded quickly and pressed my lips together.

"Binyamin."

Our grandson! My heart swelled with pride.

"And many others have followed him," Elazar added. "But we both know that a genuine confrontation with Rome will result. There's nothing anyone can do now to stop it."

War. Again. *Ribbono shel Olam*, I prayed, spare my children!

43

RACHEL ONCE TOLD ME that people can become accustomed to anything, and although at the time I had disagreed with her, now I see she was right. We have grown accustomed, in this short time, to keeping the *mitzvot* clandestinely. We are forbidden to recite the *Shema*, yet everyone I know still manages to say the prayer at least once if not twice a day. Every newborn boy, *baruch Hashem*, has been circumcised — in the tunnels, of course. Since the Day of Rest has been banned, the laymen who are unable to hide are forced to work on Shabbat, so their one opportunity to hear a *derashah* has been lost, but the learning of the Torah scholars continues in the *beit midrash* unabated. So, while the *gezerot* have brought about many changes in our life, the changes are only on the surface. In our hearts, our faith and devotion remain as strong as ever.

Elazar reminded me that this was not the first time that Rome believed that edicts banning the essential *mitzvot* would serve to suppress us. The conniving commander of the Roman legion just after the *Churban*, Turnus Rufus, had urged the Roman authorities to ban Shabbat and *brit milah* too, as a means of undermining our faith. The governor of Judea hadn't thought it necessary or advisable; such a ban was likely to incite us, just when we'd finally been subdued. He had suggested a debate between Turnus Rufus and Rabi Akiva, who was fluent in their language and even then was known to be a well-spoken debater.

Elazar said that someone in the yeshiva who had been with Rabi Akiva at the time recalled the entire debate verbatim, as well as the events that followed. This is how it went:

Standing before the governor, Turnus Rufus opened the debate. "These Jews revere an invisible being," he began. "They say He is the Almighty, the Omniscient, the Creator of the universe." He turned to Rabi Akiva. "Tell me, whose work is better, the Creator's or man's?"

"Man's work," Rabi Akiva answered.

"Jew, do you realize what you are saying? Can man build the vault of heaven, set the stars and planets on their course? Can man shape the earth, raise up mountains, fill up oceans and seas?"

"We are not discussing things which are out of man's grasp, but those which are under his control. You asked me whose work is better, God's or man's. I did not say that man can *create* — that is beyond his powers. But the things man makes are an improvement on what the Almighty creates."

Rufus scowled. "Is that why you Jews perform circumcision?" he challenged. "Do you think you can improve upon the Creator's work?"

"I sensed that your questions were aimed at that," Rabi Akiva said. "All that man does is inspired by God and is therefore also God's work." Then Rabi Akiva presented some stalks of wheat and a flour cake. "This wheat," he said, as if teaching a child, "is God's work. He made it grow in the fields. Human beings winnowed the chaff, ground and sifted the flour and made this cake. Which would you rather eat? Is the cake not preferable? We mine raw ore and smelt it and refine it into precious metal; a builder erects splendid palaces of stone and marble; garments are woven from wool after the rough fleece is first sheared and washed, combed and carded and spun. The ability to do all these things is God's gift to man.

"We are commanded to bring every Jewish male child into the Covenant on the eighth day after his birth, to bear a sign on his body that he is part of our People and must follow the Almighty's commandments. You ask if we improve on God's work? Yes, we do, but we do so according to God's will."

"You have answered well," the governor said. "This practice is not merely superstition then, as Turnus Rufus suggested. There will be no prohibition of circumcision."

Rufus then said, "What difference is there between one day and the rest?"

Rabi Akiva replied, "What difference is there between one man and the rest?"

That answer confused Rufus. "What did I tell you," he asked, "and what did you tell me?"

"You asked me what makes the Sabbath day different from all the others," Rabi Akiva replied, "and I asked you what makes Turnus Rufus different from all other men."

"My master, the Emperor, wanted to honor me," Turnus Rufus said indignantly. "He therefore gave me title and position and all that goes with it." To which Rabi Akiva replied, "And God wanted to honor the Sabbath."

"Can you prove that your God chose this day to honor above all others?" Rufus demanded.

Rabi Akiva smiled. "Yes," he said. "The river Sambatyon is my proof. All week long it casts up rocks and stones, but on the Sabbath it rests."

Rufus scoffed, "You're only trying to put me off by bringing proof from something which I do not even know exists, and if it does, is too far away for me to examine."

"Very well," Rabi Akiva said, and without a moment's hesitation, offered another proof. "The sorcerers who contact the dead know that all week they are successful," he said, "but on the Sabbath the souls rest and do not answer them. Try it with your father's spirit."

Rufus of course did not believe him, so he found such a sorcerer and indeed, during the week his father's spirit answered him but not on Shabbat. Still he was not convinced.

"Go and examine your father's grave," Rabi Akiva suggested. "You'll see that all week smoke rises from it because he is suffering in Hell. But on the Sabbath, even the sinners rest and are given a respite from Purgatory, so no smoke comes from his grave on that day."

Rufus went to examine his father's grave and it was as Rabi Akiva had said. However, he returned with a new challenge. "If, as you say, your God truly honors the Sabbath, He should not make it rain nor cause the winds to blow nor the grass to grow on that day!"

"In his own domain," Rabi Akiva answered, "a man may carry freely from place to place on the Sabbath. The entire universe is God's terrain and therefore he can bring things from one part of it to the other, even on the Sabbath. Despite this," he continued, "when God fed our ancestors the manna in the desert, He did not send it down on the Sabbath, in order to show us how much He truly honors this day above all others."

And with that, the debate was won. The governor declared that no ban on Sabbath observance would be instituted. But Rufus was unwilling to concede. Once again he challenged Rabi Akiva. "I read in your Scriptures that one of your prophets said in the name of your God, 'I love Jacob and I hate Esau.' Why does your God hate us?"

And Rabi Akiva replied, "Tomorrow I will answer you." (That was a surprise. It wasn't like Rabi Akiva to postpone his rebuttal. Could it be that Turnus Rufus had baffled him?)

The next day Rufus strutted into the governor's chamber with a defiant and scornful expression on his face. "Well,

Akiva," he derided, "what did you see in your dreams last night?"

"I dreamed that I had two dogs," Rabi Akiva answered. "The male was named Rufus, and the female Rufina."

Rufus became livid with rage. "Had you no better names to give your dogs than mine and my wife's? For your impudence you deserve to be killed!"

"Come now," Rabi Akiva replied calmly, "what difference is there between you and them? You eat and drink, and so do those dogs. You procreate and so do they. You will die one day just as they will. And yet, simply because I named them after you, you were infuriated. Imagine, then, God creates the heavens and the earth, He alone causes life and death, and yet you take a piece of wood and call it by His name. Is it not obvious why he despises you?"

The governor laughed out loud and Rufus shamefacedly stalked out.

When he returned home, his wife saw that he was very downcast. "What troubles you, my dear husband?" Rufina asked. "Is it something to do with the governor?"

"It's that cursed Jew, Akiva! Whatever I say, he always finds an answer for it. Oh, how I'd like to kill him! Whenever we meet, he puts me to shame!"

"Then I will get rid of him," Rufina said.

"And how will you do that?" Rufus asked. "The governor is on his side."

"You will see, my husband. I will find a way."

Rufina knew she was a very attractive woman. She dressed herself in exquisite clothing and jewelry, and went to visit Rabi Akiva.

But when he saw her, Rabi Akiva did something entirely unexpected: first he spat, then he laughed, and then he began to cry!

Rufina was stunned. "Why-why did you react in this way?" she stammered.

"I spat when I thought of your origins," Rabi Akiva replied, "and I cried for your beauty which is destined to be consumed by worms in the ground." But he would not reveal why he had laughed.

Rufina was so moved by his words that she burst into tears. "What shall I do, Rabbi, to save my soul? Is there a way to atone for the past?"

"The Almighty is merciful," Rabi Akiva told her. "He forgives a sinner who is truly repentant. You can act now to fulfill the purpose of your existence, to become worthy of His gifts."

This story suddenly jogged my memory. "Elazar," I exclaimed, "I *know* this woman! I met her, very briefly, a long time ago at Rachel's. Rachel wouldn't tell me her name, but I remember now that I overheard her servant refer to her as Rufina. All Rachel would tell me about her was that she was planning to convert and was secretly studying Judaism. Rachel was teaching her, and Rufina was such an avid student that Rachel said, 'If she were not already married to a gentile, she would make a wonderful wife for a *talmid chacham*.'"

Elazar burst out laughing. "What's so funny?" I asked.

"Why, Leah, don't you know? Rabi Akiva and Rufina are about to be wed!"

"Oh, my! *Rufina* is the 'rich widow' everyone is talking about?" The irony was inescapable.

We both laughed then, and when we'd calmed down a bit, we suddenly realized why *Rabi Akiva* had laughed when he first met Rufina: he must have seen what the future held.

I know all this must come as a shock to you, as it did me. When I first heard that Rabi Akiva was marrying a rich widow, my reaction was: How could a man so quickly forget his wife — and a wife like Rachel? But then, when I thought about it, I realized how long it's been that Rabi Akiva is alone. Maybe in remarrying at this time of his life, he's trying to recapture some of the happiness he had with Rachel.

"Rufina must have come back to Rabi Akiva," Elazar said, "to tell him she had repented as he'd advised, and wanted to convert. He probably sent her to Rachel for lessons then. When Turnus Rufus died and she was a free woman at last, she began to study intensively, until she felt herself worthy enough to return to Rabi Akiva. I suppose it was destined that they should marry, but I wonder if Rachel had sensed it somehow."

Destined? Of course, everything is "destined." But just between us, I can tell you the years have been kind to Rufina; she may not be the young beauty Rabi Akiva beheld years and years ago (who is?), but she's still quite lovely.

I decided to be extra nice to Rufina, to make her feel welcome in our community. She has turned out to be a very devoted wife and companion, and I've become rather friendly with her. We've met several times and talked about — guess what? — Rachel! And she asks questions incessantly about the *halachah*. I try to answer as best I can, but sometimes her questions are so sharp that I have to consult Elazar. We don't have much time for socializing, though. There's a war coming and everyone can feel it.

44

WHAT BEGAN AS SMALL, individual acts of self-defense quickly escalated, as Elazar had predicted, into a genuine confrontation with Rome, but the people were ill-equipped for battle. After all, we are farmers, basically, and Torah scholars; what could we know of military strategy, troop movements, weaponry? There was no choice but to learn these things, because we were clearly engaged in a war of survival: the survival of Torah. Never before has the Nation faced so dire a threat of annihilation. Titus destroyed our Holy Temple, but his own father Vespasian granted the establishment of Kerem B'Yavneh, thereby assuring our continued existence. Hadrian, however, is bent on eradicating Judaism entirely.

The task of turning Torah scholars and farmers into warriors fell to Shimon bar Kosiva, a *talmid chacham* from the House of David who possessed an uncanny knowledge of all things military. In an amazingly short time, Shimon transformed the People into skilled soldiers, besting the legionnaires in battle after battle. It seemed that Hashem had truly blessed our undertaking.

Bar Kosiva's successes were astounding. Jews from all over the country and other parts of the Empire rallied to his side, and then gentiles who saw their chance to throw off the yoke of Rome joined him too, swelling the ranks of our army. Each new victory strengthened our resolve and boosted our morale. Shimon appeared to be invincible. (Elazar asked Rabi Akiva privately if he thought Shimon might be the *Mashiach*, but Rabi Akiva said it was too soon to tell.)

And then, with the swiftness, brilliance and might that could only have been Heaven-sent, Shimon bar Kosiva led the Nation to the greatest victory of all: he recaptured the Holy City. Yerushalayim was ours again! He cast out the Romans and every sign of their loathsome idolatry, declared his sovereignty over the Land of Israel, and struck new coins that proclaimed our freedom.

Freedom! The very word was intoxicating. For over 500 years our People had been ruled by foreign powers and now, at last, we were on the threshold of annointing our own king, a king from the royal House of David, a king who would rule with justice and mercy in accordance with Hashem's Torah, a king whose every endeavor had the Almighty's blessing: Shimon bar Kosiva. He was the Redeemer; he would rebuild the *Beit Hamikdash*.

Rabi Akiva, as the spiritual leader of the Nation, was consulted. "Is Shimon the *Mashiach*?" the Sages asked. "Is he truly Hashem's annointed one?"

It was the question on everyone's lips. The subject was discussed extensively in every place where Jews assembled, in the *beit knesset* and in the halls of study, in the market, on the street, and at the table, but especially in Jerusalem, to where the Sages had gone to see for themselves the man who would be king.

All waited breathlessly for Rabi Akiva's decision, and the word was not long in coming. Baruch, who had traveled to Jerusalem to see this momentous event with his own eyes, brought us the news. This is what he told us:

The Sages gathered in the Holy City and Shimon was

brought before them. His noble bearing, his blazing eyes and radiant face made a tremendous impression. An aura of glory seemed to surround him. The people began shouting: "The king! The king! He is the Redeemer! *Mashiach* has come!" The uproar was deafening, but with one glance Rabi Akiva silenced them. Everyone strained to hear his words.

"Concerning the Second *Beit Hamikdash*," he began, "the *navi* Chaggai prophesied in the words of Hashem: 'Yet again, in just a little while, I will storm the heavens and the earth and the sea and the dry land. And I will storm all the nations, and the dearest things of all nations will come to Jerusalem....'

"The meaning of these verses," Rabi Akiva continued, "is as follows: 'I will give but a little honor to this House, and then it will be destroyed. However, right after that, I will storm the heavens, the earth and all the nations, and the *Mashiach* will come and redeem Israel forever.'"

The people understood that they were witnesses to the "storm" that had shaken the "heavens, the earth and all the nations," a storm named Shimon bar Kosiva, the only man alive who could catch the stones cast by the Roman ballistae with his bare hands and hurl them back at the enemy with equal force.

"Yes!" Rabi Akiva exclaimed. "He is the king, the *Mashiach*! '*Darach kochav mi-Ya'akov* — a star has come forth from Jacob, and a scepter from Israel. Edom will be your booty; Israel will do deeds of valor.'"

Rabi Yochanan ben Torta heard these words and began to tremble. "The time for the Redeemer has not yet arrived!" he declared. "Grass will grow from your cheeks, Akiva, and the *Mashiach* will not yet have come." But no one paid him any heed.

Shimon bowed before Rabi Akiva, who raised his hands over the king's head in blessing. For a moment, no one breathed. Then an exultant cry arose:

"A star has come forth from Jacob!"

From that moment on, he was called bar Kochva, the Son of a Star.

Elazar looked up from his studies and asked, "What are you writing, Leah? Do you still keep that old journal of yours?" And quite suddenly, I burst into tears.

"Leah, Leah, are you ill?" He hurried to my side solicitously.

"No, Elazar," I said, drying my eyes, "not ill. Just sad...and frightened."

"Sad? When all of *Eretz Yisrael* is rejoicing? When plans are underway for rebuilding the Holy Temple? And what could you possibly be afraid of, now that we're secure in our Land with our own king."

I closed my eyes for a moment and tried to regain my composure. "I was hoping to confide my foolish thoughts only to my journal," I said, "but since you asked, I'll tell you: I feel in my heart that this is all a mistake. That Rome will not leave us in peace, that danger is lurking on our doorstep and that — please don't laugh, or try to minimize this — I feel that Shimon is not the *Mashiach.*" My words came out in a whisper.

Elazar was silent for a while, his eyes boring into mine. "No, Leah, I won't laugh. I know that women were given an extra measure of wisdom, and you perhaps more than most. Don't look so surprised," he went on. "With each passing year I realize more and more how fortunate I have been to have such a wife. How wise you were to encourage me to learn. And look at our children and grandchildren, *baruch Hashem*, all living pure Torah lives. Surely, that's to your credit. And as to your worldliness, well, your 'feelings' about the political situation have proven accurate time and again — you were the only one who voiced concern over the *metivta* in Yavneh, and you were right, not once, but three times!

"So now, when you say you have doubts about King

Shimon and fears of Roman retribution, you cause me to stop and think. Maybe there's something to your 'feelings'."

Elazar's words meant more to me than you could possibly imagine, but part of me had hoped he would dispel my fears. Instead, he intensified them.

"True, Shimon has reigned more or less peacefully for over two years now," Elazar continued pensively. "And you know how strong his army is. He would only accept recruits who demonstrated their valor by severing their own thumbs, and 200,000 did so before the Sages called a halt to this mutilation. Another 200,000 proved themselves by uprooting cedar trees while galloping by on horseback. And all have shown fearlessness in the face of the enemy."

"Since when does our fate depend on the strength of our warriors?" I asked. "I overheard one soldier say to another: 'Let Hashem not help us or our enemies,' and when I reprimanded him for not acknowledging the Source of his success, he defended himself by saying that he was only quoting his commander, bar Kochva! If that's true, well, I for one cannot believe that Hashem's *Mashiach* would say such a thing. But there's a much greater matter that should make *everyone* realize that something is amiss. Am I the only one who can see it?"

"What is that, Leah?" Elazar asked, genuinely interested.

"Rachel taught me long ago that when King David brought peace to the land and began to make plans for building the Holy Temple, Hashem forbade it, because David had blood on his hands. Only his son, Shelomo, who had never fought a war, could have that *zechut*. Surely bar Kochva's hands are as bloody as David's; how can he possibly be destined to build the Holy One's dwelling place on earth?"

Elazar shook his head. "Leah, there's a difference between King David and the *Mashiach*..." But before he could explain, Baruch, who had apparently entered the room without our realizing it, cleared his throat. "Imma's intuition is right," he announced in a voice choked with emotion. "The Romans have killed Rabi Shimon ben Hasegan, and also Rabi Yishmael ben Elisha, who was Rabi Akiva's old friend and *chavruta.* When Rabi Akiva heard this, he rent his garments and declared: 'If good were destined to come to the world, the first to receive it would have been Rabi Shimon and Rabi Yishmael. And now, it was clear to Him Who spoke and the world came into existence, that in the end, great calamity will come to the world; therefore these two were removed from this earth.' Then he quoted from *Yeshayahu*: 'The righteous perish, and no one takes it to heart.' That means we must all take to heart the reason that these *tzaddikim* were removed from this earth, and do *teshuvah* so that we might nullify the evil decree."

"And the boys?" I asked anxiously, meaning our grandsons. "Are they still with bar Kochva?"

"No, Imma," Baruch replied. "When they heard Rabi Akiva's words, they understood that their place now is in the *beit midrash.* For sure, there will be many who will stay to fight at Shimon's side, but few to pray for their safe return and fewer still to strive to merit the Nation's salvation."

Within months, all that Rabi Akiva had said had come to pass. The Romans attacked and recaptured Jerusalem, and Shimon and his army retreated to the fortified city of Betar. A terrible battle ensued.

For over three years, the army held out against the Romans (many said that it was only in the *zechut* of Rabi Elazar Hamoda'i's prayers), but then the fortress was breached. Betar ran red with the blood of our People. Hundreds of thousands lay dead in the dust, and the Emperor forbade us to bury them. Our eyes grew dim with tears and our spirit grew faint with fear.

On Tisha b'Av, the fortress fell and with it, our last hopes. Shimon bar Kosiva was no "son of a star"; bar *Koziva*, perhaps — son of a liar — but not the *Mashiach.* His lies had led us to throw caution to the wind and now everything, *everything* was in jeopardy.

When the Romans arrested Rabi Akiva and threw him in jail, I felt as though a piece of my heart had been imprisoned along with him. "Is this the end, then, Elazar?" I cried.

"Not quite, Leah," my good husband replied and his eyes shone as he told me of the secret ceremony he had been privileged to witness: In a clearing in the woods, Rabi Yehudah ben Bava gave *semichah* to a handful of outstanding students. And among the *talmidim*, the new standard-bearers of Torah, was our own Binyamin.

"But the Romans have banned *semichah*!" I exclaimed. "Is our grandson now a fugitive?!" The thought screamed in my head. I felt suddenly faint.

"No, Leah," Elazar soothed. "Before it was his turn, Roman soldiers appeared and everyone had to flee for their lives. Rabi Yehudah was killed. The others are now fugitives and have fled the country, but Binyamin, who is equally qualified, is free to carry out his mission right here in *Eretz Yisrael*."

Praise Hashem, Who has given me life and sustained me to see this day.

EPILOGUE

... both shall be good.

I AM VERY OLD NOW. If I take ten years off my age as I've been doing lately, I'm well over ninety, but people tell me I can pass for seventy-five. Yet, deep inside, I still feel like that girl of so long ago…

Strange, what tricks memory plays! I can recall the smallest detail of whatever happened when I was young; but the later years are only a blur — they seem to run together, so that I can't tell where one begins or one ends. Not that I want to think about them. They are one long darkness like that in Egypt, where a person couldn't see his own hand in front of his face.

My eyes have seen the Holy Temple in all its splendor; I was among the throngs streaming to Jerusalem from all over the land, carrying the *bikkurim* in gilded baskets with songs of praise and thanksgiving. I have seen the *kohanim* bringing the *korbanot,* and I have heard the sweet melodies of the *levi'im.* I beheld Jerusalem in all its glory, and that is how I choose to remember it.

When the Holy City was besieged by Titus, it was like distant thunder over our home in the Valley: we knew that the lightning would strike, but we dared not think of the havoc it would wreak. When we heard about the destruction of the Temple, we mourned and tore our garments; but we were certain that it would soon be rebuilt. Hadn't Ezra and Nechemiah come from Babylon to a wasteland, and begun again, and succeeded? And now, with all the great men of the Sanhedrin among us, teaching His holy Law in Yavneh, the "new Jerusalem," surely Hashem would be merciful, and restore His glory to Zion, or so we thought. We did not know — and it was good that we did not — what the future had in store for us.

I think of our early married years, Rachel's and mine, and of raising my children. How silly and ignorant I was! Fussing over little things, crying about a broken cup or a torn dress...I wonder: if I had another chance, would I do any better? Had I known how it would all turn out, perhaps I would have been less critical and anxious, and much happier.

But no; I *was* happy then. I look back on those years as the best years of my life. I often wondered about Rachel and the miserable time in Geva. But for her, they were not miserable. Once, long ago, I asked her: "How were you able to bear it? Your husband away for years and years, with barely enough food to keep you alive — it must seem like a nightmare, looking back on it now."

"No," said Rachel. "Those were the best years of my life. It is not so much reaching the goal that makes us happy, as the striving and struggling towards it. Yes, those were the best years..." Her eyes seemed to gaze inward, and there was a smile on her face.

Then Elazar going to learn, first in Lod and then in Yavneh, and our children growing up and getting married — how proud I was of them! And then their children, and their children's children. Hashem has been kind to us. Soon my first great-great-grandchild will be born — a boy, I hope. There is no doubt what name he will be given — may it be in a good and happy hour!

Five times I have sat *shivah* — no, six, if I count Rachel. For my parents, who died peacefully, in the fullness of years, with children and grandchildren gathered around them; for Elazar; and for my two children. It is said that only the widow truly mourns for her husband, but when a parent sits *shivah* for a child, that is against the order of nature, and there is no grief to equal it.

Baruch and Batya were born moments apart. They died on the same day, although we didn't know that until later on. Strange, isn't it?

Baruch, who had been Rabi Akiva's loving disciple for so many years, was with him at the end. Rabi Akiva had been arrested for teaching Torah publicly. Pappus had warned him of the danger, but Rabi Akiva had a mission to fulfill.

"Pappus," he said, "we cannot stop learning Torah. That is what has kept our People alive! Listen to this story: A fox stood by the river bank and saw schools of fish swimming rapidly downstream. 'Why are you all swimming so fast?' asked the fox. 'Are you trying to escape some danger?'

"'Yes,' the fish replied, 'we're fleeing the fishermen who want to catch us in their nets.'

"'I have a good idea,' the fox said. 'Come up on the bank and live here with me safely.'

"'And you are the fox that's supposed to be so smart?' the fish laughed. 'If we are not safe here in the water, which is our element, how can we be safe on dry land?'

"Do you see, Pappus? We are like the fish. Learning Torah is our element. Without it, we are lost!"

Rabi Akiva's defiance of the Emperor was no idle gesture. The five students of his later years cast their light on Israel: Rabi Meir and Rabi Elazar ben Shammua, Rabi Yehudah ben Illai, Rabi Yosei ben Chalafta and Rabi Shimon bar Yochai all provided the Nation with the foundations of the Oral Law which would last forever. All took their inspiration and their methods from Rabi Akiva, their teacher and master. Through them, the Torah lived on, and as long as the Torah lived, the Nation would survive. But there were more seeds to plant; Rabi Akiva dared not desist.

And so, he had continued his teaching. The Procurator Tineus Rufus dispatched soldiers to arrest Rabi Akiva and on the fifth day of *Tishrei,* he was imprisoned in Caesarea.

Even as their *Rav* languished in the heavily guarded jail, the *talmidim* found ways to learn from him, but Rabi Akiva was careful not to jeopardize their safety. One of his disciples, Yehoshua Hagarsi, received permission to attend his master. Every day he would bring water, and Rabi Akiva used half to wash and half to drink. Once, the prison guard, out of spite, deliberately spilled half the water, and Rabi Akiva used the remainder to wash his hands.

"But what will you drink, Rabi?" Yehoshua asked.

"My colleagues have determined that we must wash before we eat. It is better that I cause my own death than violate their decision." Even though he was not among those who had thus decreed, he was prepared to give his life out of respect for his colleagues.

Finally, Rabi Akiva was brought to trial, with the evil Tineus Rufus as the judge. Yehoshua Hagarsi prayed that a *nes* would occur to save his master, but then a cloud suddenly descended from the heavens and enveloped them. "My prayer was in vain," Yehoshua said. "As it is written: 'You have covered Yourself with a cloud so that no prayer can pass through.'"

The Romans tore the flesh from Rabi Akiva's body with iron combs, but he made no outcry. It was time to recite the *Shema,* and he called out in a clear and steady voice:

"*Shema Yisrael!* Hear, O Israel! *Hashem Elokeinu, Hashem Echad!*"

The *talmidim* cried, seeing the agony of their master. But Rabi Akiva smiled and said, "All my life I have yearned for the opportunity to fulfill this commandment: 'You shall love Hashem, your God, with all your heart, and with all your soul, and with all your might' — even if He takes your very soul from you. Now that I have the chance, should I not fulfill it happily?" And his voice rang out again: "*Shema Yisrael! Hashem Elokeinu, Hashem Echad!*" Then his pure soul ascended...

Of all the lessons Rabi Akiva had taught in his lifetime, the greatest by far was the one he taught at the time of his death.

When the guards were asleep, they say, Eliyahu *Hanavi* and Yehoshua Hagarsi took Rabi Akiva's body out of the prison and buried it in a cave high in the mountains overlooking Tiberias. The Romans tried to capture the students they suspected of this "crime." All were able to escape, except for Baruch, who had not been involved but, because of his closeness to his master, was arrested as the prime suspect. The Romans tortured him to make him reveal Rabi Akiva's burial place, but he remained silent. They executed him, and left his body as prey for wild beasts. His friends buried him alongside their master.

It was on the same day, although we did not realize it until much later, that Batya went out to gather kindling for a fire. By then, we were reduced to eating rotten produce left in the fields, and roots and berries from the woods.

Oh, my beautiful Batya! She had been raised so tenderly; she never lacked for anything. And even in middle age, her skin had been fine and soft as a baby's. But then, after all the troubles and the years of famine, her face became deeply lined; at barely eighty, she was gaunt and stooped and she walked like an old, old woman.

Hours passed, and she had not returned. Elazar went to search for her. He found her lying under a tree, with a little bundle of twigs next to her, and she looked as if she were sleeping. She had died of hunger.

With sticks and flints, we scraped out a shallow grave. We placed her in it — her body was light as a child's — and covered it with many small stones. We took home the bundle of twigs to make a fire and cook some turnips and barley for the little ones, Batya's grandchildren.

Elazar lived for less than a year after that. He was buried next to our daughter. Now, here's another strange thing: My parent's tomb was in our cemetery right outside the town, with a big monument over their resting place. And Rachel's grave was in a place of honor in the *beit olam* of Bnei Brak. But today no one knows where these graves are. The Romans built barracks for their occupying forces over the cemeteries; the tombstones were used to pave their horses' stables.

But the graves of my husband and daughter, there on the edge of the forest, are not forgotten. The grandchildren built a cairn of rocks over them, and I often go there, to think and to remember...

Elazar, my Elazar! Remember how you gave little Binyamin rides on your back, Binyamin, the light of your life, the hope of the future! Why could you not have lived to see this glorious day, when the new Emperor Antonius Pius abolished Hadrian's vile decrees and permitted the burial of Betar's martyrs, and the Sages returned to Usha. And Binyamin, dear Binyamin, has taken his rightful place among them, teaching the next generation of Hashem's standard-bearers. You would have been so proud!

Every year we go together, Binyamin and I, to the cave in the mountainside where Baruch lies to the right of Rabi Akiva. There, I pour out my heart like water, and I am comforted. On the way home, I always turn back and look up at the mountains, and it seems to me that Rabi Akiva is still there, looking out over the Land, smiling down upon his students who are rebuilding Torah in *Eretz Yisrael*, guarding and guiding his People.

And Rachel, his wife, is by his side.

GLOSSARY

The following glossary provides a partial explanation of some of the words and phrases used in this book. The spelling and explanations reflect the way the specific word is used herein. Often, there are alternate spellings and meanings for the words.

ABBA: father.

ADAR: the sixth month (counting from ROSH HASHANAH) in the Jewish calendar, corresponding to February-March.

AGGADAH: Talmudic passages dealing with ethical or other nonhalachic topics.

AL KIDDUSH HASHEM: martyrdom for the sake of HASHEM and Torah.

ALEF-BEIT: the Hebrew alphabet.

AM HA'ARETZ: a Jew who lacks a religious education.

AM YISRAEL: the Jewish People.

AMAR RABI AKIVA: "Rabbi Akiva said."

AMEN: "So be it."

AMIDAH: the principle prayer; the *Shemoneh Esreh.*

AMMOT: cubits.

AV: the eleventh month (counting from ROSH HASHANAH) in the Jewish calendar, corresponding to July-August.

AV BEIT DIN: the foremost Sage of the SANHEDRIN.

AVERAH: a transgression.

AVINU: our father.

AVINU MALKENU: "Our Father, our King."

BACHUR YESHIVA: a YESHIVA student.

BAR MITZVAH: a Jewish boy of 13, the age at which he assumes religious obligations.

BARUCH DAYAN HA-EMET: "Blessed be the True Judge," said upon receiving bad news.

BARUCH HASHEM: "Thank God."

BEIT DIN: a court of Jewish law.

BEIT HAMIKDASH: the Holy Temple in Jerusalem.

BEIT KNESSET: a synagogue.

BEIT MIDRASH: a house of study.

BEIT OLAM: a cemetery.

BELI AYIN HARA: a phrase used to ward off the "evil eye."
BERACHAH: a blessing.
BESORAH: news.
B'EZRAT HASHEM: "With God's help."
BIKKURIM: the first fruits.
BIRYONIM: militants; radicals.
BITACHON: faith and trust in God.
BITTUL TORAH: the misuse of one's time in non-Torah pursuits.
BRIT, BRIT MILAH: the ritual of circumcision.

CHAG (CHAGIM): Jewish holiday(s).
CHALILAH: "Heaven forbid!"
CHAMETZ: leavened foods, forbidden on PESACH.
CHANUKAH: the eight-day Festival of Lights.
CHANUKIYAH:the eight-branch candelabra lit during CHANUKAH.
CHAS V'SHALOM: "God forbid!"
CHATAN: a bridegroom.
CHATUNNAH: a wedding ceremony.
CHAVRUTA: (A.) a study partner.
CHESSED: compassion; lovingkindness.
CHIDDUSH: a novel explanation or interpretation.
CHINNUCH: Jewish education.
CHITON: (Gr.) a tunic.
CHOL HAMOED: the intermediate days of SUKKOT and PESACH.
CHUMASH: the Five Books of Moses.
CHUPPAH: the wedding canopy; the wedding ceremony.
CHURBAN: the destruction of the BEIT HAMIKDASH.
CHUTZPAH: audacity.

DALET AMMOT: lit., four cubits; boundaries.
DENARIUS (DENARII): (L.) Roman coin(s).
DERASHOT: complex Torah interpretations; sermons.
DERECH ERETZ: courteous behavior.
DINIM: Jewish laws.

ECHAD: one.

ELUL: the twelfth month (counting from ROSH HASHANAH) in the Jewish calendar, corresponding to August-September.
EMUNAH: faith in God.
ERETZ YISRAEL: the Land of Israel.
EREV: the eve of a holiday or the Sabbath.

GABBAI TZEDAKAH: the treasurer of a charity fund.
GALUT: the Exile.
GAM ZO L'TOVAH: "This, too, is for the best."
GAN EDEN: the Garden of Eden; Paradise.
GEI HINNOM: lit., the valley of Hinnom, where fiery sacrifices of children were offered to the pagan god, Molech; purgatory.
GER: a convert to Judaism.
GET: a Jewish writ of divorce.
GEZEROT: edicts.
GVIR: an important or wealthy personage.

HAKADOSH BARUCH HU: lit., the Holy One, blessed be He; God.
HALACHAH: Jewish law.
HALACHAH L'MA'ASEH: practical law.
HAMAN HARASHA: the evil Haman.
HANASI: the prince; head of the SANHEDRIN.
HANAVI: the prophet.
HAR HABAYIT: the Temple mount.
HASHEM: God.
HASHEM YITBARACH: "God, may He be blessed."
HATMADAH: diligence.
HAVDALAH: the ceremony marking the end of the Sabbath.
HAZAKEN: the elder.

IMMA: mother.
IMMENU: our mother.
INYAN: a subject.

KALLAH: a bride.

KASHER: fit for consumption by Jews.
KASHRUT: the Jewish dietary laws.
KAVANAH: intention; sincerity.
KAVOD: respect; honor.
KEREM: a vineyard.
KETORET: the incense used in the BEIT HAMIKDASH.
KETUBBAH: a marriage contract.
KIDDUSH: the blessing recited over wine on the Sabbath and Festivals.
KLAL YISRAEL: world Jewry.
KODESH HAKODASHIM: lit., the "Holy of Holies"; the innermost chamber in the BEIT HAMIKDASH that only the KOHEN HAGADOL was permitted to enter at certain times and under certain conditions.
KOHELET: the Book of Ecclesiastes.
KOHEN (KOHANIM): member(s) of the priestly tribe.
KOHEN HAGADOL: the High Priest.
KORBAN PESACH: the special sacrifice offered in the BEIT HAMIKDASH on PESACH.
KORBANOT: sacrifices.
KRIAT YAM SUF: the parting of the Red Sea.
KUSHIYA: (A.) difficulty; apparent contradiction in Jewish learning.

LAMED-TET MELACHOT: the thirty-nine categories of activities forbidden on the Sabbath.
LASHON HARA: malicious gossip.
LEVI (LEVI'IM): member(s) of the tribe whose job it was to serve the KOHANIM in the BEIT HAMIKDASH.
LIFNIM MESHURAT HADIN: beyond the strict letter of the law.
L'SHEM SHAMAYIM: lit., for the sake of Heaven; with pure motives.

MA'ARIV: the evening prayer service.
MA'ASIM TOVIM: good deeds.
MAGGID: an itinerant preacher.
MALACHIM: angels.
MALSHINIM: informers; slanderers.

MARCHESHVAN: the second month (counting from ROSH HASHANAH) in the Jewish calendar, corresponding to October-November.

MASHIACH: the Messiah.

MASORAH: the Tradition.

MATZOT: unleavened bread.

MAZAL TOV: "Congratulations!"

MECHUTANIM: in-laws.

MELAMED (MELAMEDIM): teacher(s).

MESIRUT NEFESH: self-sacrifice.

MET MITZVAH: a forsaken corpse, whom it is a great MITZVAH to bury.

METIVTA: (A.) an academy of higher Jewish learning.

METZIAH: a bargain.

MEZUZAH: a parchment scroll containing certain TORAH verses, which is affixed to each doorpost in a Jewish home.

MIDDOT: Jewish values; positive attributes.

MIDRASHEI HALACHAH: explanations beyond the literal meanings of Jewish laws.

MIKRA: Scripture.

MIL(IN): measure(s) of distance equal to 2,000 paces.

MINCHAH: the afternoon prayer service.

MINYAN (MINYANIM): a quorum of ten Jewish men, the minimum for communal prayer.

MITZVAH (MITZVOT): (one of) the 613 Torah commandments.

MITZVAH RABBAH: a very worthy MITZVAH.

MIZBE'ACH: an altar.

NACHAT: pleasure; satisfaction.

NASI (NESI'IM): prince(s); head(s) of the SANHEDRIN.

NAVI: a prophet.

NES: a miracle.

NESIUT: the position held by the NASI.

NIFTAR: deceased.

NISAYON: a Divine test of one's spiritual strength.

OLAM HABA: the World to Come.

OLEH REGEL: one who makes a pilgrimage to Jerusalem during SUKKOT, PESACH, and/or SHAVUOT.

PARNASSAH: livelihood.
PAYOT: sidelocks.
PESACH: the Festival of Passover.
PETIRAH: demise.
PIDYON HABEN: the redemption of a firstborn male child thirty days after his birth.
PIDYON SHEVUYIM: redemption of prisoners.
PITTAH: traditional flat, Middle-Eastern bread.
PRUTAH (PRUTOT): small-denomination coin(s).

RABBAN: the respectful form of address for the chief rabbi.
RABBENU: our teacher.
RACHAMANA LITZLAN: (A.) "May Hashem spare us from such tragedies."
RASHA (RESHAIM): evil person(s).
RAV: an outstanding Jewish scholar.
RIBBONO SHEL OLAM: lit., Master of the Universe; God.
ROSH HASHANAH: the Jewish New Year.
RUACH HAKODESH: prophetic insight.
ROSH YESHIVA: the dean of a YESHIVA.

SANHEDRIN: the assembly of seventy-one Jewish scholars which functioned as the Supreme Court and legislature.
SECHAR LIMUD: tuition fee.
SEFER (SEFARIM): sacred book(s) or scroll(s).
SELA: an ancient measure of weight.
SEMICHAH: rabbinic ordination.
SEUDAH: a meal.
SEUDAT SIYYUM: a celebration at the conclusion of learning a section of Talmud.
SHABBAT: the Sabbath.
SHACHARIT: the morning prayer service.
SHADCHAN (SHADCHANIM): matchmaker(s).

SHALIACH (SHELICHIM): messenger(s).

SHAVUOT: the last of the three pilgrimage Festivals, commemorating the giving of the Torah.

SHECHINAH: the Divine Spirit.

SHECHITAH: the ritual slaughter of animals.

SHEMA YISRAEL! HASHEM ELOKEINU, HASHEM ECHAD: "Hear, O Israel, the Lord our God, the Lord is One"; the fundamental Jewish prayer which proclaims the unity of God.

SHEMONEH ESREH: lit., eighteeen; the principle daily prayer.

SHEVA BERACHOT: a festive meal, held in honor of the newlyweds on the first seven nights after a wedding, at which seven traditional blessings are recited.

SHEVUT: a Rabbinic prohibition.

SHIDDUCH: a proposed marital partner; a marital match.

SHIR HASHIRIM: the Song of Songs.

SHIUR: a Torah lesson.

SHIVAH: the seven-day mourning period.

SHOFAR: a ram's horn sounded in the synagogue on ROSH HASHANAH and YOM KIPPUR.

SIMCHAH: happiness; a joyous occasion.

SIMCHAT BEIT HASHOEVAH: celebration of the water-drawing ceremony during CHOL HAMOED SUKKOT.

SIMCHAT TORAH: the Festival day after SUKKOT marking the annual completion of the reading of the TORAH in the synagogue.

SINAT CHINAM: baseless hatred.

SUKKAH: a temporary dwelling erected for SUKKOT.

SUKKOT: the Festival of Tabernacles.

TAGIM: calligraphic decorations which crown certain letters in the TANACH.

TALLIT: a prayer shawl.

TALLIT KATAN: a small, four-cornered garment with TZITZIYOT knotted on each corner, worn by Jewish males.

TALMID CHACHAM (TALMIDEI CHACHAMIM): Torah scholar(s).

TANACH: the Hebrew acronym for the Holy Scriptures.

TEFILLAH: prayer.

TEFILLIN: two small, black leather boxes, containing certain TORAH verses on parchments, worn by men during the morning prayers.

TEHILLIM: the Psalms.

TENA'IM: the pre-marital contract.

TERUTZ: an explanation.

TESHUVAH: repentance.

TISHA B'AV: the Ninth of Av, a day of fasting and mourning for the destruction of the First and Second Temples.

TISHREI: the first month (counting from ROSH HASHANAH) of the Jewish calendar, corresponding to September-October.

TORAH: the Written and Oral Law.

TORAT MOSHE: the TORAH given by God to Moses; immutable.

TUMOT: ritual impurities.

TZADDIK: a righteous, pious man.

TZARAT HABAT: the daughter's co-wife.

TZEDAKAH: lit., righteousness; charity.

TZITZIYOT: fringes knotted on the four corners of a TALLIT or TALLIT KATAN.

TZORER: a troublemaker.

YAM HAGADOL: lit., the great sea; the Mediterranean.

YESHIVA (YESHIVOT): academy(-ies) of TORAH study.

YICHUS: distinguished lineage.

YIMMACH SHEMO: "May his name be expunged," said of an enemy of the Jewish People.

YIRAT SHAMAYIM: lit., fear of Heaven; observance of HASHEM's commandments.

YOM KIPPUR: the Day of Atonement.

YOM TOV: a Festival day.

ZECHUT (ZECHUYOT): merit(s).

ZECHUT AVOT: merit attained through the righteousness of one's ancestors.

Z'MAN: a semester in a YESHIVA.

ZOCHAH: (f.) to merit.

ZUZ: a medium-denomination coin in Talmudic times.

REFERENCES

The following is a comprehensive list of sources for events, quotations and *halachot* cited in this book or used as a basis for parts of the narrative.

Abbreviation Key:

ADRN	Avot d'Rabi Natan
JT	Jerusalem Talmud (Talmud Yerushalmi)
BT	Babylonian Talmud (Talmud Bavli)

PAGE KEY PHRASE

4 four *beit kur*... — PIRKEI D'RABI ELIEZER 2
5 philanthropy — BT GITTIN 56a
5 erudition — ADRN 6:3
8 the *kohanim*... — JT TA'ANIT 4:2
8 scent of the *ketoret* — BT YOMA 39b
9 ...room for everyone — AVOT 5:5
9 *Simchat Beit Hashoevah*... — BT SUKKAH 51a
9 the torch-juggling Rabbis — BT SUKKAH 53a; 51b, RASHI
10 Upper Galilee — BT SHABBAT 127b (SHE'ILTOT D'RAV ACHAI, SHEMOT 40)
13 spinning — BT KETUBBOT 59b
14 ...we become their slaves — YALKUT SHIMONI, MELACHIM, 181
14 First question — first answer — AVOT 5:7
14 tall — MIDRASH RABBAH, BEMIDBAR 9:24
15 Akiva ben Yosef — BT KETUBBOT 29b
15 descended from Sisera... — BT SANHEDRIN 96b (RAV NISSIM GAON, BT BERACHOT 27b)
15 the heathen general... — SHOFTIM 4:21
15 he became a ger — RAMBAM, INTRODUCTION TO MISHNEH TORAH
15 he worked for a man... — BT SHABBAT 127b (SHE'ILTOT D'RAV ACHAI, SHEMOT 40)
17 he'll find you — BT KIDDUSHIN 2b
17 old — ADRN 62, BT KETUBBOT 62b
17 bald — BT BECHOROT 58a (RASHI, TOSAFOT)
17 Moshe *Rabbenu*... — MIDRASH RABBAH, SHEMOT 2:2

18 Father personally made sure... — BT BAVA METZIA 29b
18 purposely dropped grain — PE'AH 4:10
18 Who needs all these scholars... — BT PESACHIM 49b
18 they're so proud of themselves — BT KETUBBOT 62b, TOSAFOT
19 The Replete Dog... — BT GITTIN 56a
20 Rabban Gamliel the *Nasi* — BT SHABBAT 15a
20 his son, Shimon — BT SHABBAT 15a
20 There is no compensation... — BT HORAYOT 13a
20 ...exhorbitant sums for funerals... — BT MO'ED KATAN 27b
21 the only reason Akiva is angry... — BT KETUBBOT 62b, TOSAFOT
21 his own son — ADRN 6:2
23 I'd want to share my life with him... — BT KETUBBOT 62b
23 I never studied... — ADRN 6:2
23 the study of Torah is essential... — AVOT 6:7
25 This was in *Marcheshvan* — BT NEDARIM 50a
25 her father was so opposed... — BT KETUBBOT 62b, NEDARIM 50a
27 he went off with his son... — ADRN 6:2
27 his son, Yehoshua — BT BECHOROT 58a (RASHI, TOSAFOT), BT PESACHIM 112a
28 at the stream... — ADRN 6:2
29 He gathers fallen branches... — ADRN 6:2
30 ...stiff, dry stalks... — BT NEDARIM 50a
30 a stranger named Eliyahu... — BT NEDARIM 50a
32 in these hard times... — BT TA'ANIT 10b
34 Geva — BT YEVAMOT 62b
34 Rachel must have sold... — JT SHABBAT 6:1 (KORBAN HA'EDAH)
36 Shimon — JT BERACHOT 6:8
38 half the *Chumash*... — ADRN 6:2, BT NEDARIM 50a
38 Lod — BT SANHEDRIN 32b
38 twelve years — BT KETUBBOT 62b, NEDARIM 50a
40 Peace, peace... — YIRMEYAHU 6:14
40 ...more is expected of us — BT BAVA KAMA 50a
40 with a mighty Hand... — DEVARIM 5:15
44 we mustn't do that... — BT BAVA METZIA 83a
44 A worker must be paid... — YECHEZKEL 20:34
45 In much wisdom... — KOHELET 1:18
45 a person who has Torah knowledge... — BT TA'ANIT 7a
48 studying with...Nachum in Gimzo — BT CHAGIGAH 12a
48 Rabi Nachum is called...*Gam zo l'tovah* — BT TA'ANIT 21a

49 You've sold your hair! —JT SHABBAT 6:1 (PENEI MOSHE)
51 Akiva was walking along the road... — DERECH ERETZ ZUTA 8
52 ...*l'shem Shamayim* — AVOT 5:17
52 accept the rule of the majority — SHEMOT 23:2
53 The B'nei Beteira... — BT PESACHIM 66a
54 Behold! The Guardian of Israel... — TEHILLIM 121:4
54 Hillel...was a wood-gatherer — RAMBAM (PERUSH HAMISHNAYOT), AVOT 4:5
54 Once, when he couldn't even afford... — BT YOMA 35b
54 like a fish in the sea... — MIDRASH RABBAH, BERESHIT 97:3
55 The *kohen*...was...Rabi Tzadok — BT GITTIN 56b, BECHOROT 36a
55 may you bring them up to Torah... — BT SHABBAT 137b
57 ...retain the status of High Priest for life — BT PESACHIM 57a
57 Sanhedrin of *Tzadokim* — BT SANHEDRIN 52b
58 Armed bands of *Tzadokim*... — BT PESACHIM 57a
58 ...the sacrifice after childbirth — VAYIKRA 12:6
58 no Jew can partake of the *korbanot*... — VAYIKRA 12:4, BT MAKKOT 14b
58 ...ruled that no woman was required... — BT KERITOT 8a
59 *sinat chinam* — BT YOMA 9b
65 gleaning... — VAYIKRA 19:9, DEVARIM 24:19
66 For lo, the winter is past... — SHIR HASHIRIM 2:11-13
69 he resembles a poor man... — ADRN 18:1, BT GITTIN 67a (RASHI)
69 when the aged Rabi Nechuniah... — BT MEGILLAH 28a
69 *keves* — BEMIDBAR 28:4
69 He who despises gifts will live — MISHLEI 15:27
74 ...You've been miserable... — BT KETUBBOT 62b
77 ...one day a diamond... — MISHLEI 3:15
81 Sicarii... — ENCYCLOPEDIA JUDAICA (JERUSALEM: KETER, 1972)
88 Rabi Eliezer had not recognized... —JT PESACHIM 6:3
88 In his thirteenth year... —JT PESACHIM 6:3
88 This is the People... — SHOFTIM 9:38
89 the huge rotunda of the *beit midrash* — MIDRASH RABBAH, SHIR HASHIRIM 1:1(3) (MATNOT KEHUNAH)
89 Once Akiva came late... — MIDRASH RABBAH, SHIR HASHIRIM 1:1(3) (MATNOT KEHUNAH)
98 I thank you... — TEHILLIM 118:21-24
99 rejoice in Him — YALKUT SHIMONI, YESHAYAHU, 505
99 ...ultimately for the good — BT TA'ANIT 21a
108 Rabi Akiva was systematizing the Midrash... —JT SHEKALIM 5:1

108 one of the fathers of the world — JT SHEKALIM 3:1
108 a sealed treasury — BT GITTIN 67a
108 he teaches his students... — BT GITTIN 67a, RASHI
113 *Perushim* — YADAYIM 4:6-8
115 She didn't say a word... — AVOT 5:7
115 Hashem's help... — PIYUT, SIFTEI RENANOT
115 even one who has been led astray... — PESIKTA D'RAV KAHANA
115 *Ya'ancha Hashem b'yom tzarah* — TEHILLIM 20:2,10
122 Four weeks after the *tena'im*... — BT KETUBBOT 57b
124 *Yam Hagadol*...special *berachah* — BT BERACHOT 54a
125 *V'ahavta l're'acha kamocha*... — JT NEDARIM 9:4
125 She hurled herself to the ground... — BT KETUBBOT 63a
125 ...tried to drag her away — BT KETUBBOT 63a, NEDARIM 50a
125 Leave her be... — BT KETUBBOT 63a, NEDARIM 50a
126 ...I made a vow... — BT KETUBBOT 63a
127 like olive shoots... — TEHILLIM 128:3
127 *Kol d'avid Rachamana l'tav avid* — BT BERACHOT 60b
130 His students were spread out... — BT YEVAMOT 62b
130 For thirty-three days — COMMENTARIES ON TUR, ORACH CHAYIM 493
130 during the Counting of the Omer — BT YEVAMOT 62b
130 At night we buried the dead — TUR, ORACH CHAYIM 493, ELIYAHU RABBAH 11
131 *24,000*...Rabi Akiva's *talmidim* — BT YEVAMOT 62b
132 Rabi Zechariah's forbearance... — BT GITTIN 56a
132 ...his friend, Kamtza... — BT GITTIN 55b
133 it was all right... — BT GITTIN 56a, RASHI
134 built a huge tower... — JOSEPHUS, ANTIQUITIES, XX,8,11
135 The people demanded... — JOSEPHUS, WAR OF THE JEWS, II,17
136 ...Vespasian... — BT GITTIN 56a
137 Fools!... — ADRN 4:5
137 Then they burnt down the storehouses... — BT GITTIN 56a (IYUN YA'AKOV)
139 The Lebanon... — YESHAYAHU 10:34
140 On the ninth day of *Av*... — BT TA'ANIT 26b
140 Our sacred...vessels... — BT GITTIN 56b
140 some were sold as slaves... — BT GITTIN 58a
144 The *Beit Hamikdash* was built... — MIDRASH RABBAH, EICHAH 4:14
145 only if we mourn for the Holy City... — BT TA'ANIT 30b
145 There were those who decided... — BT BAVA BATRA 60b

146 From men such as they... — BT BAVA KAMA 50a
146 ...their lack of respect... — BT YEVAMOT 62b
146 In the morning plant your seeds... — KOHELET 11:6
146 He understood them to mean... — BT YEVAMOT 62b
146 Yishmael...is a descendant... — ADRN 38:3
146 During the war... — BT GITTIN 58a
147 *Who has given Jacob*... — YESHAYAHU 42:24
147 an enormous ransom... — BT GITTIN 58a, TOSAFOT
148 ...raising funds for the needy — BT KIDDUSHIN 27a
148 *mitzvah rabbah* of *pidyon shevuyim*... — BT BAVA BATRA 8b
149 Rabi Yehoshua ben Alam... — SEDER HADOROT
152 When they asked Akiva to be... — JT PE'AH 8:6
152 The purpose of learning Torah — BT BERACHOT 17a
152 ...no one else... — BT MO'ED KATAN 9b
152 I warned him, though... — JT PE'AH 8:6
153 He went to Arabia, to Gaul, to Africa — BT ROSH HASHANAH 26a
153 to Tyre — BT YEVAMOT 98a
153 and Cyprus — BT BAVA KAMA 113a
153 Rabi Tarfon, his former teacher... — BT KETUBBOT 84b
153 Rabi Tarfon is well-off — BT NEDARIM 62a
154 I have an excellent investment... — KALLAH 2
154 Barboohin was very rich... — JT PESACHIM 4:9, MIDRASH RABBAH, ESTHER 2:3
155 In Antioch...Abba Yudan... — YALKUT SHIMONI, MISHLEI, 956
156 even a poor person is obliged... — BT GITTIN 7b
156 Better a Shabbat without celebration... — BT SHABBAT 118a
157 I only ask of you Yavneh... — ADRN 4:5
158 ...the Sanhedrin had met there... — TOSEFTA SOTAH 13:5
158 ...would...come on every *Yom Tov*... — PARAH 7:6, BT CHULLIN 48a
158 reinstate the Sanhedrin... — TOSEFTA BERACHOT 2:6
158 ...the *shofar* could be blown... — BT ROSH HASHANAH 29b
158 the progeny of Rabban Gamliel — BT GITTIN 56b
159 Rabban Gamliel was the newly crowned Prince — BT SANHEDRIN 32b
159 He would appoint the mayors... — BT ROSH HASHANAH 22a
159 doctors to heal Rabi Tzadok — BT GITTIN 56b, MIDRASH RABBAH, EICHAH 1:31
159 Rabban Yochanan...*Av Beit Din* — DOROT HARISHONIM, PART I, VOLUME 5, SECTION 1, CHAPTERS 13-18
159 Bror Chayil — BT SANHEDRIN 32b

159 his five great students... — AVOT 2:8
159 With their teacher's passing... — MIDRASH RABBAH, KOHELET 7:7, ADRN 14:6, BT SHABBAT 147b
160 *Kerem B'Yavneh* — BT BERACHOT 63b
160 Students sit...in neat rows... — BT BERACHOT 63b, RASHI
160 a thousand members of the royal family... — BT BAVA KAMA 83a
160 ...so that they may mingle... — BT BAVA KAMA 83a, RASHI
162 the beautiful gold ornament... — JT SHABBAT 6:1
164 triannual pilgrimage to Yavneh — PARAH 7:6, BT CHULLIN 48a
164 *Rachila batar rachila azla* — BT KETUBBOT 63a
164 the uprooter of mountains — BT ERUVIN 29a, RASHI
165 ...why don't you practice... — BT YEVAMOT 63b
167 he gave her the *get* — BT SOTAH 4b, KETUBBOT 63a, TOSAFOT
168 The first *mitzvah*... — BERESHIT 1:28
170 the *Masorah*...is a fence to the Torah — AVOT 3:13
170 *Kabed et avicha v'et immecha* — SHEMOT 20:12
170 the *et*... — BT KETUBBOT 103a
170 older sister too — BIRKEI YOSEF, YOREH DE'AH 240:17
170 *et Hashem Elokecha tira* — DEVARIM 6:13
170 the *et* before *Hashem*... — PESACHIM 22b
170 even the *tagim*... — BT MENACHOT 29b
170 A fence for wisdom is silence — AVOT 3:13
171 *V'ahavta l're'acha kamocha* — VAYIKRA 19:18
171 ...this is a great principle of Torah — JT NEDARIM 9:4
171 Rabi Akiva urges his students... — MIDRASH RABBAH, BERESHIT 61:3
171 Don't do to others... — BT SHABBAT 31a
172 ...I actually wanted to *bite*... — BT PESACHIM 49b
172 a student must take care...spotless garments — BT SHABBAT 114a
172 ...speak in a pleasant manner... — BT YOMA 86a
174 the yeshiva had been dealing... — TOSEFTA EDUYOT 1:1
174 For the past three years... — BT ERUVIN 13b
174 A Heavenly Voice... — BT ERUVIN 13b, JT YEVAMOT 1:6
174 Rabi Shimon Hapekuli had standardized... — BT BERACHOT 28b
174 eighteen original *berachot*...Ezra — BT MEGILLAH 17b
175 ...the additional *berachah*... — BT BERACHOT 28b
175 Turnus Rufus, to plow the Temple Mount... — BT TA'ANIT 29a
175 they sought to arrest Rabban Gamliel... — BT TA'ANIT 29a
175 the plowing...on Tisha b'Av... — BT TA'ANIT 26b

175 a Roman senator... — BT TA'ANIT 29a
184 Rabi Dosa ben Harkinas... — BT YEVAMOT 16a
184 when Rabi Akiva... — BT YEVAMOT 16a
185 he sat at his *Rav*'s feet... — JT PESACHIM 6:3
185 Make for yourself a *Rav* — AVOT 1:6
186 It's the father's job — BT KIDDUSHIN 29a, PESACHIM 113a
190 making a *shidduch*... — MIDRASH RABBAH, BERESHIT 68:4
195 It's about a *shidduch*... — CHAFETZ CHAIM, HILCHOT RECHILUT 10:4
197 You shall have no other gods... — SHEMOT 19
197 Love your fellowman... — VAYIKRA 19:18
197 Yishmael ben Elisha... — BT GITTIN 58a
198 *Ein kol davar omed*... — JT PE'AH 1:1
199 I placed my burden on His shoulders... — TEHILLIM 55:23
199 *Makom sheba'alei teshuvah omdin*... — BT BERACHOT 34b
201 Can the Ethiopian change... — YIRMEYAHU 13:23
201 a delegation to Rome... — MIDRASH RABBAH, DEVARIM 2:24
201 leopard who'd changed his spots — YIRMEYAHU 13:23
202 a decree for the annihilation... — MIDRASH RABBAH, DEVARIM 2:24
204 there was a gnat eating away at his brain — BT GITTIN 55b
206 When he broke the terrible news... — MIDRASH RABBAH, DEVARIM 2:24
208 Rabi Elazar speaks *seventy* languages — SHEKALIM 5:1
209 forty days before a male child... — BT SOTAH 2a
214 engaged to Yehoshua ben Kefusai — BT SHABBAT 147a
214 a poor man came to the gate... — BT SHABBAT 156b
216 Charity delivers from death — MISHLEI 11:4
217 moved to Usha — BT ROSH HASHANAH 31b
218 Rabi Eliezer...*Chacham Hava'ad* — DOROT HARISHONIM, PART I, VOLUME 5, SECTION 2, CHAPTER 23
218 Rabi Yehoshua the *Av Beit Din* — BT BAVA KAMA 74b
218 The Rabbis separated themselves... — BT BAVA METZIA 59b
219 Conflicts arose between the *Nasi*... — BT ROSH HASHANAH 25a, BECHOROT 36a, BERACHOT 27b
219 the people began to demand... — BT BERACHOT 27b
219 ...he is lacking in *zechut avot* — BT BERACHOT 27b
219 like seventy in wisdom — BT BERACHOT 12b
220 the full assembly gathered...accumulated — BT ZEVACHIM 11b, YADAYIM 3:5
220 ...resolved their differences — BT BERACHOT 27b

220 on Rosh Hashanah... — JT ROSH HASHANAH 4:8
221 ...nearby towns — BT SHABBAT 115a, ERUVIN 101b, TOSEFTA TERUMOT 2:13
222 *shaliach mitzvah*... — BT PESACHIM 8a
227 And all the nations of the earth... — BERESHIT 12:3
230 what shall a man do... — BT AVODAH ZARAH 10b
232 For like the four winds... — ZECHARIAH 2:10
237 Rabi Akiva had once done... — BT TA'ANIT 25b
239 *Hashem, Hu HaElokim!* — 1 MELACHIM 18:39
240 human beings...in Hashem's image — AVOT 3:14, BERESHIT 9:6
240 like clay in the potter's hands — YIRMEYAHU 18:6
241 Rabban Gamliel... — BT MAKKOT 24a
241 the Sages' first stop was Jerusalem — BT MAKKOT 24b
242 The stranger who comes near... — BEMIDBAR 1:51
243 And I will take true witnesses... — YESHAYAHU 8:2
243 In truth, because of you... — MICHAH 3:12 (see TOSAFOT, BT MAKKOT 24b)
243 Thus spoke the Eternal One... — ZECHARIAH 8:3-4
243 Rabi Akiva...began to build a *sukkah* — BT SUKKAH 23a
244 Rabban Gamliel had paid *a thousand zuz*... — BT SUKKAH 41b
244 When the Rabbis arrived in Rome... — BT MAKKOT 24a
244 the Sages were...deluged by Romans... — BT AVODAH ZARAH 54b
248 the *metivta* did move back to Yavneh — BT ROSH HASHANAH 31b
249 relocated to Lod — TOSEFTA PESACHIM 3:9
249 Rabi Tarfon... — BT BAVA METZIA 49b, CHAGIGAH 18a
249 the five elders... — JT BEITZAH 3:5, TOSEFTA MIKVA'OT 8:5
249 the wedding of Rabban Gamliel's son... — BT KIDDUSHIN 32b
250 He set it before them... — BERESHIT 18:8
250 Rabi Eliezer became ill... — BT SANHEDRIN 68a
250 My father... — 2 MELACHIM 2:12
251 thirty-two Sages — TOSEFTA MIKVA'OT 8:6
251 the upper floor... — BT SHABBAT 29b
251 they destroyed the exquisite *beit knesset*... — JT SUKKAH 5:1
252 Trajan had a son and a daughter... — JT SUKKAH 5:1
252 ...several theological debates — MIDRASH RABBAH, BERESHIT 28:3, 78:1, et al.
253 two of Rabi Akiva's *talmidim*... — MIDRASH RABBAH, VAYIKRA 21:8
253 courteous behavior precedes Torah — MIDRASH RABBAH, VAYIKRA 9:3
255 Sarah *Immenu*... — YALKUT SHIMONI, TEHILLIM, 730

255 Hadrian is going to grant us permission... — MIDRASH RABBAH, BERESHIT 64:10
256 He amended his decree... — MIDRASH RABBAH, BERESHIT 64:10
256 Rabi Yehoshua spoke to them... — MIDRASH RABBAH, BERESHIT 64:10
257 *Deracheha darchei noam*... — MISHLEI 3:17
258 it would be back in Usha — BT ROSH HASHANAH 31b
258 Their son Shimon...was *niftar*... — SEMACHOT 8
260 May it be rebuilt swiftly... — BT SUKKAH 41a
260 new edicts banning the performance... — BT ME'ILAH 17a
263 forbidden to recite the *Shema* — TOSEFTA BERACHOT 2:13
263 ...has been circumcised... — JT SHABBAT 19:2
264 Rabi Akiva, who was fluent in their language — BT SANHEDRIN 17b
264 whose work is better... — MIDRASH TANCHUMA, TAZRIA 5
265 What difference is there... — MIDRASH RABBAH, BERESHIT 11:5
266 I read in your Scriptures... — MIDRASH TANCHUMA, TERUMAH 3
266 I love Jacob... — MALACHI 1:2-3
267 ...his wife saw... — BT NEDARIM 50b, RASHI, RAN
268 ...about to be wed...rich widow — BT NEDARIM 50b
270 a *talmid chacham* from the House of David — RAMBAM, MISHNEH TORAH, HILCHOT MELACHIM 11:4
271 ...too soon to tell — RAMBAM, MISHNEH TORAH, HILCHOT MELACHIM 11:4
271 ...struck new coins... — BT BAVA KAMA 97b, RASHI, JT MA'ASER SHENI 1:1
272 Concerning the Second *Beit Hamikdash*... — BT SANHEDRIN 97b, RASHI
272 Yet again, in just a little while... — CHAGGAI 2:6-7
272 ...catch the stones... — MIDRASH RABBAH, EICHAH 2:4
272 He is the king... — JT TA'ANIT 4:5
272 *Darach kochav mi-Ya'akov*... — BEMIDBAR 24:17-18
272 Rabi Yochanan ben Torta... — JT TA'ANIT 4:5
273 women were given an extra measure... — BT NIDDAH 45b
274 He would only accept... — JT TA'ANIT 4:5, MIDRASH RABBAH EICHAH 2:4
274 Let Hashem not help us... — MIDRASH RABBAH, EICHAH 2:4
274 only quoting his commander — JT TA'ANIT 4:5
274 ...because David had blood on his hands — 1 DIVREI HAYAMIM 22:8
274 The Romans have killed Rabi Shimon... — SEMACHOT 8

275 The righteous perish... — YESHAYAHU 57:1
275 Within months... — SEMACHOT 8
275 For over three years... — MIDRASH RABBAH, EICHAH 2:4
275 Betar ran red with the blood... — MIDRASH RABBAH, EICHAH 2:4
275 On Tisha b'Av... — BT TA'ANIT 26b
275 ...son of a liar — MIDRASH RABBAH, EICHAH 2:4
276 When the Romans arrested Rabi Akiva... — BT BERACHOT 61b
276 Rabi Yehudah ben Bava... — BT SANHEDRIN 14a
276 the Romans have banned *semichah* — BT SANHEDRIN 14a
278 carrying the *bikkurim* in gilded baskets — BIKKURIM 3:8
280 only the widow truly mourns for her husband — BT SANHEDRIN 22b
280 Rabi Akiva had been arrested... — BT BERACHOT 61b
280 The five students... — BT YEVAMOT 62b
280 ...the foundations of the Oral Law... — BT SANHEDRIN 86a
280 All took their inspiration... — BT SANHEDRIN 86a
281 on the fifth day of Tishrei... — SHULCHAN ARUCH, ORACH CHAIM 5
281 the *talmidim* found ways... — BT PESACHIM 112a, YEVAMOT 105b, JT YEVAMOT 12:5
281 One of his disciples, Yehoshua Hagarsi... — BT ERUVIN 21b
281 Even though he was not... — CHAYEI HAMUSSAR, VOLUME 1, 9
281 ...the evil Tineus Rufus... — MIDRASH RABBAH, EICHAH 3:60
281 Yehoshua Hagarsi prayed... — MIDRASH RABBAH, EICHAH 3:60
281 You have covered Yourself... — EICHAH 3:44
281 The Romans tore the flesh... — BT BERACHOT 61b
281 he made no outcry — JT BERACHOT 9:5
281 It was time to recite the *Shema*... — BT BERACHOT 61b
282 When the guards were asleep... — YALKUT SHIMONI, MISHLEI, 944
283 ...abolished Hadrian's vile decrees — BT ME'ILAH 17b
283 ...permitted the burial of Betar's martyrs — BT TA'ANIT 31a